AFRICA'S EMBRACE

BY MARK WENTLING

A PEACE CORPS WRITERS BOOK

AFRICA'S EMBRACE
A Peace Corps Writers Book
An Imprint of Peace Corps Worldwide

Printed in the United States of America
by Peace Corps Writers of Oakland, California
No part of this book may be used or reproduced in any manner
whatsoever without the written permission except in the case of brief
quotations contained in critical articles or reviews

For more information, contact peacecorpsworldwide@gmail.com.
Peace Corps Writers and the Peace Corps Writers colophon are
trademarks of PeaceCorpsWorldwide.org

ISBN-10: 1935925318
ISBN-13: 978-1935925316
Library of Congress Control Number: 2013939712
Peace Corps Writers, Oakland, CA

First Peace Corps Writers Edition, May 2013

Dedicated to my children, Elsa, Sudie, Clyde, Jemina, Mitch, and Mark, And their African mothers, and all African women who taught me so much about the continent.

CONTENTS

AUTHOR'S NOTE

This story has been in the making for over forty years. I do not mean I have been working on it for forty years, but I have been waiting until my forty years in Africa had expired before writing it. Most importantly, there are some things in this story I took an oath not to tell for forty years. As I am now relieved of my oath, I am at last free to share some of what it has been like for this kid from Kansas to be embraced ever so tightly by Africa for so many years.

There is much truth in what I write, but this is a work of fiction. In order to avoid confusion and protect the innocent, and myself, I have used invented names for people and places. Much of what I write is based on fact and the realities I experienced personally in Africa, yet it is sometimes hard to distinguish the truth from what is make-believe. For me, all parts of my story are true in one way or another, although in rational terms so much is truly not possible.

After looking back over more than four decades in Africa, the line between the real and the imagined has grown very thin, and it is harder than ever for me to distinguish between the two. I feel as though I have been lost for a long time between the dimensions of what we know exists and what is not possible but observable (sometimes). I know what I observed and experienced, even if it is not explainable or true. Perhaps by reading this feeble attempt to capture and convey how this life in Africa started for me, the reader can help me find my way and discover what really happened.

This book would have not been possible if I had not lived in an African village and spent a lifetime in Africa. I also could not have written it if my life had not been so closely entwined with Africans for so many years. In particular, my marriages to African women and the raising of our children in Africa while dealing with their extended families and communities were a great and unforgiving teacher of Africa's realities.

I owe much to the many people who crossed my path in the dozens of places I have had the privilege of knowing in all parts of Africa. This book has been churning within me for many years, but it was some tough talk from my older sister, Ethne Barnes, who made me get serious about putting words on paper. I hope this book helps her and all members of my family in America to understand better why they have lived without me for decades.

I am indebted to my college friend in Kansas, Martin Limbird, as without his encouragement in 1970 to go to West Africa, this experience of mine may have never happened. I would like to thank Bob Fakundiny, who had also served in West Africa and encouraged me to go there. There is one thing he told me nearly forty-five years ago on our first encounter that has stuck in my mind. He said if I could write a book like I talk, it would be a best seller. I am afraid that my "talk" is not as colorful and exciting as it was when I was much younger.

I note the influence of my good friend, Kelly Morris, who I first met in Africa in 1970. His writings on African subjects served as a motivation for me to tell my own African story. I would also like to thank another dear old American friend, Denis Hynes, who arrived on the continent before me, for taking the time to proofread my first full draft. I must thank another close friend and fellow adventurer, Dick Feutz, who proofread many versions of my manuscript and encouraged me in all I have done since we first met in 1967. I also thank his wife, Debbie, and his ninety-eight-year-old mother, Alice, who worked her entire life as a librarian, for their reviews of my manuscript. I owe a special thank you to Marshall Williams for his unfailing friendship and support in those lean days in Wichita before I left for Africa. I also want to mention my best Kansas childhood buddy, Chuck Morgan, who never lost faith in me and also tried to come to Africa, but missed the opportunity to do so.

Lastly, but certainly not least, I want to thank my mother, Georgia, for encouraging my interest in Africa and for her insights while she stayed with me in Africa for nine months in 1974. Sadly, my mom passed away just a few weeks before I completed the first full manuscript of my book. I will always miss her review of my book.

There are other Americans, like myself, who have spent their lives connected to Africa. They don't know it, but their experiences have influenced my thinking and writing. There are many I could cite here, but those names which come quickly to mind, in no particular order, are as follows: John Mullenax, Sidney Bliss, John Schiller, Al Miller, Malcolm Versel, Peter Wright, Gary Engelberg, Leslie McBride, Bill Stringfellow, Don Clark, Kevin Mullally, Lee Yellott, Louis Siegel, Tom Shaw, Joel Strauss, John Heermans, Bill Aughenbaugh, Willie Russell, Jim Tolliver, Dean Christ, and Phillip DeBarros. Like me, they initially came to Africa with the Peace Corps for a couple of years but ended up staying much longer. In many ways this is their story too.

I also want to recognize those American women I know who came to Africa and ended up making it the center of their lives. Here I am thinking mostly of Lillian Baer, Ellon Dedo, Doris Goukounous, Christy Collins, Pam Alio, Sue Rosenfeld, Marily Knieriemen, Bess McDavid, Kateri Clement, Molly Glenn and Janet Trucker. I am sure they, and many others who crossed my path in Africa over the past forty years, can easily identify with this book.

I cannot conclude these acknowledgements without recognizing the profound impact Chinua Achebe's widely acclaimed book, *Things Fall Apart*, has exercised over me for decades. Everywhere I have traveled in Africa, I took his book with me. It is next to me now. For reasons hard to explain, it is an endless source of inspiration to me. I was hoping that someday I would have the great honor of having him read my book. It is exceedingly sad for me that this will not be the case. Chinua Achebe left this world on March 22, 2013.

Many of these people, and others who know me, may be surprised to see this book, as I have kept it mostly my secret. I underscore that this book is entirely my own idea and writing it was a lonely, solitary pursuit. I am, therefore, fully responsible for its content and how it affects others. I hope all those who know Africa well will enjoy this book, and those who do not know Africa, will benefit from this surreal tale of an American white man's entanglement in Africa. This book is intended to entertain, educate, and enrich. How this book appeals to the reader is important to me, but what really matters to me at this late stage in my life is having been able to complete this long-postponed labor of love, thereby keeping my end of the bargain with all the Africans I have known, living and dead. At long last, I find myself free and at peace.

Mark Wentling
Ouagadougou, Burkina Faso

PROLOGUE

always believed this story began in Africa, but I now know it really began in Kansas. David, who was re-baptized "Bobo-vovi" in Africa, was born and raised on a farm on the plains of Kansas. His all-white farming community was smack dab in the middle of the Bible-Belt. He was a good all-American boy, graduating at the top of his high school class and winning a university scholarship. In 1970, one semester before he was to graduate from college, he stunned everyone by dropping out to accept an invitation to join the Peace Corps as a volunteer in a West African country.

Deep down David knew this was his calling; therefore, he could not say "no" to what he had been waiting for his whole life. David never told anyone, but he could hear voices in the wind beckoning him to adventures in foreign lands. The wind blowing through the grass and trees told him things. Full-moon nights were also special for him, making his heart throb faster. Once, for no reason at all, he danced like a madman fully naked on top of the highest hill in his home county under the light of a full moon.

David was waiting for something to take him far away, but he did not know what or when it would be. For him, this opportunity to join the Peace Corps was the opportunity that would enable him to meet his destiny. Nothing could stop him from responding to this call and going on an African adventure. He could not explain this to anyone. All he knew was he had to go. He took his first jet plane ride in 1970, not knowing when he would be back to Kansas again.

David's plan was to go to Africa for a couple of years, do as much good as he could, and return to continue his studies and life in Kansas. He did not count on how things would transpire to keep him in Africa for much longer than he planned. He made many plans to leave Africa, but something always happened to thwart his plans.

Come and join David in a rollicking adventure as he follows his humanitarian heart and searches for answers to what the wind had told him many times in Kansas. Join him after he has already been in Africa for a couple of years and is about to have a profound, magical encounter with the power of a full moon. Come with Bob-ovovi and be embraced by Africa.

CHAPTER ONE
MOONBEAM MAGIC

Everyone in the village warned me not to go. People were coming by my house every day, telling me not to go. Even strangers from neighboring villages sought me out to warn me. The old woman beggar on the corner, who never left her place, came to confront me in a language I did not understand. Grandmother Aba, who lived next to my house in the palm-thatched lean-to that blew away every time there was a storm, made it clear to me I should not be so crazy as to go. My loyal, unruly African dog, Agogo, looked at me differently with sad eyes that seemed to be begging me to stay home.

My good friend, Lumasi, one of the most respected traditional sorcerers in town, said in no uncertain terms in her raspy, but authoritative voice, "A Whiteman has no business going."

There had been a close bond between Lumasi and me ever since I added to her already immense powers by providing her a pebble and small vial of water from an American river. Lumasi said, "I know your spirit is strong, but that is no reason for you to tempt the spirits."

For her, the nighttime climb to the top of the mountain for the next full-moon ceremonies was just too risky. She was afraid my soul could be altered forever and the few powers I had would be taken from me. She was also concerned it might be the start of something that would end in a way I would not like.

I could not disagree with Lumasi, and I told her she was right; it was better not to go. After all, I was scared and soon my plan was to leave the village forever. No sense risking my safe-and-sound exit from the village because of some full-moon shenanigans on the top of Mt. Ataku. But, on the other hand, after a couple of years in the village, I had participated in about all the local ceremonies without any lasting, ill effect. I had always wanted to join the full-moon trek up the mountain, but I had always been dissuaded from doing so. It was now or never.

I was a bit frightened and uncomfortable, especially as I had told everyone I would not go. But, when I felt the light of the full moon on me, I could not resist and immediately took a back path leading to a mountain path behind the village. I was careful to avoid any snakes, which were often out at night to hunt and seek warmth. I waited in the dark for the group heading to the mountaintop for the monthly drumming ceremony on sacred ground. I kept telling myself I would be all right and nothing bad would happen to me. I had climbed the three-thousand-foot mountain many times in daylight. A two-hour climb at night up its damp, slippery slopes through the cocoa plantations was not any great physical feat.

I could begin to hear the approaching revelers with their noisy drums and chants. In the dim light of their kerosene lamps, I could see they had dressed themselves in the clothes of the ancestors, mostly in bark cloth and oil palm leaves. They had also smeared their bodies with orange palm oil and cocoa pod ashes. I reached down in the moist ground and grabbed some mud to wipe on my face and tore off a couple nearby tree branches to wave, so as to better fit in and show them I was serious about accompanying them. When the long file of people was halfway past me, I tried my best to enter among them unnoticed. But, the women behind me immediately saw my white skin glisten in the moonlight. Seeing that I was among them brought forth a joyous ululating that quickly changed to a song of praise for me, their white Tuesday's child, Bobovovi.

Their very animated song alerted everyone to my presence and served to increase the level of loudness and lively movements of all those who chose that night to test the powers of the mountain spirits and the moon gods. I had entered the file of people between the pack of leading drummers and the women in the back who were carrying large clay pots of fresh palm wine. The women's song became louder, and they repeatedly shouted my name. They were overwhelmed with joy, because I had defied everyone and obeyed the call of the full moon.

Seeing how well I had been accepted, it was not hard for me to get into the rhythmic mood and antics of this very high-spirited group, which appeared to be intoxicated, even before any palm wine had been served. There was much singing, joking, and added laughter when someone inevitably slipped and fell backwards on the steep inclines, where water seeped from every pore of this fertile ground. This loud chorus of joy grew as we neared the summit. People were happy to be returning to the place where their first ancestors had settled and saved themselves and future generations by successfully fighting off powerful warriors from other ethnic groups, which came to make war on the peaceful people of this region.

There were other reasons for all this noise. Under normal circumstances, nobody would venture very far from their houses at night for fear of the wicked nighttime spirits and those evildoers who hunted heads to trade to unscrupulous sorcerers. These feared headhunters paid almost any price for a human head, which they would use to increase immeasurably their occult powers. Yet, here we were out at night, hurrying to make it to the summit by midnight. We would stay on the mountaintop all night, even beyond 2:00 a.m., which was the peak time for the wicked night spirits to do their worst kind of black magic. The idea was to make as much noise as possible to show we were utterly happy and unafraid. Moreover, the names of important ancestors, "grandfathers," were called loudly, beseeching them to protect us and join this monthly honoring of them and their ancient traditions.

Suddenly, we were on the holy ground where the first ancestor had dwelt. Upon arriving at this hallowed ground, the group became immediately silent. For a few minutes, only the breeze in a few nearby trees could be heard. The eeriness of this silence was quickly broken with a loud instruction from an old man, one of the few remaining who possessed the secrets required for the conduct of this mountaintop ceremony. Everyone in the group responded instantly with a loud cry of affirmation and began moving about quickly to put everything in place that was needed to ensure the ceremony would occur in a manner most pleasing to the ancestors and the spirits inhabiting this much-worshiped site.

First, there was the special sweeping to clear the grounds of any unwanted spirits. For reasons all had forgotten, the ground was swept with a special palm branch that had a chick tied to one side and a toad to the other. Behind this ceremonial cleansing came a battery of women bent over from the waist, furiously sweeping all the loose dirt on the surface into small mounds with short, straw brooms. Following these women were groups of men who piled the mounds on to sheets of cloth, binding the sheets carefully to avoid any leakage. When the old man gave the order, they responded in unison with a loud shout and proceeded to the east side of the sacred ground, tossing the collected debris as far as they could. Bad spirits always come from the east; therefore, the best way to get rid of them was to sweep them up and throw them back in the direction from where they had come.

Next, with the cleansing of the area completed, the women with their clay pots of palm wine were placed on the west side. The men with their drums, bugles, and assorted noisemakers were huddled along the east side. I was told to sit near the far end of the group of men. Next came the setting up of the holy three-forked tree trunk on the north side of our circle. It was buried deeply in the ground and made to stand firmly straight up. A clay bowl containing water blessed by the oldest of the village elders was carefully placed in the fork of the tree while prayers were mumbled. The oldest of the women then put leaves in the water from a sacred tree known only to a select few. The bowl was gently balanced in the middle of the triple forked "tripod" tree.

No sooner had this been done when an almost naked man carrying a white rooster with blood dripping from its throat ran madly around the group. He sprinkled the rooster's blood along the outer circumference to protect us from unwanted, bad spirits. The old man began pouring on the ground, here and there, drops of potent schnapps in honor of the ancestors. Following these necessary libations, the drums began playing softly. The women brought wood and built a big bonfire in the middle of our circle.

The loudness of the drums mounted as the fire grew. When the fire was fully ablaze, the drums stopped for a second and then started again in a very different cadence. With this new beat and rhythm, everyone became very agitated, greeting one another as if they did not know each other. A few people greeted each other with their secret names, which only those who had been initiated with them could understand. When all the greeting was done, the dancing began.

The women began to sing praises and dance in unison: two steps to the right, two to the left. They moved toward the fire with their hips moving in a rhythmic way only mastered in Africa. They danced a few times around the circle in single file. The men then joined in, dancing in the same mesmerizing fashion. As we approached midnight when the full moon would be overhead, the dancing became more animated, as did the drumming and singing. At the same time, calabashes of palm wine were passed from one person to another. It did not take long for the effects of alcohol to add to what was already an unbelievable rapturous state.

Some people broke off from the counter-clockwise movement of the dancers to jabber loudly in a language only the oldest could understand. I was told they had been possessed by the ancestors, who were now speaking through them. This very favorable occurrence made everyone all the happier, if not delirious. There was so much happening I could not understand. Everyone was so caught up in the spirit of the moment that it was not possible to ask for any explanation. I, therefore, tried to stand calmly aside, observing as closely as I could. I kept my mind open, so my ignorance as to what was really happening did not diminish how very much I was spellbound by the wonder of it all.

It would have been very impolite to refuse a sip from the palm wine bowls being passed about and it would be totally unacceptable to drink before pouring a few drops of wine on the ground for the ancestors. At some point my serenity began to erode, and I became very much seized by my surroundings. There is something about the beating of drums and a fire at night that appeals to the deepest part of our inner selves. All of a sudden, my right foot began moving in time with the drumbeat, as if it were not part of my body. Then my left foot began to do the same. I immediately found myself in the ring of the circling dancers, following along in a manner in which I did not know I was capable. My unexpected presence among the group brought shouts of exceeding joy and praise. If I had ever contributed to the ecstasy of others, this was the moment.

As I turned around and around, dancing steps I had never practiced, it was as if my body was not my own, and I feared I had lost control of myself. Everything seemed to move faster and faster. The land around us seemed to be twirling in an opposite, clockwise direction. Things seemed so much brighter, almost like it was midday instead of midnight. I could see every detail of my surroundings much more clearly than before. I began to feel deeply how special this moment was. At the same time, I was a little apprehensive because I did not really know what was going on. I was thinking of fleeing, but I could never make it down the mountain on my own.

The moon was overhead now, and it seemed so unbelievably close. I kept raising my hand to see if I could snatch a bit of the moon. I began jumping higher and higher as I called on the moon. I could see the moon smile at me. I began laughing uncontrollably and running crazily about, blurting out strange words that had no meaning to me. I was really having such an unusually good and exciting time. This moment was really special and almost too good to be true. Suddenly, I stopped all movement as I noticed the drums were no longer beating and everyone was standing still, staring at me. Just as I gave a look that expressed total surprise at finding I was the only one still dancing, there was a bright flash. I looked up to see a sparkling beam of white light coming from the moon straight for me. I was transfixed by this sight, and in a twinkling of an eye, this miraculous moonbeam pierced my body and gently lifted me up.

The next thing I remember was waking up in my bed in my little house in the village. I did not know how I returned home. Maybe it was all a dream. I was like Dorothy waking up in her bed on her farm in Kansas after her adventures in Oz. I believed I had passed out and had been carried back down the mountain, but that would have been an almost impossible feat.

The bright morning sunlight was pouring through my window, and I could hear people talking outside my house. I stood up to see who was talking. I was amazed to see a large crowd from the village assembled in front of my house and all eyes were directed at my bedroom window. A loud cheer was made when I appeared at my window. I was asked if I was alright. I said, "I am fine." This affirmation of my good health engendered an even louder cheer. Everyone seemed very happy indeed. I could see I was now the talk of the town.

Later in the day, I asked Aba why all the people came to wait outside my window until I woke up. She asked, "Do you know how you returned home?"

I said, "No, not really. I thought I had collapsed and was carried home by some of the men who had been on the mountain with me."

She laughed and rapidly said, "You ignorant Whiteman, do you not know how special you are? Don't you know the moon god showed you his highest favor and put you on a moonbeam ride from the top of the mountain to your house? The people came because they wanted to see if you were still sane and healthy after this extraordinary experience. They are happy because you are alright, and this brings great honor to our village, as it has been decades since anyone has been chosen to ride a moonbeam."

I was dumbfounded since none of this could possibly be true, but I diplomatically accepted my status as the village hero and accepted to go along with this fantastic story. It was one of those times when the truth did seem to be the enemy of what was best.

I did not tell anyone, but I still believed I was carried down the mountain and the people made up the moonbeam story to glorify their village and embellish their history. I tried to put all this out of my mind, but every time there is a full moon, I cannot help but think about what happened to me on that magical night. I still find myself avoiding exposure to a full moon. Even a glimpse of a full moon sends my heart racing, and I feel as if it is pulling and pushing me around. I try to ignore this, but with each passing day, the power of the moon on me seems to grow stronger. It is as if the moon is telling me the moonbeam ride from the top of the mountain was true, and I should stop denying it and learn to live with it.

There seems to be no way of escaping the hold the full moon has on me. I still cannot bring myself to believe I actually rode a moonbeam. That is impossible! But I never cease to wonder why I always feel more comfortable staying inside on those nights when the moon is full. The mystery of that night on Mt. Ataku still haunts me. I now know all the people who warned me not to go up the mountain on that moonlit night were right.

CHAPTER TWO
RAINS OF WRATH

Not long after that moonstruck night, the rains came. The first droplets fell like random bits of saliva spewing involuntarily from an open-mouthed sky. We all looked up to listen to what the heavens were whispering, but we heard nothing. There was only one gray cloud lost against an endless backdrop of blue sky, tainted softly by months of the dried Earth's shedding of countless coats of reddish-brown dust. There were not any signs to suggest the long and harsh dry season was ready to end its cruel and unmerciful hold on the land and all its dependents.

People carried on with their business, trying to ignore the thunder of their inner wishes for an end to the drought and all the suffering it caused. Droplets fell, and all who were about stopped to peer at the heavens again. Birds flying speedily overhead brought laughter, as everyone thought they had dropped something on her or him. "It was not rain; it was the birds!" People moved on, thinking it would be many days yet before the rainy season would begin. Then there were more droplets, seemingly falling from an empty sky pierced by the glorious scarlet rays of a lingering sunset.

By nightfall, dark clouds had gathered and droplets turned into weighty, miniature water bombs, forcefully opening tiny craters into the hard skin of the thirsty Earth. Before the sun bid its daily farewell, the clouds burst forth a deluge of water, leaving no doubt all would be saved by heaven's long-awaited baptism of a scorched Earth. Down came the rain with a force nobody could recall, scouring layers of dust from all things and covering all with its mighty blessing.

The hearts of the people swelled with joy. The village was full of loud thanks to God and all the lesser deities and generations of ancestors for the abundant rainfall. People sang and danced as they rejoiced in the rain. Some took baths. A few could not restrain themselves, running amuck fully naked up and down the slippery slopes of the village. Others clanged together iron cymbals used on special occasions of praise and happiness. Others darted about with more practical ideas in mind, placing buckets and clay jars in the open to catch the much-needed water and moving precious firewood to the dry corners of their thatched dwellings. Others began sharpening long-handled machete knives and short-handled hoes on deeply worn sandstones embedded in the earth in a corner of their compounds. They would need these key farming implements the next day to work the moist soil of their fields. The urge to cultivate their fields following a first rain was irrepressible.

The deep darkness of this rainy night could not suppress the festive mood of a people whose very lives depended on every drop of rain. They had already suffered many losses during a long period of drought and now profound hardship was at an end. Men, women, and children celebrated with all the energy they possessed, as if they were on some sort of energy-enhancing drugs. But, they were not alone. In their midst were many spirits which had always dwelt in the village. Joining them were the ghosts of the ancestors.

The gifted ones among the living clearly sensed the presence of these visitors from the other side, and their joy was multiplied and passed on to those around them. Everyone was lifted to a high level of ecstasy not previously known. All were beside themselves with the knowledge that this was an unprecedented occasion marking them and their village forever. They did not know that a critical turning point in the history of their village was occurring.

There could be no sleeping on that night! Thirsty mouths and souls could not rest while such miracles were showering down on a long-suffering people. Some people became drunk from imbibing palm wine and other locally made alcoholic beverages kept hidden for special occasions. Others were so moved by the sense of profound revival, they acted drunk. All the people of the village became an integral part of one communal, psychic mind. This spiritual unity made them forget their miseries and blinded them to the realities surrounding them. Outside the boundaries of their elevated state of grace, a very different story was unfolding.

This was not an ordinary rain that broke the dry season, bringing life back to the Earth. This was a rain sent by angry gods to punish people. While the people rejoiced, the darkness of night hid the wreckage that had begun. Branches and entire trees crashed unheard to the ground. Fields were flooded; rivers and streams overflowed their banks. The earth was breaking up, and landslides were crashing down the mountainside. Birds fell from their roosts, and animals of every kind were washed away. The destruction caused by the downpour was massive. Nothing could stop the damage.

A bright early morning sun revealed there had not been the salvation of life-giving water as all believed. Quite the contrary, God had unleashed His terrible wrath on a people struggling to survive. People stood in disbelief as they witnessed how their world had been terribly disfigured and washed away. Gone was most of what they needed to live. Disbelief and denial turned into depression and fear. People began moaning and screaming, as they would do at the funeral of a respected elder. Sometime later, Chief Yofu and his head fetish priest, Kontor, appeared to view firsthand the severity of the disaster that had changed the village forever.

Kontor represented a formidable force in the village. His magical powers and remarkable abilities as a sorcerer were known far and wide. Many times he had demonstrated his mastery of the occult forces. His high reputation as a good and able fetish priest attracted many people in search of his services from everywhere in the region. His demeanor and physical appearance reinforced his reputation.

Kontor was very old, but looked young. He had a pointed head and the face of a child. His small, green eyes were like those of a serpent. He was the tallest man in the village, well over six feet tall, and was very thin with very dark, deep black skin. It was easy to recognize him, because he always wore a simple, long white gown made of local hand-spun cotton. The long cap he wore all the time on his bald head was made of the same material and flopped from side to side as he moved about in his usual quick stride.

Later, the chief met with his elders and other wise men in the village to contemplate why God had punished their village so severely. After a lengthy palaver, I was summoned to appear before the chief and his council. All were silent; their eyes were riveted on me as I stood before them for what seemed the longest time. Finally the chief, wrapped tightly in his colorful kente cloth, walked toward me, staring straight into my eyes. He said very loudly for all who could hear, "What happened to you on that full-moon night on the mountain never happened. Everyone should wipe from their memories what happened and never speak of it again."

I was required to take a blood oath on the spot. A small incision was made on the underside of my forearm. Drops of my blood were collected in a small clay vial. These drops would be used later by Kontor in a ceremony that would bind me to never speak of this event for forty years. They had come to the firm conclusion that what happened to me on the mountain, and all the talk about it, were the sources of God's anger with them. By not talking about it anymore, they might be spared further punishment. For them, this was a life-and-death matter. Everything had to be done to appease God and the spirits, otherwise they were doomed.

From that day on, not a word has been spoken about what happened. The magic of that moonlit night was forgotten and deleted from the collective memory of the village and its oral history. It is only now I dare mention this glorious night, and I do so with great trepidation. For many years I have kept deep inside me the secret of that night and not spoken of it to anyone. I, too, was afraid that speaking of it would result in some kind of grave misfortune for me and the village. And, as nobody would believe me anyway, not speaking of it made my life easier. The villagers had no such problems. It was deeply embedded in their nature and their traditions that once the chief makes a decision they must adhere to it without fail. Moreover, all were genuinely afraid that God would mete out more suffering for them if they spoke of it.

I have been lucky to dodge God's punishment for crossing the line into what had always been prohibited for humans to do: ride the moonbeams. With every full moon, I expect something bad to happen to me, and I always do my best to avoid going out at night when the moon is full. Even when I am inside, and there is a full moon, I can feel it pressing against me and calling me. All this makes me think of that night, but I try not to remember anything. I fear the full moon and what it can do to me. Most of all I fear the full moon can silence me forever by making me go mad. Perhaps madness is my only escape, as death will only make me more exposed to punishment in the next life. (I am tempted to erase these words. They scare me.)

The chief looked at me very closely for a while before telling me, "Forget the past and focus on the future. Go back to the work you are supposed to be doing to help poor people become less poor. I hope your presence will not inflict any more calamities on our village."

The chief turned and said in a much louder voice, "I encourage everyone to begin working to undo the damage done by the heavy rainfall."

Almost immediately, people began cleaning up the mess the deluge had caused. Moans turned into religious songs of hope. Everyone believed the worst was over. With hard work and perseverance, they could repair the damage done and get their lives back on track. Everyone was saying all would be fine. That proved to be true, except for one very unusual case.

CHAPTER THREE
GUILTY OF DYING

One of the leaders of the big village cleanup in the aftermath of the floods and landslides was Emmanuel Bagbo. He was a well-known, good family man in his early forties. He was highly respected by everyone and often volunteered his time to help others. Emmanuel was a dynamic, energetic person on whom you could always depend. He was a deacon in the church and worked as a nurse in the local hospital, often making house calls after work. Everyone liked Emmanuel and expected him to be named to a special place in the chief's inner circle.

One day, for no apparent reason, the very healthy Emmanuel suddenly dropped dead. The chief and his key elders launched a full investigation into the cause of his death. The only deaths considered natural in the village were those of very young children and very old persons. Some kind of manipulation of bad spirits caused the death of anyone else, particularly if he or she was healthy. Therefore, the chief's investigators were questioning anyone who could say anything about any grievances held against the saintly Emmanuel.

Deaths were usually caused by people upset with someone to the extent they would pay a corrupt fetish priest to place a hex on someone so he or she would fall ill or die. The chief regularly judged village court cases involving people accused of paying a fetish priest to conjure evil spirits to cause harm. The practice of the dark arts was a thriving business, and its secrets were passed along family lines from generation to generation.

In most cases, the accused were found guilty and fined several dollars, and a few bottles of schnapps and whiskey. These fines helped underwrite the chief's administration and essential traditional ceremonies. The chief's compound had a spare room full of alcoholic beverages needed to satisfy the endless need to pour obligatory libations on the ground for the honor and happiness of the grandfathers. The depletion of this strategic ceremonial stock was something to avoid at all costs.

For the first time in living memory, the chief's investigators could not find any evidence that anyone had anything against Emmanuel. It appeared his case was unique. Nobody had any arguments with him or negative things to say about him. It was as if he was too good to be true, and for this reason, unknown forces eliminated him. Africa is a hard place for a good man, but this did not mean Emmanuel had to die.

These unusual findings caused a great quandary for the chief's court. The only conclusion it could draw was Emmanuel had no reason to die and thus, he was very wrong for having died. The chief's counselors determined the only way to bring closure to this tragic case and appease any unhappy spirits was to hold an unprecedented public trial of this dead man. Emmanuel was formally accused of dying before it was his time to die, and consequently, he must be tried in open village court for his woeful transgression.

A space was prepared under the shade of a huge kapok tree in the village's public meeting and ceremony place. Elders carefully considered how to outline a square large enough to accommodate the jury, judge, and almost everyone from the village. The elders used their walking sticks to trace the four sides of a very large square. Kontor performed a number of ceremonies to sanctify the ground inside the square. He slit the throat of a number of white roosters and walked along the lines traced by the elders, holding the roosters so their blood would drop along these lines. Once he was finished with all his mysterious mumblings and blood sacrifices, the space within the square became protected from evil spirits, and a welcoming area for good spirits and the ancestors.

Village volunteers firmly buried tree poles in each corner of the square and along its boundaries at intervals of about ten feet. These poles provided the initial support for fencing of the square and its palm thatch cover. Carpenters brought freshly sawed hardwood lumber from the yellow iroko tree to build a solid, elevated stand for the placement of a carved chief's chair, hewn from a single section of the trunk of a large red mahogany tree. It was in this ceremonial chair that Emmanuel would sit to go on trial for dying too soon. A special white cloth, hand-woven from local cotton spun by the oldest village women, covered the chair and stand.

It took several days to complete the court grounds. The chief and his key counselors came to inspect the grounds and discuss all the details needing attention before the trial could take place. The chief said he would consult his ancestor's house to determine the date of the trial. Each compound in the village had a small outside house reserved for the ancestors. Something belonging to, or some body part of, each "grandfather" since the beginning of the village was placed in these sacred houses. No one dared enter these houses without offering libations of alcoholic beverages on the ground in front of the door of the house while reciting the names of all the grandfathers who have died since the village was founded. In addition to these grandfather rooms, in the center of each compound, mounted high on the top of a tall tree stump was a totem symbol representing the god of the clan to which each family belonged.

The chief poured drops of whiskey from the best imported brands of spirits he possessed, calling to all the grandfathers to show him a sign to convey to him the date the trial should be held. He also wanted to make sure the spirit of the man who wrongly died did not object to the trial. For days after the chief pleaded for intervention of the grandfathers, he waited for a sign to tell him the date to hold the trial. One day he was eating white corn bread made by women at the weekly market. Inside one of the pieces of the steamed corn bread, just under its banana-leaf wrapping, was a small piece of wood in the shape of a cross. The chief interpreted this as meaning the trial had to be held on a Sunday.

Village criers walked back and forth through every passageway of the village, vigorously striking the two-tone iron gong used to alert people of important news. They announced in loud voices that the trial would be held the coming Sunday after early morning church services. People were told they should go straight from the old church high on the mountainside to the trial ground at the foot of the mountain. As all lived in a complex world where Christian and traditional beliefs were valued and practiced with equal fervor, having the trial on a Sunday was accepted without any complaint or even a second thought.

Church services in the old, whitewashed temple built over a hundred years ago by European missionaries were held as usual, but every person in the overcrowded church was only thinking of attending the trial that would follow. There was no less fervor than usual in the praises to the Christian God, who was regarded as being the same as the African supreme god. Prayers and preaching were executed with the same high level of vigor. The chorus was in perfect harmony and sounded like their recordings, which were popular throughout the country. The musicians were on perfect key, and the dancers were in full synchronization, mesmerizing all in attendance with how they moved in flawless unison.

The syncopated sounds resonated loudly off the thick walls of the old church. It was hard not to be spiritually uplifted, even when one's thoughts were elsewhere. The Holy Spirit seemed to understand, as this was one of the rare Sunday church services when not a single person became possessed by the Spirit. It was as if God understood what was going to happen next and was turning things over to lower level spirits, which had dwelt in this place for hundreds of years, long before the Whiteman arrived with his religion. You could almost feel the other dimension closing in around you and the gathering of all the grandfathers overhead. In the end, it would be the judgment passed by beings not of this Earth that would count.

With the last "amen," people rushed from the church and down the mountainside to jostle for a good place to observe the trial. There was no going home to change clothes or eat. Some had already foreseen the need for food and carried small bags of cassava flour and groundnuts to snack on. Many people were buying food and water from the many vendors who had come to make money by selling their goods to the crowd. The excitement level was high. It was like a magic show had come to town. Nobody knew what to expect, but they expected to see things today they had never seen before.

People gathered around the square traced by the elders and the structure that had been erected. Nobody dared getting too close until the chief, his top elders, and fetish priests arrived to open the white curtains hanging over the large entrance way. In spite of the scorching heat and high humidity, people waited patiently for a couple of hours. People were asking many questions about how the dead man would be represented and how his trial would unfold. After a long, unappreciated delay, the chief's procession could be seen coming toward the court square.

The crowd backed away to give ample room for the dozens who came with the chief, who was dressed in his most special hand-woven and colorfully dyed ceremonial clothes. He wore his golden crown with carved wooden badges showing all the animal totems of the village, including the one never mentioned. The chief and his entourage stopped in front of the curtain in front of the judgment enclosure and yelled out the name "Emmanuel" five times. Then they summoned the dead Emmanuel to come to face his judgment. After a few minutes of unintelligible words by Kontor, the chief threw open the curtain. He and those with him took their seats on the wooden platform built about ten feet in front of the chair where the accused would sit.

So nobody could see what was inside, a thick black curtain covered the stand on which the dead man would sit. Everyone assumed that for the purposes of this ceremonial trial, the curtains would remain closed. The chief and his assistants would talk to the curtain as if the dead man was sitting behind it. After all, how could the man, who was dead, be resurrected to sit in the big chair? Suddenly, the chief rose and proceeded to drop the curtain surrounding the dead man's chair by a quick pull on a string. As soon as the curtain had fallen away, all those assembled exhaled a loud, collective gasp.

Some fainted and others quickly fled at the sight of what they saw. People were stunned, because in the dead man's chair was the dead man. How could that be? How did he get here? But there was Emmanuel, or an exact look-alike, dressed in his finest kente clothes, sitting stiff as a board with his eyes wide open and staring straight ahead. He was covered with the powder of white ashes and looked like a ghost, but it was indeed a man in the chair. It was boiling hot and everyone was perspiring profusely, but not a bead of sweat could be seen on the dead man's face. Even the flies pestering everyone could not make him blink or lift a finger. He was like a frozen statue produced by some kind of magical holograph.

Sitting on some benches next to the chief's group were Emmanuel's wife, children, and other relatives. The women among them were wailing loudly from what was either profound grief or fear over what was happening. All the children in the group were bawling as if they had been severely whipped. After one quick glance, all of them were too afraid to take another look and covered their eyes or looked elsewhere. Tension was rising as the crowd waited for the trial to begin.

Just when the suspense was at its peak, the chief stood and looked straight at the dead man and said five times...each time raising his voice higher...in a loud voice, "Emmanuel, you were wrong to die!"

After this strong pronouncement, the chief sat down, and each member in his entourage passed in front of the dead man, looking at him and shaking their fists in anger and repeating what the chief had said. Then the town crier rose, struck his iron cymbal and asked the crowd if Emmanuel was wrong to die. In loud unison the crowd answered, "Yes, he was wrong to die!"

The chief stood and turned to the crowd, asking, "Does anyone have anything to say in the defense of the dead man?"

There was only silence. He paused for a good number of minutes, as he wanted to be seen as acting fairly, giving anyone who wanted to speak up in the defense of the dead man the opportunity to do so. As the chief prepared to return to his seat, a young girl, no more than ten years of age, stepped vigorously forward, and in a loud, crackling voice called the chief by his secret name—a name known only to members of the age group who had been initiated with him. All were shocked to see the girl do this, especially the chief, as he knew this could only mean one thing: possession.

Very quickly the girl ran up to the chief, speaking rapidly in a crazed manner a dialect only a few of the oldest people understood. The chief became fearful and turned his head to beckon the most senior elder to come and help him deal with this girl. As soon as the elder was close enough to hear the girl, several other girls began babbling and acting in the same bizarre manner. It was now obvious the grandfathers had possessed these girls, and they were trying to speak through them.

While the oldest people in the village tried to listen to what the girls were saying, the girls became more agitated and began shaking and rolling around on the ground. Their dirt-laden appearance made them more frightening. Some ripped off their clothes and became catatonic, foaming at the mouth. Others pulled out their hair. Nothing could be done but to wait for the ancestors to finish saying what they had come to say. After more than thirty minutes of this unnerving situation, all the possessed children fell to the ground like quiet lumps of earth, exhausted from an experience none of them would remember. For a moment, the silence was so pronounced you could hear in the distance the chilling cries of the evil black crows.

The families of the children came to take them away to places far from the crowd where they could calmly wake up. The chief huddled with the old people to attempt to piece together what the grandfathers were trying to communicate. There was some heated discussion, as not all agreed on the grandfathers' message. One old man became so overcome by emotion that he fainted;

some believed he may have had a heart attack. The collapse of this old man helped calm the tense situation. The chief yelled loudly, "There is too much disorder! Everyone return to their places!"

After the crowd settled down, the chief continued, "I will now pronounce judgment on the dead man."

The crowd became quiet. All wanted to hear what the chief would say, but at the same time, they were wondering what the grandfathers had communicated. The chief turned to face the dead man again. Even this stately man was not able to keep his composure when he observed that the dead man's chair was empty. He and all others looked at the dead man's chair in disbelief. Where had the dead man gone? It was now apparent that during all the commotion with the possessed children, the dead man had disappeared while everyone was looking elsewhere. Only his clothes remained on the chair. It was as if the dead man had been taken by the grandfathers. The crowd was stunned into absolute silence and fear gripped each and every one like a cold, hard steel trap.

One senior elder muttered that the dead man's disappearance might be the work of spirits contained in the wood of the iroko wood chair he was sitting on. Many people believed that all the iroko trees possessed spirits and they remained in the wood after the tree was chopped down and made into furniture or drums. There were plenty of stories of people claiming to hear items made from iroko wood talking in their houses at night.

The chief was now puzzled as to how to proceed. He gathered his elders around him again and asked for their advice. After a lengthy discussion, a consensus was reached…the trial must go on. The chief turned again to face the dead man's chair and pronounced his judgment as if the dead man were still there.

He said in a loud voice so all could hear, "Emmanuel, you have been found guilty of dying years before your time. The grandfathers confirmed this verdict; they honored us today by speaking to us. You are hereby fined twenty dollars, two bottles of schnapps, and one bottle of Johnny Walker whiskey. In your absence, the younger brothers you have so wrongly left behind will be responsible for paying your fine. Furthermore, I am very sad to announce that no funeral will be held in your honor."

When the chief said Emmanuel would not be given a funeral, there was a loud and spontaneous cry of astonishment emitted by the people. They had never heard of a dead person not being honored with some kind of funeral. Families often saved for years to hold a respectable funeral for their beloved deceased. Usually, the size of the funeral depended on the importance of the person. Funerals ended up being huge parties with lots of food, drink and music and dancing, and many ceremonies could go on for several days. Much of the prestige of a family depended on how grand a funeral celebration it was capable of throwing for its dead. It was indeed a time to give all one had, show off, and make the dead proud and happy, as the dead were watching and celebrating too. Many families became deeply indebted by holding conspicuous funerals.

The chief's pronouncement of the verdict brought closure to this extraordinary trial, especially for the family members present who were relieved to have this event come to an end. They were happy that village custom and good manners would make it so nobody would ever speak again of what happened here today. Once a judgment was rendered, it was final. Anyone who dared to speak of this trial would be denounced and severely punished by the chief's bodyguards. Punishment of such offenses usually consisted of a whipping and being tied to a pole with a rope around one's neck for a week in the chief's compound.

The trial lasted longer than expected. Darkness was falling quickly on the village. People were rushing home because they did not want to be caught away from their homes at night. For them, nighttime was when the evil spirits were making their rounds. It was best to avoid them. There were also rumors about headhunters on the prowl in the environs of the village. But, on this night, most people scurried home, because they did not want to have an encounter with the lost dead man.

I, too, rushed to my modest little house on the edge of the village. I rushed not because I was afraid to be out after dark, I rushed because I was troubled by what I had observed. I needed time alone at home to think about all I had seen that day. I sat on my narrow bed in my tiny bedroom contemplating all I had observed at this bizarre trial. I could not come up with any rational answers for all that had happened. I knew what I saw, but I did not have any explanation for it. Maybe things could happen if everyone believed in them. I did not believe what I saw, but I could not deny the existence of what I saw.

It was like some occult world existed that could only come alive if enough people strongly believed in its existence and importance. Maybe this world has always been there but died away as people stopped believing. Today, those who know about this world and how to engage with it are almost all gone, and thus, this world lies dormant and mostly forgotten. I pondered this unusual day until late in the night as I watched the dancing shadows on the wall caused by my flickering kerosene lamp. It was hard for me to sleep. I was profoundly tormented. I did not have any satisfactory answers for what I had witnessed.

I awoke early the next morning in time to see members of Emmanuel's family walking quietly toward the nearby field of broken pots. One thing not prohibited by the chief was the traditional ceremony where clay pots would be broken to mark the end of a life and the impossibility of that life ever being brought back to the world of the living. The family carried a large clay pot it had been using in its compound. Generations of clay pottery shards covered this field; they remained where they fell after families broke them into many pieces to recognize the loss of their kin.

Emmanuel's family found a spot relatively clear of pottery shards. Emmanuel's oldest brother took the pot and lifted it high over his head and, after saying loudly "Goodbye Emmanuel," he slammed the pot hard to the ground, shattering it into many pieces. At that moment it was done. Emmanuel was dead and gone forever. Death was like a broken clay pot; it can never be mended.

CHAPTER FOUR
CHAMELEON
HEAT WAVE

After Emmanuel's family passed by, I heard the hushed whispering of many people outside my front window. I looked out the edge of the window to see who was there. It did not take me long to see a chief from a neighboring village with some of his elders. They had arrived before dawn to camp in my front yard, waiting to meet with me. This was not the first of such early morning visits. It was customary to go to someone's house very early in the morning and wait for them to wake up. In this way, you were sure not to miss the person. Many people believed if important things were not done early in the morning, it was best to postpone them until you could take action at sunrise.

I quickly gulped a bowl of cassava flour mixed with groundnuts and sugar cubes soaked with boiled and filtered water. With this crunchy, homemade breakfast cereal consumed, I was ready for what could be a long traditional palaver with another group of African village leaders. I quietly exited my front door and pretended to be surprised at seeing such an important delegation waiting to see me. I offered in the local language the usual long-winded morning greetings, wishing all the best. Some benches were brought for us to sit on. I was offered the seat of honor, a special hand-carved chief's stool. After some typical friendly exchanges and a long pause, the chief rose to present the reason for their early morning visit.

The chief started by saying, "We are happy to see you healthy and still living among us. It is good to have a Whiteman living in our district. In the past all white men we have known helped us improve our lives. We assume you too are here to help us. That is good, as our needs are many. We need a water well, a health clinic, market hangars, schools, and much more."

The list of needs and their magnitude was overwhelming, but very true. And this was only one village of twenty in the small District of Ataku I was attempting to help.

The chief's remarks were punctuated with nods and varying grunts of agreement by the dozen men who accompanied him. There were also some quick gasping inhalations, which I had learned meant you understood and acknowledged the truth of what was being said. The chief ended his remarks by thanking me again for receiving them and listening so well to what he had said.

He, then, had one of the men bring forth a clay pot containing fresh palm wine, which he poured into two calabash bowls, one for him and one for me. He handed me a bowl of the foamy, white brew. I followed his lead by pouring a few drops on the ground for the grandfathers and then took a swallow myself. Although it was very early in the morning to be drinking alcoholic beverages, for me to not partake of this wine in this fashion would be insulting and a gross violation of cultural norms.

One swallow was enough for me. As I carefully balanced the wobbly calabash bowl on the ground in front of me, I was thinking of how I would now reply to the chief. I was trying to think of a story or a parable that would relate well to the topic at hand, but I could not think of any. In this society a good speaker must be able to weave stories into his (rarely her) oral presentations in order to hold a high position in this society. I did not have any stories to tell. Moreover, my ability to speak in the local language was weak. They would make many exceptions for me, as I was an outsider. Nonetheless, I was very ill at ease as I began my choppy reply.

In my usual soft, meek voice, I basically said, "I understand your needs and I wish I could help, but I am unlike the other white men you have known. I have few resources at my disposal."

This was hard for them to believe, because all white men were rich compared to them.

I said, "I know it is difficult for you to believe that I really do not have the wherewithal to help you. I have already been asked by my village to help build a new three-classroom primary-school building. It would be hard for me to help any other village before I help my home village."

They were not happy when I said this, but they seemed to accept the logic of what I said.

Our exchange lasted over two hours, and the temperature was rising as the sun rose over Mt. Ataku, telling us it was time to move on to something else. As we were saying the many departure greetings and shaking hands with the usual mutual snapping of fingers, something fell from the mango tree branches above us. At first, I thought it was one of the mango fruits falling to the ground. But, there in our midst on the ground was a chameleon. Upon seeing the chameleon, all gasped and stepped backwards, except me. I was fascinated by chameleons, but the villagers feared them. They believed spirits occupied them, and their bite could transmit the essence of a spirit into your body. This chameleon looked different. It had an unusual splotch of red coloring on its head crown, and oddly, this splotch did not change color when the rest of its body adopted the coloration of its surroundings.

To the horror of all, I quickly pulled my blue bandana from my back pocket and threw it over the hapless chameleon, carefully wrapping it up, so it could not escape. They could not believe what I had done. They were convinced I was totally crazy when I took the chameleon from the handkerchief and held it in my hand. To show them they had nothing to fear, I allowed the chameleon to bite one of my fingers with its toothless mouth. This was more than the chief and his elders could bear. They all left my compound in a hurry, saying there was no sense asking this crazy Whiteman for anything. And, anyway, the falling chameleon was a bad sign that trumped all they had sought.

I had been looking for a chameleon to put in a small bamboo cage I had built. I took the chameleon into my house and put it in the cage with some grass. I enjoyed watching it rotate independently its protruding eyes. It was amazing how it could see in all directions at once and its flexible prehensile tail acted like a fifth leg. Its long sticky tongue could unroll and whip out in a split second to reel in an unwary insect. Its tongue was easily longer than its body, and its five-toed feet were a rarity in the animal kingdom. I understood it could see things no other creature on Earth could see.

Clearly, chameleons were among the most ancient and weirdest creatures on Earth. Given the special nature of the chameleon, I was not surprised the villagers were very superstitious about this singularly odd reptile. Of course, for the villagers there were not any notions which could be considered "superstitions." All their beliefs on this and everything else were real and needed to be taken seriously.

The sound of loud clapping at my front gate rudely interrupted my pleasure in observing this marvel of nature close up. Clapping instead of knocking was used to ask if anyone was at home, and if it was alright to enter.

I replied, "I am at home; enter in peace."

I was very surprised to see a woman from the village who was the most revered fetish priestess, Babagan, enter my compound. I could not fathom why she would bother herself to visit me.

Babagan was the female counterpart to Kontor. She was very short and dressed in multi-color cloth made of many discarded patches of cloth that local tailors put aside for the making of such dresses. She was very old and wrinkled from head to toe like a dry prune. She was fearless and fierce in her behavior. She was clearly a no-nonsense person, full of impressive energy, who did not take "no" for an answer.

She came swiftly to within inches of me to confront me about reports of my harboring lost spirits which inhabited a very rare redheaded chameleon. I was speechless. I did not know what to say, and I did not dare quarrel with this powerful woman.

"Turn the chameleon over to me immediately!" she demanded.

There was no arguing with her. I removed the chameleon from its cage. She quickly grabbed it from my hand and thrust into its mouth a thin, sharp stick she was holding, pushing the stick through the chameleon's mouth until it came out its anus. With the chameleon skewered like a shish kebab, she asked me to show her the spot where it fell to ground. I indicated the spot where it had landed, and she stuck the stick firmly in the ground at that spot.

She firmly instructed, "No one should touch the stick, as the spirits in the chameleon were meant to come out at this spot."

I promised to make sure the chameleon impaled by a stick would not be touched. She said, "I will return in a few days to collect the chameleon's remains."

In the hot tropical sun, the chameleon quickly expired and began to shrivel. When Babagan showed up a few days later, it had dried to a crisp. She carefully removed the chameleon's remains and placed them on a small, white cloth. She gently dropped the remains into a miniature wood mortar she was carrying. She took from the cloth wrapped around her waist a small ivory pestle that she used to crush the chameleon's remains into a fine powder.

She poured this powder into a small glass vial, and said, "This powder can be used as a strong ingredient in a very powerful medicine."

My dream of raising chameleons had been quickly reduced to some kind of mysterious medicinal powder.

As I started to enter my humble dwelling, a hot wind came blowing hard around the mountain. I found this odd but thought nothing of it. I entered my house and the heat brought from the wind enveloped me like a warm blanket. My limbs became heavy, and my eyes could not stay open. I staggered toward my small bed to lie down for a few minutes before going to look for lunch. The weight of this tropical heat wave penetrated every pore of my body. It was as if I was in a heated cocoon, undergoing some sort of metamorphous process. I felt paralyzed. There was no resisting the deep sleep which felled me in the middle of the day.

There were times that afternoon I wanted to wake up, but I could not get any of my body parts to move. As hard as I tried to raise my arms and legs, I could not move them. I lay immobilized, sweating profusely. My clothes and mattress were soaked, and I was drenched by the pool of sweat that enveloped me. Yet, as uncomfortable as it was, I could not break the hold this deep-sleep coma had on me. It was almost dark before I could begin freeing myself from this death-like slumber. I was finally able to stand up, but I was nauseated and dizzy, as if I was recovering from being sedated by some kind of powerful drug. I stumbled out the door to see what the women, Aba and Assi, living next to me were doing.

I found them recovering from the same deep sleep stupor I had just experienced. Later, we learned this tropical heat wave had put every living thing in the village to sleep. The chief called a special meeting of the elders' council to examine what possibly could have triggered such a rare phenomenon.

After much deliberation, the chief communicated forthrightly the conclusion. He said, "The hot wind was caused by angry spirits which had come to collect their brethren who had been released at the wrong time from the strange chameleon Bobovovi had mistakenly captured."

I feared a strong admonition from the chief, and perhaps, some kind of punishment. I even feared the worst: being banned from the village.

But, again, my ignorance saved me. I was viewed as the "dumb Whiteman" who was interfering with the natural order of village life because of his ignorance. The people were fond of saying that even a small child knew more than the highly educated Whiteman. The joke in the village was I was so dumb, I could not tell the difference between a goat and a sheep. What good was education if it meant you did not know even the basic fundamentals of living with the ancestors and spirits? I did receive a brief, but stern message from the chief via his official messenger.

The message basically said: "Africa likes you, and the village likes you, but you must learn our ways or leave!" I did not want to be perceived as a threat, so I promised to learn even more about local ways and to be more careful in the future. For sure, from then on, I looked at chameleons very differently and gave any chameleon I encountered a very wide berth.

CHAPTER FIVE
HEAD IS HEAD

A few days later, I awoke to find three people waiting for me. One was the chief's next-door neighbor, who was also the village historian. Another was a respected elder and master keeper of village customs and traditions. The third person was a woman who knew the woman knowledgeable of the uses of plants.

The village historian said, "The chief has sent us to instruct you on the basic information one needs to know to live in the village in a way that avoids trouble. We should have given you such instruction a long time ago, but we did not think you would be the cause of so much spiritual commotion. We now understand your spirit is strong and attractive to the ancestors, village gods, and the good and bad demons of the spirit world."

Having said all that, they rose and bid good-bye, saying my instruction would start first thing tomorrow morning. While I had other things to do tomorrow, I had no choice but to agree and say I was eager to begin my instruction.

On the surface, the village looked like a simple and very backward place. It was a collection of mud-brick dwellings, mostly with straw roofs, and without any modern amenities. Most of its three thousand inhabitants had not been to school and could not read or write. I found out the hard way that first impressions are important, but easily deceiving. Indeed, the more I learned of village ways, the more it became an exceedingly complicated place in which to live. The slightest move could not be made without thinking of the impact of that move on the ancestors, animistic spirits, and large pantheon of gods and lesser deities. One had to keep an eye on neighbors and all with whom you contacted. Even the smallest misstep could make someone jealous or put them in enough opposition to you to have them resort to fetish or ancestral manipulation aimed at affecting you in one way or another.

Making everyone like you and keeping them happy was an impossible challenge. Nobody could avoid crossing someone sometime. This fact kept the village in constant turmoil and off balance, as the flow of occult attacks and counter attacks was constantly in excess. The village was always waiting for some new case to surface and, usually, the waiting period was short. These attacks were the sources of many cases being pursued for judgment by the chief and his council of elders. People loved litigation, and they could not wait to accuse their neighbor, or even someone they just met for the first time, so they could take them to village court or even to the higher state courts. Deep down, simple village life was really very complex and demanding.

For me, as an outsider, much of this was nonsense. Initially, I believed I was excluded from any involvement with the litigious nature of village life. Later, I found it was impossible to live in the village without being the object of some evildoings. In fact, some preferred targeting outsiders to see what would happen. Testing various local powers on strangers was not unusual. I was considered fair game for the mischievous. It was something of a sport for them to pay fetish priests to play with my life. Sometimes, without knowing it, animistic practices were focused on me to test my character and measure the strength of my innate spirit. Some wanted to see if they could alter the natural-born destiny of a human being who was not from their world.

The next day I was surprised to see the inimitable Kontor at my front gate early in the morning. His presence sent a chill up my backbone. He had been sent by the chief to begin my instruction. I was a little surprised by his unexpected appearance and dress. The old, white clothes he wore were ragged. He looked like he had just come from working in the fields.

Apologetically, he politely told me, "I have not come from the village but from the countryside. We usually clean ourselves and change into clean and neat clothes before entering the village."

Nobody wanted to be seen dirty or as having done manual labor. I assumed he had received his instruction from the chief the day before and had gone in the bush before coming to get me. He indicated we would be going on a walk into the woods and, accordingly, I, too, should put on some old clothes.

Before we left my compound, he demanded, "Are you careful to dispose of your fingernail cuttings and any body hair?"

I meekly replied, "I know to do this. Anything coming off my body is burnt or thrown into the latrine. This is not hard to do in secret as I always cut my own nails and hair."

He nodded his approval, saying, "One could never be too careful. There are always people around looking for body parts to use to gain power over those from whence the parts came."

There was also a thriving clandestine market in human and animal parts. People would buy them for use in ceremonies to gain power or specific favors from concerned gods or spirits. I really did not believe any of this, but I always found it easier to err on the side of safety by disposing of my hair and nails in ways that made them uncollectable by others.

Upon leaving my compound, we immediately took a bush path headed toward the woods. As we entered deeper into the bush, we came across other footpaths leading in various directions. Each time we would come across another path, he would ask me which path I would choose.

Each time I responded, "I cannot choose because I do not know where the path leads."

In his melodious voice, he sternly replied, "You are not giving me good answers. Look closely at the entryway of any path for telltale signs of what it is used for and where it might lead."

I closely examined the bushes and trees on either side of the paths and could not see anything to give me any clues about the path.

He then said in a more serious tone, "Look at the stems of grass tied subtly in knots on the left side of the path. They are barely noticeable to the untrained eye, but the way they are tied means this path leads to a place to defecate. Every child knows this."

As we arrived at a fork in the path we were on, he gave me a stone-hard look and asked, "Which path should we take?"

I looked carefully at the left fork. I could not see anything identifying the course of this path. I hopefully said, "I would take the left path as it seems free of any signs."

In an angry manner, he quickly said, "You are wrong. See those two twigs tied together with grass, stuck in the ground at the side of the right fork? This means this path is the best one. The other path would shortly end. Therefore, to avoid a dead end, we should continue along the path on the right."

He stopped to show me a certain kind of tree stump that was hidden in the tall grass. He pointed at the small stump and informed me, "This is a special kind of small tree with deep roots that farmers use to mark the sides of their fields. If you have not planted these trees in a line to mark the perimeters of your fields, you cannot claim to be using the field. The presence of these tree markers are often used to determine who has the right to farm a given piece of land. The stumps of these trees endure for many years."

Later, we came upon another path that veered sharply toward a clump of trees. We stopped. He waited as I looked for signs as to what this path was all about. I was pleased to note, "See this clump of tall grass bent and pinned to the ground by a stone? It must mean something."

He said, "Good. This means there is a fetish sanctuary at the end of this path. Only those engaged by that fetish spirit to represent them on this Earth should use this path."

I replied, "This is a good thing to know."

He then surprised me by saying, "Follow me."

He led me along this forbidden path. He said, "As long as you are with me, it will be alright, but you should never be so foolish as to follow such a path on your own. I want to show you what lies at the end of this path so your curiosity would not someday lead you to do something stupid."

He was a great teacher, and when he talked at length, I grasped his meaning quickly.

At the end of the path was a round clearing with open ground of about twenty yards in circumference. In the very center of this circle was a tree with three upward growing branches shorn of its leaves. At the base of the trinity of branches was a clay bowl containing sacred water with some leaves from the tree. (I had seen the same arrangement on that extraordinary moonlit night at the top of the mountain, but I could not say this.)

Ten feet from the base of the tree, a circle had been established by burying old wine bottles upside down so only about one inch of their bottoms was protruding from the ground. As the sun was overhead, these bottle bottoms reflected light. It looked like a sparkling, fiery circle. Off to one side of the circle was a small grass lean-to that was used by those who had been engaged by the spirit which occupied this sanctuary. They stayed here when they came to give offerings to the spirit and wait for its bidding.

I wanted to enter the circle and see up close what was in the clay bowl in the triple-tree fork. Kontor stopped me from doing so, saying, "You would put your life and sanity at risk by stepping into the sacred circle."

He continued, "I know this is hard to understand, but it is the truth. There are many cases in our village's oral history that prove this true."

I responded by asking, "What would happen to me if I did step over the boundary formed by the bottles."

He said, "I am not sure, but whatever it is, it will follow you the rest of your life until it consumes you."

Since hearing this, I have found it made no sense to take any risks, and thus, it has always been easy for me to give such sanctuaries a wide berth. Why tempt the unknown?

After we left this secret sanctuary, we headed down a path taking us to an open, treeless savanna area where only tall straw grasses grew. In the far distance, I could see where my house was located. Just as he asked me to find a path to lead us back to my house, we heard shouts coming from a wooded area about one hundred yards away. We saw a small group of people running through the tall grass as fast as they could go. The few women among them were wailing a high-pitched warning, repeating the word "danger" at the top of their voices. We quickly moved down a path leading in the same direction as the people fleeing the danger. We ran so we could catch up with the people as they came out of the tall grass onto the wide path that passed by my house. Running fast was difficult because we were both wearing flip-flops.

When we caught up with this group of farmers, they were so out of breath, they could not speak. Finally, Kontor heard a word that told him the whole story. This word was: "headhunter."

He quickly told me, "Go with these people and stay within your compound."

Then he sped off to alert the village and inform the chief. All along the eight hundred yards between where we were and the center of the village, he was shouting out "headhunters." As soon as people heard this, they stopped what they were doing and rushed home to make ready their defenses. Groups of men with machetes and handmade muskets gathered to wait for the chief's orders to go to the spot where headhunters were observed.

I remained behind within my compound walls until I heard the armed group approaching my house. I stepped outside to observe what was going to happen next. With the group were some of the chief's most important elders, his top security guard, and Kontor, who quickly entered into the tall grass, dispersing smoke over the grass by waving a wire brazier full of burning embers, like a priest blessing the faithful. At first I thought he was going to set the grass on fire, forcing those hiding within to come out and be captured. But no, this was just the start of an elaborate ceremony that included blowing various powders into the grass and pronouncing a fast stream of magical words. We were all very silent and intimidated by the very powerful magic we observed being worked by a man who obviously possessed great powers.

After a short while, we could see in the distance what looked like a big piece of blue cloth slowly sailing through the air towards us just over the top of the grass. As this bizarre image came closer to us, we could see it was a man dressed in a large blue boubou gown that was flapping in the wind. The fact that he was wearing a long boubou gown told us he was probably a trader who belonged to a distant northern ethnic group. But, more important than this was the impossible fact he was floating through the air suspended and propelled by some unknown force. We appreciated greatly how Kontor had somehow conjured up some strong magic to make this amazing scene possible. I could not believe my eyes. The tall man hovered for a split second in suspended animation in front of us before being dropped suddenly to the ground with a hard thud.

As soon as the intruder was released from the force that held him, the armed men in our group pounced on him and beat him from head to toe with the huge sticks they were carrying. They tied his feet and hands tightly together and placed him on a long pole like a large animal being carried to the butcher. As they carried him through the village, people spat and threw stones at him. He was taken to the section of the chief's compound used to punish people, and his neck was tied tightly to a post firmly buried in the ground. His punishment would be quite severe.

No matter what he said, or if he might be innocent, he was guilty in the eyes of the villagers as a stranger who had no business being where he was found. The fact he came from the distant north and possessed a very tall and slender physical form versus the short stature of most of the local inhabitants, incited deep-seated prejudices that added greatly to the deep divide between coastal and northern ethnic groups. There was no bridging of the gap between coastal agriculturalists and northern pastoralists. The people of Ataku were profoundly incensed that such a northern intruder had violated their land with his foreign presence.

Furthermore, everyone hated in the extreme those who came during certain times of the year to hunt for heads they could sell in neighboring countries for a good price. Wicked fetish priests used these heads to increase their powers and undertake ceremonies to conjure up evil spirits. Headhunters would wait along isolated paths and jump on anyone coming by and cut off her or his head, and run away with it in a burlap bag. Every year several headless bodies were found discarded in the bush.

The chief and his elders kept all this in mind as they considered what to do with the headhunter they had captured. For them, this man was obviously a murderer and had to be dealt with accordingly, and, as murder was only for the gods to judge in the afterlife, his sort was beyond their jurisdiction. They, therefore, had no choice but to turn him over to the government security authorities. But, first he was stripped of his clothing and beaten repeatedly with a bamboo stick. He was never given a chance to say a word.

I was escorted back to my house by one of the chief's advisors. My head was aching as I tried to make sense out of all I had just observed. How can a man be brought out of his hiding place in the tall, thick grass by magical powers? I asked the man with me how is this possible.

All he could say was, "I do not know and I cannot know. Only those chosen by the gods to have such powers can know. You should not stress yourself so. This is not unusual, and as you can see, the result was very good."

Somehow, this made me feel more at ease. I said, "Anyway, I was never in any danger as I am sure the headhunter did not want a Whiteman's head."

In reply to this, he shook his head vigorously and looked directly at me and sternly said, "No, you are very wrong, head is head. If you have learned nothing else today, please know that!"

CHAPTER SIX

SCHOOL OF JEALOUSLY

The next day I awoke to the usual daybreak sound of women sweeping my compound grounds. I found the rhythmical and smooth way the women swept my compound very soothing. Bent fully over from the waist, they seemed to glide across my compound like swans on a still lake. It was like being awakened by quiet waves rolling up and down a sandy beach. I peeked out my bedroom window to see if anyone was waiting for me this morning. I was surprised not to see anyone. I was expecting another one of the chief's "teachers" to be there for another day of learning what all children know. I guess all the commotion of yesterday with the capture of a headhunter had upset the plans of a number of the chief's associates.

I was thinking today was a good day to get back to what I originally was supposed to do: build a three-classroom school. When I first came to the village, I was asked, "What can you do to help us?"

I replied, "What do you need?"

Their answer was, "A school."

The only primary school they had was a collection of straw-covered, mud-walled shelters that did not hold up well in the rainy season and often blew away in the dry season. I had, therefore, been trying to raise for months the $2,000 needed to build a three-classroom, concrete structure with a tin roof.

My agreement with the village school construction committee, named by the chief, was that it would provide all the gravel, sand, and labor. These items had to be delivered before I would bring the things it could not provide, such as cement, steel rebar, nails, lumber, and tin roofing sheets. Almost immediately after the conclusion of our agreement, all women in the village were mobilized to scoop up sand from a streambed located several miles away and carry it to the construction site. The women came with their big metal washbasins, filled them with sand and carried them on their heads to the work site. Each woman made several trips each day. In a few weeks, it was as if sand from several dump trucks had been delivered. I was learning that progress in the village depended on the hard and courageous work of women.

The sand was too coarse and full of debris, so screen mesh sieves had to be built. All the sand had to be sifted through these fine wire meshes. Throughout, the women seemed tireless in their efforts and made work look like fun. They sang songs in unison and often times did a little dance after relieving their heads of heavy loads. For the women, this was the easy part; the hard part was making the gravel needed to make concrete. Making gravel required collecting hard stones and crushing them into small pieces with a heavy hammer. As the women only had a couple of old hammers, I found myself obliged to buy a dozen big hammers for them to pound stones into jagged pieces of gravel.

Making gravel was hard work. Much care had to be taken to avoid eye injuries caused by fragments of stone ricocheting into your face. Nevertheless, several women suffered eye injuries as they reduced big piles of stones into small mounds of gravel. Each woman was assigned by her leader to produce a specified number of washbasins of gravel each day. Everyone worked hard, because they did not want to suffer the humiliation of their peers by not filling their gravel quota. But, as hard as they worked, gravel was not being produced fast enough. I, therefore, offered an incentive of about ten cents per washbasin of gravel produced. This was a small amount, but for these women, it was an important sum. Many of these women had no money at all and did not participate in the monetized economy. The incentive was welcomed with much happiness and gratitude. The pace of gravel-making picked up significantly.

When enough gravel and cleaned sand had been stockpiled, I met with the village school committee so it could provide me with the male laborers, carpenters, and masons who would actually build the school. As many of the laborers were old, I asked why younger workers could not be provided. I noted that every day there were dozens of able-bodied young men sitting under the big shade tree in the village center, doing nothing. They replied these men could not do manual labor because they had been to school. It was then I learned that even a few years of schooling meant you were destined for greater things in life than manual labor. One should not harm your prestige, shame yourself and family, and waste your time by working with your hands.

I found these young men, and so-called "future leaders," to be arrogant and useless. Their lazy behavior and insolent demeanor made me fear for the future of the village and the country. If this was the result of primary-school education, I was forced to question the value of that education. What good future could a country have if its youth would not do manual labor when it was not qualified for anything else? The whole idea in the village was that children, particularly boys, should obtain their primary-school diploma, go to the capital city, and find a salaried job permitting them to send money back to their family in the village. This was more of a dream than a reality. Paying jobs were scarce and becoming much harder to find as the population was growing very fast. For me, things in the village had been turned upside down, with the most intelligent and able people never having seen a classroom, while those, who had some education, were a burden to society.

I consulted with Aziz, the Lebanese owner of a small hardware store, 'Aziz and Sons,' located in the nearby regional capital of Kpolomo. Although the store carried the name of Aziz's sons, I never saw anyone in the store except Aziz. I arranged with Aziz the purchase and delivery of cement, wire, and form lumber. I was obliged to buy picks, shovels, levels, heavy twine, and a variety of hand tools. Aziz was always very helpful. He allowed me to buy on credit, and he transported everything to the work site in the village. In addition, I consulted a local blacksmith for the fabrication of a metal, rectangular mold needed to make the sand-concrete blocks that would form the school's walls.

Making blocks required workers experienced with this task. It was something that had to be done at the onset so enough blocks could be made and cured by the time they were needed to build the walls. The block makers provided by the village committee arrived early on the site and began clearing a flat space under a nearby tree for placing the blocks as they were released from the metal mold. This area was pounded hard with the backs of shovels, so it could support the hundreds of bulky blocks to be laid closely to one another like dominoes being readied for a cascading chain reaction.

The key to making blocks was a proper mixture of sand and cement mixed together with the right amount of water. You had to know how many shovels of the mix to put in the mold and how to pack the mix in the hand-mold by hitting it on the top with the back of the shovel. The tricky part was taking the mold full of mix to where the block would be placed in an upright position on the ground. This was done by turning the mold over gently and sliding it off the newly formed block in one swift and very straight, upward motion. Once a block had been placed on the ground, it would begin to harden. As the hardening process must occur slowly, the new blocks were doused with water for several days and covered with burlap bags and palm branches. The fresh blocks also had to be protected from errant goats, sheep, and chickens, which could break them up by simply walking on them before the blocks were sufficiently hard. It was thus required to erect a thorn-branch fence around the block-making area.

As work progressed, there were many expenses I had not foreseen in my budget such as hammers, sand sifts, water barrels, and the daily provision of food and palm wine. Many of these expenses were funded from my own pocket, but I did not care much about this as long as good progress was being made toward building the school. I was not a construction expert, and I had no previous experience with building. I did have some books on construction that enabled me to know when something was done wrong or to question some work when I noted any task not being done correctly. I found my presence at the work site also helped keep discipline and order. People did not like to work if I was absent. Often times when I would leave the work site, I could hear the laborers dropping their tools and walking away. I was the outside catalyst who kept things moving ahead. I did question how difficult it would be to achieve progress if they could not work on their own.

There was one time when I was overseeing the work site that everyone yelled something at the top of their voices and ran away into the surrounding bush. For a brief minute or so, I was puzzled by this bizarre behavior, but when the first bunch of bees descended quickly on me, I was also running for my life. African bees are much more aggressive than the bees we had when I was growing up in Kansas. African bees swarmed frequently and terrorized every living being in their path. The people at the work site could hear the distant buzzing of the bees and this signaled to them to take cover immediately. I didn't hear anything and ended up with several painful bee stings. I had heard a dozen or more stings from big African bees could stop your heart.

The school was being built according to government plans. In many ways, it was a simple structure with half walls on either side of each classroom and a narrow veranda providing a passageway in front of the classrooms. As with any building, the important thing was the digging of a deep foundation trench on solid ground and the pouring of well-mixed concrete into the trench and the holes dug for the footings that would support the pillars. Again, getting the right proportion of sand, cement, gravel, and water was fundamental, as was pouring the concrete in the correct thickness and curing it with water for a number of days before any load was placed on it. Construction work had to be done in the right sequence and with much patience.

Once the foundation was complete, the masons could begin laying the blocks that would form the walls. Mainly, the blocks had to be laid straight and the joints cemented firmly. Once the walls were up to window height, a reinforced concrete lintel would be poured into wooden forms built by carpenters. Ironworkers, who had the tools and knowledge of how to bend and attach the rebar with metal wire, assembled the rebar for these lintels. After the lintels were poured and cured for several days, the rest of the blocks could be placed, and the building could be prepared for the roof.

The difficulty in constructing the roof was finding wood cross-beams long enough to span the thirty-foot width of the school. Sometimes long eucalyptus tree poles were used, because they grew tall and straight, but they were not as strong as desired. The preferred material was the strong, but splintery wood from the tall fan palm. These palms were, however, hard to find. They were more expensive, and people did not like to cut them down, as they provided some fruit and their spiny leaves were used to weave baskets. Carpenters also did not like working with this rough-hewn, grainy, black wood because its hardness ruined their tools. Yet, given its durability and its resistance to termites, the fan palm was chosen for the trusses that would support the roof structure. These sturdy trusses would be attached tightly with rebar to the walls of the school.

Laborers nailed long wooden slats as level as possible to this structure and tin roofing sheets were attached to these slats. Placing the galvanized tin roofing sheets was something of a specialty. The sheets required a specific overlap to prevent rain from leaking into the classroom. Fixing the sheets to the slats required special nails to be hammered in place firmly but not so hard as to dent the sheets. Placing small blocks of wood between the slats and sheets was also required to keep the sheets level and the slope steep enough to allow for the quick runoff of rainwater. The workers had to walk carefully on the sheets so as not to disturb their position or make an indentation which could lead to rusting and an eventual hole in the roof. The big test for the roof was to pour buckets of water on the roof to see if any leaked into the classrooms.

With the roof on, the masons could move ahead with plastering the floors and walls. Only masons experienced with using a cement-sand mixture to plaster could do this work. Each mason required several apprentices to prepare the mix and bring it to them, so their work was uninterrupted. The plaster mix required a finer sand than the one used to make the blocks. Sand was passed through a much finer sieve to produce the grain of sand required for plastering. Plastering the entire school took weeks, and once this was done, the school was painted with a bright coat of whitewash. Once whitewashed, the school was ready for the final blessing ceremonies by selected fetish priests who slaughtered several white roosters for the occasion. With the obligatory, traditional blessings completed, the school was ready for occupancy following the receipt of instructions from the chief.

The chief sent word that he and his council would arrive to inspect the school. The opening of the school would depend on the results of their inspection. The next day the chief arrived as announced. He and his elders walked slowly around the school, going in and out of all three classrooms. Following their close scrutiny of the building, they huddled under a nearby tree. After a short discussion, they asked the school director to come and talk with them.

They asked him, "Can you confirm sufficient teachers are available for the six primary-school grades, and there are enough desks for the students who would be crowded into each classroom?"

The school director responded, "Yes, I can confirm this is so. All is in order. We are ready to move into the school and begin instruction."

The chief and his elders thanked the school director, who was much respected because of his high level of formal education. In the village, besides the chief and his elders, the other most respected people were teachers, preachers, and veterans of foreign wars. Perhaps the most respected man in the village was an elderly man who had been a well-known teacher and the only villager to have been educated in France. Another very old and respected man had fought with the French army in colonial times in Indochina and Algeria. He had some medals from his days in the French army and wore them every day, regardless of his attire. He impressed everyone by traveling to the capital city every month to collect his army pension from the French embassy. These two men and a few others always were given special places to sit at any important village event.

After further discussion with his entourage, the chief announced, "All is well, and I am very happy to see that after many months of hard work, the school has been nicely finished. I thank Bobovovi and all others for doing such a good job. I will consult with the grandfathers as to the best dates for the final inauguration and subsequent occupation of the school."

He and his elders re-wrapped tightly the traditional dress cloths covering their bodies, leaving their right shoulders exposed. They began their slow walk back up the wide path leading to the chief's compound, several hundred yards up the foot of the mountain. I was honored by being asked to join them in their walk back to the chief's compound.

Instead of entering directly into the chief's main compound area, they passed through a side door for direct access to the grandfathers' section of his compound. There were dozens of small houses with locked wooden doors that were crowded together all along the exterior walls. They turned to their right to place themselves in front of the door of the house reserved for the grandfather who, according to oral history, was the oldest of all their ancestors and first chief of the village. They waited there as women from the chief's compound came meekly up from behind the group to place a large basin of fresh palm wine and small calabash bowls in front of the house's door.

The women were asked to leave, as the chief did not want to jeopardize this solicitation of the grandfathers' advice by the presence of any woman who might be having her monthly period. Unless a high fetish priestess of some sort, women rarely participated in any village ceremony. The one exception to this general rule was the annual fertility festival which aimed to ensure a good harvest. All women who had proven their fertility by bearing healthy children were welcome during this festival to walk in the fields and allow their blood, sweat, and tears to drop onto the farmland. The more women participating, the higher the probability the fertility god of the land would bless the fields and produce a bountiful harvest.

The chief poured a small calabash of palm wine on the ground in front of each door, offering along with this libation a greeting to the individual grandfather, asking him when would be a good time to start using the school. Kontor then proceeded to cast an assortment of cowrie shells and kola nuts on the ground in front of the door. The positioning of these shells and nuts as they fell to the ground told Kontor the response of the grandfather. He would intensely study the arrangement and the way in which each individual shell and nut lay. He affirmed that he understood the message being communicated by making a loud grunting noise and saying loudly at the end: "Aha!"

After consulting the senior grandfather, the group moved into the chief's compound meeting room where they considered at length what the possible opinions of the grandfather might be. The chief listened to all that was said and ended the meeting by saying, "I will sleep on this and wait for any additional information the grandfathers might communicate to me in my dreams."

The chief awoke early the next day and summoned the village crier, "Make rounds in the village and inform all the people they should come to the school the following Sunday after church for the final blessing of the school."

On the following Monday, the new school would, therefore, be put into use. All the people were very happy to know that at long last their children would have a decent school to attend.

There was a party atmosphere in the village as the day approached for inaugurating the school. But early Sunday morning their glee turned into depression and anger as shocking news spread like a wild bushfire throughout the village. During the night vandals had done extensive damage to the school building. This devastating news had people wailing as if someone had died. For the first time ever, church services were canceled. The village was at the breaking point in trying to cope with the magnitude of this devastating news. The chief and his elders held an emergency session, and a team of the chief's most trusted bodyguards were sent to investigate what happened to the school.

The investigators found that during the night the brand new school had been reduced to ruins. Big holes had been poked through most of the tin roofing sheets. Walls had been knocked down by sledgehammers. Large holes had been dug in the floors. Messy, old engine oil had been poured in every classroom. Small fires had been set throughout the building. Desks had been broken and burnt. The damage was shocking! It was beyond comprehension why anyone would want to destroy the school. Yet the chief's men knew immediately who the culprits were.

For them, there was no question that this nasty work had been done by men from their neighboring sister village, Aniko. The people in the two villages were interrelated, but long ago they had a great feud, and they followed separate ways with different chiefs.

It all started over a century ago when they were all part of one village perched on the top of the mountain behind a complex bastion of terraces and protective stone walls. They settled on top of the mountain after fleeing a wicked king in a far eastern part of the country. Their gods and ancestors led them to their mountaintop refuge. They were able to survive there, because their elevated position enabled them to defend themselves against attacks coming from all directions. Their fortified mountaintop location and defense systems developed over many years gave them the advantage they needed to repel the wicked king's warriors, other warring ethnic groups, and slaving parties.

Only after fifty years of peace and the arrival of foreign missionaries did people begin venturing down the western slope of the mountain to find more land for cultivation. At first, timid forays were made a short distance down the mountain. Little by little, groups crept farther down the mountain until they reached flatland in the fertile valley below. After a while some groups would stay for weeks at the bottom of the mountain before returning to their homes on the mountaintop.

Each time they returned, people would ask them how things were at the bottom of the mountain. They would reply, "Not good! There are too many mosquitoes and snakes."

In reality, things at the base of the mountain were quite unlike what was reported. The land was rich; mosquitoes and snakes were not a big problem, and life was easier. There was no climbing up and down all the time or tying oneself to trees in order to cultivate on a steep slope. The truth was that the people going down the mountain were trying to keep others from joining them, so they could enjoy the land for themselves. It was only after the villagers came down the mountain at the invitation of the European missionaries to attend church that they discovered some of their brothers and sisters had established a thriving small village. At that moment the village divided, selected different chiefs, and a separate village was started less than three hundred yards from the one already established.

Over time, memories became blurred over which village was founded first by "liars," who came down the mountain first. Nonetheless, faulty memories did not dim the ardor of the feud between the two villages. Since that time, one village would do all it could to prevent the other village from getting ahead of it. This story and the disheartening loss of months of my work taught me that jealousy was a powerful force at work. Jealousy made it harder for people to move above a subsistence level of day-to-day living. It did not pay to accumulate wealth. Jealousy of the possessions and progress made by others would make people work to cause the loss of what others had acquired. People would hide any goods acquired and live much poorer than they were to avoid the envy of friends and neighbors, especially if there was any possibility that their jealously would encourage them to pay fetish priests to cause them harm in one form or another.

All this made me reflect on what possessions I should keep. I arrived in the village with only a small bag. My own poverty did not allow me to procure much. I did possess some items that made me look relatively rich in the villagers' eyes. The fact that I had a 50cc motorbike and small Swedish kerosene refrigerator made me look rich. The refrigerator rarely worked, and when it did, I only kept drinks and my snake bite kit in it. But that made no difference. The owning of a water filter also set me apart, but I needed the filter to purify water for drinking. I was poorer than I had ever been, but all the people in the village considered me well-off. I found it was useless to try to convince them that a Whiteman could be poor.

Village households were often known by the level of poverty in which they lived. Having a tin roof and your own water well in your compound made you well off. The same could be said of being able to eat three meals a day. A well-off man would eat a corn or cassava flour meal mix for breakfast, and yam fufu or rice with a tasty meat or chicken sauce for lunch and dinner. A poor person would eat only corn porridge at every meal with okra and a fish sauce made from small, smoked sardines. A very poor person would eat the same, but without the nourishing smoked fish.

The poorest person would be one who did not have matches, and thus, had to borrow embers from a neighbor's cooking fire to prepare any meal. Sometimes poor people would avoid being pitied by making cooking fires without cooking anything, because they wanted their neighbors to see the smoke and, thus, think they were eating. There were also other measures of poverty that included how much land you had to farm and how many trees you owned. Land and tree ownership were often distinct from one another. I discovered "poverty" could be a very relative thing. It did not take much of a change in one's household situation to make one more or less poor. People were used to living on the edge of survival, prepared to fall to a lower level with the occurrence of the slightest upset.

The strong jealously factor often prompted folks to leave the village and live far away so their fellow villagers would not know what they possessed. They could not accumulate wealth and build a better life if they lived close to the extended family, as they would have to share anything they earned with all members of the family. Anyone not sharing could suffer the ultimate punishment of being ostracized from the village. Even those living far away had to be careful to hide their possessions. They never knew when someone from the village would visit and talk of all the things money required, like funerals, illnesses or special ceremonies. Money spent on funerals and the costs of hiring fetish priests and traditional healers often was more than all other household expenses combined.

I expected the destruction of the new school to lead to open warfare between the two villages. I would not have been surprised to see bloody battles take place between the warriors from each village. But, on the contrary, all remained peaceful and nothing happened between the two villages. Oddly, no fighting was allowed between people of the same blood descending from the same grandfathers. The village leaders understood the destruction of the school was one act in a long series of revenge attacks the villages had committed against each other for generations. They stoically accepted this attack on their school as a reaction to their destruction of a cocoa-plant nursery that the Aniko village had developed with disease-resistant seedlings it had stolen on a rainy night from a distant government agricultural research station. The people of Ataku could not stand by and see their neighbors increase their production of cocoa, the main cash crop, while their cocoa yields continued to stagnate.

The village leaders knew they would have to wait patiently for an opportunity to enact their revenge. Until that day they would be keeping a close watch on any advancement achieved by their neighbors. In the meantime, the school could not be repaired until revenge had been taken, as it would not be wise to do so until the score was equalized. In other words, the only way the school could be spared destruction a second time was for something in Aniko to be destroyed, thereby moving the revenge game up to another level of play where it would be started over again.

I was puzzled and angered by all this, as it made no sense to me. I found it most distressing and frustrating that there were so many inconceivable and unpredictable events one could not possibly anticipate when planning anything to improve life in the village. I was very discouraged from doing anything more for the village. I had certainly learned how excruciatingly hard it was to help people help themselves enjoy better lives.

CHAPTER SEVEN
CHIEF'S COMPOUND

The destruction of the school put me into a deep funk. I did not want to leave my house, and I avoided everyone. People became quite concerned over my depressed state. The chief sent a messenger to summon me to his compound. I did not want to go see the chief, but I had no choice. I trudged up the mountain slope to his compound. The path leading up to the chief's compound was once a small road that was used in the distant past by European missionaries who would drive their cars up to the church that still stood on the mountainside, just above the village. It had been many years since any four-wheeled vehicle had come this way. Now, it was a wide, weedy swathe with a well-worn footpath in the middle.

I left quickly to walk to the chief's house. I knew I would be obliged to greet everyone I met along the way. The familiar greetings were quite intricate, taking up much time. The greetings were complicated, and any misstep in saying them would convey a sense of impoliteness or ill regard for the dignity of the other person. These were among the worst sins that could be committed in this society. The greeting would vary according to the time of day, the status, age and sex of the person, and when you had last seen the person.

At the minimum you needed to ask about one's health, the well-being of the household and all its members, and one's work. In particular, women would be asked how their husbands and children were. Men would be asked about their wives and children. The responses to any greeting were equally involved, as the same kind of information was required. Being polite in the village meant nobody could be in a hurry. Haste did make waste when it came to maintaining relationships with others. For sure, patience was divine and politeness was more important than one's intelligence.

All along the pathways from my house to the chief's compound were the usual women vendors sitting at the side of the road with some of their children, selling a wide variety of foods and other items, such as small cans of tomato paste, salt, sugar, matches, cigarettes, and cooking oil. I was puzzled by how any of these women made any money. Their tubs and tables were always full, and there were dozens of them selling the same item.

I once asked a woman vendor, "How much money do you make in a day?"

She laughed and said, "It is more about having an identity and something to do than making money. Participating in the market-place makes me feel less poor."

Some of the items the women were selling were broken down into the smallest units and wrapped in miniature bundles of paper or banana leaves. For example, one match and one cigarette could be purchased. I bought a handful of peanuts from one woman, not because I really wanted them, but I wanted to show I was a good person who knew he needed to share a little of his money. As usual, I was careful to receive the peanuts with my right hand and give the money with my right hand. Giving or eating anything with the left hand was totally unacceptable. I had been told that the left hand was for wiping one's butt, and thus, it should not be used when dealing with other people or touching food to be consumed.

One group of women was in an isolated area, off to the side of the other women vendors. These women were selling strips of red rags, which were obviously for use by women on their periods. If a woman wanted to alert people that she was on her period, she would lay one of these strips on her doorstep. Women would wash these rags and their panties when they took a shower. No woman, no matter how high her station in life, would allow anyone to wash her red rags or panties. It was now imminently clear to me where the expression "on the rag" originated.

There was the usual throng of children who came to join me on my walk, as it was a great novelty for them to see up close a White-man. Also, since all white men were believed to be wealthy, they hoped I could give them a small coin as a gift. They were fond of singing over and over in their language a catchy little ditty about where their word for a white person originated.

The song sounded something like, "The banana turned ripe and became all black, and then the skin was peeled off to reveal a white fruit inside; this was how the Whiteman was made!"

This made me think they thought a Whiteman was produced by peeling off the black man's skin. I was a bit embarrassed by all this, especially since I knew many people also thought whites looked like corpses and smelled liked wet dogs. Was I really perceived as an overripe banana, a dead person, and a smelly dog after a rain?

I stopped at the chief's outer door and stood amidst a number of sleeping, short-legged dwarf goats. I clapped my hands in the usual fashion and asked for permission to enter. Goats like the ones at my feet marauded everywhere in the village, eating anything they could find. They joined the errant dogs and pigs to keep the village clean of any trash or dumpings. The people did not eat pigs. Pig meat was taboo, but they sold pigs to other villages which did eat them. If there were any rotten flesh leftovers, the vultures roosting in tall trees at the edge of the village would swoop down to finish the cleaning job.

A comely, well-dressed young woman came to welcome and escort me to the chief's reception room. As I entered his large compound, I was impressed by its vastness and the number of people and activities taking place. All of the many eyes in the compound stared at me for a brief moment. It was as if time had stopped for a couple of seconds and people were frozen still in a photo. But, quickly, this twinkling of suspended animation ended, and they resumed what they were doing, acting as if I was not there. I knew it was an unusual moment for them. It was rare to see a white person in their compound. Just by being there, I had made their day and given them much to talk about for days to come. I knew they were studying my every feature and would take long hours in the days ahead going over every detail of how I looked and acted.

As soon as they saw me, it seemed they redoubled the energy they were applying to their multitude of tasks. All the younger women immediately pulled up their waist cloths to cover their breasts. Perhaps they did this as my eye kept returning to the wide variety of female breasts dancing in front of me. It was the custom for women not to cover their breasts in their own compound, but I could see they were not comfortable being topless in the presence of a white stranger. The older women could care less and remained as they were. For them, breasts were only for nursing children, and some were indeed nursing babies and toddlers. Knowing most of these women were among the chief's many wives, I did my best to restrain the natural ogling of my corrupted Western eyes.

The compound was full of busy women and children. In one corner women were thrashing orange palm fruits in an earthen conical pit lined by stones. The palm oil would be extracted and kept for cooking and making sauces. The fibers would be used to make brushes. The nuts would be hulled and the kernel consumed or sold. The shells of the nuts would be broken and used by blacksmiths to make the super-hot fires needed to forge metal. Some of the palm oil would be mixed with the ashes of cocoa pods to make a local soap. The uses of the oil palm tree were multiple. Next to the yam, oil palms were the most exalted of indigenous crops.

Next to these women were others working on reducing Shea butternut down to a thick cream used for making body lotions and shampoo. Shea butternut trees grew naturally in wooded areas, and people competed over the rights to harvest their nuts. These nuts had become an important export crop, and thus, a new source of much-needed cash. Everyone in the village applied Shea butternut cream to their entire bodies following their showers, especially in the dry season when this cream protected the skin from cracking. People also treated with Shea butternut cream the cracks in their feet that were caused by a lifetime of walking barefoot.

In another corner of the compound, women were distilling palm wine into much stronger, colorless alcohol spirits. They were also heating old palm wine to keep it from going bad. Having enough palm wine and all its derivatives were important for the many ceremonies the chief was obliged to conduct. A steady stream of palm wine was necessary to keep the chief's court in full operation. The main drawback to making palm wine was it required killing oil palm trees.

Male palm-wine specialists would buy the tree, cut it down carefully, and place it on a slight incline so the sap would run toward the top of the tree. Near the top of the tree, they would punch a small hole. Under the hole they would place a clay pot to collect the dripping sap, which would be given to women for fermentation into palm wine. It was very important for the hole not to become "infected," so every day the wine specialist would go to each of his felled palm oil trees and use a burning blow reed to cauterize the edges of the hole. This daily disinfecting chore was essential to reducing bacteria and producing top quality palm wine.

Many women were busy cleaning metal pots and pans, buckets, and kitchen utensils. Keeping things clean was very important. All metal items were scoured with soap and rubbed hard with the strong bristles of the akudja pods that grew on vines most people had growing on their walls. For stubborn stains, lime juice was applied. All kitchen utensils were stacked to dry in large straw baskets and hung in the outdoor kitchen in places that could not be reached by chickens and the dwarf goats marauding within the compound. Roasted goat meat was very popular and in constant high demand.

I could see there were several shower stalls in the very back of the compound, next to the latrines. A woman's wrap-around cloth draped the open entrance to one shower stall—a clear indication the stall was in use by a woman. I could hear faint sounds of water splashing on the cement floor of the showers, as a woman splashed water on her body from a galvanized bucket with a calabash bowl. I could imagine in the corner of these stalls were clay jars filled with special water and leaves women used for female hygiene. This thought intruded my mind as a rude reminder of how embarrassed I was during a visit to another compound when I used the water in the clay pot to top off the water in my shower bucket. As usual, this gave many people a good laugh and added to the amusing talk about my ignorance of local customs.

Near another shower stall was a woman vigorously scrubbing clothes on a big flat rock. When she was finished washing clothes, she would rinse them in a big washtub of water next to her. She would twist and shake the rinsed clothes out, and hang them on the bushes that grew here and there in the compound, or throw them over the exterior wall to dry. There was one short clothesline made of an old piece of insulated electric wire strung between two fan palm poles in the compound, but it was already full of clothes hung out to dry. When the woman finished with her wash water, she threw it in the shower stall.

Clothes dried quickly in the hot tropical sun. One woman would snatch the drying clothes and take them to a small shady spot under a neem tree in the compound. She had an old, heavy metal iron that had been filled with charcoal embers. From time to time, she would swing the iron back and forth in the air to help keep the embers burning hot. The iron was so heavy that it pressed clothes flatter than I had ever seen before.

There were several neem trees in the compound. This imported tree found its way to Africa decades ago from India with the arrival of the earliest colonists. The neem was popular as a shade tree. It could grow anywhere and in the driest of conditions. Its small leaves were closely bunched on its many branches, shading the ground completely. People were careful to keep the tree away from their farms, as nothing could grow under it. Its leaves were slightly toxic and used in storing grain to discourage infestation by insects. Its seeds were harvested and sold for export as an ingredient for non-toxic pesticides. Neem and eucalyptus trees were grown around houses to keep mosquitoes away. One tree that was never used was any species of a fir tree. The eerie sound of the wind blowing through these trees was just too spooky for most people.

I could imagine that behind the shower stalls was the very strategic compound garden, which was essential to good nutrition. These gardens were small, usually made in a circle of less than ten yards in diameter. Household residues were constantly spread on the garden, and thus, over the years very rich soil had been built up. Fences made of thorn tree branches carefully protected these gardens from animals and thieves.

The gardens were placed behind the shower stall so they could benefit from the water runoff, following along small irrigation canals. The main crops in these gardens were okra, tomatoes, African eggplant, and hot chili peppers. Along the garden perimeters, papaya trees—grown from seeds women would collect from the best papaya fruits they had tasted—were usually planted. Papaya fruit was always recommended for any digestive disorder. Papaya leaves and the white sap secreted from the skin of its fruit were used to tenderize meat.

All these items were essential ingredients of the required sauce that accompanied the main starchy staples of yams, cassava, and corn. These staples would be pounded or mashed into gelatinous lumps to be consumed by tearing off a bite-size piece with the well-washed fingers of the right hand and dipping it into the sauce before swallowing without chewing. There were a variety of sauces, or soups, all necessary for good health and making what would be a rather tasteless, starchy meal into a savory culinary delight.

In front of the shower stalls were some naked children standing on concrete blocks, squirming and screaming as their caretakers were energetically scouring their bodies from head to toe. Although they lived in an environment which gave them no choice but to cohabit with dirt and animals, cleanliness was highly valued. Bathing two or three times a day was common. I was often accused of being the dirtiest person in the village, because I bathed only once a day. Some people would come up to me and tell me my body odor was offensive and I smelled like a goat. My bad personal hygiene habits were unacceptable to many people, particularly as it was widely believed a Whiteman was so clean and pure the consumption of his or her excrement could result in beneficial effects.

Since it helped to keep people healthy, I thought the tradition of cleanliness was a very good thing. The heavy health toll posed on human life by the warm, humid tropics was formidable, as it was the perfect environment for the year-round multiplication of germs. People were in a constant combat against a wide variety of tropical ailments, as every disease vector thrived. Flies were everywhere, mosquitoes were inside and outside, and cockroaches showed how abundant they were every night. I often thought what was needed was one freezing winter to kill off all the disease carriers. There were just too many things to make you sick and kill you, and I expected there were some diseases that had not yet been catalogued in my medical dictionary.

Malaria was one of their biggest health scourges, and the local missionary clinic was always jammed with people seeking treatment. I had succumbed to malaria several times and received quinine injections at this clinic. Malaria added to a high infant mortality rate. Few people could afford a mosquito net, and window screening was out of the question. Staying clean was also necessary to avoid being infected by yaws or other tropical sores which created open wounds on your skin. Surviving childhood was a fifty-fifty probability. Only the strongest lived long enough to gain the natural immunities needed to enjoy a long life, which, on the average, was fifty years. Anyone over fifty was considered an elder, and those people much older than fifty were revered.

Villagers were accustomed to seeing many of their children die, burying their bodies immediately without notice. The deaths of small children and the very old were considered normal. Any deaths between childhood and advanced old age were believed to be due to evil spirits having been manipulated in one way or another to kill you. (The only exception to this rule was the death of Emmanuel Bagbo.) People could perform all kinds of ceremonies with powerful fetish priests to change the path to their destinies, but one could not change one's ultimate and final destiny that the gods set at birth. The only way to miss your destiny was to have the power to change into an animal, but that possibility happened rarely. Most people were not interested in doing this, because the animal you usually became was a goat or a cat.

People resorted to all kinds of local remedies. Those who could afford the money took both the local remedies and what the modern clinic offered. Some had small scars on their bodies, exhibiting their submission to the incisions used by traditional healers as part of a cure. A very popular wide scar was cut deeply in the middle of the chest; it looked like a big, one-inch-long welt. This was a sign of protection against all forms of evil. A sure sign that someone was raised in a village (versus a town) was the unsightly scars on their legs left by tropical sores.

As I had suffered, and almost died, from malaria, I was more open to trying some local remedies and allowed a traditional healer to make some small cuts with a razor blade just behind the back part of my elbows and on my pelvis. I also drank the bitter malaria tea made from boiling the bark of the mango tree and had my daily dose of lemon grass tea which was believed to ward off malaria. I, too, wanted to increase my chances by partaking of medicines from both worlds.

I never tired of watching all the activities taking place in a household compound. It was impressive and instructive to observe what people had to do every day to survive and conform to local traditions and values, and how the smallest upset in the survival routine could be devastating. While I continued to wait for my audience with the chief, I became engrossed with watching women braid their hair. I had been told many times by women their biggest problem was what to do with their hair. In those days, hair straightening products and weaves were unknown. The only thing women and girls could do to change their normal short-hair style was to braid it, either with the hair itself or with tiny, shiny wire threads that were coated with a sleek black plastic coating.

Sometimes, for special functions, women would braid their hair tightly with wax wires and then remove them to get a temporary big Afro look. The key for the hair-braiding specialists was to braid beautifully in a way that lasted a long time, but not too tight. If the braids were too tight, the woman would suffer bad headaches and be obliged to take the braids out, wasting the hours or days it took to braid her hair, not to mention the cost. Once a hair specialist was known for braiding too tightly, she would lose her business. It was this factor and other techniques which made braiding an art form.

Hair concerns were constant, and there were many women who specialized in braiding hair. In fact, a whole industry had been built up around helping women with their hair. The local manufacture of hair products was a thriving business, and hair specialists were consulted as often as healers and fetish priests. The specialists competed with one another to create new demands for something to do with hair. Many concoctions were developed, purportedly to treat all kinds of hair problems. Services for men were not totally neglected. Older men also wanted to cover their gray hair and sought out specialists who could blacken their hair. It was not unusual to see men getting their hair color toned up by a brisk brushing with black shoe polish. No matter that the hair polish left unsightly, inky black stains on the skin surrounding the hairline.

I began to notice the young woman, who received me at the chief's entrance and stayed with me while I waited to see the chief, was very pretty. She had deep black, unblemished skin with a nice bright tone. She had not been given the usual tribal scar, a half-moon indentation under the left eye. She was very well shaped and had a lovely smile with beautiful, white, and nicely formed teeth. Her hair had been freshly braided, and she had applied some local makeup. She impressed me as being very healthy and well nourished. She wore nice clothes and carried herself in a graceful and attractive manner. She was truly exceptional!

I often thought women in the village walked like models because they were experts at carrying things on their heads. I admired the heavy loads they could carry, and I had been embarrassed a few times when I did not have the strength to lift a loaded washbasin up and onto their heads. Sometimes it took two persons to help place the load on a woman's head, but once the load was placed and the woman had her balance, she glided away. For me, it was a beautiful thing to see women walking in a file with heavy loads on their heads in such a graceful and fluid manner. They stood tall and straight in a stately posture, embodying grace and composure in spite of their heavy burdens. The babies they often carried on their backs and the things they carried in their arms accentuated this effect on me.

I thought how wonderful and useful it would be if I could carry things on my head so my arms would be free for other uses. I was like a handicapped person, because I could not walk a single step with anything on my head. Men and women were carrying all kinds of things on their heads, and I could not even begin to do the same. I really felt inept as I observed people going by on bicycles and motorcycles, carrying huge, awkward loads on their heads. As much as I tried to learn to carry items on my head, I could not do so. I concluded if you did not begin at a very early age to carry things on your head, you could not do it. Even a three-year-old could carry things on the head, but I could not. It was like being the only kid in town who did not know how to ride a bike.

CHAPTER EIGHT
CHIEF'S COUNSEL

I enjoyed observing the myriad of activity in the chief's compound. A few times while I sat, waiting for the chief to summon me, I caught the young but mature beauty sitting next to me darting quick looks at me from the side of her eyes. I could see she was very shy. After this happened a few times, I told her, "Please be at ease, and do not be afraid to talk to me."

After a few minutes, she asked me, "Is it okay for me to touch your hair?"

I was not surprised by this question. Many people, especially children, had already asked to touch the hair on my head and arms. They were really interested in knowing how white people's hair felt. She lightly brushed the hair on my arm and then quickly touched the hair on my head.

She said softly," I wish I had hair like yours."

The way she touched my hair and the sweet way she said her words made me think something else was going on. I could sense some warm feelings for this woman ginning up within me, and, consequently, I was now the uncomfortable one. This made me think the chief wanted to offer this woman to me.

A few weeks earlier, one of the chief's many emissaries had come to tell me, "The chief is worried about your health. He has not received any reports about you having sex."

According to local beliefs, if you did not have sex regularly after the age of about eighteen, you would become ill and perhaps die. I was encouraged to pick one of the unattached village women to be my partner.

The emissary continued, "If you cannot find a woman who pleases you, the chief will select a woman for you."

I was now thinking this was why the chief summoned me and purposely delayed receiving me so I could spend time with this local beauty. Her graceful ways, her nicely braided hair, and her nice clothes and makeup all made sense now.

The signal finally came for me to enter the chief's chambers. As I entered, I was told by his oldest counselor on which stool to sit so I would not be higher than the chief. The young woman escorting me was dismissed. I was always nervous in front of the chief, not so much from fear of anything in particular, but of the unexpected, as one never knew what he would decide. I was uncomfortable because I would have to do as he said, even if it made absolutely no sense. The chief had to be obeyed no matter what. People had learned over many generations to blindly submit themselves to authority. Everyone had to do as the chief decided. It was considered very bad manners to do differently or to show the slightest criticism of the chief.

The chief was old by local standards and had been chief for forty-four years, replacing his father while still a teenager. His grandfather and great grandfather had also been chiefs. Any male member of the royal clan who had sworn allegiance to the clan's god and ancestors could be elected chief by the council of elders that represented all village clans. In some ways I thought this was a democratic process. Everyone in the village was represented and all accepted the chief would sit on the chief's stool until his death. This lifetime of service was considered natural. A chief had to be in place a long time to protect the village's traditions and maintain peace and stability. In this way, the village could grow and prosper. Most importantly, the chief had to be someone the grandfathers accepted.

The chief had to be respected by all and someone who had never been accused of any evildoing. He had to be sexually active and capable of producing children. He could not be a drunkard and must be in a good mental state. Perhaps the most important selection criterion for a chief was his oratory skills. A high value was placed on knowing how to speak well. This meant being able to utilize in an appropriate and effective manner proverbs and parables in one's speech. Short quips were not an acceptable style of speech for a chief. It was the long and intricate palaver that was respected, even if the matter being discussed was a simple one. The greatness of a chief depended on the ability of his tongue and mind to make an interesting story out of almost every utterance.

Verbal communication had been elevated to a high art form in the local culture. The tonal language required speaking in an elaborate manner. The number of written words in the local language was not large, but the meaning of many words could be changed according to the context and tone with which they were expressed. Therefore, the possibilities of expressing oneself were almost limitless. Enunciating each tone exactly right was essential to be considered a good speaker. This rule escaped most people. Also important was being able to end each word with a nice-sounding syllable, even if this meant artificially adding one. Speaking the local language well, in a musical manner pleasing to the ears, was a challenge few met.

Selecting a new chief was not an easy business for the village. There were many candidates for the chief's stool who did not want to be selected. The chief's job was fraught with relentless headaches, and he was obliged to live off what the villagers contributed. Sometimes, if a man thought he was going to be selected as chief, he would flee and go into hiding. However, this did not make any difference, as one could be selected even if he was working in some faraway country. And, if selected, he had to return to be chief or be banned forever from the village and risk condemnation by the ancestors. There had never been a case of a man selected to be chief who declined the offer.

As I sat a few minutes in front of the chief on a low stool, which wobbled a bit on the uneven, pounded earth floor of his reception room, I pondered the simplicity of the bare-thatched room. I also thought about the role of the three very old men sitting next to me on a higher wood bench. The chief sat on his much higher and very ornately carved stool. The chief's stool was painted with a black, sooty substance. Carved into the surface of his stool were the reliefs of a large variety of animals. It was not clear which animal might be his clan's totem; this was kept an absolute secret by the chief and his head fetish priest. In contrast to the simple cloths which draped his three elderly advisors, the chief was in a multi-colored gown composed of hand-woven strips of cloth painstakingly sewn together. The making of such a cloth required years of tedious labor by those who were born into this specialty.

From the designs stitched into the cloth, I could tell this was a very old cloth that had probably been handed down from previous chiefs. There were few elders still around who could interpret the meaning of each design. I imagined the designs told an important story about the accomplishments of former chiefs.

At the chief's side was a hand-carved wooden cane with some of the same animal figures carved into it and highlighted by a thin coat of gold lacquer paint. On top of the cane was the figure of a rare red-headed chameleon that matched the one on the chief's printed cloth wrap. Pinned to his fedora-like cloth hat was an assortment of small wooden animal forms also painted with gold lacquer. I had been told that in the old days when gold was plentiful, all these symbols had been made of real gold. In any event, much of the meaning of these symbols had been lost over time. With the passing of each elder, much knowledge of the village's customs and past history was lost.

I was an out-of-place oddity, as I sat awkwardly with these very regal wise men. I was there in all my whiteness in my one pair of long pants, long-sleeved shirt, and simple rubber flip-flop thong sandals. These were my few remaining good clothes I brought in my small suitcase from the States. In this cultural setting, my style did not meet minimum standards. My gestures were foreign and I lacked in elegance and eloquence. I could never qualify for any role in the chief's council. There were times I wished I could stop being "white," or at least stop being treated like a white person. Yet, it was believed for reasons nobody could fathom that I was liked by the grandfathers and the spirits. I knew I looked very laughable in their eyes. My self-esteem was rock bottom because I knew I did not measure up to their minimal standards. It was beyond me why they even put up with me.

The chief sat as if he had been grafted to his stool and gravity was pulling him tightly downward. His face had many folds, drooping down in layers, falling over one another in a waterfall fashion. In some ways he looked like an old, but well-fed bulldog. The weight of his sagging, brownish skin seemed to stretch his watery eyes downward. His front teeth were crooked, with one turned to one side and the other protruded outward. His teeth had been stained red from years of munching on bitter kola nuts.

Looking at his face, you would think he was in a permanent state of remorse, but for sure, looks in his case were deceptive. I was thinking he was lucky good looks were not among the criteria used to select a chief. The name given to him when he was enthroned was Yofu, meaning "bold and brave," but I never saw him exhibit any of these characteristics.

After the usual greetings, which were a cultural must in this society, the chief honored me by extending his hand for me to shake. I shook it firmly. I was proud of the way I affirmatively ended my handshake by making a loud snapping noise by rubbing my middle finger against his. Having shaken hands like this with the chief meant we were closer than I thought. The chief began by saying he was worried about me. I, then, expected him to give me a talk about how I threatened my health by abstaining from sex with a woman, and thus, he would offer me the young woman escort. But he had something else to say.

He said, "I am worried about the impact of the destruction of the school on your well-being. This is a good time for you to take a break for a few days and go visit the capital city, Melomti."

I was taken aback by his concern for my well-being. His encouragement to take some time off in the lively capital city delighted me.

He continued by saying, "The village does not want to lose you and the help you can provide the village. We want you to stay happy and healthy."

I responded, "I am grateful for your concern for me and your good suggestion that I take a few days off in Melomti."

The few elders sitting next to him grunted their assent and nodded affirmatively.

Before I asked permission to leave, his words lifted me, and I felt bubbly inside. I thought this was the time to raise the sex topic myself, especially as I did not want to come back again to talk about the risks I courted by not being sexually active.

The chief could see I had other things on my mind and called me by my local day name, saying, "Bobovovi, do you have anything further to say?"

I squirmed on my stool, as I did not know how to express my interest in the woman who had escorted me. I finally just blurted out, "I found the woman who accompanied me to the door to be very attractive."

As soon as the awkward words came out of my mouth, the chief and his elders laughed loudly. I interpreted this as meaning they were happy I had shown an interest in this woman. After their lengthy series of chuckling ceased, the chief cheerfully said, "I am sorry for the laughter, but we find it funny that you like my newest wife."

I was more than shocked by these words and my own irreverence in thinking of his wife in this way. How could I be so dumb and wrong? I should have known only one of his many wives could have escorted me to his chambers. The chief called out a name and a very old woman appeared at his doorway.

The chief said to me, "I had my youngest wife bring you in, so I will have my first wife escort you out."

He quickly added, "Many young women in the village would be happy to be with you. Choose one that pleases you."

We shook hands again and the old, heavily wrinkled wife led me out of the compound. As I left the compound, I tried to look away so my eyes would not meet those of the chief's newest wife, but I did spot her out of the corner of my eye with a big smile on her face waving good-bye.

CHAPTER NINE
CHEZ ANDRÉ

On my way home from the chief's compound, I stopped at the village's general store, Chez André. This store was also a bar and a small restaurant. It was a good place to get a refrigerated cold beer and sit on its front terrace, whiling away the time by watching people pass by. As I gazed at my surroundings and out across the village, many random thoughts and past memories flooded my mind. There was so much to think about and so much more to understand about the village and its inhabitants.

Skin Tones

I liked to talk to the light-skinned mixed-raced woman, Lydia, who worked at Chez André. She was very charming, but all business. Her father was German and her mother a local woman. She had never known her father. Her fatherless example was one reason families were leery of having their daughters go with foreign white men, as they would often leave their women and kids and never come back. It was not always easy to be a mixed-raced person living among blacks. Lydia, like all other women with her heritage, was called in the local language "white sister."

You cannot change your skin color, but many women tried. In general, people believed a lighter skin was desirable, and, accordingly, people were jealous of the naturally light-skinned mixed-raced women. For some reasons hard to fathom, men found lighter-skinned women more desirable, and their prestige could be enhanced by marrying a woman with light skin. It was a fact that bigger dowries were given for lighter-skinned women. All this worked to help create thriving businesses in skin-lightening creams. Women experimented with all kinds of lotions to lighten their skin. Sometimes the use of the lotions would ruin and permanently discolor a woman's skin, making her undesirable. Nonetheless, the number of women who took the risk was countless.

Men were careful to check for telltale signs of skin lightening treatments when courting women with light complexions. The best way was to check those parts of the body that were normally covered by clothes to see if they were the same color as the exposed parts of the body. Sometimes one could tell by seeing if the hand knuckles were a darker color. There were funny stories about men who became upset after finding the woman they married was not truly light skinned. There was a story about a man discovering the true color of his wife when the skin on his belly became lighter after rubbing repeatedly up against his new wife while having sex. This man actually took his wife to village court because making love to his new wife had turned his belly white. This caused everyone in the village to have a good laugh.

I admit I also played the skin-color game. To me, the color was not as important as the quality of the skin. A healthy, unblemished skin of any color was attractive to me. I don't know why, but I favored mixed-raced women with nice skin and teeth. Philosophically, I thought the mixing of the races was the way to go. When everyone was mixed, there would be much less racism. I thought miscegenation was the way to true world peace. There were exceptions for me. One was naturally copper-toned African women with real red hair. But this kind of skin and hair color was so rare as to not really be a consideration. The same might also be said of any nicely-featured, black African woman with natural long hair.

There were, of course, people who had skin diseases causing depigmentation of the skin, turning them into unsightly splotchy white beings. There were some effective local medicines for such cases, but their application to the skin burned so badly many of those in need of a cure chose to live with their ailment. If the depigmentation was not too widespread, afflicted persons would use makeup and special body paints to cover up their discolored spots. Depigmentation was considered a normal, non-contagious ailment, and people who were affected received the same consideration as everyone else. In fact, for the most part, the disease was a normal part of life, although its causes were unknown.

The big exception to all the rules governing skin depigmentation concerned albinos, who were both respected and feared. These were black people who had been born without any skin pigmentation. It was easy to tell they were albinos and not whites, as their speech and mannerisms were like everyone else's in the village. As they were thought to have been born with special powers, their body parts were sought by those involved with the clandestine trafficking of human organs. There were others who thought they were natural-born witches, and thus, needed to be destroyed. In fact, most albinos were well educated and quite accomplished.

These threats caused albinos to stay hidden most of the time. Also, they could not be overexposed to the sun. The dangers faced by the village's small albino population prompted the chief to require all families with albino members to stay in a protected compound near his. He believed having the albinos close to him ensured any powers they possessed would come his way. The killing of albinos had become so prevalent in recent years that the government had mounted a special campaign to protect albinos, passing legislation that made albino killing a crime meriting a lifetime sentence in prison, instead of the usual fifteen-year sentence for murder.

The most special kind of person in this category was the extremely rare albino dwarf. In general, dwarfs were considered as sources of good fortune. If families had a dwarf, they would build a separate house for her or him, construct high walls around it and have this dwarf compound guarded day and night. Dwarfs could generate a lot of money for their families. People would line up all day long and pay a fee to have an opportunity to pat a dwarf's head. Patting a dwarf's head was believed to bring good luck. An albino dwarf was so exceptional that people would pay much more to pat the head of this kind of dwarf. Some of the richest people were dwarfs. After hearing this, I also wanted to pat a dwarf's head, but as far as I could discover, there were not any dwarfs in the district of Ataku.

Insults

There were other exceptions to skin discoloration etiquette. For example, it was rude to refer to any skin problems caused by leprosy and smallpox. Accusing anyone of having either of these diseases could lead to one's immediate expulsion from the village. One of the worst insults one could make was to say someone had one of these frightening diseases, particularly if a woman made the insult to a man. In general, women were never supposed to criticize or insult a man, and if they did so, they risked physical punishment by the chief's guards. It took me a long time to learn this and even longer to learn about the worst possible insults one could pronounce.

It was hard to learn this, or other insults, as nobody would dare say the words composing the insults. Once I learned the worst insult, I found it hard to say, because it had something to do with defecating in the insulted person's mouth. This was such a serious insult that in living memory only one woman had dared utter these harsh words to her husband in a fit of rage. She was severely punished and tied to a pole in the chief's compound for three days without food, water, and whipped with a car motor fan belt. Later, I was told she was so ashamed she abandoned her children and left the village. I almost wished I had never learned these dirty words.

Of course, there were plenty of lower-level, everyday insults that were common utterances, particularly from adults to children. Calling a child who did not perform well a "meathead" or "monkey brains" was a daily occurrence in most families. A heavier insult would be to call someone a dog belonging to a northern ethnic group that ate dogs. This particular insult fell into disuse when a man from this ethnic group became the country's newest dictator through a military coup.

Children were insulted all the time and strictly disciplined. Their absolute obedience to their parents and family elders was remarkable. Even the slightest misstep on the part of the child could result in a beating. Kids were very much loved, but they were definitely to be seen and not heard. I was always impressed by how still and quiet kids could be when adults were around. If you wanted any kid to go away and stop what he or she was doing, all you had to say was that you were going to get a stick. Every household kept a stick ready for beatings.

Once I observed a kid being beaten severely by his mother with a heavy stick for a long time. After about ten minutes, I could no longer bear hearing the kid's wailing and seeing his body swell up with welts. I intervened and stopped the whipping. His mother was so surprised by my action she looked hard at me with a questioning, hurt face and turned around quickly, stomping off toward her nearby house. I was told later that what I had done to stop the whipping of this child was unprecedented and unacceptable. The news of what I had done was relayed to the chief. He sent one of his messengers to tell me to never do anything like that again.

Village Idiots

Today, I came to Chez André to splurge and celebrate my impending trip to Melomti by having one cold beer. Yet, sitting on the front terrace watching village life going on before me reminded me of so many other things. I could see across the dirt road that ran by André's place one of the handful of village idiots. This one was a tall, fully naked man who roamed the town with a short log chained to his ankle. Mental illness and insanity were considered ailments imposed by the gods for their own particular purposes. It was believed these "fools" could communicate with the gods. For this reason, mentally deficient people were allowed to go about naked or clothed as they pleased.

It was considered a civic duty to give them food and water, and make sure they were well. If any of them were a menace, logs were chained to their legs to restrain their mobility, allowing others to move away from them if need be. In particular, male village fools who became sexually aggressive were fitted with restraints that would keep them from harming women. Of course, these restraints did not keep them from playing with their genitals. People just ignored them and gave them a wide berth. I tried to do the same, but it was hard at the moment for me to enjoy my cold beer while the male fool across the road masturbated and made sounds like a coo-coo bird.

Woman of Mercy

I turned to see who was coming up behind where I sat on André's terrace. It was the angelic, but horribly disfigured, Tchichi. The young woman had been burnt badly over her whole body when she fell into a wood fire as a child. Every part of her body was deeply scarred except her exposed breasts, which were beautifully formed and perfectly symmetrical. Her behavior had become so saintly and her disposition so sweet following her ordeal with fire, people believed she had also been touched by the gods, and thus, everyone had a high regard for her. Moreover, it was believed it was possession by the gods that caused her to fall into the fire in the first place. She constantly walked from house-to-house in the village, seeking out people who needed help. She was always topless and her well-shaped breasts served to remind people that she was once very beautiful. I did find her a beautiful person to know.

There was a different story I had heard about the cause of Tchichi's misfortune. This version of what happened to Tchichi related to an old village custom of female excision. A generation ago all girls in the village would be taken at an early age to the village's traditional healer to undergo a clitorarectomy, which had been the traditional practice for centuries. Previously, having the clitoris removed from a young girl was a serious family responsibility and necessary to protect the family's reputation. In those days, a girl who had not been operated on was considered to be unclean and could never find a husband.

The colonists began a massive campaign to prohibit female genital mutilation, which continued until well after independence was declared. This campaign ultimately was effective, and today, only a few families continue to violate the prohibition against this ancient practice. Tchichi's family was one of those families, and the story goes she was very upset when her mother took her to a hidden place in the forest where she was excised. After her excision operation, she came home very angry and immediately threw herself into the cooking fire. Since that day no other cases of excision have been reported in the village.

Meanwhile, the practice of male circumcision continues. All males are obligated to submit to initiation ceremonies when they are adolescents. The ceremonies last for about a week at a hidden location in the forest. A select group of elders leads these ceremonies. It is at this time young men are instructed as to what is involved with being and acting like a man. They are deprived of food and water, and put through a number of physical endurance tests. The final event of this initiation week is the full circumcision of their penises with a rough blade made by local blacksmiths. Each boy is expected to endure the pain of this crude operation without showing any pain.

Each year a number of boys end up in the clinic because their circumcision wounds become infected. There are also cases where the infections and stress caused by these initiation rites result in death. Nonetheless, the halting of this important traditional practice is unthinkable. The thought of any man being uncircumcised was outside the realm of the acceptable. Any uncircumcised man could never be a chief or hold any position of importance. Nobody dared to decry this sacrosanct practice.

God's Messenger

As I turned to greet Tchichi, my eyes stopped to focus on part of one wall on the side of André's store that had been filled with words written in Greek and Latin. This told me one of the village's most famous fools had spent some time at Chez André's. I had seen such writings before at various places in the village. I had once met the author of these erudite inscriptions. I learned he was the chief's oldest son, Isaac, who had gone to Germany to train for the priesthood. He had the habit of writing these same words everywhere he could. He always dressed in his frayed brown monk's habit, wore a big wooden cross, and carried in his big pockets small pieces of charcoal with which to write.

This demented man of God was constantly talking in languages nobody understood. He had been such a brilliant student at the nearby missionary school that the European priests teaching there arranged for him to go to Germany for advanced studies. After many years of study in Germany, he suffered a breakdown and became insane. People blamed the cultural shock of living in Europe. He was, therefore, brought back to the village and now wandered about freely, espousing his message everywhere he passed. I often thought that what he wrote should be deciphered. Maybe he was revealing some great truth. I, for one, really wanted to know what he was trying to communicate. I revered him, as did all the villagers. Yet his experience had made people reluctant to send their children to the Whiteman's world.

Women Really Rule

On another wall at Chez André's was a famous large cartoon drawing that made me laugh, but its message was also something I often pondered. Life size, color figures were painted on the wall, depicting an older man and a young woman. There were bubbles outlined next to arrows drawn to the mouths of the man and woman, displaying the words of each.

The woman was saying to the man, "You are too old for me."

The man responded, "But my money is not old."

It was true the possession of wealth enabled men to have many women of any age and all the wives they desired and could support well.

For many women, the age of a man was not a critical factor. Of the most importance was how well he could support her and her children. The best kind of man was one who cared for her well, gave her many children, helped her set up a business and assisted her extended family. Finding a man capable of doing all this was the main objective of every woman. It was as if love was a secondary consideration or not a consideration at all.

It seemed marriage from the very beginning was all business, starting with a payment of the bride price and paying for an expensive traditional wedding party and gifts. Men saved money for years to pay the dowry and offer the woman the required full trunk of cloth and gold jewelry. To an outsider, marriage in the village might have looked like a business project whose main 'raison d'être' was to produce many children, especially boys, enhance the man's prestige, and generate economic wealth. It was a man's world, but all depended greatly on the good graces and hard work of women.

Women entrepreneurs dominated commerce in the village. Almost all roadside vendors and sellers in the weekly market were women. When it came to making money, the women were very serious and hardworking. They learned business and money management at a very young age, usually at the side of their mothers, from the time they could walk. Indeed, many of the vendors were young girls who watched over the business while their moms tended to other chores. They learned in their childhood how to keep accounts in their heads. They had proven that written records were not necessary to being successful in business.

The wealthiest people in the country were unschooled market women who rode around in chauffeured Mercedes Benz' and owned many properties. Women represented a powerful force to be reckoned with. Even the poorest women in the village worked day and night, seven days a week, to get ahead. Women did all the household work, all the business work, and most of the work on the farms. I often thought women expended more calories each day than they consumed, but the corpulence of some of the wealthier women belied this thought. Of course, they did less work when they became richer, as they could then hire poorer women to work for them.

Many times I thought if women could run the country, progress would be achieved much more quickly. I asked women why they did not go into politics and try to get into government. The response I often heard was, "Politics is the folly of men and a waste of time. Too little money is made in doing politics. As far as we are concerned, men waste their time in politics, sitting around talking all the time and practicing the art of the long palaver. All we need from men are children. The rest is not of much importance."

The Art of Wood

The corner posts holding up the roof to André's terrace were carved with some of the same animal figures on the chief's symbolic staff and hat. Again, figures of chameleons and bats were prominent, making me think these two creatures have some hidden meaning for the village. I thought I might pay a visit to the village wood carvers again, as they might be able to tell me what these carved figures meant. There was a family of very skilled wood carvers who lived at the edge of the village. One had to be a member of this family to learn the art of wood carving, as the skill took years to master and was passed on from one generation to the next.

I was amazed during my first visit with them to see the carvings they could make with the crudest of locally made hand tools. I did not know such beautiful and intricate wood carvings could be produced by iron chisels, adzes, and knives made by village blacksmiths.

I asked the head carver, "How do you know what to carve?"

He answered, "The piece of wood selected tells me how to shape it. In every piece of wood there is a carving waiting to show itself. It is my job as a carver to produce what the wood is destined to be."

Wood carving used to be a big business, with many tourists coming to buy their products. But now, the scarcity of hardwoods like red mahogany and the yellow iroko made it impossible to produce their most popular item: a huge chair carved out of one large section of a tree trunk. The chairs would have lions or elephants as legs with carvings of other animals all over them. Outsiders came years ago and logged all the big hardwood trees and took away all the rare ebony trees. Local timber cutters took the rest, including the trees high on the mountain that were usually outside the reach of loggers.

Local woodcutters would fell the trees where they grew and cut them into planks with a long two-man saw blade. This would require digging a large hole under the tree in which one man could stand upright. This man would hold one end of the long band saw while the other would mount on top of the log to work the saw from that end. They would go up and down, producing some rough, but usable planks. They would then carry the planks down the mountain for sale. The main wood available was white planks from soft wood trees. These planks were used for cheap furniture or forms for pouring concrete. Unlike the scarce hardwood, they would rot easily and were subject to rapid termite damage.

Today's Hunters

As I began to dig into my pocket to pay for my beer, a dozen boys passed by and asked me if I wanted to buy any cooked rats or mice. These boys had been amusing themselves, digging up places where rodents hid, catching them for a quick kill, and skewing them on long, slender sticks. They would cook the rodents over an open fire by slowly rotating the stick in the flames. The rodents would be cooked, hair and all, and sold to those who enjoyed them as a snack. As I was not among those who ate hairy, grilled rodents, not even if they had been gutted, I passed on this delicacy.

Just behind these boys were hunters carrying several *agoutis*, which were large grass cutting rodents they had killed by burning off their grassland habitat and shooting them as they fled the flames. Agoutis were among the most favorite local foods. If they could not be consumed right away, their meat would be smoked and saved for sale to the highest bidder at a later date. For me, the taste was too gamy and their smell too strong. I often thought if anyone could domesticate these large rats, they would make a fortune. Villagers could not get enough agouti meat, especially as the supply was limited to what hunters could shoot in the dry season.

I tried many foods I had not known before, including cat, bat, and snake meat. I also had once consumed warthog meat. I liked the huge land snails and was disappointed that they were only available for a few months in the year. There was always a plentiful supply of nutritious grubs living under the bark of the oil palm tree. There were many fruits growing around the village; some I knew and some I did not know. Avocadoes were abundant, but I grew tired of eating them all the time. I was told in former times monkeys were eaten, but when the people observed every time a monkey was eaten, a twin child would die, they stopped this practice. In any event, this didn't matter much now as it had been many years since anyone had seen a monkey or any other of the wild animals that used to inhabit this area. The great hunting clans of large African animals of former times had been reduced to hunters of rodents.

A Man's World

In many ways life was easy in the village, particularly if you were a man. Agreeable women and food were plentiful, and a man did not have to work very hard. When one was hungry, fruit could easily be picked from the trees, or cassava tubers could be pulled out of the ground. There was also an ample supply of palm wine. Older men could not understand why younger men wanted to go to Europe to do menial jobs for low wages, and suffer bitter winter weather and racial abuse. Certainly, they would not do such demeaning work in their own country. For those men who were strong and in a position of some power, the village was still something of a tropical paradise.

Elders had enjoyed better times years ago, especially when cocoa production made a lot of money, and their culture and customs had not yet been diluted by modern ways. Twenty years ago, one family could earn enough from harvesting three acres of cocoa annually to buy a car. Today, the total harvest of the same acreage of cocoa does not earn enough to buy one car tire. When the world prices for cocoa are low, the village becomes more impoverished.

The government encouraged the village to diversify into cotton production, but they found cotton reduced soil fertility and was too labor intensive. Moreover, their first cotton harvest was ruined by a heavy rainfall, as the government truck scheduled to pick up their small mountain of cotton never arrived. I believed the elders when they said life was harder and less happy in the village, and it was becoming harder to care for the fast-growing population.

They said there was much less laughter than before. It was becoming much harder for the center to hold. The people could neither fully have all which was new nor could they cope with the loss of the old ways of life. Many had left their old world, but they still had not arrived in the new world. All the hopes and dreams generated by independence had dissipated, and new "hopes" for a better future had not yet materialized.

CHAPTER TEN
LOTTO AND JOSEPH

Just as I was about to leave Chez André, a man dressed in the latest European fashion came from the road to greet me. This debonair middle-aged man was known as "Lotto," because he was one of those very rare persons who had won the popular London football-pool betting scheme. He was formerly a clerk, but when he won big in the lotto, he quit his job, built a big and very modern villa in the village, and bought himself a fine car. He was the envy of everyone, yet people disliked and feared him.

They thought he had made powerful juju to win so much money. Nobody knew how much money he won, but it had to be a lot, as he lived in such a grand style. In most other ways, he lived a sad and lonely life. To avoid jealousy and pressures to share any of his wealth, he spent most of this time behind the high walls of his villa. He had withdrawn from all village activities and lost touch with the chief and his elders. In general he was resented by everyone in the village.

As I was the only Whiteman in the village, Lotto felt safe with me and offered to buy me another beer. I was torn, but local courtesy required I accept his offer of a beer. I was uncomfortable with him as I knew how the people perceived him. He was just too pompous for me. He had with him one of his friends from a distant village who had arrived in his new "*deux chevaux*" (two horsepower) Citroen car. Having a car like this one distinguished the man as belonging to the country's slim upper class of elites.

His friend, Joseph, also dressed like a well-heeled government official. He wore a well-pressed, gray polyester safari suit cut in front just enough to reveal the heavy, but short one-inch protection scar in the middle of his chest. On his right wrist was a quality watch, in his breast pocket was the latest fountain pen, and he wore horn-rimmed eyeglasses. He smelled of the cheap cologne he had splashed amply on his body. All these items were considered necessary to demonstrate that one was high class.

In my conversation with Joseph, he revealed his car was a recent acquisition. Before buying this car, he drove a Vespa motorbike, which was also considered high class, but not as high as having a covered, four-wheeled vehicle providing protection from the rain and sun. Actually, his Citroen car was one of the cheapest French cars, akin to the Renault 4L, which was also popular for those who could afford it. Besides being very economic, these cars were very easy to repair and so light they could be lifted by a couple of people from the muddy roads in which they often became stuck. Many preferred the Citroen, because it had a standard stick shift on the floor, while the Renault 4 L had an awkward shifting handle protruding from the dashboard.

I learned from Joseph that he had been among one of the initial groups of Africans to be educated at the prestigious William Ponty School in Dakar, Senegal, former capital of French West Africa. The French colonial administrators sent to this school only those Africans they considered to be the most brilliant. Most of the first wave of senior colonial assistants and post-independence leaders came from this school. The requirements of this school were the same as similar schools in France; so for an African to graduate from this elite school was quite an honor. This was one element of the French colonial policy to assimilate Africans. In other words, this policy aimed to turn Africans into French. I could not believe they really thought assimilation was possible. For me, it was just another noble colonial ideal that was not practical. In any event, the French language endures, especially as it provided a neutral way for one ethnic group to communicate with another.

The multitude of diverse languages spoken by the dozens of ethnic groups jammed into a relatively small geographic space posed difficult development challenges. For the government to favor any local language would inevitably result in making other ethnic groups angry. There was a need to begin school instruction in the local language of each geographical area, but the cost to train teachers and develop course materials for so many languages was cost prohibitive. And people were not interested in seeing their children learn to read and write in their own language, because there was no profit in doing so. Everyone wanted to learn French or English, so they had a chance of finding a paying job. In addition, with proper French or English they could travel outside their home areas and blend more easily into the educated elite.

Both Lotto and Joseph made for an exceptionally odd pair. They seemed to be men in charge of their own worlds who cared little about what others thought of them. Like many elites, they let the nail on the small finger of their left hand grow several inches long. The growing and maintenance of such an awkwardly long finger nail was not easy, but for them, it was necessary to show they did not do any manual labor, and thus, they were true elites. In contrast, the fingernails on their right hand were trimmed well back like everyone else. This was a clearly visible testament to the fact that people ate with their right hand. The right hand was for eating, greeting, giving and receiving, but the left hand was for personal hygiene. This hand-use rule was true, even if you were naturally left handed.

Somehow, it was as if Lotto and Joseph had achieved the impossible and changed their destinies. There were many who tried to change their destinies by paying huge sums to the most powerful fetish priests. Using occult means to manipulate the road taken to one's destiny was an accepted practice, but one's ultimate fate could not be changed. People were constantly paying sorcerers to divine their destinies and tell them which spirit or god would accept their sacrifices in order to improve their destinies.

The largest cash expenditure for any household was for payments to fetish priests for one thing or another. If added to this cost was the money spent on traditional healers, funerals, offerings to clan, and local gods and spirits, there would be very little left in most household budgets for any productive investment or even the schooling of children. Like many, I speculated on how the grandfathers regarded Lotto and Joseph and how they would be accepted among them and others in the afterlife. I thought their lives would become very difficult when they ran out of money. They, too, did not seem to be making any productive investments.

The fancy, modern way Lotto and Joseph dressed also projected their contempt for the president of the country's edict for people to adopt indigenous names and wear traditional clothes. In fear of retribution, most people did adhere to the strong authenticity campaign promoted by the president and his all-powerful political party, the only one allowed in the country. In a recent election, the president presented himself as the only candidate for national presidential elections, and the people voted either "yes" or "no."

Those wanting to vote "yes" had to go to the church courtyard to vote, and those desiring to vote "no" would go to the school on the edge of town. Lotto and Joseph said they had not participated in such electoral charades, but gave no hint about how they were spared from this misguided civil obligation and avoided suffering the cruel wrath of the "President for Life."

Lotto and Joseph knew very well the chief had received an order from the president to ensure all people over eighteen years of age in the village voted "yes." The chief's messengers had instructed each clan chief to tell all household heads that all adults in their families must vote "yes," and this meant nobody should go to the school to vote. Of course, people knew anyone showing up at the school to vote would be severely beaten by the group of presidential thugs who were in the village for this purpose.

As we discussed this electoral event, I told Lotto and Joseph I was surprised when one of the chief's messengers had come to me with the firm instruction, "Bobovovi, you must vote. The president's order to the chief indicates all people in the village must vote, including any foreigners. So, you are required to vote. We must have one hundred percent in favor of the president's reelection."

I revealed that the pressure to vote in the presidential election caused me a great deal of stress. I knew it was not possible for me to vote in the election, but, on the other hand, I did not want to disappoint the chief and let the village down. I told them I had spent days agonizing over what to do. I did not tell them that I decided the day before the election to walk far into the bush and lie about some problems I had which prevented me from returning to the village in time to vote.

I also did not tell them about the deceptive option I chose on Election Day. On that day I decided to say I met a beautiful woman in a neighboring hamlet and she invited me to stay the night with her. In this way I would not only get out of voting, but also get people off my back about not having sex with a woman.

I reminisced over how well my plan worked. I spent a creepy night in the bush in a distant seasonal farm camp, fighting off mosquitoes and keeping a watchful eye out for snakes. I stayed up most of the night, as I was afraid something could happen to me if I fell asleep. When I returned to the village late the next afternoon, some of the chief's people were waiting for me. I braced myself for some hard questions. My fear quickly evaporated as they rejoiced at seeing me safe and sound.

I told them my big lie, "I met a beautiful woman last night."

They all reacted in unison, "We are happy for you." There were a lot of nodding, positive grunting sounds and many smiles.

Continuing my lie, I said "I am dreadfully sorry I missed the big voting day."

I recalled they did not appear to detect my faked despondency as they replied, "That is okay, Bobovovi. We had someone vote for you. The village is very happy as it registered a one hundred percent 'yes' vote."

This important village achievement made me angry and sad. I knew they did not like the hated dictator, but they had no choice but to see him continue his stranglehold on power. I did not dare say anything negative. It was another day when what was good and reasonable did not count as much as allowing peace and stability to prevail. Strict obedience to the chief's order had been demonstrated. Balance was maintained, and things did not fall apart. It was not about what anyone liked or wanted. It was about preserving the status quo and being a team player. Security was more important than freedom. Chaos was to be avoided at all costs. The most important thing was to maintain the village's survival dynamics.

CHAPTER ELEVEN
CHICKEN IS NOT CHICKEN

I wanted to quickly say my good-byes at Chez André and head home before it became dark, but the usual obligatory hand-shaking ritual with all whom I met delayed my departure. Handshaking embodied politeness and respect for the dignity of each person. I spent much time every day shaking hands and exchanging greetings. Being in a hurry in the village was not an option; time had to be given to others.

There was a saying in the village: "The most important thing you can give is your time." Patience and taking time for others were signs of wisdom and humanity. Anyone acting otherwise would be considered rude and ill-tempered.

I arrived at home in time to light my kerosene lanterns and a couple of candles before darkness fell. The first thing I wanted to do was make sure my Honda 50 was clean and full of fuel. I passed a lantern close to my motorbike to examine each part, checking to see if everything was in good working order. The fuel in the motorbike tank was low, so I brought from my outside storeroom my ten-gallon plastic fuel container and began pouring fuel into the tank. I carefully moved the lantern away, as I did not want gasoline fumes to ignite. I had heard stories of people holding their lanterns too close to their tanks and the fumes caught fire, exploding and destroying their houses. There was one famous case where such a fire started near a cooking gas canister. It exploded like a huge bomb, shattering the entire house and killing all its occupants.

As I finished readying my motorbike for my big trip the next day, Assi, one of the two women who shared my compound with me, brought me my nightly meal of grilled chicken and boiled yam slices. The freshly killed chicken was small and tough, but very tasty. I found that African chickens had a very different taste, due to the fact they ranged freely and scratched the ground for their food. Every household compound always had a flock of chickens pecking the ground as they scavenged for something to eat. Chicken droppings were everywhere. Raising chickens was a woman's job, and thus, their sale was an important source of income for women.

At one point I decided that I could make a useful contribution if I could help women improve the manner in which they raised chickens. What they needed were bigger and healthier chickens. Each year many of their chickens would die from Newcastle disease, which was easily preventable with vaccine drops absorbed through the chicken's eyes. With bigger chickens, regular health checkups, and better feed rations, they could raise larger chickens which produced more eggs. I decided I would set up a demonstration in my own compound to show how to improve the raising of chickens.

My first task was to obtain an improved breed of chicken to mix with the local chickens. I knew of a commercial farm that raised white leghorn chickens in the regional capital, Kpolomo, located about twenty miles away. I made a trip to Kpolomo to see if the farm owners could sell me some chickens I could use to begin reproducing them in the village. I mainly wanted roosters which could mate with local hens. My idea was to keep the roosters in good conditions in my compound, and women would bring their hens, leaving them with me for a few days for mating purposes. When I discussed this idea with some of the women, they mostly laughed. The word spread that the crazy Whiteman was pursuing another screwball scheme, which they dubbed, "Operation Cock."

As it turned out, the commercial farm did not have any roosters to sell me, but it did offer to sell me fertilized eggs that I could incubate to produce chicks and raise them into full-grown chickens. They offered to loan me a kerosene incubator that would keep sixty eggs warm for the twenty-one days needed until they hatched. As this was the only option, I accepted it and arranged for the eggs and incubator to be delivered to my house in the village. As the fertile eggs must be turned every few hours, I set up the small coffee table-sized incubator next to my bed in my bedroom so I could easily tend to it during the night. I had to lightly mark each egg with numbers, one through four, around its middle section so I could turn them precisely one quarter of their circumference every three to four hours. It was important that the eggs be carefully rotated and heated evenly at a prescribed temperature.

Before carefully placing the eggs on the wire mesh tray that slid into the incubator, I viewed each egg in candlelight to verify that it was fertile. The hard part was keeping the incubator wick adjusted so the flame maintained the correct internal temperature. Every time I woke up to attend to the incubator, I would check the temperature gauge inside the tray to ensure the eggs were not too hot or cold. I was constantly trimming the wick, cleaning the soot out of the chimney pipe and making sure the incubator fuel tank had enough kerosene. This work was intense and time consuming. I could not get a full night's sleep or leave the house for a long period. I was like a mother whose babies depended solely on her.

One morning I woke up very ill, and I could not breathe well. I was very weak and I could not tend to the eggs. I left my house to get some air and found, after a few deep breaths outside of the house, I felt much better. I consulted my Merck medical manual to see what might be wrong with me. I was reluctant to read this manual because I found, as I read about the symptoms of so many aliments, I would start having them and suffer from a type of hypochondria. In this instance the manual did help me conclude that by sleeping next to the incubator, I was exposing myself to carbon monoxide poisoning by breathing in the fumes put out by the incubator. From then on, I moved the incubator to the adjoining sitting room next to my bedroom and made sure to leave the wooden shutters on the windows open.

On the twenty-first day I could see eggs beginning to hatch as the chicks inside began pecking the shells. In rapid order I was a proud mother, with twenty-nine of forty eggs hatching baby chicks. I had already prepared a space on the floor in my sitting room for these baby chicks. I had put down some plastic sheeting in a corner and surrounded it with concrete blocks so the chicks could not escape. I poured some water into inversed jar lids and placed pounded corn and millet meal on some pieces of cardboard. Maintaining feed, water, and keeping this chick corner clean was almost a full-time job. The village had a lot of laughs when it learned I was raising chicks in my house. Some villagers started calling me the "chicken man."

The chicks grew rapidly. Within a few weeks, I transferred them to a pen I had constructed behind my house. This is where I planned to keep them until I finished building my masterpiece, an elevated bamboo chicken house. My idea was to build a chicken house in such a way the chickens would stay in one place, above the filth of the ground and be easily watered, fed, and vaccinated. Moreover, the eggs could be collected without entering the chicken house. Also, the chicken manure would drop to the ground, where it could be collected and be used to fertilize gardens.

The design of the bamboo chicken house was simple. It required a four-post frame made of small tree trunks with bamboo strips nailed to the frame at exact intervals. The floor was four feet off the ground and was made of bamboo strips, allowing chickens to walk from one strip to another, while their droppings fell to the ground through the gaps in the strips. Bamboo strips were nailed to the sides to permit enough space for the chickens to pass their heads through, so they could eat and drink from half-bamboo feeders placed at floor level along the sides of the chicken house. At one end of the house, compartments for egg laying were installed, so the eggs could be reached from outside the house. The roof was covered with straw thatch, helping keep the chickens cooler, as did the aerated nature of this house. Since chickens did not tolerate heat well, this was an important feature..

After experimenting with this bamboo chicken house for eight months, I thought I had introduced a very innovative improvement villagers would be eager to replicate. People came from far and wide to observe the chicken house, and they all seemed to like what they saw. The hardest challenge I faced in keeping my chickens healthy and productive was providing them with the nutritious diet needed for them to thrive and produce eggs daily. I found they needed more protein and calcium. Without enough protein they would not produce eggs, and without enough calcium, the egg shells would be too soft and break. I concluded that neither the chicken nor the egg came first; it was protein and calcium that had to come first.

I tested various rations. The best ration I could come up with included small dried sardines and crushed sea shells. I would mix the latter with sorghum and corn. One problem was this mixture had to be ground, and the operator of the village diesel-powered mill did not want to grind my feed, as it messed up the mill blades. Moreover, nobody would grind grain after me. My mixture left a bad taste in people's mealy meal. I was finally able to get the local mill operator to grind my mixture at the end of the day, after satisfying all his usual customers. I had to pay extra, because when he finished grinding my feed, he had to disassemble and clean the circular mill blades.

I was able to collect and offer as gifts some very nice big, white eggs. This was a novelty to the village. They only knew small, dirty brown chicken or guinea fowl eggs. I also cleaned my eggs so they were very white. The clean whiteness of the eggs made some people refuse them as gifts. They said, "We believe these clean white eggs were made by some machine. They do not look like they could have possibly been laid by chickens."

The word circulated that I had a machine to produce eggs, violating natural laws, and I should be forced to stop. I thought this was hilarious. To counter these accusations, I invited the chief and his elders to see that my chickens indeed produced such big and clean eggs. They easily agreed, but expressed in so many words, "The eggs are coming from your chickens, but as your chickens were spawned in a machine, they are indeed unnatural machine chickens. This is an acceptable, but an unneeded manipulation of the laws of nature."

My chickens were, therefore, looked upon as outsiders, just like me. In other words, for them, my chickens were not chickens.

I kept the roosters separate from the hens and fenced in an open pen so women who wanted to breed their local hens could easily stop by and drop their hens into this pen. I found it difficult to get the local hens to produce fertile eggs. They also lacked protein, especially as the enclosure prevented them from scavenging far and wide for their food. I was told by one woman that termites were a good source of protein, so I devised a way to collect termites. I filled some large clay pots full of decomposing earth and set them next to a nearby termite hill. Termites were attracted to the earth mixture in the pots and soon they were full of termites. I would then empty the pots in my cock pen, and the chickens would work quickly to devour the termites as they scurried in all directions. This system actually worked very well and was positively commented on by many villagers. (At last, maybe the Whiteman had something to offer.) There were also some people who thought the big white roosters would be good for sacrificial rituals.

In the past, sufficient termites could only be collected for human and animal consumption with the onset of the early rains when termites would leave their hills and fly away in swarms. When this would happen, women and children would fill wash basins with water and put a large stone in the middle of the basin. When night fell they would place a lighted kerosene lamp on the stone, just above the water. The termites would be attracted to the light, hit the lamp, and then fall into the surrounding water where they would be scooped up by the handfuls. Some of the termites would be immediately fried and eaten while others would be dried and saved for later consumption. I thought termite-raising and harvesting could be a good business endeavor.

The cock-pen reproduction process did not work very well, as few local hens produced fertilized eggs. I, therefore, came up with the idea of allowing a few cocks to roam freely in the village, impregnating as many hens as they pleased. At first, this new cock venture seemed to work well, but after a few weeks, all my cocks had died. Obviously, this imported variety of rooster did not have the immunities needed to survive on its own in the local environment. And, the few mix-breed chickens produced showed they could not survive as long as local chickens. Moreover, the people who ate the chickens which perished said they tasted terrible, and they much preferred their tasty local chickens. I knew very well that changing taste preferences was an insurmountable hurdle.

After a few months, even the well-cared-for and protected hens in my bamboo chicken house suffered, and helping them survive was too expensive. Nobody could afford to invest the time and money I had invested in my new chicken-raising scheme. Clearly, what I was trying to introduce was neither practical nor sustainable. Of course, the villagers knew beforehand that my chicken project was destined for failure, but, just in case, they wanted to see what I would do. Also, my chicken project gave them much to talk about and was great amusement for them. It was like I was the only entertainment in the village. They enjoyed having me around just to break up the monotony of their daily routines.

I found I was more a catalyst for laughter than for development and change. This was not a bad thing as the people considered laughter a great gift, and even in the most stressful situations, they would find a way to laugh. I was often surprised how they could laugh in tragic situations that would bring most people to tears. Maybe the amount of daily laughter should be a development indicator. They also found solace in singing their many songs and dancing.

I once asked a woman, "Why are you singing all the time?"

She said, "Music is one good way of combatting our misery."

I could not argue with her on this point, and increasingly, I turned to singing in times of stress and sadness.

All these thoughts came to me as I munched on my tasty grilled chicken. I savored every bit of it. I had learned from the villagers to suck all the remaining meat off the bones and chew the small bones into a pulp to swallow. I would also bite into the leg bones and suck out the nutritious marrow. In this way, when I finished eating my chicken, there was hardly anything left to dispose. The children living near me were upset when I began eating a chicken like they did. They previously stood by to pounce on my chicken leftovers when I still ate like a Whiteman. They made me feel so guilty I wanted to go back to my old ways of eating a chicken in the Whiteman's incomplete way. It was as if the children's well-being depended on me eating less.

I was torn between being nice to the kids and showing everyone I was not as dumb as I once was. This is one case where they could see the Whiteman was getting smarter, but they wished he had stayed dumb like he was before. It was customary for men to eat first, and children and women would eat what the men left. The nutritional outcomes of such a practice were obvious. This is one of many instances where I had to ask myself if I wanted to be like them or stay as I was before I came to this ordinary African village on the edge of the forest at the western foot of Mt. Ataku.

CHAPTER TWELVE
DDT MOMENT

After crunching and thoroughly sucking each chicken bone, I heard Assi entering and setting down a galvanized bucket with my bathwater on the hard concrete floor inside my shower stall. The dull clunky, scraping sound made by the galvanized bucket hitting the floor was a signal to me to take my evening bath. I quickly entered my bedroom, undressed and wrapped my towel around me and picked up one of my kerosene lanterns. I placed my kerosene lantern on top of the high wall ledge dividing the shower stall from the toilet stall. In this way no water would splash on it while light was cast on my body. I took from the same ledge next to my lamp my huge bar of strong French soap, Mon Savon, which had been around for a half a century or so. I also had my local *akuja* fiber-washing sponge, made from the insides of cucumber-like pods growing on vines that one observed covering large stretches of most compound walls. With these essential items in hand, I was ready to begin my nightly bathing ritual.

Unlike most people, I bathed with hot water. Assi would always place a full bucket of water on the dying embers of the charcoal fire she used for cooking dinner, so my bath water was hot. I took the calabash dish floating in the galvanized bucket and began to pour water on my body from the top of my head so it would wet my entire body. I would start by washing my hair and rinse it, then move downward, thoroughly scrubbing each part of my body. I would rinse each part of my body as I proceeded. I was surprised at how well I could wash with half a bucket of water. I became so used to washing like this that I later found modern shower systems bothersome and wasteful, with water needlessly falling on me constantly.

I was fortunate as the water in my bucket tonight was clear. In the dry season, when our compound well was dry, Aba and Assi had to walk long distances before sunrise to find water in muddy creek beds, and I was obliged to use water that was brown in color. During these times it was very hard to wash and maintain the color of clothes. My clothes quickly faded and were discolored and frayed by the hard pounding they received on flat stones. I marveled at how anyone could keep white clothes spotless and bright. As most fetish priests always wore white, I often thought that among their powers was the ability to keep their clothes white in spite of the dusty air and dirty water.

Brown, dry seasonal water also presented added challenges to producing clear potable water for drinking. I would boil a pot of this water and pour it into my upright filter where the water would drip into the lower compartment of the filter by passing through a soft, porous, white stone element. I would use some of this boiled and filtered water to scrub the element and boil it again with the filtered water. Then I would filter the water again through the cleaned filter element. Keeping a supply of essential clean drinking water required an important investment of money, time, and effort.

The water from the second cycle of boiling and filtering was what I drank after it was cooled. I learned the hard way not to drink any other water and that I could not drink the water the villagers drank without falling ill. Water-borne diseases were a major reason for mortality and morbidity, particularly among children. Everyone needed the same clean water I drank, but nobody could afford to replicate what I did to obtain potable water. I did not see how much progress could be achieved as long as people did not have reliable access to clean drinking water. If water is equated with life, the lack or absence of potable water could be equated to misery and death.

Besides bathing in hot water, I allowed myself one other modern amenity: a sit-down, white porcelain flush toilet. When I arrived in the village, I found it hard to use the squat-type latrines commonly employed. I really needed to sit down to have a comfortable and good bowel movement. I, therefore, incurred the trouble and expense of building a buried septic tank just outside my house and hooking it up to a toilet anchored solidly in concrete inside my house. I had Assi always keep a bucket of water sitting next to the toilet so I could flush it by pouring water into it.

People came to see and use my toilet, but they did not like it. Unlike me, they could not defecate well sitting down. My toilet seat was partially ruined by people standing on it and squatting down to do their business. I was glad people stopped using my toilet, saying my sit-down toilet was inferior to a squat toilet, as squatting allowed a more thorough evacuation of the large intestine. Anyway, as most villagers did their business at designated places in the surrounding bush, and small children did it anywhere they chose, a relatively expensive flush toilet with a septic tank was not on anyone's wish list.

I admit being caught with the need to have a bowel movement in the bush was a problem for me. I was never at ease sitting in the bush and defecating, even though I always carried toilet paper in my back pocket. It also bothered me that flies would come and possibly spread disease from the dump I left in the bush. All this prompted me to devise what I called an "air mail" method of shitting in the bush. When I had to go, I would step into the bush, and after finding a good hiding place, I would defecate into one of the large manila envelopes I always carried with me for this purpose. After finishing my business, I would seal the envelope and toss it as far into the bush as I could. As I tossed it, I would loudly shout out the words, "air mail." I asked myself what people would think if they ever came across one of these strange yellow envelopes. Maybe they would think they were droppings of the gods.

I had a hard time sleeping. I was overly excited by thoughts of my trip to the capital city of Melomti. I lay in my bed as the night lantern flickered odd shadows on the wall and the translucent gecko lizards chased the shadows in search of insects. For me, the geckos played a useful role in the house. They always came out of nowhere at night to devour any bug they encountered. I particularly appreciated their role in keeping the mosquito population down. They only bothered me during their mating season when from their hiding places they would make provocative croaking noises.

The villagers had very different views about geckos. They thought they were evil, and every attempt should be made to kill them when they appeared from nowhere. They were in a constant battle to kill any gecko entering their house. Nobody could sleep until an intruding gecko was killed. I could see geckos were curious. They came out of nowhere, and it was a mystery where they stayed during the daytime. People believed the bite of a gecko would allow a spirit gecko to enter your body, causing itching all over the body as the spirit gecko traveled along the lymph system. People thought I was crazy to allow geckos to run freely on the walls inside my house at night.

On the contrary, ubiquitous fence lizards were not of any concern. These lizards were present everywhere during the daytime. The male fence lizard was quite visible with its reddish-orange head constantly bobbing up and down, as it tried to attract insects. I often tried to guess how many times one of these lizards would bob its head before moving on. I thought there might be some kind of numerical pattern, but I found the number of "bobs" was very random. The droppings of these lizards were everywhere. Although inconsistent with everything else I had observed, the villagers had no use for these lizards or any beliefs related to them.

I was very concerned about mosquitoes, in particular the female of the anopheles mosquito, which transmits malaria. I hoped all these lizards were consuming tons of them. Although I never saw mosquito bites on my body, I had contracted several severe cases of malaria. But my suffering from malaria did not lead to my adoption of measures designed to reduce the incidence of malaria. My claustrophobia prevented me from using a mosquito net, and I could not stand the smell of burning Chinese mosquito repellent coils in my bedroom at night. These coils burnt like incense, giving off a foul odor that nauseated me. My main complaint about mosquitoes was when they buzzed in my ears and kept me awake at night.

I did participate in the promotion of the use of mosquito nets, and a good number of people bought bed nets, but few used them as instructed. Some bought them just for prestige and folded them up so they could be like a pillow. Others bought them to make fishing nets or special wedding dresses. If anyone in the household used them, it was the male head of the household. This behavior occurred in spite of the high priority assigned to increasing bed net use by children and their mothers, particularly pregnant women. Those few bed nets actually used correctly often wore out quickly and needed replacement. The correct use of bed nets was a proven, effective way of reducing the incidence of malaria, but, like so many other simple innovations designed to improve life, they were difficult to put into practice widely.

I was a poor example in the constant fight to rollback malaria, but I was a big promoter of bringing malaria under control. It was by far the biggest killer of children and the main reason for medical consultations. For sure, the most dangerous animal in Africa is the mosquito, killing more people than anything else. One thing I promoted was the installation of screens on the windows. To serve as a good example, I had the local carpenter purchase screens and place them on all the windows of my house. In this way I could sleep with the coolness of the night air by leaving my wooden shutters open all night. Many villagers saw what I did at my house and thought it was a good idea, but for reasons other than keeping mosquitoes out. They thought it was a great way to keep heat-seeking snakes from entering your house at night. There was little they feared more than snakes, and for them, all snakes were poisonous.

The World Health Organization (WHO) decided the best way to eradicate malaria was to spray all houses inside and out with DDT, the most effective insecticide against mosquitoes. WHO had organized a huge campaign to spray all the villages in the region. A date had been fixed for the spraying of Ataku. The chief's messengers fanned out to advise every one of the date they must remove everything from their house. The inside of house walls would be sprayed with DDT, and people would have to stay out of their houses for forty-eight hours after the spraying. For the first time, I actually heard of people objecting to the chief's ruling. For them, it was inconceivable that generations of items could be removed from their houses. What about the old and sick and the "grandfathers'" houses? There was no way the latter could be opened for spraying.

When hearing of these objections, the chief sent advisors to the households of each clan chief to demonstrate why the inside of houses had to be sprayed if they were ever to reduce the terrible scourge of malaria. These advisors entered the clan chief's house and noted the usual clothes and other items hanging on nails and wooden pegs driven into the hard mud walls. They removed some clothes from a wall and held them high for all to see. When they shook them, dozens of mosquitoes could be seen flying away. As there was no refuting this hard evidence, the grumbling became less. The clan chiefs were instructed to do the same in each house of their clan so all would be convinced of the need to empty their houses. Besides, this would be a great opportunity to clean thoroughly their houses and throw all the debris collected to the east of the village so all the bad spirits would go back to where they came from. This latter point turned all in favor of the massive spraying campaign.

Everyone was in favor of spraying except for one person: me. I had read Rachel Carson's *Silent Spring*, and thus, I had some rudimentary knowledge of the possible heavy environmental consequences of spraying with DDT. I knew that once DDT entered into the food chain, it took many years for it to dissipate. I certainly did not want to be exposed to DDT and was desperately seeking a way to be absent from the village the day the spraying teams came. I did not know what to do, so on the day of the spraying I followed an impulse and disappeared for the day into the forest. I waited in the forest until almost dark before returning to my house. Oddly,

I found my house and all its belongings just like they were when I left them.

I asked Assi, "Did the spraying take place?"

She replied, "Yes."

"Did they try to spray my house?"

She quickly informed me, "No, they saved your house for last, but they ran out of DDT spray long before that. They will return, but nobody knows when."

I prayed they would never return. In the following weeks and months, people did note there were hardly any mosquitoes around, and the local clinic reported the number of malaria cases had fallen to a record low. For sure, morbidity and mortality due to malaria had been greatly reduced by the use of DDT, but the real cost of using this deadly insecticide will probably never be known.

CHAPTER THIRTEEN
RIDING THE BISMARCK

Early the next morning, I mounted my trusty Honda 50, revved up the engine, and headed for the train station about ten miles away. I bid farewell to Assi and Aba, some of their children, and my faithful dog, and hit the dusty trail. With a big smile, I waved at people as I passed through the village to join the road leading to the train station. My adrenalin levels were running high. Several dogs were taking a nap in the middle of the road I needed to use. I revved my engine and honked at them, but typically, these dogs did not show the slightest signs of movement. They seemed not to be worried about being run over by a vehicle.

I had always been amazed how African dogs would lay sleeping in the middle of the road in spite of all the traffic. It was not that people were letting sleeping dogs lie, as they were constantly beating them and throwing rocks at them so they would move. But the dogs did not care and often had to be physically carried off paths and roadways. I had tried to raise a couple of African dogs, but found them a challenge to train. I began to believe these dogs were born with psychotic traits. As these dogs were purported to have been descended from the dogs of the ancient Egyptian pharaohs, I asked myself if these Basenji-like dogs were as difficult in ancient times as they were now. The ancient Egyptian pharaohs had images of similar Basenji dogs engraved on the walls of their tombs in the pyramids. I concluded African dogs must have been more manageable back then.

To avoid the dogs and continue on my way, I drove my motorbike slightly into the bush at the edge of the path. I whizzed by the dogs, but they did not seem to notice me. I was really on my way now. When I was about halfway to the station, a big spitting cobra crossed the road right in front of me. As this had happened many times before, I did not let this snake slow me down. After all, I could not miss the train! I simply did as I usually did in such situations and raised my feet and drove over the slick black snake.

Anyway, a spitting cobra was not too dangerous. It could only injure you by spitting into your eyes, thereby causing sharp pain, temporary blindness, and some paralysis. I may have acted differently had this been a very poisonous green or black mamba, as the bite of these deadly snakes could kill in a matter of minutes. As recommended, I kept an anti-venom "snake-bite" kit in my small kerosene fridge, but if a snake were to bite me, I would probably be too deep in the bush, and thus, too far from my fridge for the medicine to do any good. Nonetheless, one main reason for operating my fridge was so the anti-venom in this kit could remain viable. I figured if a snake ever bit me I should rapidly say my last prayers and try to write a few last words.

I could see more cobras sticking their heads up as they slid through the leafy grounds of the teak plantations adjoining the road. Seeing the teak trees made me think of what happened a few weeks ago at this same spot in the road. I was told one of these teak trees sprang up and ran in front of a pickup, causing it to swerve and hit another tree growing alongside the road. I saw the pickup; it had a deep V-shaped dent in the middle of its front bumper like it had hit a telephone pole very hard. The driver swore that a tree had run in front of him. An investigation was made, and it was found someone had indeed paid a lot of money to an out-of-town fetish priest to do harm to this man. The driver's story was accepted, and he was able to demand the offending party to pay for the damages to his pickup. For most people there was nothing unusual about this story except about the innovative way a tree had been used to carry out this occult mission to do harm.

My excitement rose as I spotted the ramshackle train station on the horizon. I could clearly see the ancient train inherited from colonial times. It was in the station being swarmed by people jostling with one another as they tried to get their tickets and board the train with their baggage. I steeled myself as if I was going into battle. It would take much effort and some aggression to obtain a ticket and places on the train for me and my motorbike (locally called, "moto").

At that moment I wished there was some better way to get to the capital. There was a road, but it was practically impassable at several points, especially after a rainfall. Even in the driest conditions, it could take two rough days of bouncing around in the back of old trucks equipped with wooden benches to make it to the capital. Crooked police and customs officials, who demanded bribes, also set up numerous roadblocks. A ride on the train was fast and smooth in comparison. If the train did not have one of its frequent breakdowns, the hundred miles to the capital city could be traveled in about ten hours.

To make sure I obtained the all-important tickets for me and my motorbike, I paid one of the young guys hanging around to help me buy tickets and to get me on the train. These guys knew how to get through the crowds and cut a deal with the ticket sellers in the station, who knew them well and probably received a kickback. In no time I had my tickets in hand, and the same guy helped me guide my motorbike through the dense, noisy crowds to the open car in the back, where it would be tied firmly to the interior wall of the train. After we received a receipt for the motorbike, the guy accompanied me to one of the better passenger cars, telling some people to move so the Whiteman could have one of the better wooden benches. I did not like the preferential treatment, but I knew there was no sense fighting this custom at this time. Moreover, the seat I was offered was a good one next to the window where I could get fresh air and watch the world pass by.

I looked out the window and saw the general hardware store where I bought the bulky sisal bag with a woven handle that I could conveniently loop over the handlebars of my moto. I had the bag with me now; it contained my change of clothes, a few toiletries, a towel, and an all-purpose wrap-around African cloth. I was thinking I would go to a roadside tailor in Melomti and get a new shirt and pants made. I also planned to sift through the mountains of American used clothing for some nice shirts. These used clothes were considered helpful to keeping poor people clothed. It was obvious to me that many people would go without clothes if they did not have access to used clothing imported from the States.

Well-off people would never buy used clothing, because wearing them was a sign of poverty and low status. I was able to wear such cheap clothes because they could look like they were mine. The people thought these clothes came from dead people, as nobody would ever discard such nice clothes. I gave up trying to convey the notion of people in the States discarding and frequently buying new clothes. It always gave me a laugh to be in the deep bush and see somebody walk by in a shirt with some American university name or slogan written on it. The people wearing the used clothing had no idea about the meaning of the words on their shirts. For them, a shirt was a shirt, and what was written on it was of no importance.

I often asked what children wore before the advent of the import of used clothes, and the reply was usually "nothing." I was told in the old days a young man or woman would receive a long shirt following initiation rites during adolescence, and many people wore bark cloth wrappings. I had the impression that wearing clothes was a relatively new innovation for many people living in rural areas.

Nowadays, people at all levels of the social strata were jockeying to out-dress their friends and neighbors. Women would save up to buy the high prestige imports of real Dutch wax-print clothes. They would not have their tailors make the usual three-piece skirt, blouse, and head piece right away, but would hide the new cloth until it lost its commonness. Everyone did this as one way of avoiding the awkwardness of meeting someone with the same cloth. And, to make their husbands happy, they would buy extra yards of the same cloth to make a shirt. Seeing a man and woman dressed in the same cloth was a sure sign a woman was trying to show appreciation for her man.

Every new issue of Dutch wax cloth was given a name by the people according to the designs in the cloth. An up-to-date woman prided herself on being conversant with the names of various cloths. Some important market women made sizeable fortunes selling cloth throughout the region. The heyday of Dutch wax cloth took a hit when some traders started bringing in much cheaper Chinese imitation cloth. These imitations were so carefully done one had to look closely to see what was printed in the edge of the cloth. If it did not say "Real Dutch Wax," it was a knockoff and would fade after a few washings. On the contrary, real Dutch Wax could last a very long time, especially if care was taken to wash it with a soft soap bar. I was very much interested in those cloth patterns with an obscure African proverb printed along their borders in the local language. I was always challenged to interpret what the words meant and, when I was successful in doing so, I always impressed the villagers, who also wanted to know what the sayings meant.

We were waiting impatiently for the train's loud steam-powered whistle to blow, marking the start of our trip to the capital. But, when the whistle did finally blow, we all acted very startled. The earth-shaking sound of the whistle galvanized people and animals into action. All living things began scurrying to get away from the narrow-gauge train tracks, which had been laid in early colonial times, long before anyone living could remember. Two more toots of the deafening whistle and we could feel the ancient train making a grudging attempt to move ahead. It was like some long-slumbering beast awakening from a disagreeable period of hibernation. And then there was a sudden screeching gasp, which frightened everyone, but at the same time, all were pleased when the train jerked hesitantly forward. At last, we were on our way and ready to enjoy the adventures of the trip!

It was a miracle the train could still make its daily trips to the capital. It had been scheduled for the scrap heap thirty years ago, but there was simply no replacement for it. Teams of ordinary handymen had become experts at keeping the train running. They were constantly moving back and forth on the train, checking repeatedly all moving parts. They carried with them all sorts of hand tools, bolts and nuts, and simple strands of baling wire. They never ceased fussing with one part of the train or another.

Thanks to their incredible mechanical improvisations, the train had served well beyond its planned lifetime.

We did not go far before the train stopped at the next village. The train would stop at all twenty-two of the main villages located on the rusty rail line to the capital. These stops were the main reason it took ten to twelve hours to travel one hundred miles. At every stop the train would be accosted by dozens of clamoring vendors selling their wares. If you were hungry or thirsty, you would buy something from the vendors. At the first stop, I called out to a vendor through my large open window and bought a small plastic bag filled with filtered water and a couple of handfuls of fried plantain pieces wrapped in coarse brown paper. There was never a need to worry about thirst or hunger, as the many stops offered those who had money an opportunity to buy food and drinks of every kind. I took pity on some of the poorer passengers sitting close to me and shared my food and water with them. Their big smiles and humble thanks made doing this worthwhile.

The main challenge of train travel came when you had the urge to use the toilet. There were not any sanitary facilities on the train. If you had to go, it had to be when the train stopped. That meant rushing into the nearby bushes and quickly doing your business before the train departed. If you did not have anyone you could trust to watch your things, you would have to take them with you and risk losing your seat. Honestly, one reason I shared my food was to make friends who would save my seat and protect my bag. This may all sound easy, but at each stop, dozens jumped off to do their business. There was a lot of maddening competition to find a good place to do number one or two or both. It was not unusual for people to come out from their bush toilet to find the train moving away from the station. Some never made it back in time and would have to wait for tomorrow's train.

The train was packed with people, animals, and goods. All the benches and floor space were completely filled, and some people had to stand. Most of the passengers were market women accompanied by their children, goods, and animals—mostly goats and chickens—they were taking to the capital to sell. After a few hours, the rude smell produced by this coarse mixture of organic and inorganic matter became overpowering. I found myself keeping my face just outside the open window. I was careful not to stick my head out too far, as the probability of colliding with some sort of insect was high. The wooden floor of the train became so soiled with urine, manure, and vomit (the motion of the train made some kids sick) it became too slippery to walk safely.

None of these inconveniences lessened the high level of exuberance of what appeared to be a joyful gathering on the train. People were chatting nonstop, swapping stories and laughing loudly. Sometimes, they would sing songs and church hymns. Children played with one another and many women openly breastfed their infants. There was a carnival atmosphere, making you feel like something special was happening. It was like I had run away from home and joined a circus composed of all kinds of exotic characters. It was exciting, and one of those moments in life when I felt like I had been transported to a different planet where nothing in my previous life was of any relevance.

The small children moved about and played their own games. Their mothers were constantly haranguing them to behave, making awful threats to them if they did not sit still. Little by little, the bolder kids crept closer to me, as many had never seen a Whiteman. Other kids were so scared of seeing a Whiteman they hid behind their mothers. I could hear their mothers telling them I was not a corpse, but a real person from another place. One little girl came close enough to me to achieve her mission of showing off to the other kids by touching me. As soon as she touched me, I could hear her mother telling her to leave me alone.

Her mother called her "bucket." When I heard her called by this name, I immediately knew this was a woman who had lost many children. It was believed that one bad spirit or another caused the high level of child mortality. Even if sickle-cell anemia or one of the many childhood diseases resulted in death, the child's death was still associated with the actions of a bad spirit. This prompted families with many child deaths to give names of inanimate objects to their children. This was done as a way to trick the spirits into thinking a child was not human, and thus, not seek to cause the child harm. I heard another mother on the train call her toddler "broom." This also did not raise any eyebrows, as everyone understood and would do the same if they had also had the misfortune of losing many children to evil spirits.

There were a few children who were not active; their hair was tinged with redness. This was an indicator of *kwashiorkor* (protein deficiency) and malnourishment. As well as they were cared for and as chubby as they were, they were not eating a diet providing them all the vitamins, protein, and nutrients they needed for a healthy start to their lives. Too many children were born too small and not fed correctly in their early years to avoid becoming permanently impaired by stunting. It was hard to understand how a country could advance if such a high percentage of its children were stunted. Poor nourishment reduced a child's immune system; therefore, many succumbed to disease before the age of five, making the child mortality rate very high.

One infant girl was sitting on the floor near me, playing with a razor blade. I knew it was a girl, because her ears were pierced. As soon as girl babies are born, their ears are pierced and fitted with small earrings or threads. I could not bear seeing any longer how close this baby was to cutting herself with a razor blade, so I reached over and snatched it from her and handed it to her mother, who did not seem to be paying any attention to her child. I expected the mother to thank me for my good deed, but she only laughed and gave the razor blade back to her baby.

I could not believe she had done this and asked her, "Are you not afraid your baby will cut herself?"

She laughed again and said, "If the baby cuts herself, then she is just too dumb and deserves being cut. In this way she will learn about the dangers of playing with a razor blade."

There was one song they began singing as we arrived at every stop. This song would start by naming the village we would stop at next and go on to name the villages we had already passed, as well as the ones remaining on our route. The melody of this song stuck in my head after singing it only one time. I really became tired of this song, but I joined in singing it at every stop and laughed along with everyone else. After all, this was a lot of fun and it was a useful geographic lesson. It made it so you could never forget the names of the villages this daily train passed through. At the end of each rendition of the song, all would shout the word "Bismarck," which was the original name of the train. But, as long as anyone could remember, the train was called in local language the "iron beast."

The day became long, and the temperatures rose steeply, as did the humidity. We slowly approached the coastal capital. We fidgeted in our seats and became agitated as we began to smell the salty air blown far inland by the prevailing ocean breeze. Then, we could see the tops of buildings over the tall savannah grass, which waved to and fro in the ocean wind. The swaying movement of the grass grew more vigorous as we approached the coast. We could now see the top of the highest building, the multi-story headquarters of the single political party. Spying the roof of this building reminded me of the advice one of the chief's senior advisors gave me the day before I left the village.

He told me, "Enjoy yourself, but keep in mind a few simple rules. I caution you to avoid any risks by not mentioning the president, his party, or his army in any conversation. This is a very pleasant country if you can steer away from engaging in these taboo subjects."

Of course, there was another general, additional rule about avoiding any involvement with fetish or occult practices. In other words, stay away from sorcery no matter how high your curiosity. There had been many stories about foreigners who were attracted to the local occult practices. They became too involved and ended up in a bad way. I had heard stories about some white people who had been driven crazy by some juju they had exposed themselves to and others who had been evacuated, paralyzed from the neck down. I had seen enough myself that I could not ignore the existence of the very real and strong presence of African religions and beliefs in people's daily lives. It was very hard to ignore what was so omnipresent. I knew well that even a tiny sliver of strong belief in this other world could affect one's well-being and mightily complicate one's life.

The savannah grass began to shorten as we approached the coast, and towering, sacred baobab trees appeared on the horizon, like solemn sentinels which protected the entrance to the capital. The air became thicker and visibility lower, as the dry Harmattan winds sweeping down from the north collided with the moist, salty sea air, which penetrated everything. The grass looked like it was coated with rust. About a mile from the capital, the train workers began applying the brakes, causing a loud screeching noise, which prompted many to cover their ears. The noise became louder as we approached the station. It was as if the wheels of the train were no longer turning, but locked, so the train was now on a long slide into the station. It was as if we were coming in for a dangerous belly-landing in a disabled plane.

The train maintenance men were running about crazily, attending to all the meticulous details needing precise manipulation so the train would stop in front of the station and not go on to crash into the barrier at the end of the track. This was risky business, and everyone knew to remain still and quiet. Some prayed. Others nervously chewed on short lengths of small branches used as "toothpicks." One woman near me was busy cleaning her ears with a bird's feather that had been stripped of its feathers, except for the end she was sticking into her ear.

The speed of the train gradually slowed, and there was a nail-biting super screech. Then the train shuddered as if it was in the final death throes. Suddenly, the train stopped, throwing everyone off their seats, making them tumble into each other. Immediately, all began singing praises to the Supreme God, thanking Him for their safe arrival. The level of excitement had peaked again. Everyone quickly picked themselves up, gathered their belongings and kids, and headed for the exits. It did not take long before this motley crowd vanished in a dozen different directions. I stayed behind to receive—in what I hoped was in good condition—my moto. I was happy to have arrived in the capital, but at the same time, I was a bit sad to see my train adventure come to an end.

CHAPTER FOURTEEN
WHARF FISHING

I was pleased to have my shiny red moto turned over to me in good condition. I checked it over and made sure no fuel had been siphoned from its tank. Satisfied with its condition, I gave the expected small tip to the two young men who had brought it to me. Exerting only one brisk downward thrust with my right leg on the starter pedal, my moto started and sounded good to go. I happily headed for the train station exit gate and joined the riotous city traffic. An even layer of sand covered the bumpy, rusty-red laterite road; sand was blowing constantly in from the nearby beach. Vehicles of all sorts vied for room to pass, slipping and sliding, and sometimes colliding, as they struggled to find a way through the dense jumble of traffic.

Hordes of two-wheeled motorbikes monopolized traffic. The most prevalent two-wheeler was the French-made *Mobylette*. This cheap motorbike was pedaled like a bicycle to start its engine. Sometimes entire families or groups of three to four people could be observed squeezed onto one moto. There were also hundreds of small taxi cars that people shared. Hundreds more people were on bicycles, often times carrying impossible loads while managing amazing feats of balance and stamina. Added to this maddening mix were some donkey carts and small four-wheeled flatbed wagons pulled and pushed by young men. All these vehicles jostled for their positions on the narrow, unimproved road heading south to the coast. I cautiously joined this vehicular mob where the most aggressive men and women would fiercely compete to find a way to move ahead and arrive safely at their destinations.

Of course, most people depended on what they called "God's transport" i.e., your "feet." There were throngs of people along the sides of the road, mostly women balancing a large variety of heavy loads on their heads. At the same time, they could be breastfeeding and carrying a baby wrapped tightly on their backs. It was amazing how little their heavy loads seemed a burden to them as they moved gracefully through the crowd. For me, it was a self-evident truth that the well-being of the country rested on the shoulders (or heads) of women. As far as I was concerned, as long as women could not get ahead, the country could not progress.

It was a lopsided and colorful road scene—lopsided because there was shade on one side of the road and none on the other side. Of course, everyone naturally avoided the harsh rays of the hot tropical sun, even though it was late in the day and the sun's light was less ferocious. In a land of constant heat, the sun was to be avoided as much as possible. It was colorful, because as usual, everyone was dressed in a myriad of African cloth printed with a vivid mixture of all possible colors. The energetic tempo at which people moved, gestured, spoke and walked, combined with the mosaic of colors, created a lively, vibrant feeling. It was like seeing an unending carnival in motion. Being active and colorful appeared to be highly valued qualities, particularly for women.

In contrast with this multi-colored scene, there were topless young women who wore the simplest cloth wrap made of drab homespun white cotton strips that had been sewn together. There were many of these women interspersed in the crowd, and all were carrying heavy head loads. They had two lines of scarification starting at their waists and crisscrossing between their breasts, going over their shoulders and crossing again as they continued down their back to waist level. A closely spaced succession of raised incisions made these scar lines, creating a chain composed of pimple-like bumps. The young women were referred to as "fetish children" and would submit to several years of apprenticeship and servitude before becoming full members of their cult.

They were acolytes who belonged to a fetish cult that used them to carry loads to and from the markets to make money for their fetish order. The scar lines on their bodies were part of the initiation ceremony they had endured to join this cult. It was prohibited for them to speak. They lived together in an open-air dormitory in a vacant compound managed by their leaders.

As they were inducted into the cult, they had to learn an ancient language which had long ago fallen into disuse, except for cults like this one. It was in this language they would be taught the secrets only known to sworn members. They were both feared and respected. This contradictory combination contributed to people wanting to help them by paying them money to transport their goods. In this way people were able to transport their goods, as well as gain favor with the fetish spirit the young women served.

I headed toward the coast, because I wanted very much to see the ocean before the sunset. As it was late in the day, I did not have much time. I arrived at the only paved road in the country, which ran parallel with the wide beach. I stopped and fixed my gaze for several long moments on the wide expanse of ocean that stretched before me to the endless horizon. The sound of the waves rolling in and out was therapeutic for me, making me feel calm and enveloped by a deep sense of peace and well-being.

Darkness was rapidly approaching and I wanted to take a quick stroll on the beach at the water's edge, but it was the wrong time of the day to do so. This was also one of the two times each day (the other time was at sunrise) hundreds of people came to squat at the water's edge to relieve themselves. At these times, the beaches became a community toilet, and people placed themselves at polite intervals along the beach. The arrival of higher tides would wash the nasty mess away, and the strong undertow of this part of the ocean would take all the crap far out to sea. I was impressed by how so many people could time their bowel movements with the rise and fall of the tides, as if in tune with the lunar cycle.

One reason for this massive use of the beach as a toilet was the difficulty of digging family latrines and septic tanks, as the water table was too close to the surface. The nearby ocean had seeped deeply into the coastal plain, making well water brackish and undrinkable. Fresh water had to be piped in from a long distance. Toilets in most households consisted of large metal buckets placed in elevated outhouses. The outer wall of the outhouse was facing the road, and there was a small external door so the bucket could be removed, emptied, and returned to its place.

There were filthy city trucks making regular rounds at night to collect the fecal contents of these buckets. The powerful, nauseous odor discharged by these contaminated buckets and trucks was overwhelming. Those who operated these trucks—laughingly referred to as "honey wagons"—stank as badly as the rotten fecal matter they collected, and they acted crazily, threatening anyone who approached them with fists full of human offal. One of the worst things that could happen to anyone was to be stuck in traffic behind one of these honey wagons. People caught near these trucks sometimes fainted from the overpowering stench.

Mixed with the smell of the collective seaside beach toilet was another evening odor which had a source hard to determine. In some places, I thought the rancid smell of urine was the origin of this smell. Urine saturated many areas; peeing openly in public by both men and women was tolerated. It took me a long time to realize the acrid smell occurring every evening was coming from thousands of households lighting charcoal fires to prepare their evening meal. The charcoal was first doused with kerosene so it could be readily lit with a wooden match. The smell of burning charcoal and kerosene from thousands of fires lit at about the same time rose to create a gaseous layer of pollution that hung over the city. The smell was very discernible to outsiders who had not previously experienced being smothered by such a simultaneous mass ignition of charcoal. Thus, a thousand trees or more daily went up in smoke.

As darkness fell I rode on slowly for a few hundred yards, going down the wide paved beach road passing in front of the ultra-modern building housing the president's office. The president spent his nights in a distant, well-guarded military camp. The main reason for such a nice road was to allow for parades of hundreds of people to pass by, singing and dancing in praise of the president, who was expected to rule for as long as he lived, just like a village chief. A very strong personality cult had been built up around the president.

This parade ground was also where the president would give his lengthy speeches. At a moment's notice, tens of thousands of people could be summoned to listen to one of the president's lengthy and incoherent extemporaneous speeches that often lasted for three to five hours. All were required to stand at attention and keep their eyes focused on the president while he was speaking. Anyone who failed to do this in the slightest way would be whipped by one of the president's dozens of crowd managers. People were expected to memorize everything the president said because they could be tested on the subject matter of his speech by the neighborhood political czars. When the people were sure they were not being watched by the secret police, they would joke about the speeches. One common saying was that it was too bad the president's many words could not be turned into food, because doing that would end hunger.

The single national TV channel would start each evening with a view of the Earth from a distant point in space. The camera approached Earth, and then the African continent would appear, and far below was a discernible outline of the country. Suddenly, a bright star appeared in the heavens. Descending from the light was an angelic image which progressively became a clear picture of the president who landed on a map of the country amid fireworks and the loud praises of the population. Trumpets blared while angels loudly sang his praises, exclaiming the arrival of the country's savior.

The president's portrait was posted everywhere. His book of sayings and speeches was required reading in all the schools. His praises were sung before and after classes, as well as in every workplace. Big billboards with his sayings and party slogans had been erected at every major crossroad. I was intrigued by some of the information the billboards were attempting to communicate. One slogan in particular caught my attention. This slogan contained only two words: "Development = Culture." The presentation of this inscrutable slogan was always followed by another billboard with the reverse order of the same equation: "Culture = Development." I never ceased pondering the meaning of this slogan. I thought it might be trying to convey the notion that there was some connection between achieving developmental progress and cultural values.

The walls around the president's palace were beautifully painted with colorful murals depicting numerous joyous scenes of happy crowds singing the praises of the president and his political party. I was impressed by the high quality of the painting and the intricacy of each scene. It must have taken months of meticulous work to complete murals running along several blocks. I was surprised there was the talent available locally to paint these lovely murals. I passed the murals several times before it dawned on me that there was something out of order. All the nicely drawn black faces of the hundreds of people portrayed had Asian features. Later, I asked about this and I was told North Koreans hired by the president had painted these vivid murals.

Comic books were also published to communicate to the masses the extraordinary but fabricated achievements of the president since his birth. They all started with "once upon a time, a great human being was born." The president had many flattering names, but the ones most often used for him were the "helmsman" and "enlightened guide." Since the president had miraculously survived many assassination attempts and car and plane crashes, people were convinced he was protected by the strongest spirits. This belief was bolstered by the fact that he kept the top fetish priests of the country in his super luxurious presidential palace that was located within a well-guarded military camp. They had the job of transferring to him the strongest powers they could conjure up and warning him of any impending dangers.

The people feared the president, and this fear generated a certain amount of respect, but it was hard for them to be proud of him because he was uneducated and poorly raised. The people were also rankled by the fact he had too much blood on his hands and too much money in foreign banks. Secretly, everyone wished their president had gone to school. Those who had voted with their feet and fled to safety in other countries would laughingly refer to him as the president "without a diploma." Many people were biding their time until they could revolt, but as the decades passed vested interests became more deeply entrenched, and the younger generation had not known any other way.

All these thoughts came into my head as I cautiously passed in front of the president's office building on the opposite side of the road. No one dared to pass on the side of the road directly in front, as soldiers guarding the palace would immediately pounce on you and beat you mercilessly with heavy sticks. Even worse, you could be shot if you looked like you were trying to take a photo of the president's palace. No warning signs were posted anywhere. It was assumed everyone should intuitively know the rules when passing near the president's office. All this was scary to me, but I had to drive in front of the office to get where I wanted to go: the old, rusty wharf.

The old wharf had not been used in decades, and the cast-iron pillars it rested on were rusted to the extent that it could crumple into the water at any moment. About half of the wooden planks covering it had rotted away or been stolen. Anyone venturing out onto the old wharf risked falling into cast-iron crossbars and the water thirty feet below. A good number of people had already drowned by falling off the wharf into the deep, turbulent water, where a strong undertow would pull their bodies quickly out to sea. Their bodies would usually never be seen again, or they would be found on the beach in a neighboring country.

In spite of this real danger and the big sign in front of the wharf prohibiting anyone from walking on the wharf, dozens of men could be seen on the wharf fishing with hand lines. For certain, it was much safer to go out on the wharf before it was dark. Many treaded on the treacherous planks to find a good spot to fish just before dark, and they remained there all night. For some reason, fishing was much better at night.

I carefully observed how the men walked to distant points on one side of the wharf, throwing their fishing lines out as far as they could. I really liked fishing; I could not stop myself from getting closer to the old wharf. As I approached it, a short, old man with a bundle of fishing line, small cans, and a few flimsy plastic bags tucked in the loops of his ragged pants asked me, "Would you like to go fishing?" He looked friendly and quite harmless.

I answered, "Yes, but I do not know where to leave my moto."

He quickly replied, "You can leave your moto and bag with a nearby watchman who guards all the goods of the men fishing off the old wharf. I promise to lead you safely on and off the wharf and loan you one of my fishing lines. By the way, my name is Gerard."

I shook his extended hand and accepted his offer. I was excited about learning the art and dangers of wharf fishing.

Gerard had a small, dim Chinese flashlight to help us pick our way carefully through the obstacle course of rotten and missing timbers. I stayed very close behind him, trying to step as lightly as possible, prepared to jump or grab onto anything solid in case of any sudden collapse beneath me. He closely followed the old rail line in the middle of the wharf, as this seemed to be the most solid part of the rickety old wharf's remaining structure. About sixty yards out, when we were past the pounding, coastal waves, standing over much calmer ocean water, Gerard said, "This is a good spot. Let's fish here."

It was also a spot not too close to many others who were already fishing. For me, I was fishing for fun; for them, they were fishing for survival.

Gerard demonstrated how to bait the hook and throw the heavily weighted lines far out over the ocean waters. He took from a plastic bag he carried with him a smelly piece of a dead fish and firmly attached it to a rather large fishhook. He said he always used for bait a part of the fish he had caught the previous night. He made sure the hook was fastened tightly by pulling firmly on it, while tightly holding the line in his other hand. He checked the sinkers, which were made of bolts and nuts, to make sure they were also secure. He carefully placed yards of fishing line next to him in a circular, overlapping pattern, making sure there were no tangles. He checked all this gear closely with his tiny flashlight.

He waited for a moment while his eyes adjusted to the light of a half moon. He then took about five feet of line connected to the sinker and hook, swinging it rapidly in a counterclockwise motion above his head. With perfect timing he let loose of the line, allowing the centrifugal force to carry it far away from the wharf. He threw it off the eastern side of the wharf, as the flow of the strong parallel coastal current moved in that direction.

He slowly let out more line until he was satisfied he had the right distance and depth. He took from his large pocket a small, empty *Peak Lait* milk can, which had contained the same milk I used daily for my morning coffee. Inside this tin can were some small pebbles. He tightly wrapped some slack in his line several times around this can, then he tied his line around an old metal rail in the middle of the wharf. I was puzzled by the role of the tin can, but later, its use became readily apparent.

Now, it was my turn to launch my line. I did everything I saw him do, and he said I was good to go. Like David slaying Goliath with his slingshot, I twirled the line over my head the best I could and let it go flying into the open sea. Given the strong ocean breeze, I found doing this and keeping my balance was much harder than it looked. I did not throw my line as far as my companion, but he said it was okay. He wrapped my line around another Peak Milk can, which rattled audibly with all the little pebbles it had inside, and secured my line to the metal rail.

I asked him. "What do we do now?

He laughed and said, "There is nothing to do but lie down, rest, and wait to see if we catch anything."

We lay down on our backs with our heads propped up on the metal rail. It was a beautiful tropical night. The stars seemed so bright and close. I was happy there was not a full moon, as I could never be exposed for such a long time to its light. Far out to sea there was a lightning storm, giving us a natural sound-and-light show to view. The time passed agreeably. I was getting sleepy, but I was abruptly brought out of this melancholy moment when the can on his line went wild and started rattling noisily. Gerard jumped up and quickly grabbed his line, jerking it powerfully.

He shouted excitedly, "A fish is on my line and I need to sink the hook deeper before trying to haul it in!"

When his feisty red snapper cleared the top of the wharf, he hit it on the head with a little hammer and safely stowed it in a wet plastic sack. No sooner had he finished doing this, when my can of pebbles started rattling loudly. I jumped for my line and did as he had just done. My heart was pounding with excitement. I was pleased when I saw I had hooked a bigger red snapper than the one he had caught.

He stopped my fish's wild gyrations with a swift hit to its head using his ballpeen hammer. He dexterously removed the hook which was deeply embedded in the fish's gaping mouth. He took from his pocket a black plastic bag like the ones littering the entire landscape. The wind had blown discarded plastic bags across the country and almost every tree and bush had these bags hanging from it. The trashy bags were so ubiquitous some referred to them as the "national ornament." My newfound fisherman friend tried to make a joke about putting my fish into a future national deco- ration. He quickly slid the slippery fish into the flimsy plastic bag, tying a tight knot in the top of the bag.

Gerard handed the fish to me, but I refused, saying, "Go ahead. Keep the fish. It's yours."

He insisted, saying, "It would be bad luck not to take your first catch."

I accepted the fish, but I asked, "What should I do with it?"

He replied, "Any local restaurant would be happy to clean and cook it for you."

I offered my biggest thanks for the fish and he escorted me off the wharf before returning to a night of fishing. I thanked him profusely one more time and, as I said good-bye, I expressed a sincere wish, "One day we will fish together again."

With a wide grin on his face, he said, "I will be happy to see you anytime. I can see the sea likes you."

I headed to where my moto was parked and paid a small amount to the watchman for his services. I slipped the bag holding my fish over my handlebars and headed toward the economic lodgings recommended to me a long time ago. It was a dark night, and the ocean mist reduced visibility. I carefully maneuvered my moto along the sandy road, which was slippery as my fish.

CHAPTER FIFTEEN
MELOMTI BY NIGHT

I slowly threaded my way through the noisy assortment of vehicles, cautiously heading toward the part of town where I could find a cheap room. The modest accommodation I was looking for was difficult to locate, as it did not have any sign or fixed name. It was one of many clandestine places operating on the edge of legality, trying to avoid gaining any official status so as not to pay taxes and be exposed to any government controls. These places were called "clandos." There were clando hotels, restaurants, bars, nightclubs, taxis etc. If one wanted the cheapest prices, you looked for a clando. The main risk was being in a clando when it was raided by the police.

Harsh government controls had worked to create many types of clandos. Each clando operator cut his or her own deal with local authorities to maintain its anonymity. To survive in the "big brother" living and working environment, all citizens had to apply what they called system "D." The "D" represented in local language a combination of sentiments that were something like "lying, cheating, making do, and not giving a shit." People had become so used to lying to stay out of trouble they had forgotten what the truth was. The only truth that mattered was the "president's truth." So, if need be, you only said to state officials what they wanted to hear and not what was true. This perverted survival system had been going on for so long that people no longer knew what the genuine truth was.

In this system everybody spied on everyone else to see who would overstep the "truth" boundaries. Anyone admitting the harsh realities of the political system would be reported on, and thereby, risk disappearing forever. Nobody could trust anyone, not even their own family members. The regime's secret police watched many people. They did not know from one day to the next whether or not they would be sleeping again in their own beds or in one of the hidden gulags of the regime.

Many people disappeared for long periods of time, and if they returned, they were unrecognizable from all the severe beatings they had received. You could disappear just for mentioning the president's name without adjoining all the honorifics that must accompany it. If there was a need to talk about the president, people invented imaginative nicknames for him. City life offered a lot of benefits, but it also entailed the risks created by living close to the "throne."

As I approached the neighborhood where I believed the clando lodging was located, I began stopping to ask a few of the many people along the sides of the streets if they knew of its whereabouts. I finally found it in at the dark end of a hidden side street. All things off the main arteries were hard to find, as electricity reached very few places from the main roads, which were dimly lit by a few ancient street lamps that still worked. If one judged Africa by the amount of night lighting, it could be easily referred to as the "dark continent." It was really dark, and the foggy air made it even darker and weirdly surreal. One could easily get lost in one's own neighborhood.

I banged on the metal gate until a small boy came to open it slightly so as to see who was there. Once he saw me, he timidly requested, "Please stop making so much noise. You are making people fear there is a police raid."

"Is there a room I can rent for a few days?" I softly inquired.

I heard an equally soft reply, "There is a room for about the equivalent of three American dollars a night."

I immediately accepted and began rolling my moto carefully over the concrete slab that bridged the open sewer running along the street. These kinds of concrete-walled gutters aligned all the city streets. They were about three feet wide and five feet deep. Everything was dumped into them, and they exuded a very bad smell. They would get blocked with rubbish, and when it rained they would fill up and overflow onto the streets, spreading the awful mess they contained. Children had been known to fall into them and die.

I once had the horrible experience of stepping out of a taxi parked along the street and disappearing into one of these cesspool canals. I stood knee deep in rotten, soggy waste for several minutes before being rescued by a passerby, who had heard my screams. Everyone had a good laugh about the white guy covered by sewage. I gave generous tips to my rescuers and rushed to the nearest public water spout to clean myself off. It took days for the intolerable smell to leave my body, even with vigorous scrubbing and using the strongest soap and disinfectant. The smell would never leave my soiled clothes, so I had to burn them. Hell for me would be standing for an eternity in one of these open sewers.

Ever since that unforgettable dip in a sewer, I became leery any time I was near one of them. I could not bear having to repeat such a nasty experience. When I passed over the sewer in front of the clando lodging, I held my breath until I was safely through the gate into a vast compound where single rooms lined three walls. A narrow, covered front veranda was shared by all rooms. Along the fourth wall were located shower and latrine stalls, upright water spigots, and an outside kitchen. In the middle of it all was a large thatched-covered, circular hangar with a few banged up, heavily rusted metal chairs and tables. I was disappointed the place was not better than I had imagined, but I should have known better.

The small, ill-kempt little boy, who smelled badly, silently led me to my room. He opened the roughly made wooden door with a simple old skeleton key and provided me with a kerosene lamp and a galvanized metal bucket. I learned I was to provide my own soap, towel, and bedding. There was not any bed, only what was referred to as "luxury grass mat" placed along the wall on the floor along with a soiled pillow. It was called a "luxury mat," because it had one thick, coarse reed mat covered by a thinner, finely woven grass mat. I was also given a locally made hand fan made from the leaves of the fan palm tree.

At first, I was not sure what the fan was for, but later I learned how essential it was. I was also provided with a Chinese mosquito coil to burn to help repel the mosquitoes. An old beer bottle stood in one corner. I knew this was for trapping cockroaches, which would climb up the bottle in search of the beer residue in the bottom of the bottle. They would fall into the bottle, but they could not climb out. The room smelled of kerosene, as it had been swept with a mixture of this fuel and water in order to keep down the insect population. The room was stark and dismal, but it was relatively clean and seemed free of bugs and rodents. Moreover, at three bucks a night, it was a bargain and well within my very limited budget.

Before tipping the half-asleep boy, I told him, "I have a fresh fish. I am looking for some place to have it cooked."

"That's easy," he said. "There is a small restaurant, Café Tasteful, located at the end of the street, just around the corner."

As it was getting late, I quickly parked my moto in the room with my bag still on the handlebars, grabbed the plastic bag with the fish and headed toward the café. When leaving the lodging compound, I crossed directly to the other side of the street so I could be as far away as possible from the open sewer. I picked my way slowly along the dark street until I arrived at the corner where I could easily see Café Tasteful. It was well lit with bright Petromax lamps.

I sat down at one of the outside tables and a chubby waitress, who seemed genuinely happy to be able to serve a Whiteman, waited on me immediately. I told her about my fish. She stopped giggling long enough to say, "Give me the fish. It will be ready to eat in about thirty minutes."

She gave me choices of the side dishes I could eat with it. I decided on the green beans and fried plantain pieces. She delivered my fish to the kitchen, hidden somewhere inside. I learned long ago never to look into a kitchen of a place like this. Kitchens were usually so filthy that seeing one would ruin your appetite. Returning, she shyly asked me, "What would you like to drink?"

I wasted no time in responding. "I will have a beer."

"Would that be a cold or warm beer?" she inquired.

I knew most local people who could afford it drank warm beer, as they believed it was unhealthy to drink anything cooler than your blood temperature. Nonetheless, I knew what I wanted. "Please give me your coldest beer."

There were only two types of bottled beer, and both came in unlabeled bottles. One came in a clear glass bottle and the other came in a dark green glass bottle. The latter had twice the alcohol as the former. I opted for the beer in the dark bottle, but I wanted to know if a cold beer was refrigerated or not. Usually, a cold beer was one that had been kept in the cooler waters of a large clay jar buried to its top in the ground. Somehow, the condensation process made the beer much cooler than one right out of the crate, but it was still warm compared to a beer that had been in a refrigerator. The "cold beer" I received was from the underground clay cooler. Cold or not, a beer was refreshing on this hot, muggy night, especially after such a long and tiring day.

It did not take long before my fish was served in royal style. I was surprised at how picturesque it looked on the big, flowery tin plate surrounded by green beans and yellow plantain slices. I was so hungry I could not restrain myself, shoving quickly as much food as I could into my mouth. The fish tasted delicious, but I had to be careful of the many bones. The chubby waitress sat not far from me, admiring my hearty appetite by making occasional positive grunts of approval of the way I ate. She did not seem to care that I ate with a fork and knife and not with the fingers of my right hand like the local people. As she did not offer me a water pitcher and basin to wash my hands before eating, and gave me the fork and knife, it was obvious she knew white people did not eat with their hands.

I ate every bit of my food, washing it all down with my large bottle of cool beer. I was feeling good and fully satisfied. I thanked the waitress and told her to thank the cook for such an excellent meal. I gave her a higher than usual tip and rose from my simple wooden table that was covered with a cheap, blue-colored plastic firmly attached at the edges with thumb tacks. The whole place was painted blue. The wood uprights and the plywood walls were painted blue, as were the tin roofing sheets. The floor was covered with cheap blue linoleum. The wood chairs were painted blue. The waitress wore blue. There was so much "blue" that in the future I always referred to the place as "Café Tasty Blue."

CHAPTER SIXTEEN
AFRICAN BEAUTY

As I left my bright blue environment for the dark, sandy streets of the capital, I heard strange music coming from somewhere down another side street about fifty yards away. I could see a small crowd gathered under a glass sign dimly lit by a single electric light bulb. I debated if I should go see what this was all about or go back to my dismal room to get some much-needed rest. As is often the case, my sense of adventure led me astray. I chose to investigate what was going on under the only lightbulb in the adjoining street. After all, once my curiosity was satisfied, I could turn around and go to my room.

I slowly strolled down the street. When I neared the small glass sign, I began to hear the people speaking in a language I had not heard before. Painted in yellow on the white glass box that was lit with a low wattage light bulb were the words "Bar Unika." I ambled slowly up to the entrance for a better view. I could see the single old bulb illuminating the sign, but the inside of the bar was dark, lighted only with kerosene lanterns. I knew the high cost of electricity prohibited its use inside the bar.

It did not look like a place I should venture into, so I began to turn around and walk back in the direction from where I came. Just as I started to turn around to go, I heard the voice of a young woman saying something in a very loud voice. I turned to see who was uttering these words, and there, not far from me was a tall young woman signaling to me with much vigor to come back. There was no mistaking her pleading gestures; she wanted to talk to me.

In the dim light, I could see the woman was well dressed in a three-piece outfit made from one of the latest Dutch wax cloths. It was brilliant green with dark brown patterns printed in repeated swirls. She had tied neatly on her head a piece of the same cloth in a manner I had not seen before. She motioned for me to come closer. When I was within a yard of her, I could see she had tribal facial scarring patterns unfamiliar to me. When she smiled at me, I could see her very white front teeth had been filed into sharp points.

I was transfixed by the intricacy of her facial scars. She had deep, wide horizontal scars cut at half-inch intervals across both of her cheeks. On top of these scars were thinner, vertical scars. The width of her forehead was covered by a half-dozen thin horizontal scars placed closely together. I knew this scarification had been done shortly after her birth, and it should tell me which ethnic group she came from, her clan, and the part of the country in which she had been raised. But the hundred cuts on her face told me nothing. I had never before seen a permanent facial design like hers.

The weak light casting wavering shadows on her face gave her a scary look that was repelling to me. As I approached her, she was jabbering a mile a minute, both to me and to those around her. I did not understand a word, but she stepped briskly forward and grabbed my hand, pulling me through the bar entrance. She held my hand tightly as she walked through the crowded passageway. Laughing loudly, she greeted and introduced me to everyone. She seemed to be proud to show everyone she had a Whiteman with her. I could see she had a lively personality, and I began to feel good vibes from her. She pushed her way through the crowd and found a place for us to sit on low benches made of small branches propped alongside one wall. She sat down and with surprising force pulled me down to sit tightly next to her. I was a captive in a place where no escape was possible.

The benches were made from stripped tree branches that had been nailed at close intervals to larger branches supported by small stumps buried in the ground. In the flickering light provided by the kerosene lamps, all appeared to be very shiny. Obviously, the benches had been made shiny from the daily sitting done on them. The earthen floor was also shiny from all the spilled booze, hundreds of sweepings, and the thousands of bare feet that had tread on it.

I tried to communicate my name to my boisterous companion by pointing at myself and saying my name. She laughed as if I were doing something hilarious and pointed toward her chest, saying what I thought was her name. She said her name over and over, but I could not understand or say it. Every time I tried to pronounce her name, she almost laughed herself into tears. I interpreted this as meaning I was really mangling her name, if indeed it was her name.

Before I knew it, I was handed a large calabash full of frothy *chukatu*, a locally made, sorghum-based beer favored by many northern ethnic groups. Most of the sorghum harvest was given to women who make this fermented alcoholic beverage for men to drink. Almost all the calories consumed by men in the north came from the daily drinking of chukutu. I had not drunk chukutu before, but as it was still fizzing from the fermentation process, I thought it would be okay to be a good fellow and join the drinking by having a calabash of this inexpensive local brew.

My companion, or should I say caretaker, was delighted when I took my first big swallow. The first swallow was tough to handle, as the taste was rude to the maladapted palate, but the more I drank, the easier it became to drink even more. With each swallow my companion would snap her fingers in joy and then shake her right hand in the air in such a way that her two loose fingers would bang together to make a clapping sound. I had never seen this curious gesture before. I tried to replicate it, but failed to do so. Nonetheless, my effort to do this common gesture delighted all those sitting around us.

I could feel the alcohol moving into my bloodstream. I was starting to feel pretty good. I even felt lucky. It was like I was on a date with a very congenial, happy-go-lucky woman. Who needed to know what was being said? After all, man is man and woman is woman. There is no language barrier that can block feelings and body chemistry. After a few calabashes of chukutu, I was feeling quite enchanted sitting next to this long-legged woman who was shaped like a model. As the evening wore on, she became increasingly lovely and desirable to me. I certainly had no objection to all the affection she was showering on me. There was nothing quite like being wanted by a woman, even if she was from another world.

I cannot recall how many calabashes I drank or how many times I poured the first drops of each calabash on the ground before me in honor of the grandfathers. I do recall everyone was happy as I devoured calabashes of chukutu and the manner in which I did libations to the ancestors. Suddenly, my elation turned to nausea as the buildup of the negative effects of this local brew started twisting my innards. I was near vomiting. Everything seemed to be spinning around me in a clockwise motion. It was clear I had had my fill and could take no more. My protective companion could see I needed some air. She helped me get up and wrapped her left arm around me to steady me as I limped toward the exit.

I felt a little better when I was outside, but I also thought my collapse was imminent. My guardian angel kept talking to me in a soft and reassuring voice. I grunted my assent to whatever she was saying. I tried to indicate to her the direction to take to where I was staying. As we moved away from Bar Unika, I thought she was taking me home. It is hard to recall what happened after that, but I have a dim memory of her guiding me down dark pathways through a few sand dunes, making me think we were near the beach. I was so miserable by that time I did not care about anything but getting to a place where I could lay down and sleep.

My scar-faced angel practically had to carry me the last fifty yards, as I had lost all control of myself. If this was some kind of scam, and she was taking me to be robbed or worse, there was nothing I could do. I was totally helpless. We passed some small ramshackle abodes built of scrap metal, which indicated to me we were in a place where only the poorest of the poor lived. We finally arrived at one shack to find a small boy sleeping in front of it. She yelled at the boy. He jumped up and quickly unlatched the front door. It was a poor, little home, but I could see in the candlelight that it was very tidy and well kept.

To my surprise, there was a big double bed with nice covers and pillows with intricately embroidered slips taking up about half of the floor space. When I saw the bed, I flopped down on it looking up to see my surroundings continue to spin rapidly in a clockwise motion. It was as if the whole world was whirling out of control, and I was on some sort of fast-moving merry-go-round I could not get off. Just as I was ready to cry out for help, I passed out and plunged into a deep sleep.

After a few hours, I awoke with an excruciating urge to pee. I could see my angel sleeping next to me in the nude, and somehow I was also without any clothing. It was so dark I could not see where to pee. When I got up, I caused the one lit candle to blow out, and it became pitch black. I stumbled across the room, trying to be quiet, as I did not want to wake my angel. I felt my way across the room. When my hand touched the metal wall, I thought I could pee against the bottom of the wall, and my urine would flow outside. I could not hold it anymore and let go with an almost unending flow of urine. It took me some minutes to fully empty my bladder. Then I felt my way back to the nearby bed. I was perspiring heavily in this hot, metallic room.

I returned to bed, and my angel reached over and held me tightly, in spite of the heat. Her long arms and legs were wrapped so firmly around me I could hardly move. I fell back to sleep as our sweat mingled. Before I faded away again into a deep slumber, I appreciated that her sweat actually smelled like sweet perfume. I was also impressed that her legs and arms were so smooth and hairless.

Later in the morning, there was a brusque knock at the front door. Without moving and opening her eyes, my angel said something, and the knocking stopped. At that point I was wide-awake, adjusting my eyes to the rays of sunlight piercing through the multitude of tiny holes that perforated her metal shack. I was trying hard to recall what happened last evening and how I ended up where I was now. I rolled my eyes from one side to another to gather as much detail of the room as I could. I did not move because I did not want to disturb my angel, who appeared to be still sleeping fitfully. Actually, I was finding my surroundings very quaint. I was impressed that with the little she possessed she had decorated and furnished her shack quite nicely. I was ashamed to see the homey scene spoiled by a long puddle of urine pooled on the shiny linoleum floor, stretching from the bed to the other side of the cozy room made of an innovative assembly of junk metal.

I could see it was very bright outside and began to worry about my things and my moto, particularly as I did not know where I was. I was concerned the people managing the lodge would be worried that I had not come back. All this worrying produced within me the sudden urge to leave quickly and get back to where I was supposed to be. I started to get up, but the amazingly strong angel quickly pulled me back down. She spread her legs and pulled me on top of her and starting thrusting her hips up and down so as to communicate to me what she wanted. I had such a terrible headache and hangover I was not able to perform as she wanted. I tried to get up several times, but each time she would hold me down on top of her and press down on my buttocks. I finally managed to disentangle myself from her, and when I did, she muttered some words I thought could only be some sort of insult of my masculinity.

Suddenly, she sprang out of bed, threw her arms upward, and stretched her whole body in a feline fashion. It was then, in the uneven polka-dot light, that I was stunned by how beautiful her body was. She had shiny brown skin, and I was surprised I could not see a single blemish on her body. It was hard to believe she did not have any scars of any kind and not one stretch mark. Her round breasts were plump, pert, and perfectly shaped. Her buttocks were full and nicely round. She was straight and fit, nothing on her body sagged. I was astounded. She looked so much better naked than when dressed.

The only thing interrupting my gaze of her sublime nakedness was the necklace of beads she wore around her waist. I could see tiny leather pouches attached to this necklace. I knew each pouch contained prayers and fetish powders to ward off evil, protecting her from any misfortune. Such waist necklaces were never removed. Perhaps her body looked even more beautiful because it was in sharp contrast to her heavily scarred face. Somehow, I found the exotic mixture of the face and the body on such a lanky, sexy frame very attractive. I was already thinking about coming back after I sobered up and recovered the function of the "manliness" this African beauty wanted and deserved. I needed for her to see me when I was sober and gain her respect for my virility.

She picked up my clothes and made it clear she would dress me like a mother would dress a child. She tenderly put every piece of clothing on me. As she was buttoning the last button on my shirt, she looked deeply into my eyes and gave me a big hug. It was obvious she was sad about me leaving, but she knew I had to go. She held her arm around me as she walked me the three steps to her door. As we slowly moved toward her front door, I was hoping she would not notice I had soiled her floor. I feared what she would say about my desecration of her cozy home. I owed her for committing such a nasty act. In her beautiful nakedness, she opened the metal door, made of flattened oil barrels, just enough to let me out. She released me, giving me a hard slap on the butt as I stepped outside. I have often pondered what that slap meant.

I returned every time I could to Bar Unika in search of the woman I called angel, but I never found her. I could not communicate well enough to others to give them a good indication of whom I sought. Describing her facial scars did not seem to help, as she was not the only one to have such scars. I regretted not working harder to pronounce her name. I searched the area where I thought she resided, but I could not find any clues. The shacks in this area had been bulldozed and removed by government authorities as part of a campaign to remove squatters. I really wanted to be with her again, but I never found her. She became like something I had dreamed. Her lovely and very animated image never left my mind. I hurt in my heart because I wanted her so much, but she was nowhere to be found. I miss her very much. I have never met anyone like her. I hope she is well wherever she is.

CHAPTER SEVENTEEN
HANGOVER REMEDIES

I t was sad to leave my angel like I did, but I had to get back to where I was supposed to have spent the night to make sure my belongings were secure and everyone knew I was alright. The bright sun blinded me and my head was throbbing as I dealt with the severe consequences of a heavy hangover. I left the squatter colony and followed a path leading over a beach dune to another path, passing through a vegetable garden women were watering from a shallow well. I tried to ask for directions, but as I did not know where I was or where exactly my lodging was located, this was complicated to do.

It was obvious I was lost and much farther away from where I stayed than I thought. I could not understand how I had walked so far in the night. I could see in the far distance the top of the tall political party building, so I walked in that direction and finally entered the city. Everything looked very different in the bright sunlight.

I came to a road which looked familiar. I knew if I followed it I would see another road leading toward the area where I stayed. I felt miserable and weak. I needed to eat, but before I could eat, I had to check my lodging. My clothes and body smelled like sour chukutu. I needed to wash myself from head to toe. I pushed myself and was somewhat encouraged when I saw a street I knew that led to the turnoff to where I was staying. I picked up my pace a bit, and I was thankful to arrive at the front gate of my lodging after fifteen more minutes of walking.

As it was daytime, the gate was open so I strode through it rapidly and headed straight to my room door. As I walked across the compound, the eyes of people representing maybe a dozen ethnic groups stared at me. I knew it was highly unusual for them to see a Whiteman staying in such a place. I ignored all this, especially as I was desperate to take a bath, change my clothes and go somewhere to eat. I arrived at my front door when it suddenly dawned on me I needed my room key. I became almost sick with the thought I had lost my room key. I breathed a deep sigh of relief when I found it at the bottom of my pants pocket, along with my money.

I immediately thought my angel was not only lovable, but was honest too, as she had not taken advantage of me and stolen my money. As all my money was intact, I could see my drunken evening with her had not cost me one centime. Maybe I had observed without knowing it the 'money rules' governing contacts with women in bars. These rules revolved around being sure not to tell any woman how much money you had or show her your money. If you wanted to impress women by showing your money, the prevailing practice was to take a few bills and wrap them around a stack of pre-cut newspaper strips to make it look like you had a big wad of money. The thought that my angel was ready to give of herself without expecting anything in return made me want to see her more than before. She was indeed a rare exception to the general rule.

I slid the rusty, flat iron key into the door lock and turned twice; the door easily opened. I was happy to see my moto and bag untouched, and it did not seem like anyone had missed me. I was eager to enjoy my bucket-bath, change my shirt, and go find some grub. First, I had to pee again. I locked my door behind me and headed to the outside big- bucket latrine. I made sure nobody was in the outhouse and stepped unwillingly inside, latching the door behind me. The terrible smell was so overpowering I could pee only as long as I could hold my breath. I dared to look down through the latrine hole and saw the huge metal bucket overflowing with human excrement and urine. Maggots, flies, and cockroaches were in abundance around and inside the bucket. I could not stand the putrid smell any further. I had to get out of this foul smelling place fast! I zipped up after emptying only half of my bladder and fled outside to breathe some fresh air. I knew that if I ever needed to have a bowel movement I would have to find a way to cope with this very nasty cesspool in a bucket.

I left the stink of the ghastly outhouse gasping for air, yet I tried to act in a way that didn't draw attention to me. I quickly returned to my room, undressed, and wrapped the towel I had brought with me around my waist. Sitting in the veranda, in front of me was the galvanized bucket full of water which had been delivered the evening before. I was disappointed to see the bucket coated with black scum. This told me the proprietor was not from a southern ethnic group, as only some northern ethnic groups would allow their buckets to get so scummy. Usually, Southerners would scrub their buckets daily with a shredded bark sponge loaded with soap and lime juice until the bucket was shiny. Anyway, a scummy bucket was not going to keep me from washing off the smell of chukatu.

I could see it would be a challenge to walk through people as I crossed the compound to the shower stalls. I would have to hold my towel in one hand and carry the heavy five-gallon bucket with the other hand. I put my soap bar in the bucket of water. Part of this challenge was avoiding situations where courtesy required stopping to shake hands, as this would require setting the bucket down and starting all over again. I weaved through the people mingled here and there in the open courtyard, nodding my greetings, hoping nobody would want to shake my hand. I successfully arrived at the open-roofed concrete-block shower stall without one handshake. I quickly entered and latched the tin door behind me.

I threw my towel over the door as a signal to others the stall was occupied. I found several small tin cooking pots I could use to dip water from the bucket. I poured a couple of pots of cool water over my body and soaped my body vigorously. Just as I was prepared to rinse myself with more pots of water, I heard some people talking above me. I looked up to see a dozen teenage students attending the secondary school next door leaning out their second-story windows to take a good look at me. I pretended not to notice, but I accelerated my rinse. I wrapped my towel tightly around me and exited the stall as quickly as I could remove myself from their sight. I did not take time to dry. I walked back to my room with water all over me. I knew this raised a lot of eyebrows, but I did not care. I was determined not to shake the hand of anyone. I knew then what everyone else in this compound already knew: you do not take a shower except at night or when school is out.

I entered my room and dried myself. But I was soon wet again as the heat and high humidity made perspiration flow profusely from my pores. I quickly put on the other shirt I had brought and hung my stinky shirt over the one flimsy metal chair to air it out. I was feeling so weak from hunger and my hangover I did not think I had the stamina to ride my moto. I decided I would take one of the hundreds of mini-taxis that plied the city streets. I wanted to get some good hangover foods like chicken soup or boiled rice porridge. I knew it would be hard to get either of these dishes from the food vendors who lined all the streets, so I was thinking I would splurge and try a new German restaurant I had heard about. I put on my one good pair of khaki pants and dusted off my plastic sandals, buckling them tightly. I made sure I locked my door and placed my room key deeply into my left pocket.

I tried to walk out of my lodging compound without being seen. Of course, everybody staying in this compound watched me as I headed for the exit. As I looked around, I was able to confirm to myself that at least a half dozen or more ethnic groups were represented in the compound. I was always very impressed how each group was tolerant of the other. I did recognize, however, in the event of any conflict, they would break into groups along ethnic lines.

Anytime there was a rumored threat against the president, his ethnic group would produce bows, arrows, and spears from nowhere and be ready to fight with other ethnic groups, who also kept their weapons in hiding. There always seemed to be rumblings under the surface, and it took only a minor incident to set off a major upheaval.

It did not take long to find one of those small 4L Renault taxis. The price asked by the driver was so cheap I did not hesitate to take a front seat next to the driver. In spite of the hectic traffic, the savvy, aggressive taxi driver was able to find his way forward. We arrived at the new German eatery within minutes. I paid the driver, adding a small tip. The doorman opened the restaurant door and the well-dressed waiter showed me to a small, but elegant glass table. This was a very spiffy and modern place. I was pleased that it was one of the few places in town with air-conditioning. I was feeling better already.

I explained to the waiter my miserable condition and the depth of my hunger. He recommended to me the special of the day, a rice dish with a new red sauce they had just received. He did his best to speak to me in English. It was funny the way he said "rice." When he said this word it sounded like "lice." In the local dialect, there were not any "r's," thus foreign words with an "r" were hard to say. His "r" sounded like "l."

I said, "Okay, I will take the 'lice' special with the new red sauce."

I also asked for a large bottle of cold mineral water so I could begin to rehydrate myself. My sweat still smelled of chukutu. Now I knew why many Africans smelled like they did. I was learning that we all smell like what we consume.

After ordering I looked around and saw only white expats in the place, many drinking something I had not seen before: a draft beer. I asked the waiter about this, and he said, "This place is owned by the national brewery, and it made a special effort to make it the first place in the country to serve draft beer."

A frothy draft beer in a chilled glass mug looked so very inviting. I recalled someone once told me the best way to sober up was to drink some more beer. This observation made it easier to convince myself I should enjoy the new treat of one draft beer. I could not help myself. I told the waiter to bring me one draft beer with my food. After all, one beer could not hurt anything.

While waiting for my food, I was surprised to see many flies. I thought this was indeed odd because this was a new and modern place. When I looked behind the colorful tie-dyed curtains, the reason for the flies became quickly apparent. The place was so new they had not yet completed the installation of all the glass panes in the windows; therefore, flies could easily gain entry where the panes were missing. Of course, the flies that found their way around the curtains flew straight for the draft beers. I now understood why all the beer drinkers had covered their mugs with the cardboard coasters provided to place the beer on. This protective measure was, however, not enough to keep some flies from falling into the suds.

I watched carefully what the expats would do when flies fell into their drinks. Their reactions could tell me how long they have been in Africa. The rule of thumb was a person who was new to the continent would push her or his beer away and not drink anymore after a fly fell into it. Someone who had been around a while would dip a finger into the beer and flick the fly out. The old timers would ignore the fly and continue drinking their beer. I had swallowed many flies with no ill effect.

I was studying the shoes of the expats for any clues which would indicate to me their nationality when the very outgoing waiter tried to strike up a conversation with me in his limited English.

He asked, "Sir, where do you come from?"

"I am American," I replied.

He was very happy to hear this, saying, "My name is Jacob. I want to congratulate all Americans for all their great achievements."

"What are you talking about?" I asked.

He answered, "Your ability to travel in space to visit alien beings on other planets is very impressive."

"Where did you get this information?" I asked.

He reminded me, "TV has been recently introduced in our country, and everyone can now see what Americans are doing. Just last night, I watched *Lost in Space* and saw with my own eyes some things you are doing on other planets. I also recently saw the American movie, *King Kong*. I can't believe how large monkeys are in America."

I knew it was useless for me to try to explain to him all he saw on TV and at the movies was make believe. For him, what he saw was true. At that moment he disappeared briefly before bringing me back a huge plate of overcooked long-grain, white rice, covered with a thick red sauce, and one draft beer. I was famished. I rapidly mixed the rice and sauce together and began eating as if I was dying of hunger.

Jacob was impressed by how quickly I was devouring the rice and said, "I know Americans have a high regard for 'lice,' as they have put a Bill of 'Lice' in their constitution."

I knew he meant the Bill of Rights, but I did not know how to explain otherwise to him. I let him ramble on about his appreciation of stressing the importance of food in the US Constitution.

"Everyone knows people have to be well-fed to be good citizens," he said as he emphasized his point by lightly tapping on my table. In a bizarre way, I thought he may have a point.

In a hushed voice, he continued, "I wish my country could have democracy like you have in America. We should have a Bill of 'Lice' for my country too. It is too bad we do not have a word for democracy in our language. We do not have justice here, but we do have a good word for that in our language. We suffered many injustices during colonial times, but things have been much worse for us since we gained independence. Our only hope now is to get something better after this independence phase is over. Tell me, what comes after independence?"

Obviously, he thought history worked in phases. There were the pre- and post-colonial periods, so there must also be a post-independence phase. I did not have the heart to explain to him that independence is a permanent condition.

I tried to mollify him by saying, "It takes a long time, but independence would improve after some years with good leadership, and if enough people did not like the justice they have now, they could revolt."

He snapped back, "Revolt would never happen. We are proud of our ability to submit to authority no matter what!"

I said, "If this is the case, you must like the way things are now."

He did not like my reply and grimaced, saying, "No, this is not true. It is only by falling a long ways backward that we can get the running space we need to make a great leap forward." He now sounded like he was toeing the prevalent political line.

At that point I was confused by his comments, but I could see his suppressed frustration over having known only one president for his entire life. Sadly, the chances of him knowing another president in the foreseeable future were very dim.

I found the rice sauce to be excellent and asked him how it was made. He rushed into the kitchen and came back with a large bottle labeled "Heinz Ketchup." I was dumbfounded to see this highly appreciated and very exquisite sauce was nothing more than ordinary ketchup. It was at that moment I knew I had perhaps been in Africa too long.

As I finished my "fly-less" beer, he politely asked, "Would you like another beer?"

I instantly replied, "No, I am fighting a tough hangover acquired from drinking too much chukatu last night."

He told me, "You can find some great hangover treatments in the fetish market."

I thanked him for the advice and asked for the check.

I once drove past the fetish market. Its stalls and kiosks covered a city block. I wanted to explore it, but the awful smell caused by a variety of rotting animal parts offered for sale was so strong I passed on the opportunity. Various decomposed animal body parts used for occult ceremonies or different kinds of cures covered table after table in this market. Heaps of plants and herbs used in traditional medicines were piled high on other tables. Surrounding the outer edges of the market were numerous booths occupied by a wide variety of traditional doctors, sorcerers, fortune tellers, and representatives of many different spirits and gods. For a price, consultations about any problem, ailment, or treatment could begin right on the spot.

There were offers of miracle cures for diseases modern medicine had not been able to treat. I was impressed by how many people, even very well-educated people, came to this market in search for a treatment of whatever physical, mental, or spiritual problem afflicted them. This open market was really an oasis of hope for those who had lost hope. It was like a fast food restaurant, catering to the sick and those who had tried all other options. There were no rules except for the prohibition against the use of any bad juju. Those found doing anything to appeal to the evil spirits from the east, where bad voodoo originated, would be expelled from the market and lose their license to practice. All practitioners in the market had to be card-carrying members of one of the guilds related to the profession they exercised. If anyone wanted to do bad juju, it must be done in a faraway place.

As I paid for my meal and left a generous tip of about fifty cents, I passed a guy carefully watering the nicely potted, luxurious tropical plants located throughout the restaurant. Given the lack of sunlight in the place, I was impressed at how green the plants were and how well they looked. I bade farewell to my waiter, and as I was about to exit, I took a closer look at the plants. Upon examination, I found they were very attractive artificial imitations. It was interesting that artificial plants were used in a tropical country where such plants grew naturally and were easy to obtain. Yet, for the life of me, I could not grasp why these fake plants were being watered.

I asked the young man with the galvanized watering can, "Why must you water plants that are not real?"

He emphatically replied, "It is my job to water all plants, real and not real. I am duty bound to do my job. My family depends on me to do good work and bring home my monthly salary."

It made no difference to him if the plants were real of not; he would do his job. My only thought was, "Good for him."

CHAPTER EIGHTEEN
MELO HOTEL

I was feeling much better, but as I stepped out into the burning tropical sunlight, my nausea resurged. I needed a good cup of coffee. It had been some years since I had enjoyed a cup of freshly brewed coffee. I needed something much better than the cheap instant Nescafe I drank every morning. I thought about where I could find a real cup of coffee. Then it came to me. There was one modern hotel that could offer a decent cup of coffee. I had never entered the ritzy Melo Hotel, but I thought I now owed myself its acquaintance. Another bonus of going to this hotel was its air-conditioning. Perhaps I could while away the rest of the afternoon sitting in the hotel lobby with a good cup of coffee.

I walked the six blocks to the hotel, stopping a few times to shake out the sand that constantly lodged between my feet and the soles of my sandals. I brushed myself off and stood tall as I entered through the front plate-glass door of the hotel as if I was some important Whiteman.

Immediately, the doorman offered his assistance, "May I help you, sir?"

I said, "I am looking for a good cup of coffee."

He escorted me to the hotel bar and showed me to a well-upholstered armchair with a glass-top coffee table next to it.

"Please be seated. A waiter will come to serve you," he said very politely.

I felt like royalty, but I also felt guilty. I knew they were only treating me with such deference because I was white. As I looked around this swanky hotel, I could see only white people being served by black people. I knew my cup of coffee in a place like this could feed an average African family for a day. I was uncomfortable. I repressed a desire to jump up and leave.

My discomfort increased, because I also thought most of the whites there were "spooks"—people working for embassies that traded information during the day and spied on each other during the night. This was the era of the great East-West conflict, and both sides were looking to "one-up" the other. It was almost comical how they jockeyed to collect information they could report back to their respective capitals. Sometimes they paid the same sources for the same information. All this was laughable, as most of what they reported was common knowledge among the local people. For sure, the voluminous reports they filed were of no interest to anyone except a few obscure intelligence analysts.

Just when I was about to skedaddle, a handsome young waiter in a red vest, white shirt, and well-pressed black pants appeared from nowhere. He bowed slightly and in a polite tone asked me, "Sir, my name is John. I am your waiter. What would you like?"

The thought of a good cup of coffee was overwhelming me. I awkwardly blurted out, "I would like a cup of your best coffee."

The waiter nodded and made a quick note in his little pad, saying, "I will be back with your coffee in a few minutes."

Indeed, he was back in a flash with a circular tray carrying a small coffee pot and an expensive cup and saucer, along with real cream and sugar. He told me, "I am pleased to serve you the hotel's sweetest ground coffee."

I thought he meant to say "finest" coffee, but after one sip, I understood that "sweetest" was correct.

The coffee was good, but it was unnaturally very sweet, too sweet for me. I certainly did not have to add any sugar, because somehow the coffee had been pre-sweetened before its serving. I slowly sipped my coffee, trying to make it last a long time so I could enjoy the air-conditioning. The waiter saw I was about to finish my first cup, and he dashed over to me so he could pour my second cup of coffee.

As my curiosity was getting the best of me, I asked him, "How do you make the coffee so sweet?"

He replied, "I will show you how this is done after you finish your coffee, sir."

The bar was really very nice and comfortable, and the restroom was like paradise. I spent more time than I needed in the restroom so that I could enjoy the wonders of flush toilets and running water. I could live anywhere and do anything forever as long as I had ready access to such modern sanitation facilities.

I could not complain about anything in the hotel. It was all good, but it was terribly boring. There was not all the color and clamor of Africa relentlessly engaging your senses. It was artificial, dull and light-years away from the bustling and vibrant reality of the world going on outside. It was as if I had stepped into some kind of superficial aseptic environment where the clock had stopped. I know my African friends from the village would see this as some kind of white heaven populated by people who looked like corpses. Maybe hell would be a sterile place like this where boredom killed you a little every day for all eternity.

The waiter promptly brought me something I had not seen in a long time…a nicely printed copy of my bill. My sweet coffee cost three times more than any coffee would cost anywhere else in the country. I was still curious to learn how they made their pre-sweetened coffee. As agreed, the waiter took me to a small annex at the back of the hotel and pointed out a very short and broad-faced, balding man with swollen eyes.

He said, "This is the man who can tell you about how the coffee is sweetened."

The man invited me into the small annex and showed me several big ten-gallon tins full of selected Robusta coffee beans soaking in a thick, syrupy molasses.

He said, "The beans are soaked in this sugary syrup for one month, and then, dried and ground."

Thus the secret of sweet coffee was revealed to me. I hoped one day to have the same coffee-drinking experience with the higher quality Arabica coffee.

He asked, "Would you like a cup of coffee?"

I said, "I just had two cups inside."

He then begged me, "Sir, you must try my coffee!"

I acceded to his plea and sat down on a tiny three-legged stool while I waited for him to provide me with a cup of his coffee. He brought me a large serving in a tin, Chinese-made cup. His coffee had a nice aroma and tasted much better than the coffee I had drunk inside.

He advised, "Anytime you want a good cup of coffee, come to me first. I ask for only a fraction of the price they charge inside. Always ask for me by my name, Emerson."

I gratefully answered, "I will definitely keep this in mind anytime I am nearby."

We had an enjoyable conversation while I sipped my coffee. He had some nice African music playing at a low volume on his little cassette player. I found this atmosphere, even with the heat and flies, much more to my liking. I had a vision that someday we would see Emerson Coffee Shops across Africa.

Emerson kept scratching lightly at the edges of his noticeably puffy eyes. At first, I thought he may have been in a fight and suffered from the wrong end of what was locally called a "Katanga" (a reference to a protracted and very bloody conflict in another African country). He scratched his eyes so many times I had to make a detour in our polite conversation and ask him, "What is wrong with your eyes?"

He laughed at my discomfort and quickly said, "I am getting over a bad case of 'Apollo.' You have nothing to fear. I am past the contagious stage of this form of conjunctivitis."

Everyone has called conjunctivitis "Apollo" since 1969 when American astronauts landed on the moon. Apparently, immediately after the Apollo mission landed on the moon, there was a major outbreak of conjunctivitis, and thus, a link was made between the moon landing and conjunctivitis. Henceforth, the word Apollo entered into the local lexicon to indicate any kind of eye infection.

It was getting late, so I asked Emerson, "What is the best way for me to get off the hotel grounds without going back through the hotel?"

He pointed to a dirt path going through the well-manicured green grass, but he said, "You should hang around for the big ball tonight."

Apparently, once a month the hotel hosted on its big front courtyard the national band and singers, and the public was invited to come without charge. I had heard good things about the famous national band and the highlife music it played. In spite of my weariness, I decided I could not miss this big event.

Emerson said, "The band plays a lot of popular African, American, and reggae music over big loudspeakers. I am going to stay late so I can hear the band and the latest Franco OK jazz numbers, as well as Jimmy Cliff and James Brown."

I said, "I will definitely stick around for this huge musical event, but I need to eat first."

He indicated to me the location of a nearby roadside restaurant called "100%" where I could enjoy some nicely fried yam slices and beef brochettes. I bid farewell to Emerson with a hearty handshake that ended with a louder than usual mutual snapping as our middle fingers rubbed against each other in perfect timing. I was pleasantly impressed by this satisfying snap, as such handshaking quality usually only happens between old and close friends who had been accustomed to shaking hands with one another for years.

CHAPTER NINETEEN
MAMIWATA'S SEA

Before going to the 100% sidewalk eatery to enjoy some good street grub, I wanted to walk a block to the oceanfront to see the fishermen bring in their catch. In the wee hours of the morning, the male members of fishing families would bravely struggle with all their might to paddle their pirogues a half mile or so out into the ocean to cast their expansive nets. At night the kerosene lanterns they hung on poles erected aft and stern made their boats visible far out to sea. For newcomers, these dots of lights hovering above the murky ocean waters looked like giant fireflies marooned at sea. Some people imagined they were the big phosphorus eyes of undiscovered sea serpents.

The fishermen would set their huge fishing nets before dawn and slowly haul them toward the shore by paddling furiously against the treacherous rip tide that tried to force them to go parallel to the shore instead of directly toward it. This was very hard work and only a specialized group of mariners from a separate ethnic group had been able to master over generations the formidable task of harvesting this unruly sea's bounty. It was only those belonging to this group who knew how to swim. They spent more time on the water than in their makeshift, palm-branch camps scattered among the coconut groves along the beach. They preferred being in their pirogues than staying in their flimsy, palm-frond shelters that leaked when it rained and often blew away in the strong coastal winds. For them, life on land was not important. They lived only for taking fish from the sea.

Late every afternoon they would reach the shore, and people would gather to see what they caught, and market women would come to buy their catch. There was always an air of excitement as the fishermen approached the shore with their nets. When they were very close to the shore, the fishermen would dive into the water and encircle their nets to hold them in place so as to minimize the number of fish escaping from the net. The maintenance of their nets was a full-time job. When they were not at sea, much attention was given to untangling and repairing their nets. It took strong swimming to hold up the edges of the net while resisting being washed away by the strong riptide.

I arrived at the beach and looked up and down the shoreline to see where the fishermen might be coming in with their catch. I could not spot any fishing pirogues at sea or any crowds waiting for them on the shore. I was puzzled by the absence of any fishing activity and was surprised when I spotted some pirogues lying on the beach. I thought maybe I had arrived too late to see the catch. I approached the pirogues, admiring the way they had been painted with colorful designs.

I knew the symbols displayed by the designs possessed special meanings only known to the fishermen. The pirogues were not named, as the fishermen believed the fish in the sea were for all to enjoy, and no single boat should be singled out by name because it caught more or fewer fish. Fishing was a community effort; no single individual or family should be recognized for its fishing achievements or lack thereof. It was also not good to be boastful of catching many fish, as this would anger the sea goddess, Mamiwata.

I was going to sit on the edge of the pirogue and look out to sea for any fishing activity, but when I looked down into the pirogue, I found a young man asleep on top of a pile of fishnets. Obviously, pirogues are not left unattended; a family member had to guard them. My presence alongside the pirogue startled the sleeping man. He opened his eyes wide before I could speak. I was concerned the sight of a Whiteman peering down on him would scare him; therefore, I quickly smiled and waved to indicate he had nothing to fear from me. He sat up, and we exchanged greetings. I then asked him, "Why is there no fishing today?"

He laughed, showing his very white and large teeth with a huge gap between his two front teeth. "It is prohibited to fish on Thursdays."

I was astounded by the news that fishing was prohibited on Thursdays and asked him, "Why is this so?"

He answered, "The sea belongs to Mamiwata on Thursdays. It has always been like that. Nobody would dare upset Mamiwata by fishing on Thursdays, as this would be very risky and make fishing bad on the other days of the week. If Mamiwata was made excessively angry, she could cause "Wahala." (I later learned that Wahala was something akin to lasting hell on Earth.)

Smiling widely, he added, "It is a day off for both fishermen and fish, and it is a day for the people's fetish priests to conduct special ceremonies in honor of the sea goddess. Clan chiefs would also provide her offerings of food and drink, setting them afloat in baskets in a distant, hidden ocean inlet."

I knew entry into this sacred inlet was forbidden to all except those who had been initiated into a secret maritime cult. I was told that at this sacred spot a ten-foot pyramidal shrine to the goddess had been built from white sand cemented with calcium powder made from crushed seashells and covered with rare shiny shells of an unknown origin. The center of each face of the pyramid was laced with strands of blue antique Venetian glass beads. Along the four edges of the base of the shrine were rows of white cowrie shells. The sunlight reflected off the shrine, making it appear to be a very bright lighthouse. Those approaching the shrine on a sunny day had to wear sunglasses. Its brightness also alerted strangers to avoid this forbidden place. It was the duty of each generation to maintain this shrine and make sure nobody violated the sanctity of this site.

Each time the fisherman smiled, I could not help but admire how nice his teeth were. I was always amazed how attractive local people's teeth were even without any dental care or use of toothpaste. They did use a variety of small twigs to clean their teeth and rub their gums. It was a common sight to see people chewing on these sticks.

I mentioned, "You have beautiful teeth."

He said, "Thank you. Do you know that in our country a gap between the two front teeth is considered a sign of beauty?"

It was then I learned having a wide gap between your two front teeth was considered a mark of beauty and a special blessing from God. This made me happy. I had never enjoyed the luxury of braces, and thus, for the first time, I appreciated the natural gap between my two front teeth.

CHAPTER TWENTY
100% ROADSIDE EATERY

I left the fisherman on the beach and headed inland toward the area Emerson had indicated I would find the popular 100% sidewalk restaurant. After walking a few blocks, I arrived at dusk at "100%" to find small wooden, unpainted, cheaply made tables and low benches being placed at close intervals along the side of the street. This simple sidewalk was being transformed into a nighttime bar and restaurant that catered to all walks of life. I took a seat on one bench where there was a wall I could lean my back against. With my back protected and a clear view of my surroundings, this was the perfect place to eat and pass the time.

A young girl timidly came up to me to see what I wanted. She was dressed simply in what could be called working clothes, a ragged, white T-shirt and a worn skirt-cloth tied improperly, showing excessive unevenness at the bottom. No self-respecting woman would leave her compound unless her wrap-around skirt cloth was tied tightly around the waist in a way that the bottom edges had the same exact matching length. To ease the waitress's anxiety over serving a rare white customer, I greeted her in the local language. I always found the use of my limited knowledge of the local language could score a lot of points, and this encounter was no different. My simple greeting brought forth giggles and a big smile showing, of course, perfectly formed and very white teeth.

She quickly regained her composure and asked me what I would like. I tried my best to treat her with dignity and look her in the eyes. Many Africans would have not granted someone of a low station in life such a favor. Instead, they might avoid looking at her and order her around unkindly like a serf. There was no menu. It was obvious to anyone who ate at these roadside eateries what could be available: roasted meat, chicken, and fried cassava, plantains, or yams. I said, "I will take meat pieces on a stick and fried yam slices."

Just saying these words made my taste buds salivate, making me realize I was actually very hungry. Although I was still recovering from my chukutu excesses, there was no way I could eat such food without having a beer to wash it down. I liked eating my roasted goat meat pieces after rubbing them in salt and finely sliced, fresh hot peppers with drops of squeezed lime juice. Eating this spicy combination had to be washed down by a cold beer. I, therefore, asked for the coldest of their beers, knowing I would get whatever bottled beer they had in stock.

My food came on the usual colorful Chinese enameled tin plate. No silverware was provided, as such was not used to eat these foods. A much younger girl child came to me with a washbasin, a pitcher of water, and a small bar of local soap. She poured a trickle of water over my hands as I washed and rinsed them. I shook my hands vigorously in the air and held them at my side while they dried. My plate was complete with pieces of well-roasted meat, deep-fried yam slices, and salty, chopped hot peppers and sliced limes. These ingredients made eating roasted goat meat a culinary delight. As expected, the pepper was hot, requiring a swallow of beer after every bite. It was hard to go too many days without having a hunger attack that could only be satisfied by roast meat dashed with hot pepper and a pinch of salt. I called this the "roasted goat meat attack."

Not far from where I was seated, a half a dozen women were sitting on very low stools tending to their squat charcoal grills and roasting meat and plantains. Local blacksmiths made these grills, which were akin to hibachi-type grills. The toxic smoke from their cooking was everywhere, but it did not seem to bother them in the least as they bantered back and forth, laughing often, as if they were enjoying some festive event. Their cast-iron metal cookers were of simple construction and fabricated by local blacksmiths. As roughly hewn, locally made, chunky charcoal pieces were the fuel of choice, such a cooker was essential for every urban household.

In the rural areas, only the better-off people used charcoal. Most people did their cooking in the ancient way by pushing the ends of tree limbs into the spaces between a trinity of three stones. The wealthy bought small, compressed containers of butane gas and did their cooking on small gas stoves. But even the better-off households kept, as a backup, a charcoal cooker. For all classes of people, the preferred food was the same. Poor and rich basically had the same diet. Wealth had little impact on basic food preferences.

It was obvious all the women working at this popular chop place were related. This was a family enterprise operated under the watchful eye of the "big mama," a corpulent woman who sat in the center of the place at a small table, collecting the money paid by the customers and shouting orders to her underlings. She was fat by any standards, but the local people did not use that term. It was a matter of your God given "form," not a matter of being fat or thin. Most of the commercial activity in the country was controlled by strong-willed, hardworking, no-nonsense business women like this one. All the young girls working there carried out their tasks in fear of eliciting from her any criticism. Total obedience to her was imperative. Even the slightest misstep on the part of any worker would result in a strong rebuke from the big mama. Nobody dared to cross or displease big mama.

The place had filled up with people. Motos and cars were stopping to take food away. You could see the latest Mercedes Benz pulling up to make a food order. It was rumored the president sent his guards to bring him food. The take-away food was wrapped in brown paper or any used notebook paper. The brown paper mostly came from the inside layers of paper lining used cement bags. This helped make empty one-hundred-pound cement bags a very marketable item. The other used paper was from the waste bins of offices and private homes. One always had to be careful not to throw away any documents he or she did not want to end up being used as wrappers for food, thereby revealing all the information they contained. I once entered a local taxi to see it decorated on the inside with some self-adhesive address stickers I had thrown away a long time ago.

Loudspeakers had been set up to blast out popular African music. The place was so enjoyable I ordered a second beer and some grilled bananas to munch on. I never tired of such an ambiance where an indescribable diversity of people were coming and going. Under normal circumstances I would have tarried much longer in such a lively place, but I did not want to miss the monthly shindig at Melo Hotel. I also believed many of the people at this place would be moving that way. I paid my bill, including a small tip, and told the waitress good-bye. I waved at big mama to acknowledge her authority and thank her for the good food. She returned my wave with a happy smile and a wave of her own. I was perfectly primed for a delightful musical evening at Melo Hotel.

CHAPTER TWENTY-ONE
DANCING UNDER THE PALMS

I followed other people who were taking a shortcut going in the direction of the hotel. It was very dark, but they seemed to know where they were going. The white sand covering the narrow path appeared to have a florescent quality, emitting a soft glow, making it easy to follow. In no time at all, we arrived at the road that passed along one side of the hotel. We crossed the road and headed through thick grass to the expansive patio in front of the hotel. I did not like walking through the grass. I knew we would stir up bugs that would bite my bare ankles and sandal-clad feet, but the excitement of the moment was so high that this passing thought about bug bites quickly faded away.

Mature coconut palm trees growing about every twelve feet towered over the vast length and width of the cemented patio. A variety of colored, electric lightbulbs had been strung from one tree to another in this majestic coconut grove, just a few feet above head height. The multitude of lights created a mosaic of shadows and odd reflections. On one side of the patio was an area where white plastic tables and chairs had been placed. This area was separated from the much larger patio by a rope tied to a number of palm trees. This was the area where drinks would be served to those able to pay for them. A small admission fee was demanded to enter this area, which was reserved for the better-off clients. Except for those seated in this area, the vast majority would spend the night standing up or lingering in the shadows. Most people would dance all night long.

I did not like separating myself from the masses, but the attraction to sit where I would be able to have a cold beer overruled my egalitarian principles. I paid the small fee and selected a table near the side of the patio where a low wooden platform had been erected for the band and singers. I had a great seat to observe the vast dancing space, but I was concerned about the huge coconut I observed hanging in the palm tree high above me. I heard stories about coconuts falling on the heads of people and killing them or causing serious injuries. Throughout the night I made frequent glances at this coconut dangling above my head. I hoped there would be no gusts of wind which would increase the probability of it descending on me like a kamikaze.

As was usual in this part of the world, events always started later than expected. But if measured by African time, nothing was ever too late, and things started at the time they were destined to start. When the grounds and outlying areas were over-crowded with people, the band appeared. It took some time for the band to set up, conduct some squeaky microphone checks and practice a few warm-up notes. Suddenly, music poured forth like a huge flood, engulfing us like a giant lion's loud roar. People reacted by clapping, whistling, and cheering loudly. Quickly, everyone grabbed their partner, and, if they did not have a partner, they danced alone or with others. Immediately after the first musical note shot from the loudspeakers, all began to dance as if nothing else mattered. Everyone moved in perfect timing to the highlife music. No matter how much their bodies swayed to and fro, their feet hit the pavement in unison.

All night long I could hear underneath the music and noise one foot of each dancer doing two side steps one way, and then the other foot following with two steps to the other side. Two steps to the left, and then two to the right, or vice versa. The methodical way each foot shuffled along the ground at the same time had a hypnotizing effect that made my head continue to bob left and right. Of course, the beer I was drinking only amplified this mesmerizing effect. Again and again, there was "swish-swish" to the right, and then "swish-swish" to the left. The music never stopped until the band took a break after an hour or so. One had to be very fit and rhythmical to dance highlife music for so long, but this was only a warm-up for the much tougher demands of the rhumba music that followed.

When the highlife band and its bellowing female singers took its break, loud rhumba music began to blast from the loudspeakers, transforming the world into another dimension, forcing one to forget all about life's struggles and enjoy the moment as much as possible. It was as if this was the time to take revenge on all of life's miseries by dedicating all you had to being in tune with the music, making your best effort to demonstrate your dancing prowess. Dancing rhumba required the body to move in unimaginable ways and everybody reacted differently. The variety of dance moves made for a riotous ambience, and the eye of the keenest observer was challenged to follow every move. My eyes darted right and left as they were attracted to one dancing style or another. I did not want to watch any one person dancing for too long as I was afraid I would miss someone else who may have an even more spectacular dance style.

It was hard not to focus on the women's hips, which appeared to have become unhinged from their bodies. Their buttocks gyrated rapidly in an impossible manner as never-ending tunes played on and on. As I feasted my eyes on the myriad of energetic dance moves and a multitude of body contortions, my own feet began moving in an uncontrollable fashion. Somehow my feet carried me to the dance space, and I, too, joined the crowd with my own comparatively feeble dance style. My feet and body seemed to have adopted a life of their own. I found myself making dance moves I did not know I had and feeling very good about the steps my feet had discovered.

My presence among the dancing crowd was acknowledged by all those around me with applause, positive nods, and lots of laughs. People were genuinely amused to see a Whiteman, as ridiculous as he may appear, attempt to make dance moves only those born hearing this music could master. The local people say a child's first step is a dance step. At that moment, I was like a child taking his first dance steps. It was an exhilarating moment that I wished could last forever.

The highlife band came back and all had to flip their dancing mode switches into a very different gear. This music had a slower, gentler pace, giving people time to catch their breaths and amorous couples the opportunity to dance closely together, sometimes in very sexy embraces. As this two-step shuffle music was best danced with a partner, I headed back to my table and my beer. Before I could arrive safely back to my chair, an attractive young woman smelling of cheap perfume grabbed my hand and begged me to dance with her. My first instinct was to say no, but she did not look or feel like a woman who would accept refusal easily. And, besides, I did not want to do anything to spoil this fantastic evening.

This buxomly black beauty pulled me into the dancing mass and squeezed my body against hers as she tried to lead our dancing with an excess of energy. It was all very awkward for me, particularly as I knew my dancing was laughable. "You can easily see I can't dance to this music," I openly admitted to her.

"Hey, I do not care about that. It has always been my dream to dance with a Whiteman," she said gleefully. No doubt, this was a woman who was out to have a good time.

The way she said this made me fear she was after more than money. I could see now I was getting myself into a difficult position because this young woman was really so nice and beautiful, and all the parts of her body that were supposed to be round were perfectly and fully round. I was surprised at how well she could dance in ultra-high-heeled shoes that poorly fit her well-calloused feet. Before I succumbed to her charms, I reminded myself I was almost broke and would be hard pressed to offer this well-put-together woman a beer. I, therefore, tried to discourage her from striking up a relationship with a Whiteman, particularly this Whiteman.

I told her, "You are foolish for wanting to be with a Whiteman, especially as African men are reluctant to go with women who are known to have been with a Whiteman."

She laughed loudly and said, "I don't care because all white men are rich and can take good care of me. I think they can show me more romance than my black brothers."

I tried to tell her all white men were not rich, but she would not accept that. I told her, "I am very poor and live with nothing in an upcountry village."

I made her laugh again by saying, "Black or white, the important thing is to be in love."

She laughed louder this time and said, "There could be no love or romance without finance."

I finally was able to get her to detach herself from me by showing her how empty my pockets were and my sandals were the cheapest the Bata shoe store had to offer. It always irritated me that the lowest class of Whiteman could come to Africa and acquire the prettiest girls and be treated like a king, just because his skin was white.

I made my way back to my table and found I really needed to sit down, as my legs were hurting from using all those muscles I normally did not use. I ordered one last beer, determined to nurse it slowly for the rest of the night. I told myself when I finished this beer, I would leave and head back to my clando lodge. Somehow, the night played tricks on me and hours passed unnoticed. Before I knew it, the musicians were packing up their instruments and daylight was breaking. The dance crowd had dwindled and the few remaining people were dispersing in all directions. It was like I had fallen asleep without knowing it. I became alarmed and checked my pockets to see if I had been robbed. I was relieved to find the little money I had was still in my left pocket.

I rose to leave and discovered my legs were so weak I could hardly walk. This made me wonder if I had danced more without knowing it. I was also puzzled by seeing four empty beer bottles on my table when I only had two beers. I limped toward the road. I had to find a taxi. I could not walk the long distance to my lodging place. I was totally wasted and so sleepy it was hard to stay awake. I hailed one of the old mini-taxis and gave the driver a rough indication of where I wanted to go. I was desperate to get to my room so I could pass out. I told myself I would sleep all day and prepare to leave at dawn tomorrow. I had had enough of the city and was anxious to get back to my routine and familiar surroundings in the village. I was surprised I was feeling a bit homesick for the village.

Following several explanations, the taxi man was able to find my lodge. I quickly entered the compound and headed straight for my room, hoping no one would stop me to exchange greetings. I was lucky. I was able to arrive at my room door without anyone hailing me, breathing a sigh of relief when I found my rusty key in my left pocket and heard the door lock snap open with two turns of the key. I practically ripped my smelly shirt and pants off, almost ruining my buckles on my sandals as I yanked them off and dived onto my sleeping mats. I did not want to use the soiled pillow, so I rolled up my towel to serve as a pillow. Appreciating the coolness of wearing only my underpants, I was all set to fall into a deep sleep, but there was one thing I had overlooked.

It was hot. Too hot! Then I saw the problem. There were not any vents or windows on the side of my room facing the ocean. Anytime the cooling effects of the ocean breeze were cut off, it became unbearably hot. I understood now why this room was empty and cheaper than others. It was like living in a sauna bath. I now understood the role of the hand-fan made of woven palm leaves.

I tried to engage in thoughts that would make me feel cooler. Usually, when in very hot places, I would think about how I suffered as a young man in Kansas during bitter winters when I had to rise before dawn and do my farm chores in the dark while the snow blew across the frozen plains. Thinking of a Kansas winter for a few moments was usually enough to make me not be hot anymore. This time it was too hot and none of these thoughts of winter in Kansas helped me feel any cooler.

Normally, there would be a family or a couple staying in this room and they would take turns fanning each other. I was alone; therefore it was impossible to fan myself and sleep at the same time. I was now thinking I should have picked up a girl to fan me.

I fanned myself with one hand as long as I could, then I would change hands. I did this for quite a while and I eventually dozed off into the kind of deep daytime sleep only possible in the hot tropics.

I slept for a few hours before some stomach rumblings awakened me. My sleep was so deep I had almost forgotten where I was and it took me a while to feel fully awake. I was drenched in sweat and found myself lying in a pool of my own perspiration. I was impressed I could sleep so soundly on a soaked mat with the temperature hovering around one hundred degrees Fahrenheit and the humidity near 90 percent. The increasing frequency of my stomach cramps warned me there was a bowel movement in my near future. I was also tormented by the urgent need to pee.

The peeing was the easy part. I could pee in an empty "cockroach" bottle in my room and pour the pee into the latrine later. The bowel movement had me really worried. I knew I would vomit if I had to enter the foul-smelling latrine room again. Something had to be done! Then I recalled there was a street vendor just outside the compound door who sold miniature bottles of cheap perfume. I quickly put on my clothes and rushed out to buy one small bottle of perfume.

I returned to my room as quickly as I had exited it, waiting until my stomach rumblings and painful cramps told me it was time for me to go to the nasty latrine. Not much time passed before the urge to defecate became so great I had to run to the latrine cesspool. I unrolled some of the toilet paper I had brought with me. I tore off some small pieces and soaked them in perfume before I shoved them up my nostrils.

All I could smell was sweet cheap perfume, and I was off like a flash to the latrine. I quickly latched the latrine door and lowered my drawers so I could squat across the hole situated above the unspeakable honey bucket. This was not a place to tarry. I quickly unleashed a torrent of diarrhea that never wanted to end. I begged the gods to help me finish my business so I could leave this hell-hole in the shortest possible time. The time finally came when I could wipe myself and thrust myself out of the latrine into fresher air, pulling the pieces of tissue saturated with perfume from my nostrils. I prayed I would never have to use these godforsaken facilities again.

This bout with diarrhea made me reflect on the many times I had had dysentery since arriving in Africa. It is as if the insides of my intestines turned into mush as soon as I arrived in the trop-ics. There were microbes, maybe even unknowable ones, which thrived in the tropics. They entered the digestive system as soon as anything was digested in the tropics, transforming the intestines in a way that prevented having a solid bowel movement. I had read somewhere that this change in your intestines was called "sprue."

This tropical impact on the intestines was exacerbated by recur-rent battles with hookworm and numerous parasites, which also thrived in the tropics. After one bout with hookworm, I became determined to never go barefoot again, as the hookworms entered through the soles of your feet. After being treated for roundworm and tapeworm, I was more careful about what I ingested. In partic-ular, lettuce and other leafy vegetables which may have been fertil-ized with human excrement were excluded from my diet. Boiling and filtering drinking water was not enough. Vegetables and fruits had to be washed in Clorox. The tropics are not a good place for anyone with a weak immune system.

I do think as time passed I developed immunities to a lot of ail-ments. At least, when I later became sick, it was not as bad as all the times I was sick during my first year in Africa. I had malaria sev-eral times, but later, after several bouts with malaria, I found I had higher resistance to it. Moreover, I learned to recognize the symptoms well enough to treat it quickly. I once had amoebic dysentery, but I never contracted typhoid and cholera. The latter was particularly scary as it was the newcomer disease in Africa. There was no getting around the fact that a white person living in Africa would get sick more often and seldom feel well. All the African bugs loved feasting on the fresh meat the newly arriving white people represented. Africa is no place for those prone to illness.

The omnipresent dust generated by the long dry season also made life impossible for anyone with respiratory problems. I had always thought there were undiscovered diseases in Africa that were evolving to the outbreak point. For sure, any contact between an open wound and the tropical soil would result in the worst kind of infections and permanent scarring. Any time I had a skin scrape, I immediately tried to wash my skin with surgical soap and keep washing my wound several times a day until it was healed. Staph infections were common and most people had scars on their legs from the tropical sores they had contracted as children. I never saw any antibiotic that was effective against all the infections one could contract in Africa. I am sure we will hear one day of some new disease coming out of Africa.

Enough with this medical reflection! I needed to stay focused and plan my departure from town. I would settle my lodging bill today, so I could go early in the morning to the train station for the return trip back to my village. I checked to see how much money I had to make sure I had enough for my return trip and one more meal at the nearby Café Tasty Blue. I assembled my few personal items. As the sun set, I was all ready to go, looking very much forward to returning to the village. I had had enough of city life and missed village life more than I had previously realized. My excitement level was rising. I reminded myself to buy some small gifts for the women who lived in my village compound. It was bad form to return with empty hands from a trip to the capital, which most people in the village had never seen.

Just as I was feeling good about my plans to get out of town, stomach cramps returned with a vengeance. The pain I felt in my lower abdomen was very worrisome. I told myself this was serious. I had to collect a stool specimen for examination at one of the local medical labs to verify the kind of parasite for which I needed treatment. I immediately looked about my sweltering room to see if there was something I could collect my feces in. There was a small plastic cup I could use, but this would require returning to the foul latrine I had hoped never to set foot in again. I repeated the same drill again, plugging my nose with tissue soaked in perfume. I now had to expel a small amount of my excreta into the small cup. It was always a challenge to do this without getting any of it on my hands.

I returned to the atrocious latrine shed, keeping my calm long enough to get my business done as it needed to be done. This time I did not have any more of my own toilet paper to wipe myself, so I used the squares of old newspapers hanging on a nail on the side of the outhouse. I took my half-filled cup and placed it in the black plastic bag I had brought, making sure it stayed upright and did not spill. I carefully walked back to my room to see if all was in order before asking the gateman where the nearest medical lab was located.

The gateman said, "There is a lab nearby. It is only a ten-minute walk."

I set off with my plastic bag and its stinky contents in the direction of the lab. I had to proceed slowly. I did not want to spill any of the soupy contents of the cup inside the bag. About halfway to the lab, a young man dashed up to me and snatched the plastic bag out of my hand. Some people observed what had happened and began shouting the first word I was told a foreigner should learn in the local language—the word for "thief." People were surprised that I was not upset. Instead of cursing the thief, I was laughing.

It was indeed very funny what had just happened. I could not help but laugh about how the thief would react when he opened the bag and saw what he had stolen. I related this to the people around me and they also began laughing. I yelled loudly for all to stop shouting "thief." I was afraid this would cause a mob to pounce on the thief and do him much harm. It was a frequent occurrence for thieves to suffer injuries or death at the hands of a mob. People hated thieves.

Culturally, one of the very worst things you could do was to steal. Really bad thieves would be "neck-laced" with an old spare tire that would be set on fire. Burnt spots could be observed sometimes on the roads as evidence of this kind of radical mob justice. These spots reminded everyone that thievery would not be tolerated. I thought this kind of behavior was barbaric and very unjust. I would ask myself how fair was it for leaders of the country to commit consistently grand-scale robbery of the national treasury and not suffer any consequences, while a street boy could be burnt to death for stealing a handkerchief from a roadside vendor.

I forgot about my need to get a stool-sample analysis and returned to focusing on my early morning getaway. I needed to eat early and get a good night's sleep. As it was already late in the afternoon, I headed for Café Tasty Blue for an early dinner. I ordered grilled chicken and fried yams, washing it all down with locally bottled soda water instead of the usual beer. I was conscious of the fact that I had to clean out my system so I could stay healthy and alert for my trip back to the village.

Of course, following my dinner I could not resist going again by Bar Unika to see if my angel woman was there. I knew I was being stupid, but I entered the poorly lit Bar Unika, passing closely in front of everyone to see if I could distinguish the young woman who had attracted me a couple of nights earlier. I was sure the sight of a Whiteman walking around and peering closely at every-one was viewed as weird by all those present. I was acting foolish, but I could not resist searching for "angel" one more time.

The waitress asked me, "Would you like a drink?"

I awkwardly replied, "I am looking for someone."

The waitress asked, "Who?"

I said, "A young woman, but I do not know her name."

She replied, "There are plenty of young women around. If you want one, I will bring one to you."

I, in turn, replied, "I only want the one I am looking for."

She thought this was strange, because for a man in need, woman is woman. She said. "Okay, but be sure to tell me if you change your mind about whether or not you need a 'tire change.'"

The latter was a reference to the common saying about a travel-ing man suffering a flat tire and needing his tire repaired. In other words, a man away from home may need the small sexual fixing only a woman could give him.

I slowly returned to my dismal room to get some sleep before rising early at the crack of dawn to go to the train station. In my head, I was saying my good-byes to the images of people and places I had encountered during this visit. At night the misty sea air gave the city a surreal look, making people appear as images lost in a foggy mirage. You could almost smell the rust the city wreaked of. Every metal item was in one state of rusting decay or another.

The sea had a high salt content and the prevailing breeze always blew inland, coating all with a saline dampness. People could not keep cars or anything made of metal near the coast, as the rust would dissolve them within a few months. Special workers were hired to clean all the cars and metal fixtures with fresh water every day to retard rust. But even with extra special care, the rust, like advancing age, eventually won out.

CHAPTER TWENTY-TWO
TRAIN TO NOWHERE

The long nap I had earlier made it hard for me to sleep. Also, I kept waking up to see if daylight had broken. I was afraid to oversleep. My usual rule was to get up when I could distinguish all my fingers when they were held about a foot from my face. Finally, after what seemed like an eternity, daylight appeared. I quickly dressed, washed my face by splashing some water from the bucket in my room, rubbing my eyes vigorously. I looped the straps of my bag over one side of my moto's handlebars. I pushed my moto toward the outside gate, handing my key and final payment to the watchman. I ignited the engine of my trusty moto with one downward thrust of my right foot on the starter pedal and zipped off toward the train station.

I found the same tumultuous scene at the station that I had encountered on my previous trip. I aggressively forged my way through the teeming masses to get my ticket and a place for my moto. I searched for the same approximate seat on the train so I could sit on the opposite side from the one I had sat on during the inbound trip so as to see the side I did not see on the inbound train. I took my preferred seat among the usual squish of people. I relished all the pandemonium while the train grudgingly repeated the same noisy, grinding process to come alive and move out of the station. I was delighted to be heading toward my home village.

The train chugged up to higher ground and picked up speed as it moved beyond the city limits. The first stop was about twenty-five miles away. Already people began singing in reverse order the-naming-of-the-towns jingle. The song reached its peak as we pulled into the first station, but the singing came to a sudden halt as the train came to a jolting stop, spilling people and goods in a pell-mell fashion everywhere. I had the feeling this was unusual, but not without precedent. Nonetheless, such a hard jolting was not a good sign.

As we stayed longer in the station than usual, I was beginning to worry there may be something wrong. I was not surprised when my worst suspicions were proven correct. A railroad employee passed through our car announcing, "The train has a technical difficulty and has no longer the ability to move forward."

This announcement was met with shock and a very agitated mixture of words and cries of alarm. People simply did not want to believe what their ears were hearing.

The trainman continued in a robotic manner, "The train can still go in reverse, and therefore, it will go backwards to the capital where it will be repaired. All who want to get off can do so here. Those who return to the capital will be reimbursed for the ticket or given a new ticket for the next departing train."

This news was a sour, depressing pill to swallow. I could see I had no choice but to return to the capital, although that was the last thing I wanted. Furthermore, I did not have the funds to stay any longer in the city. As the train started its slow movement backwards, I had plenty of time to contemplate my fate and what I would do once I was back where I did not want to go.

I did not have money to go to the same cheap lodging place. In any event, I had to avoid anything akin to the infernal conditions of a room there. I recalled the name of a guy I had met once who told me to look him up if I was ever in the capital. This was definitely the time to look him up and see if he could help me, but I could only vaguely recall the neighborhood he lived in.

It took hours of crawling backwards to reach the station in the capital, but as soon as we arrived, I headed quickly out the door to fetch my moto in an attempt to beat the crowd. I was having a hard time accepting that I had been on the train all day and had not gone anywhere. I quickly grabbed one of the reimbursement tickets being handed out and headed for the neighborhood I thought this guy, Felix, lived in.

Along the way I encountered, at every street crossroads, the usual swarms of street beggars, and children who hustled each passerby for a few coins. Although they could be a nuisance, I always tried to be kind and sympathetic to them and give them any small change I might have. This time of year there were more beggars than usual, particularly women with small infants strapped to their backs and in their arms. These seasonal beggars came from distant northern arid lands where food was always in short supply during those months referred to as the "hungry season" or the "season of skinny cows."

There were beggars with all kinds of physical deformities. Some were so horribly disfigured it was painful to look at them. Some were in wheelchairs. Others, without the use of their legs, moved about by sitting on small skateboards, propelling themselves with their well-calloused hands. Many had been afflicted by some horrific diseases that had eaten away their faces and limbs. There were those who had been blinded by onchocerciasis (river blindness), holding on to sticks by which small children led them. I always

hoped the rumors were false about babies being horribly muti-
lated at birth so their value as beggars would increase. I found
abhorrent the thought some of the beggars surrounding me were
victims of some mafia-like organizations only interested in maxi-
mizing their profits.

The challenging part for me was deciding which beggar to hand a
coin. Once the mob of beggars saw you reach into your pocket, you
would be besieged by dozens of beggars at once. And giving to only
one could lead to conflict between the one you gave to and the rest.
Sometimes it was better to not give anything to avoid being mobbed.
I tried to develop some criteria to help me select which beggar to
give my pittance. But I could never decide which beggar deserved
more than the others. Was it the old blind man or the young woman
nursing twin infants, or was it the horribly disfigured cripple who
could not walk? Choosing which beggar to give to was something like
trying to decide which country to provide development assistance.
Both processes were fraught with cruel choices. Certainly, any positive difference made by my charity would be fleeting.

There were exceptional times when no beggars could be
seen. The same applied to the hordes of streetwalkers who could
be observed every night in certain areas of the city. By order of
the president, every time there were important visitors arriving,
the entire town would be cleaned, and any undesirables found
would be trucked off to their home villages. The trunks of all the
trees along the roads would be whitewashed, and where the visitors would pass, the roads were swept and lined with whitewashed
stones. In this way the visitors would only see happy people lining
clean roads, singing, and dancing. This helped visitors gain positive impressions of the country and its president-for-life.

During these times all trash and debris would be collected and
hauled to distant areas in the bush. There was not any modern

trash collecting service in town. Sporadically, hand-pushed carts and small wagons pulled by donkeys would be hired to remove trash that had piled high on every street corner. Modern refuse collection companies were not interested in collecting trash because of its high content of dirt and the absence of anything valuable to recycle. Local trash was mostly dirt and sand, as every compound would take the morning sweepings of their compounds to the corner dumping ground. Moreover, extreme poverty made it so there was little of value to discard.

One trash collection company did express an interest in managing the city's waste, but its condition was to be allowed to import trash from the US. Evidently, the US had a surplus of "rich" trash it wanted to export on barges to any country. The company thought it could sift through this trash, find much of value, and use what was left over to fill the huge craters created years ago by mining companies. The government rejected such a deal. It did not want its country to be known as a dumping ground for waste from other countries.

Government officials were proud of their country and did not want anything to spoil what they considered the good image of their country. I marked up most of this to "false pride," which was to me, along with excessive jealousy, holding the country and society back. I believed these factors and others were among the key causes of the country's "false start" after gaining independence. In any event I thought an interesting measure of a country's development level might be the quality of its trash.

CHAPTER TWENTY-THREE
FELIX TO THE RESCUE

As soon as I entered the neighborhood of my destination, I began asking roadside vendors, every block or so, where I could find a Felix, who I described as short, old, and balding with a big stomach. He had told me he was well known in his neighborhood and I only had to ask around to find him. I was pleasantly surprised when someone replied that he knew him and would show me his nearby compound. At first, I thought I would be taken to the wrong Felix, but after moving a short distance, I could see the "right" Felix walking toward me.

The famous, speedy African grapevine had done its work. He had already been alerted that a Whiteman was looking for him. The joke was the grapevine often times worked so well that you could hear the news before it happened. Felix welcomed me warmly, as if I were some long-lost close friend. He jumped on my moto behind me, and we headed toward his house as I struggled to stay upright as my moto tires sank deeply into the soft, sandy soil. He indicated the gate I should approach and we entered his expansive compound to the loud welcome of his large extended family. There must have been fifty people of all ages spread across his compound busying themselves with one task or another.

Felix had four wives who gave him thirty children, aged from almost newborn to thirty-five years of age. This high number of children elevated his prestige and added to his notoriety. He was considered a wise man. People from all walks of life often sought his counsel. He was proud of his home compound, as it had been deeded to his grandfather in early colonial times. Deeds were rare, as there were no modern laws governing land ownership. Felix had a bubbly personality and completed almost each sentence with an unusual, chortling laugh. He looked much younger than his age and possessed the energy of a teenager.

When I asked him, "How do you stay so young and active?"

He replied, "I never sweat the small stuff. I never desire more than I have. If I get more, that is okay. If I do not get more, that is okay too."

I heard him being called by his popular local nickname, which meant "old young man." This nickname summed up much about his character and outlook.

I briefly described to him my train ordeal. He sincerely sympathized but said, "I am very upset with you for not coming to my place when you first arrived in the capital. No matter, you have nothing to worry about now. I have a nice little house for you, and if you like, you can sleep in a hammock tied between two coconut trees in front of the house."

His compound was nicely swept, covered with clean, white, fine sand and shaded by closely spaced and regularly harvested coconut palms. Felix and I sat under a small grove of palms in low wooden-slat lawn chairs, inclined at a forty-five-degree angle, allowing for air to circulate around us.

Shortly after my arrival, a number of women began scurrying around the outdoor kitchens, prompting Felix to note very soon we would be eating delicious yam fufu with a special sauce for which his first wife was locally famous. A couple of women brought us calabashes brimming with a dark local brew made from fermented corn. After pouring some drops of this drink on the ground for the ancestors, we enjoyed sipping this sweet, low alcoholic beverage as we made small talk. The welcoming I received in this pleasant compound was so warm and reassuring that I briefly forgot about my bad day and my almost penniless state.

When we finished drinking, he said, "Let me show you your quarters while the women prepare our food."

In one corner of his compound was a tiny blue house, consisting of a breezy, well-lit bedroom and a real bathroom with a flush toilet and adjoining shower stall. There was also a nice bed with a mattress covered by clean sheets. In the middle of the room dangled an electrical wire with a single clear light bulb. It was as if I had entered a five-star hotel. I kicked myself for staying elsewhere when I first arrived. Of course, I would have never had the transcending experience I had with my angel if I had not stayed in that dismal lodging place. I muttered to myself a local proverb that basically means "everything in life happens for a reason" and roughly repeated Proverbs 19:21 from the Bible, which was something many local people were fond of saying: "Many are the desires in a man's heart, but it is God's purpose that prevails." Or more commonly, "man proposes but God disposes."

I repeated my sincere thanks to Felix several times for offering me such a nice place to stay for the night. We returned to settle again into our comfy lawn chairs as we waited for our food. Life was feeling very good at that moment…so good that I did not want to relate to Felix all my needs about getting back to my village.

I reluctantly told him, "I am broke. All I have is my return train ticket but, given my experience with the train, I am reluctant to give it another try."

After hearing about all my troubles, he let out a string of high-pitched laughs, which at first frightened me, but when I realized he was genuinely amused, I laughed with him. The sustained, odd quality of his laugh was such that anyone passing by who did not know him would probably question his sanity. When he finally stopped laughing, he heavily criticized me by saying, "Stop worrying so much over such small details. If you want to live a long life, you have to do like me and not worry about anything. The ancestors will always look over us, and God would not fail to provide. Think with your head, not with your heart. You should not worry. I will take care of everything for you."

Then he quickly rose and said, "I will be back in a few minutes." He handed me a local newspaper he had snatched from a nearby side table and said, "Here, you can read the paper while I am gone." I saw him step out of the front gate of his compound. I could hear him hollering the names of various people.

I picked up the local daily and quickly thumbed through its ten pages. I found it very boring, as it mostly reported on what the President for life was doing, praising him ad nauseam. It also reported on the events of his single political party. The only page I found of any interest was the obituary page. In particular, there was an interesting obituary about two guys who had both died of heart attacks in prison on the same day. I was thinking that this was quite a coincidence. How unfortunate it was they were not able to live out their sentences, especially as jail terms were normally short.

Felix came marching back at a quick pace, laughing as usual. He told me, "You have nothing to worry about. I have arranged for you a good spot on one of the passenger trucks a close friend of mine operates on the road going to your village. This truck will pick you up early in the morning. All your transport problems are solved; therefore, you should relax and enjoy yourself. Is there anything else you need? If you wish, I can find you a young lady for the night."

I said, "I'm fine. All I need is a good night's sleep, so I'll be well rested for my overland trip tomorrow."

He replied, "There is absolutely no problem. Everything will be as you want."

I handed his newspaper back to him and said, "I saw something very curious in the obituary section."

He asked what and I replied, "It was reported that two men died of the same cause on the same day in prison."

As soon as he heard my words, his habitual smile fell from his corpulent face, and he looked me straight in the eye and said in no uncertain terms, "You have a lot to learn about Africa. Maybe Africa likes you so much, because you are so innocent and gullible. By now, you have been in Africa long enough to be able to see below the surface and know what the real guts of African life are like. I cannot believe you actually think it possible for two guys to die at the same time in prison of a heart attack."

He quickly changed the subject by saying, "I know how Americans are. I once traveled to the States when I was a young man. I won a contest offered by the American Embassy and a few others and I were taken on a two-week tour of the States."

He named all the States he had visited and rattled off all the things he had done there. It was like he was happy to tell me all this, but, at the same time, afraid to do so. I was really impressed that this average man had been to the States and actually had visited many states I did not know. He concluded his story on his US adventure of more than thirty years ago by saying, "Americans have life too easy, and thus, they do not know what the true core of life is all about."

For Felix, the States was so overdeveloped people had forgotten the real ingredients composing the fundamentals of life. He had much to say about his impressions of the States. He continued, "I was shocked people did not know their neighbors. Everything was artificial. The buildings were tall and perfectly good buildings were destroyed to build new ones. There was far too much concrete and asphalt. Much land was wasted by planting grass when it could be used to grow food crops. There was too much food available, making people fat. People exercised to lose weight when they could get the same result if they worked. I was amazed there was water to drink everywhere and so many old people were about. I visited a refinery and thought it was a wonderful thing as there were eternal flames burning all the time. Of course, every house received cooking gas in its kitchen stove. Truly a miracle! I saw the Grand Canyon and thought God must have been very angry to cut such a deep trench into the Earth."

Felix was on a roll and added, "The thing I liked most about the States was law and order, and the fact you could drive long distances, going from one state to another, without any police roadblocks. I was surprised everything was so orderly and people respected the law. And there were so many churches! It was very different than the few American movies I had seen."

He also talked about his visit to a court of law saying, "I was surprised to see the law was applied to all people in the same way, as this was not like my country, where all the big shots did as they pleased with impunity. I could not believe you could actually get your mail delivered to your house. I was astounded by the fact you could call 911 and actually get help. Calling the police in my country often results in greater losses and problems. I liked the fact everything in the States was so predictable, whereas in my country, too much cannot be anticipated. There is too much upheaval on a regular basis, making it hard to plan and invest."

Some of his views on his US experiences gave me a lot to ponder. He acted like he was glad he had finally found someone with whom he could convey his long pent-up story about his US experience. But before he could say more, and I could comment, his first wife beckoned us to come to another shaded area of the compound where small tables and benches had been placed for our meal. As we sauntered over to this eating spot, Felix called to his oldest son to bring us the coldest bottles of beer. Evidently, he had a small store near the entrance to his compound where he sold beer and other items.

We squatted down to sit on small low stools while the women set before us piping hot mounds of fufu already sitting in thick, oily orange sauce full of chunks of meat. For this occasion, the women had brought out new Chinese tin enamel bowls covered with colorful designs. A young woman came with a pitcher and a basin for the washing of our hands, as this is food you could only eat well with the thumb and two forefingers of the right hand. As the big glass bottles of cold beer were set on the table, Felix wished me a hearty appetite as he started eating. I quickly followed, trying to show I was adept as anyone with eating with my right hand, forming the right bite-sized balls of fufu I could swallow without chewing.

With the first bite, I almost fell off my stool. The sauce was so overdosed with the strongest hot peppers the smallest taste was extremely painful to the untrained palate. I tried as much as I could not to show how much the hot pepper was making me suffer, but I could not hide my profuse sweating. Felix was also perspiring but was eating away with much gusto. I tried to contain the fire in my mouth by constantly taking swigs of cold beer. Every bite was like volcanic lava rolling through my mouth and down into my stomach. I could not help but cry; my ample tears joined my heavy perspiration. When I could not bear the flames in my mouth anymore, I put all manners aside and asked to be excused for a few minutes.

I fled to my little house to weep and run in circles, jumping up and down in an effort to calm the effects of the super strong hot peppers. My predicament was such I became hysterical and laughed at myself. I was surprised to find my laugh sounded like Felix's chortling. I made a mighty attempt to calm myself and regain my bearings so I could rejoin Felix. I tried to put on a happy face and return to Felix to finish my food in a manner that would not hint of anything gone awry.

When I returned to my bowl of fufu, I found Felix had finished eating. My fufu was sitting in a different bowl with an orange palm oil sauce lighter in color than the one I had left in the previous bowl.

Felix said, "I can see my first wife's special hot pepper sauce was too much for you. I had her bring another bowl with a sauce that is much less hot."

I thanked him for this and began eating again without any problems, except the portion of fufu provided to me could have fed three men. I was determined to finish it so his wives would be honored.

In the nearby kitchen area, I could see they were cooking sauce and yam slices in large aluminum pots on cast-iron charcoal grills. I had once observed how these pots were made. Local artisans would collect aluminum junk, melt it down and pour it into molds made from the original cast-iron pots imported generations ago. A wax model was made from these old pots and surrounded by sand in a wooden frame. Using the lost wax process, hot aluminum liquid was poured through a small hole to fill the space occupied by the wax. The mold was knocked away. All the rough edges were filed away, and the pot would be polished and put up for sale. These pots were used by all. I often pondered what people would do without them and what was used before their advent.

I always thought the original mother cast-iron pot should be in a museum or enshrined in some form of a statue. Why not? There were statues of the president all over the town as well as signs plastered everywhere with slogans reminding everyone of the virtues of the president and the wisdom of his party. I had even seen one small statue in honor of the mosquito. It was a bronze statue in the shape of a mosquito with an engraved inscription thanking the female anopheles mosquito for preventing white people from settling in the country in large numbers. Thanks to this mosquito malaria was prevalent, and the first white settlers perished from this ancient disease in large numbers, thereby discouraging their further settlement. Hurrah, the humid tropics win again!

Felix sagely observed, "It is good to eat the hottest peppers. They kill any internal parasites and build up your resistance to disease. They have a high content of vitamin A. All the people I know who lived a long time ate the hottest of hot peppers. My people survived all these generations because of eating fufu with the hottest possible palm oil sauce. Yams, hot peppers, and palm oil trees are among our last remaining indigenous food crops."

What he said about the benefits of hot peppers was all new to me, but I nodded, inhaled, and grunted my agreement to everything he said. I was about to question some of his homespun wisdom when there was a loud noise I had not heard before.

The loud calls I heard continued for several minutes. During this time nobody tried to talk as the magnified voice of somebody calling out in a melodic fashion would drown out their voices. After about ten minutes, the sound stopped and I asked Felix, "What on Earth is this all about?"

He hesitated but finally said, "Northerners have recently established a mosque just a short distance away and they use loudspeakers to call their Islamic faithful to prayer five times a day."

I expressed surprise. "I have always been told this was a Christian country."

He said, "Yes, this is a Christian country, but there is nothing we can do about the northerners practicing their religion."

I could see he was not happy about these new arrivals, but he could not say much as these people belonged to the president's ethnic group.

Changing this awkward subject, I told Felix, "I am thinking of taking a short ride on my moto to see the ocean one last time before departing again tomorrow."

"This is a good idea," he said.

Just as I was getting up, a large python snake slivered by me. I tried to act nonchalant about this because nobody in the compound was paying any attention to the snake. I knew pythons were considered sacred and everyone who could manage to obtain a python would keep one or more snakes in their compounds to help ward off evil spirits. This harmless snake was also useful to keeping down the rodent population. People would often keep them in their household granaries to deter mice and rats from damaging their food stocks.

Felix saw me watching the snake wide-eyed and said, "My family and I are devout Christians, but we are still obliged to follow traditional customs, as the old African spirits are still around to contend with. One can never be too careful. As a matter of fact, just last week a witch fell off her broom at night in a neighboring compound and she had to be put to death. My own python had somehow impregnated a neighbor woman, and she had to do many ceremonies and get an abortion."

I tried to act knowledgeable of such frequent events by saying, "I have heard of people changing into goats and cats to escape being apprehended by the authorities."

He replied in a natural and unperturbed manner, "Such events are nothing. They happen all the time."

For no reason at all, I responded nonchalantly with an awkward "amen."

He said, "All kinds of things are happening all the time, making it necessary to appease the African gods and the ancestors. Christianity is essential but not sufficient. It is a constant challenge for us to balance all the worlds we live in. For everything, we seek answers in both worlds. If I am sick, I seek both a traditional healer and a local physician. If my children want to make a good grade at school, they study hard, but they also pay the fetish priest to perform ceremonies that will enhance their chances of success on an exam."

He continued by saying, "It is like walking on a tight rope. It is easy to fall off on any given day. At every step one has to consider the seen and unseen, never letting your guard down. The spirits and ancestors are in constant movement, being manipulated by their own world or by the world occupied by humans. Vigilance and striving consistently to take measures for self-protection are necessary for your sanity and survival."

This kind of talk made my eyes dart around the compound to check for what else I had missed. I could see an unwieldy structure built of iron bars that could only be in honor of Felix's clan totem. Also, in the middle of the back wall was the usual small edifice built for the ancestors. In a corner near the front was a fetish shrine with offerings surrounding it and chicken feathers stuck to it from the last offering of a white rooster. I could see practicing Christianity, ancestor worship, and keeping up with all the African deities could be a full-time occupation. I also thought the ancient world was much more complicated than today's world. There was no doubt in my mind that if Africa could harness and direct its immense spiritual powers toward achieving progress, it would be one of the fastest developing continents in the world.

After the big python passed by, I went to fetch my moto to take a little spin toward the ocean side. All the kids gathered around and cheered me on, singing that jingle of greetings tailor-made for white people. As soon as I pushed my moto out the front gate, I mounted and started it with only one thrust of my right foot. I dashed quickly off to the corner. Trying to show off my motorbike skills, I turned quickly onto the main road before the arrival of some oncoming cars.

Somehow, as I turned the corner my wheels slid and the next thing I knew I was sliding along the road surface while my moto was skidding along a different path. The car behind me came to a screeching halt, almost running over me. All the traffic stopped and a large crowd gathered around to see what had happened. Luckily, I had not been hurt, but I was very embarrassed by my stupid fall. With every intention of continuing my little outing, I went to pick up my moto. As I leaned over to stand it upright, I was surprised to see the right side of the handlebar completely severed.

I was shocked to see my handlebar broken like this. I was at a loss as to how I could fix my broken handlebar. I needed my moto, but it could not be driven without a handlebar. At that moment Felix appeared through the crowd. He called to some young men to help push my moto back to his compound.

Felix held my hand as he walked me back to his place, consoling me, "Do not worry. I know a blacksmith who can weld your handlebar back together. He can work on it tonight. Your moto should be ready for your departure early in the morning."

I was heartened by this information. A smile came back to my face. I liked the way Felix was always upbeat.

As soon as we entered the compound, darkness fell like an opaque curtain pulled rapidly across a stage. I was feeling queasy. I told Felix, "I am feeling tired. I need to sleep now so I can rise early and be rested for my trip."

He quickly agreed. I slowly walked to my cozy little house. I guessed I was suffering from some post-accident trauma as my legs were trembling. I had trouble removing my clothes. I just wanted to lie down on the bed. I stripped down to my underwear and fell onto the bed and passed completely out. The next thing I heard was someone clapping loudly at my door and saying, "Hurry, the lorry truck has arrived!"

How could the night have gone by so quickly?

CHAPTER TWENTY-FOUR
SEA NEVER DRY

I quickly threw on my clothes and splashed some water on my face, wiping it off with my hand. I hustled out the door toward the outside gate. As I passed through the gate, I stopped suddenly to behold in front of me, in all its hulking beauty, a genuine 1950s British-made Bedford truck that had been restored to its former glory. Its chrome bumpers and hubcaps were shining. Its side panels were painted blue, and all its edges were painted bright blue and yellow. Its name, "Sea Never Dry," was painted in dark blue letters on a white background on the top wooden panels, front and back. I was very intrigued by its name.

The wall-to-wall benches inside the lorry were already crammed with passengers, and there was a mountain of goods piled on top. I was surprised it was already filled with passengers. Much time was usually lost waiting to fill up a passenger lorry. There always seemed to be room for one more person. I was concerned about the whereabouts of my moto, but I was assured by Felix it had been fixed and was packed between other goods on top of the lorry. My next concern was where I would sit, but Felix said he had arranged for me to sit in the front seat next to the driver. Thanks to Felix, I was being given special treatment. All the passengers were probably wondering why an extra stop had been made to pick up a short, scrawny, and ill-kempt Whiteman.

I was shown my seat next to the burly driver, who shook my hand with a healthy snap and introduced himself as Martin. Of course, this was his Christian name, and like everyone else, he had to have at least one African name. For sure, he would have his day name and probably another name related to the circumstances surrounding his birth and his position as a child in his family. Many factors were considered when determining each baby's African name. Their mothers would often be renamed so they would be the "mother of so and so." As the occurrence of events and the intervention of the spirits at the time of birth determined names, the president's authenticity campaign to oblige all citizens to reject their Christian names and adopt African names was hard to apply, as one could not simply choose an African name long after they were born. Anyway, Martin was also Atsu, which meant he had a twin brother.

I squeezed myself onto the shabby front seat, which had patches of yellow plastic covering a few holes exposing below some wire springs. I thought I would have my space on the front seat to myself, but right after I sat down, a shapely young woman squeezed in next to me. At first, I imagined Felix might be trying to set me up with a female friend. Later on I thought this attractive young woman was being done a favor in exchange for some favors she had done previously for Martin.

Martin was assisted by three apprentice boys who hung onto the sides of the truck until they were called upon to do some work. Martin was a rotund, short, and jovial sort, who appeared to be made to drive this lorry. He held the wheel like a smiling captain, eager to tackle the journey ahead. His large potbelly interfered with turning the black vinyl steering wheel, as it scraped against his much callused belly. He kept a towel near him to wipe off the heavy perspiration streaming down his face. Martin nosily cleared his raspy voice, yelling, "Our departure is imminent."

Upon hearing Martin's shouts, the apprentice boys swung into action. Two of them stood at the ready to remove the wooden wedges, stuck under the back tires to prevent the lorry from rolling. The third, larger apprentice boy pulled from under the truck bed a large metal crank. He walked to the front of the lorry and inserted the crank into a hole, signaling to Martin he was ready to 'crank-start' the motor. He had to crank several times before the old engine rumbled reluctantly to life. Everyone became silent as they wanted to hear if the motor sounded as it should.

Although the rumbling sound of the motor sounded very bad to me, Martin grinned and waved away the apprentice boy. He then used both of his hands to push, with all his strength, the gear stick into place. I quickly moved my left leg out of the way so he could manipulate the spindly floor shift-stick without interference. This required that I press up against the appealing young lady sitting next to me on my right. She did not seem to mind and remained emotionless.

The screeching noise made by forcing the gear stick in place joined the tractor-like sound of the motor to hurt the ears. In fact, the sounds this old lorry made sounded to me like the antique John Deere tractor we had on the farm where I grew up on in Kansas. Finally, after pushing with all his strength, the gear was engaged and Martin stretched his left leg so he could slowly release the very worn and wobbly clutch. Suddenly, the lorry lurched ahead, and everyone let out a loud cry that sounded like a mixture of joy, relief, and fear.

As the motor produced a nauseating smoke screen, the lorry moved ahead in fits and starts. The motor seemed out of tune, coughing up an uneven mixture of hits and misses. Everyone was jerked constantly backward and forward. I could not help bumping into Martin and the young woman, who, between bumps, conveyed to me in local language her name, Celestine. Trying to avoid biting my tongue, because of the constant ups and downs, I replied she had a nice name. Given all the shaking going on, I was almost glad I had Celestine next to me to absorb some of the shocks of the incessant bouncing.

As the creaking old truck moved grudgingly forward, Felix ran up to the open side window shouting, "I wish you a safe trip. I put a small sack of cassava *gari* flour meal into your bag, which I stashed behind the driver's seat. Please do not forget Africa likes you, but you have to like Africa too."

He repeated this several times and begged me, "Do not forget what I say."

Of course, I never forgot what he said, but I was deeply puzzled by why Africa could like such a misfit from Kansas. I did feel many times like Dorothy in the "Land of Oz," but I could not find the equivalent of the red slippers I needed to find my way back home and extricate myself from a world that was not my own.

The lorry picked up speed. I was happy I was once again on my way back to the village. I could not wait to get "home." But my hopes were dampened when we turned into the first filling station we encountered to take on enough fuel to get us to our destination. I should have not been surprised, as it was the custom of all bush transport vehicles to collect upfront the money from the passengers, thereby enabling the driver to pay for fuel for the trip. The cost of fuel could represent over fifty percent of the transport cost. When the lorry stopped to refuel, there was no breeze. My sweat began to mingle with the attractive young woman pressed against my right side. I was intrigued by the woman. Out of the corner of my eye, I tried to size her up.

The most remarkable thing about her was her smooth and unblemished skin. Becoming an adult with such unmarked skin was a rarity in this tropical climate and cultural setting.

I could easily spy the tops of her ample breasts pressing firmly against the front of her low-cut blouse. As there were no stretch marks to be seen on her breasts, it was probable she had not ever been fully pregnant or grossly overweight in her life. I estimated her age at about eighteen. I knew age was considered just a number and almost nobody paid much attention to one's age. Most people did not know their birth dates. If they needed some official papers, they would often put down the approximate year of their birth.

Celestine was dressed in a brand new bluish Dutch wax cloth with the latest bluebird design imprinted on it, and she wore new matching blue shoes. The use of this expensive imported cloth placed her in a higher class than most women, but all women tried to scrimp and save to buy this prestigious cloth. Her hair had been recently braided into one of the latest hairdo fashions. Her eyebrows were heavily penciled with black eyeliner and her eyelashes had been unevenly colored with black mascara. Her whole face had a heavy layer of makeup. Her lips had a ridiculous amount of messily applied red lipstick. Her feet were not overly calloused, which meant she had not spent much time growing up in a rural village. She had small, round earrings that were made from what looked like real gold. Obviously, she was dressed to impress those who would be waiting for her at her destination.

I really could not figure her out from her looks and demeanor, but for sure, she was a young woman who had some man with means who cared for her greatly. I started thinking of her as the "special one." I also began thinking she was out of Martin's league. I tried to learn more by striking up a conversation with her, but I was surprised to find she only spoke the local language; therefore, our conversation was limited. I reflected on how such a sophisticated young woman could be unschooled. I summoned all the local words I knew as I tried to make conversation with her while the lorry waited silently to be fueled. Finally, I asked her, "Where are you going?"

I was shocked by her response, "I am going to Aniko where my father is the village chief."

Her reply sent a chill down my spine. I immediately thought of how the people of Aniko had destroyed the new school I funded in Ataku. I was afraid our sitting together could be used by Aniko in its lengthy traditional feud with my village of Ataku. I feared being accused of associating with the daughter of the chief of the enemies. For the remainder of the trip, I carefully minded my behavior with her and weighed with much caution every word I uttered. It was a challenge to keep my distance when the seating arrangements glued us together like sardines in a can. I took care not to reveal where I was going or why. I acted like I was a stupid tourist on a little outing. I now had her figured out more than I wanted.

Martin jumped in beside me and gave the signal for the apprentice boys to get ready to go. He smelled of diesel fuel. I looked around and saw the filling station was without electrical power. This meant siphoning fuel with a hose from the station's elevated tank where fuel was stored when there was electricity. I could see the sebaceous film left around Martin's lips. He had to use his mouth to get the fuel going from the tank to the lorry by sucking on the hose. He kept licking his lips and spitting out the window in an effort to get rid of the fuel taste in his mouth. I thought this was nothing new to him. He had probably done this a thousand times. He saw I was watching him, and he laughed, telling me, "Don't worry, a little diesel is good medicine."

While I had my doubts about the benefits of ingesting diesel fuel, I did recall seeing a woman in the village screaming bloody murder and running around like a chicken with its head cut off with her hand over one eye. I joined the crowd gathered around her to see what had happened. At first, I thought she had been possessed by some mischievous demon. Once the commotion settled down, I was told she was reacting to the pain of treating cataracts in one of her eyes with diesel fuel. I was assured a good cure for cataracts was filling a bottle with diesel fuel and holding its opening upside down over one eye so it could be fully washed with diesel fuel. The challenge was to hold it over the eye for at least a minute, as it burnt mightily. I saw this as useless pain. Cataracts could be easily treated at a local clinic where a trained doctor could remove them using, if need be, a clean razor blade.

The lorry rumbled to a start, just as it did before, and we rolled onto the reddish laterite road leading out of town. I had learned that laterite was a plentiful, low-grade iron oxide excavated in great quantities for surfacing roads. We began to move along at a good pace as we passed the city limits, heading through the tall savannah grass toward the places we all hoped and prayed to reach before dark. It was not long before we hit our first long stretch of washboard. The lorry shook in a much different and violent way. It was as if the lorry and everyone in it were in some huge vibrating machine intent on breaking them down into smaller pieces. I did not know how the baggage piled on top of the lorry could stay tied down under such a beating or how the lorry resisted being torn apart.

I could see the apprentice boys scurrying about like spiders on a web blowing in the wind, miraculously holding onto the fringes of the lorry with their fingertips. They were on the lookout for any baggage or vehicle parts falling off, making sure the baggage ropes remained tight and key bolts and nuts on the lorry did not come loose. If things did fall off, an apprentice boy would quickly jump off to retrieve whatever the fallen object was and run to jump back on the lorry. I worried about how my moto would fare on such a rough road trip.

The formation of washboard on the road surface was a phenomenon for which there was not any good explanation. The road was covered with perfectly formed mini ridges and valleys. The ridges were spaced about six to ten inches apart, causing any vehicle to constantly shimmy. Somehow wind, rain, road surface composition, and the passing of vehicles conspired together to produce this washboard effect that led to the demise of many vehicles. A road grader could flatten the washboard bumps, but the plethora of mini speed bumps would return within weeks. Certainly, the only answer was all-weather, paved roads that would save the transport industry much money and ease the circulation of goods and people. It was hard to understand how a country could advance without a good road system. The country roads in Kansas were better than the national highways here.

There was always a debate over how to handle traveling on washboard roads. Some drivers believed you should go fast enough to fly over the washboard. But high speed on these unimproved roads was considered to be one of the causes of washboard. Others thought the best approach was to go very slow. The fast approach stirred up too much dust; the slow approach took too much time. Just as I was about to raise these issues with Martin, the washboard tapered off and we spied the first of many roadblocks in front of us that would slow down our trip considerably, as well as increase its cost. This was a combined customs and police roadblock. Everyone moaned at the prospect of having to get off the lorry and unload all their goods for inspection.

Fortunately, Martin had plied this route for years, and thus, was well known by those manning the roadblock. Martin stopped the lorry at a spot indicated by the officers in charge and got out, but left the motor running. He greeted the officers, intimating they were all good friends, chatting about the weather and exchanging the latest gossip. There was much laughing. Martin came back to the truck and grabbed a plastic bag from behind his seat, taking it to the officers who pulled from it a huge bottle of Johnnie Walker Red Label whiskey. The officers expressed their thanks and signaled to the boy holding the rope across the road to release it so our lorry could pass.

Everyone aboard was happy to have such a capable driver like Martin, who could navigate his way through this roadblock without hardly any delay. At the same time, they knew the cost of the whiskey was part of the cost of their tickets, and there were many roadblocks ahead. The police and custom officers operating these roadblock scams were generally despised and considered to represent some of the worst aspects of bad governance. The people resented this kind of overt corruption, especially as customs and police officials were among the wealthiest people in the country.

It was difficult to see how the country could advance when nobody could travel more than twenty miles without being shaken down by customs and police agents. These official "holdups" added insult to the problems posed by very bad roads. In many ways, poor governance, corruption and excessive expenditure on military and paramilitary forces were killing hopes for a better future. The government spent more on maintaining its army than it did on education or health services. Without any external enemies, the role of the army was hard to justify.

As we left this first roadblock behind us, we also began to leave the savannah and enter into a different ecological zone where more trees grew. This higher rainfall zone also changed the nature of the road surface, which turned from red laterite washboard into a darker, thicker type of earth. Although this was the dry season, rainfall was still possible on this stretch of road. Standing water in the road indicated it had rained recently. Any rainfall was feared. Rain would cause long delays and the possibility of the lorry getting stuck in the mud. All eyes were now scanning the sky for any hint of rain.

The change in the road surface brought a new rhythm to the trip. The red, gritty laterite transitioned to dark clay and one big pothole after another. Some potholes were actually craters almost large enough to swallow the entire lorry. While the previous washboard part of the road rattled your teeth, this stretch of the road was like navigating a rough sea in a small boat. The lorry lumbered wildly up and down, rolling widely from right to left. At times there were huge drop-offs, bouncing all passengers violently into the air. Several times I hurt my head when I bumped up against the metal roof of the lorry. Everything and everyone was in a jumble. It was like being inside a tin can that an uncaring, super-being was shaking vigorously.

There were times when Celestine and I ended up intertwined by the force of all the road bumps. She was constantly holding onto my upper right thigh and her hand was frequently forced to brush against my private parts. In almost any other circumstances, I would have been aroused by such intimate touches, but nothing of the sort occurred this time, as I held on for dear life. Celestine had abandoned all her reserve and now made a squealing noise every time we hit a big bump. I bounced up and down, and back and forth, ricocheting off Celestine and Martin. I tried hard to not interfere with Martin as he held tightly to the steering wheel. Martin struggled to navigate the lorry along the smoother parts of the rough road, and most of all, he worked mightily to stay out of the ruts left by other vehicles.

Falling into these ruts would be catastrophic. It would require stopping the lorry to allow the apprentice boys time to dig a path the lorry tires could follow to get back on the better part of the road. Worse than falling into the ruts was meeting an oncoming vehicle, which would represent a genuine calamity. One of the vehicles would have to back up until there was a wide spot in the road where one vehicle could pass the other. Deciding which vehicle would back up was fraught with tension, sometimes resulting in violence between drivers and their passengers. Often the side in the biggest hurry would pay a bribe to the other side to get it to back up. The bargaining between the two sides could be quite fierce, as each side would take turns to bid up the price. I assumed Martin was one of the most artful bargainers plying this road, and thus, could get us through any impediment blocking our way.

Another scare of back-road bush driving was to encounter a vehicle involved in an accident or broken down. There was usually no way of getting around such a vehicular obstacle. If the vehicle was broken down, the best thing to do was try to help fix it. This was one reason why Martin and his apprentice boys were also very skilled mechanics. At one point I thought we were approaching a disabled vehicle because some fresh broken branches had been strewn in the middle of the road at regular intervals for about thirty yards. Any broken-down vehicle would put branches like this in the road to warn any approaching vehicle there was an obstacle ahead. But happily, in this case, the vehicle in question had already moved on, leaving the branches scattered in the road.

The apprentice boys had their hands full. They made sure any baggage on the lorry roof and vehicle parts falling off were recovered. For me, it was a miracle they were not thrown from the vehicle, as they were being bucked about violently. They were like rodeo pros who knew how to stay in the saddle when riding an unbroken horse. Meanwhile, many passengers suffered from minor injuries and became ill as they struggled to stay in their places. This was no trip for the weak or children. Even veterans of this trip became sick and vomited more than once. The train was looking very good compared to this hard road trip. More than once I wished I had given the train another try.

Martin was a driving marvel. It took great strength and concentration to keep the lorry moving forward along the best possible path. The steering wheel had worn a hole in the white undershirt covering his potbelly, exposing the heavily calloused belly that he had developed from years of guiding this road beast to and from points in the hinterland. I was amazed by the sheer enjoyment he seemed to derive from his capacity to get the lorry to obey his commands. He was always smiling and frequently let out loud, maniacal laughs. Sweat was always pouring off him, but he did nothing to rehydrate himself. I was also amazed at how this sturdy old Bedford lorry could suffer such a beating and not break down. These types of Lorries were truly the old workhorses of Africa, just as the American Dodge power wagon had once been. If one wanted to say in local languages how strong something was, the words often employed were "Bedford" or "Dodge."

Martin said he trusted his lorry one hundred percent, but he feared flat tires, although the apprentice boys had everything needed to fix a flat. The main problem with a flat tire was that it required removing all the people and baggage so the lorry could be jacked up. This meant losing a lot of time. Suddenly, Martin applied the brakes and brought the lorry to an abrupt stop. In front of us was a flimsy roadblock consisting of pieces of rags tied together and stretched across the road between two small saplings. When we stopped, two poorly dressed guys appeared out of the adjoining bush and bleated, "This is a rain barrier. It has rained up the road and no vehicles are allowed to pass. Any vehicle would cause damage to the wet roadbed and sink deeply into it."

Martin asked, "How long will it take before the road will be open again?"

One of guys answered, "At least twenty-four hours."

When everyone heard this, there was a collective sigh of disappointment.

Mighty Martin jumped out of the lorry and began a lively discussion with the operators of this surprise roadblock. After some talk and laughs, I could see Martin reach into his pocket and give them some money. This transaction promptly led to the lowering of the rope of rags and we were good to go again. The passengers cheered. I quietly thanked God. I turned to see how Celestine was reacting. She looked deeply into my eyes and smiled ever so sweetly. Her reaction scared me. I interpreted it to mean she liked me and was enjoying sitting next to me. I now saw I had more to be concerned about than arriving at my destination.

The road continued to hammer our bodies, but everyone was happy to be moving again. We had not gone far before we encountered another, more substantial roadblock composed of big tree trunks lying across the road. Moreover, the two guys manning this roadblock were wearing the uniforms of the dreaded national customs agents. As Martin pulled to a stop, they immediately came up to Martin's window and stated loudly in no uncertain terms, "All baggage must be removed and inspected."

For the first time, the permanent smile on Martin's face faded, and his jovial demeanor became somber. Celestine whispered into my ear, "This is bad. I can see by their facial scars that the policemen are from a distant northern ethnic group which delights in making southerners suffer."

One of the policemen stared at Celestine and she stopped talking. When the policeman stopped looking at her, she rapidly used a series of gestures to tell me these guys were a different sort of people. She pulled down the bottom eyelid of her left eye. She then pointed at them with her forefinger in a way they could not see. This gesture was quickly followed by rubbing two fingers against her forearm, and then, wagging her right forefinger sideways. All these gestures meant these men were not like us. When the policemen stepped away from the vehicle, she whispered, "Can't you smell how they stink? They smell like the rotten sorghum and the dogs they consume." Obviously, she was quite prejudiced.

She was also very agitated. I did not know what to think. I nodded agreement with what she said and emitted quiet humming sound bites to indicate in the local way my low-key agreement with her remarks. But I thought she was being unfair and exaggerating her perceptions of these agents. Anyway, what did we have to fear? I did not think it was possible that we were carrying any drugs, arms, or contraband of any kind.

Martin slowly stepped out of the truck, giving instructions to the apprentice boys to begin unstrapping the mountain of baggage on the lorry roof. He also asked all passengers to disembark. He did everything to show the two policemen he was going to obey their instructions to the maximum degree. After bellowing out orders, Martin turned to the two policemen and said, "It is really too bad all this is required as it will mean not arriving at our destination as planned today. We have already lost time at a rain barrier road-block a few miles back."

When the policemen heard this, they laughed and said, "That roadblock is a fake. You are a fool for allowing such roadblock amateurs to swindle you."

When the policemen observed Martin was proceeding to unload his lorry, they called him to talk with them. After a brief hush-hush talk, Martin came back and softly advised everyone, "We can pay our way out of this situation, but the amount demanded requires a contribution from everyone."

He turned to me and whispered, "You do not have to pay any-thing, even though they are expecting a higher bribe amount because a Whiteman is aboard."

Although I was broke, I began to protest. Martin stopped me by gently commanding, "Be quiet. I promised my brother Felix I would take good care of you!"

I responded quickly, "I did not know Felix was your brother." (He did resemble Felix in many ways.)

He said, "We neither have the same father nor the same mother, but we were raised together in the same compound."

I could not find anything more to say except, "Oh."

Martin explained the situation to the passengers and asked each to give something so we could continue on our journey. People moaned but saw no choice but to contribute some money. All the money collected was handed over to the senior of the two corrupt officials. Everyone waited in suspense to see if the amount paid was enough to satisfy them. There was a huge sigh of relief when one of the policemen said, "You can remove the roadblock, but you must put it back after your lorry has advanced."

The apprentice boys sprang into action, and with the help of some passengers, dismantled the roadblock and reassembled it after the lorry moved a short distance forward. Once again we were able to continue our torturous road trip home.

After a while the road did improve slightly and we made better time, even though we were also gradually gaining altitude. All of a sudden, Martin brought the lorry to a stop and shut off the engine. He informed all of us, "The last stop with the two policemen consumed too much fuel. I need to ensure we have enough fuel to make it to our destination. Perhaps, I can get some help from where you can see the white flag flying over there."

I could barely see a ragged flag flying from a tall pole above a small shack located a short distance from the road. I knew such white flags indicated the residence of some kind of fetish priest, but since Martin had stopped here, maybe this particular priest also sold fuel. I asked Martin if I could go with him, and he said, "Yes, you should see what I am going to do."

We walked briskly to the shack, and Martin called out to alert the occupants of our need for help. A fetish priest, dressed in a soiled white robe, came out of the shack and graciously said, "Welcome to my modest compound. Please sit on these benches beneath this breadfruit tree."

Martin explained, "We are short of fuel. Can you be of any help?"

The fetish priest responded, "I can definitely help you."

At that moment I expected for him to call to the young man sitting near the front door of his shack to bring a jerry can full of fuel. But instead, he pulled from the deep pockets of his robes a handful of kola nuts that had been cut in half.

He cupped the kola nut pieces in both hands, shook them for a few seconds, and then tossed them on the ground in front of him as if he was playing craps. He repeated this ritual several times. Each time he uttered some magic words when he tossed the kola nuts, closely studying the positions in which they landed and the collective arrangement they made.

Martin whispered to me, "A positive positioning of the kola nuts guarantees whatever the quantity of fuel left in the lorry's tank will suffice to get us to our destination."

I was dumbfounded by what he said. I was at a loss to understand what was going on in front of me.

Before I had any time to question Martin on this, he was giving the fetish priest some money and thanking him for his help. I was asking myself: "What help?"

As we walked back to the lorry, Martin tried to explain to me how the fetish priest had worked to get a favorable interpretation from spirits through his divination of the meaning of the positions of the kola nuts. I could see Martin was happy. The spirits had communicated he did not have to worry about fuel. We climbed back into the truck and took our seats next to the smiling Celestine. Everyone in the lorry was feeling good, as they could see Martin was happy. I was probably the only one who was worried. From where I sat, I could see the fuel gauge indicator pointing to empty.

Not long after the apprentice crank-started the lorry, we turned around a curve in the road and the shaking stopped. We had reached a section of the road that had been improved for use by the large oil palm plantation the government had developed by taking land away from hundreds of peasant farmers. At this point I could begin to see in the far distance a faint outline of Mt. Ataku. This was a clear sign I was not far from the village. My heart began to beat faster in happy anticipation of getting home. It was like I was coming home after a very long absence. I found it hard to control my emotions. Home was indeed where the heart is, and for now, my heart was in the village. For the first time, I realized I really liked being in the village.

Martin reassured me that we were getting close to my village by saying, "We are only about forty 'telephone poles' from your stop."

I did not understand what he meant; therefore, I asked him what distance he was referring to. He chuckled and said, "It is common here to use the approximate distance between telephone poles as a unit of measure. Thus, "forty telephone poles long" represents the approximate distance taken up by a stretch of forty telephone poles."

I appreciated this way of measuring distance, but I still would have liked to know how many miles were covered by forty telephone poles.

Both sides of this improved section of the road were covered with chunks of white cassava. Women were using the sides of the road as a drying platform for cassava they had already fermented. Once dried they would grate the cassava pieces into a gritty gari meal, a favorite snack food and the main food of people traveling long distances. The women grated the fermented cassava pieces on old sheets of tin roofing they had perforated densely by driving nails through them. The opposite side from which the nail was driven left a rough surface upon which the cassava could be grated. After grating, the resulting cassava flour would be heated in a large pan over a charcoal or wood fire. The final flour product was easy to conserve and could be stored for long periods without going bad. Seeing all this cassava made me reach behind my seat and grab from the plastic sack Felix had given me, a handful of gari to munch on.

Before arriving at the side road that led to my village, Martin stopped the truck so all could relieve themselves. I took advantage of this break to thank Martin and to congratulate him on his excellent work as a super driver. I was really indebted to him. I conveyed to him, "I can see we are nearing my village. I am very happy about that. Can you tell me more about the well-polished young woman sitting next to me?"

He said, "She is the well-kept daughter of the chief of the village located next to yours. Do not worry. She has traveled with me before. She is no trouble. A group of people will be waiting for her at the crossroads. They will whisk her away before your moto is unloaded."

I mentioned to him, "This is the roughest road trip I have ever been on."

He laughed and said, "The road is rough, but I prefer it to some of the sandy roads I often ply in other parts of the country. On these roads the going is very slow. We have to lay down metal tracks to drive on to keep from sinking into the sand and there are thorns hidden in the sand that cause many tire punctures."

I finally asked him the question that had been pestering my mind since the onset of the trip, "What is the underlying meaning of the name of this lorry? What does 'Sea Never Dry' mean?"

This question made him chuckle at some length. He said, "Just as the sea is never dry, life is never without problems. Life is an eternal struggle. It is constantly filled with problems, just like the sea is always filled with water."

I was profoundly struck by this meaningful interpretation of the name of his lorry. From then on, whenever I encountered too many problems, I would always mutter to myself: "Sea Never Dry."

Martin yelled out, "We are about to move ahead!"

Everyone scampered to climb onto the lorry to take their places for this last leg of the trip. People chatted more and their liveliness increased, as spirits grew with the knowledge that the end of our trip was near. With each passing telephone pole, I became more excited. Thoughts of being home soon and seeing everyone in the village warmed me through and through. Finally, we reached the spot in the road where it crossed the smaller road going to the village. Celestine was the first person to leave. Just as Martin had said, she was quickly whisked away on the back of a moto, while others from her village waited for her baggage. There was no time for any good-byes between us. That was fine with me.

It was a big job extricating my moto from all the baggage on top of the truck and descending it carefully to the ground. The apprentice boys were experts at doing their job. They carefully brought down and parked my moto alongside the road. I bade farewell to all, grabbed my bag from behind the seat, looping it over the handlebars of my moto. I could not wait to be on my way. I could see the heavy weld on the right side of my handlebars and was happy they were whole once again. I was even happier when my moto started with only one downward thrust on the pedal. I quickly mounted my moto and waved good-bye to all and took off toward the village.

I had no sooner taken off when I almost ran off the road. My handlebars had been nicely welded, but they were no longer straight. I quickly discovered to drive straight I had to tilt my handlebars at about a thirty-degree angle to the left. There was no changing this. I would henceforth drive my moto by holding my handlebars aimed in one direction while I headed in a slightly different direction. All thoughts of this directional anomaly dissolved as I began to enter the village. I could not believe tears were welling up in my eyes. I was so happy to see the village again. Maybe I did like Africa.

People gathered along the path toward my house as the word spread quickly that I was back. Children sang my praises and waved as I passed. Women gave a welcoming ululation reserved for special guests. I arrived at my place, and everyone came out of their compounds to welcome and help me enter my modest dwelling. People were genuinely happy to see me back. I thought for sure there was nowhere on Earth where I would get such a warm welcome. My dog was very excited to see me. He leaped higher than I had ever seen him do before.

I entered my house, which had been kept spotlessly clean and ready for my return at any time. The women and children of my compound gathered around as I unpacked my bag. The women expressed great joy when I gave them some cheap imitation gold earrings and a loaf of bread from the city. The kids were ecstatic with the pieces of hard candy I handed them. I had never spent so little on gifts and seen people so effusive in their thankfulness. For days after my return, people continued to thank me, and God, for giving me such a generous heart.

I was so very tired. All I could do was eat, bathe, and go to bed. My food was brought and put on my table before I had even finished unpacking. I quickly ate the fried yams and sauce and took a quick calabash bath before crashing into my much-missed bed. I was out like a light. All was now well in the world.

CHAPTER TWENTY-FIVE
RAINS MAKE LOVE

A sound I did not expect to hear awoke me the next morning. Raindrops were making a loud racket on my tin roof. This was something I should not be hearing in the middle of the dry season. I sprang out of bed and looked out my window to make sure it was indeed raining. I could see rain pouring down in a steady drizzle. Most of the time it rained at night, but this exceptional rain had started at sunup and it looked like it would fall all day.

On a rainy day like this, there was nothing to do but stay inside. Like many others I enjoyed these days and appreciated the cooler weather the rains brought. I was looking forward to snuggling under my blanket with a good book to read. One reason I liked these rainy days so much was I could count on no one bothering me. Daytime rain meant nobody would venture out and all meetings would be canceled. Even if there was a meeting next to where you live, rainfall was an acceptable reason for not attending. Nobody would expect to see anyone else on a rainy day.

Everybody knew on a rainy day like this many couples would stay in bed and make love. What else was there to do? For sure, about nine months after such a daytime rain, the number of additional births was noticeable. Lovers would seek out each other during such rainy days, as rainfall helped hide their movements, and nobody would be outside to see them. People jokingly called these "love rains." All those who had the "itch" would try to find a mate for the day. I was probably the only single young male in the village who was inside alone without female company.

I was well into my book and thoroughly enjoying my rainy day when I heard my front gate creak. I thought it must have been left unlatched and the wind had blown it open. I looked out my front window to see if this was indeed the case. Instead of seeing my front gate swinging in the wind, I was shocked to see a fully soaked woman standing in the rain and shivering. I could not believe my eyes. There was the "special one," Celestine, dressed in the same cloth she wore while she sat next to me on the "Sea Never Dry." In an odd and uncomfortable way, I was happy to see her, but her totally unexpected presence in front of my house in the rain spelled danger. Alarm bells sounded in my head.

I was debating what to do. It would be cruel to leave her standing in the rain, and she would talk badly about me if I did so. Allowing her to come into my house on a rainy day to dry off would create an impossible situation for me. But maybe nobody knew she was here, and she could come and go without being seen. My good heart finally bested me and I opened the front door of my house. As soon as I opened the door, she scampered through the rain and entered my house like a pet happy to get out of the downpour.

Once she was inside my house, she smiled at me and shyly said, "Thank you for allowing me to get out of the rain."

I brought her a towel so she could dry off. She asked, "Do you have a cloth I can wrap around myself so I can take my clothes off and hang them inside so they can dry a bit?"

I brought her my indigo cloth I rarely used. As soon as I handed her the cloth, she surprised me by undressing without hesitation in front of me. As she took off an item of clothing, she handed it to me. I thought she would keep her panties on, but she didn't. After undressing, she took the towel and dried off before wrapping my cloth around her very shapely body, just above her very symmetrical and full breasts. This whole time I stood spellbound as I watched her peel off her clothing. I could not help but closely observe her movements. She saw me watching her and smiled seductively at me while she hummed a sweet melody I had not heard before. Softly, she said, "You know how to look at a woman. I appreciate that."

I was beginning to feel an attraction between us. I asked her, "Would you like a cup of hot coffee or tea?"

"A cup of tea would be nice," she answered. So I entered my small kitchen to heat some water on my little propane gas burner.

She followed me and told me, "Please stand aside. I will make tea for both of us."

My kitchen was small, so it was hard for her not to brush up against me, but I perceived as intentional the way she stayed very close to me. She brought the tea kettle to the small table in my sitting room and told me to sit down while she finished making our tea. When the tea was ready, she placed everything on the table and sat across from me while she poured my tea. Her presence made me feel very good. I could not deny it was good to have a woman in my house.

It was hard to carry on a conversation, but the language barrier did not keep her from talking constantly in a very low, soft voice. She said, "I like the dark blue plastic sheeting you have placed on all your tables." I had bought a roll of cheap plastic and cut it into pieces for all my tables and the top of my bookcase.

While we were sipping our well-sugared tea, she stretched one leg under the table so her bare foot touched mine. When her foot touched mine, it was like a hot streak ran up my leg, warming my entire body. I was beginning to think she had put some love potion in my tea. There were plenty of stories in the village of women putting potions in a man's drink or soup to gain his affections. I was fully on guard. I was very cognizant of the risks I was taking by associating intimately with the daughter of the chief of Aniko.

Suddenly, she exclaimed, "This tea makes me hot!"

She dropped her cloth below her breasts and started fanning herself with the part of the cloth freed up. I doubted that she was really hot. For me, this action of hers was part of her effort to seduce me. Or, maybe she was so relaxed with me she felt uninhibited to the extent she exposed her breasts just like she would do at home. I could not help myself. I stared shamelessly at her bare breasts, as they swayed gently back and forth as she fanned herself. This was becoming too much. I could feel my own body temperature rising.

She said sweetly, "I can see you are hot too." She rose gracefully and came over to remove my T-shirt. As she did this, one of her heavy breasts brushed up against my cheek and momentarily touched my shoulder. I was indeed sweating now, as irresistible forces of nature were taking control of this situation, making it increasingly harder to think straight.

She timidly asked, "May I see the rest of your house?"

With tightness in my throat, I managed to say in a squeaky voice, "My house is very tiny. There is nothing else to see except my very small bedroom."

In a syrupy, sincere voice, she said, "I would like to see your bedroom."

I walked the few steps to my bedroom door and opened it to show her inside. She stepped quickly inside and looked at my very narrow bed and made a "tché-tché" sound by sucking her tongue against her upper front teeth. I knew this sound meant disapproval.

She gently criticized, "Your room is a mess. Look at the cobwebs in the corners and the dirt on the floor from the crumbling mud brick walls. And you are too skinny. Many women would marry you just for the opportunity to fatten you."

She grabbed my thin grass mat rolled up and standing in one corner of my room. She rolled the mat out on the concrete floor next to my bed. She took my pillow from my bed and laid it at one end of the mat. By this time I had become mesmerized by her very attractive topless form and the very feminine and graceful way she moved about.

In the same sweet tone of voice, she said, "I am feeling tired." In all her beauty, she lay down on the grass mat. She removed her cloth wrap and covered her hips with it. She looked up at me and sweetly asked, "Would you like to take a rest with me?"

By that time I was a goner, fully under her control. I reclined next to her, and she turned on her side and glued her body to mine, putting the inside of her right thigh directly over my groin. I heard her say something about 'war.' I swallowed deeply as I knew in the local language the words for 'war' and penis were the same. I could see she was talking about making war, which meant making love.

She gently rubbed the hair on my chest and arms. She was very aroused and happy. Her smile was captivating. How could I resist a beautiful woman who wanted me badly and walked a mile in the rain to my house? I was helpless. She put her cloth wrap to one side and pulled my shorts and underwear off in a single motion. She then gently straddled my body on her knees. She looked closely at my genitals, and for the first time, raised her voice to say how nice my war looked. She continued on her mission to make war with me no matter what. I could do nothing but enjoy the pleasure and let her do what she was so capable of doing in such a loving way.

She made war against my war, and there was no doubt about the outcome of the battle. My war expended itself long before she had finished her battle. When the war-making was over, she lay closely next to me with her right arm over my body. The way she looked at my naked body told me she had not been with a Whiteman before. I continued to admire her smooth, unblemished body. The striking contrast between her black skin and my milky white skin excited me. It was hard to believe this was the same young woman I spent a day sitting next to in a truck. She impressed me as a really lovely and sweet person. Any man would enjoy her company.

The rain began to taper off, and she said, "I must go before the rain stops. I do not want anyone to see me. I must hurry."

She quickly dressed. I helped her pull up the back zipper on her blouse. She gave me a very affectionate and strong, full body hug and said, "I hope you will want to see me again." She beamed with happiness while I was sinking into a very worried state.

I nodded, indicating I really did want to see her again. She rushed out my front door with her top body wrap covering her head so nobody she might pass on the way home could see who she was.

As she disappeared out my front gate, the risk I had just taken by allowing her to have her way with me left me in a queasy state. It was like I had slept with the enemy. A sense of foreboding over this intimate encounter with the daughter of the Aniko chief quickly replaced my sense of great pleasure. If my chief ever learned of what happened in my house on this rainy day, there would be severe consequences for me. Moreover, many of the eligible women in my village would be enraged to learn I slept with a woman from Aniko. My world had truly been shaken on this rainy day. I knew that from this day forward life could never be the same. One day I would have to pay the price, one way or the other, for sleeping with the "special one."

CHAPTER TWENTY-SIX
WRONGLY ACCUSED

I n spite of the full moon, I slept soundly throughout the night. It was so nice to sleep in the much cooler air brought by the daytime rains. As usual, the first sounds I heard at the crack of dawn were the roosters crowing and the women sweeping the compound. These sounds reminded me I should catch up with the news. I pulled out my tiny transistor radio from the drawer in the rickety nightstand next to my bed. Just as millions across Africa were doing at the same time, I tuned my radio to a short-wave band that captured the British Broadcasting Company (BBC) so I could listen to the daily Africa report. I was glad the two double "A" batteries in my radio were still strong.

I knew most African leaders also listened to BBC, or its French sister, Radio France International (RFI) first thing in the morning. They listened to BBC and RFI not only to hear what was happening in other countries, but in their own countries as well. Some of the more authoritarian heads of states tightly controlled the media in their own countries. They feared people would hear some home "truths" on these international broadcasts.

I stayed in bed longer than usual on this cool morning, but my prolonged slumber was disturbed when there was a loud clapping at my gate. I found at the entrance of my compound one of the chief's messengers who informed me, "The chief would like to see you this morning about a very important manner."

I politely replied, "I would be very happy to see the chief. I will be at his compound within an hour."

The messenger thanked me and departed. This was indeed a serious summons, as it came right on the heels of my amorous couple of hours with Celestine. How could the chief have found out so quickly about what happened between me and Celestine yesterday? I felt sick to my stomach. I tried to brace myself to face some harsh music in the chief's compound.

I quickly dressed and washed my face with water from the bucket always sitting in the shower stall at the back of the house. I quickly ate a snack of gari flour mixed with sugar and filtered water. I told everyone in the compound I was going to the chief's house. I petted my dog before setting off on foot. The going was slow, because I had to perform more than the usual greetings for each passerby and person along the roadside. The greetings were longer as many people wanted to ask about my trip and express their happiness to see me back. They all asked in a half-serious, but joking manner, about what I had brought them from the capital. My usual polite response was I had many problems in the capital and my money ran out before I had time to buy their gift. I was sorry, but they would have to wait until my next trip to the capital.

As I walked I was thinking maybe the chief wanted to see me about something else. Sometimes he would call me on short notice to be what he called his "village's white ambassador" to visiting foreigners. He liked showing me off as the village's white person, using me to explain village customs to visitors. At first, I liked doing this, but after I was in the village for a long time, I grew to dislike this onerous chore. It was impossible to explain to foreign visitors, who were only around for a brief time, how things really worked in the village. As far as I was concerned, it was pointless to try to explain anything to anybody coming from outside Africa. People were probably better off staying the way they were: not knowing a goat from a sheep.

The chief summoned me once to play this ambassador role with a group of black Americans. These people were on a trip to discover their roots in Africa. This was an awkward meeting as these Americans did not see how a Whiteman could tell them anything about Africa. The chief kept asking me to explain things to them, but they did not want to listen to me. I understood how this was difficult for them, but it was also difficult for me. I just wanted to leave and let them try to figure things out for themselves. The way they acted made the chief and his elders suspicious. This was the first time they had seen black people who were not Africans. They could not figure out why black people made gestures like white people and knew so little about their customs.

When I arrived at the entrance to the chief's compound, one of his guards was waiting for me. I knew he was one of the chief's traditional guards because of the multi-colored robe he wore. He greeted me coldly and told me, "Follow me."

I walked behind him, surprised he was leading me to the big circular "judgment" house in the chief's compound that was reserved for trials. This was a bad sign. I began to worry. A knot developed in my stomach. The guard stopped at the doorway to the house and commanded, "Take your sandals off and enter."

I stepped inside the house. Once my eyes adjusted to the darkness of the poorly ventilated, dank house, I could see the chief sitting on one side with his most important elders. In front of him were all the heads of all the clans in the village. They were all dressed in their best traditional clothes. On the other side was a middle-aged man sitting alone. The serious nature of this august assembly was readily apparent. My only thought was they had somehow found out about Celestine and me.

One of the senior elders motioned to me to sit on the low stool placed about five feet in front of the chief. I sat down and stared directly into the chief's droopy face. From the way he looked at me, I could see this was quite serious indeed. I was scared. There was no doubt in my mind this was about my brief affair with Celestine; otherwise, I would not be the center of such dramatic attention. I now believed Celestine had purposely led me into a trap. Only this "quickie" with Celestine could oblige the chief to mobilize such a formidable group of village leaders on such short notice. The chief nodded to one of his oldest elders and this ancient, wiry man, who was all wrinkled skin and bones, rose to speak.

The ancient man held onto his staff for support as he began to speak in a voice so scratchy it was hard to understand. After about ten minutes he finished speaking, and I was asked, "Do you understand?"

I quickly admitted, "I do not understand."

Upon hearing this, the chief asked his male secretary to interpret for me. The secretary said, "The chief has been waiting for your return to judge this serious accusation brought against you by the man sitting at the opposite side of the round room. The man has accused you of making him ill. He has many hospital and doctor bills to prove his illness. The only good explanation he could find for his sickness was you had slept with one of his young wives."

Hearing this I breathed more easily. One of his wives could not possibly be Celestine.

The chief firmly asked, "What do you have to say about this?"

I lost no time in saying, "I am shocked to hear this. I do not know the man. I have not slept with any woman who could possibly be his wife."

Everyone could see I was visibly shaken by the accusation. They believed my jittery reaction was due to my guilt. After some discussion I learned most people in the room believed I had made this man sick by sleeping with his new wife. One elder said, "We all recall the day you were not around when WHO sprayed our houses with DDT. You said you were absent because of your intimate encounter with a nice young woman that lasted all night. This man fell ill about the same time you had this encounter. The evidence is therefore heavily in his favor."

I was flabbergasted and a bit unnerved. I was snared in my own lie about this fictitious encounter, but I could not ever reveal the truth. I was condemned to live with my lie and accept whatever punishment this lie brought me. I swallowed hard and said, "I do not think this was possible. The woman I met said she was not married or living with anyone."

I, therefore, complicated my lie with another lie, but I had to say something in my defense. One elder immediately blurted out, "All women are snakes and should not be trusted."

I was heavily criticized for trusting this make-believe woman. They noted the plaintiff had not yet consummated his marriage to the young woman and they lived far apart, but he had paid the family of the woman a respectable dowry.

I knew if he had paid a dowry he was recognized as the husband, and thus, there was no sense contesting this point. The cost of a dowry could be quite high, involving the provision of cash and animals, and filling a trunk full of cloth and jewelry for the bride. Some men saved for years to have enough money to pay a dowry and fill the marriage trunk. This huge trunk had to be filled with the best cloths and bedcovers. The man would also have to provide the bride with a necklace and earrings made of gold. This expensive jewelry had to be designed according to traditional styles which had been in use for many generations. Of course, the man had to have a house for the lodging of his new bride.

For all those in the room, except me, it was a well-known fact that sleeping with another man's wife causes her husband to fall ill. Finally, the chief spoke, "For me, this is an open-and-shut case. You are guilty as charged. The only matter remaining is to announce your punishment."

Upon hearing his words, I wanted to rise and run swiftly away, but I had no choice but to sit there and face head-on the harsh judgment meted out to me. The chief's senior elder rose, as if all this had been rehearsed beforehand, and stamped his wooden staff against the ground three times saying, "I'm ready to announce the verdict of this court. It has been decided by this court to fine Bobovovi the equivalent of one hundred dollars. This sum will be given to the man concerned to help him defray his medical costs."

The chief and all his elders assented loudly their agreement with this verdict, and the chief declared, "Justice has been served fairly!"

I sat there stunned by this announcement, asking myself where I would find one hundred dollars, but I was also relieved none of this was related to what had happened between Celestine and me. The chief asked for the judgment house to be cleared. He and a few elders remained behind to counsel me. The chief began by saying, "We are happy to see your return to our village. While you have caused a number of disturbances in the village, we know you must stay with us. Normally, we would have asked you to leave the village, but we have not done this because we can see the ancestors and a number of spirits like you. We do not know why this is so, but we have no choice but to be patient and wait until the spirit world reveals its reasons for liking you."

I meekly tried to say the right thing, "I am happy to be back. I also do not know why Africa likes me, but I am beginning to like Africa. I am sorry for all the trouble the trial we have just endured has caused you."

The chief told me, "Do not worry about the trial. It was really nothing. Just pay the fine and all will be forgotten."

I did not say I was incensed, as I saw this as a ploy by the plaintiff to get money from the Whiteman. I believed others were involved in this setup of the Whiteman. I could only agree with the chief, and I noted, "The payment of this fine will deplete all my savings."

He said, "I know this will cause you some financial hardship, but payment is necessary for you to remain at peace in the village."

I replied, "I have the money in my house. Please send someone to get it."

I learned much from this bizarre trial. After this unusual day, I considered more than ever that I had paid my dues. I was now a full member of the village and subject to its ways and laws, just like anyone else. As tradition required, nobody ever mentioned this trial again and it would not have any bearing on how I was treated. I was broke, but life was still good for me in the village. By the time I had returned home, I was feeling better and thinking I was comfortable with staying in the village for a little while longer. I knew that someday I would have to leave the village and Africa. I had already stayed much longer than planned, but I was prepared again to postpone my departure.

I, too, was beginning to believe I was liked by many in the spirit world and wanted to know why, as I saw nothing special about myself. I did not understand why I was being pulled more toward

Africa than toward my roots in Kansas. I was also puzzled as to why I was no longer homesick for Kansas. I was really somebody here, so why go back to Kansas where I was a "nobody"? On the other hand, what kind of future would I have if I stayed in Ataku?

CHAPTER TWENTY-SEVEN
YAMS REIGN SUPREME

I returned to my house with severe hunger pangs and the sound of Assi and Aba pounding fufu with another woman. This sound reminded me that I needed to eat. The thought of swallowing a nicely pounded bite of yam fufu with a spicy meat sauce intensified my hunger and made me approach the women who were doing the pounding. Assi and Aba always made sure I had food to eat, and in return, I gave them a modest amount of money each month for this essential service. I could see they had peeled several big yams, as the goats were already eating the peelings. I could also see a nice meat sauce was cooking on the remains of the charcoal fire in a small iron grill used initially to boil the yam slices. A good plate of fufu, with a great sauce on the side, was just what I needed to give myself a more positive outlook.

All three women were perspiring profusely as they lifted and slammed down their heavy wooden pestles onto the boiled yam chunks lying at the bottom of the huge wooden mortar that had been made by hollowing out a section of a mahogany tree trunk. The yam chunks had to be frequently dampened with a small cup of water to keep them from sticking to the mortar. To help them stay in the perfect unison of motion needed to avoid any collisions, as they took turns thrusting the pestles into the mortar, the women sang a little song, moving their feet ever so slightly to the rhythm of this song. The song was a simple one mothers often sang to small children, but it was something of a catchy tune. They repeated this little ditty in time with the slapping sound of pounding fufu. The words of this one-line tune were sung repeatedly and went something like: "Do you want your yam boiled or fried?" After hearing it a few times, it was hard to get this tune out of my head.

This song was as ancient as the yam, which was one of the few remaining indigenous crops still cultivated. Before the arrival of the colonists, a couple hundred years ago, yams and oil palm sauce were the major staples. The colonists brought many other crops like corn, cassava, coffee, cotton, and cocoa, but none could match the exalted traditional prestige of the yam. Before the arrival of white people, when the population was much lower, people subsisted by eating plentiful wild game, wild rice and millets, and many natural products of the forest and savannah. The domestication of local Guinea fowl also brought meat and eggs. A plate of grilled Guinea fowl was still more welcome than chicken.

Today's rural population has a much less diversified diet, with consequent nutritional implications. Many more people are living today thanks to modern medicines, but few are as strong and active as their grandfathers were. In the old days, many died in childhood, but many among those who survived their childhood years went on to enjoy advanced age. It was not uncommon a couple of generations ago to find a man in his eighties in the best of health with many wives and dozens of children. These men had never experienced modern medicine and depended totally on traditional remedies. They were seldom sick and were strong and virile until they died. These days it is rare to see men like this, as many rely on imported foods and modern medicines. It is troubling to see that the much more numerous, younger generations are, in many ways, weaker than the one that preceded it.

Since ancient times, the yam was worshiped as a source of life. Once each year there is an important yam harvest festival to celebrate the yam and all the benefits it has brought people since the time of the first grandfathers. The cultivation of yams involves a lot of work. Each step requires special prayers and ceremonies. As I progressively observed how important the yam was, I decided I needed to know firsthand how to cultivate and harvest yams.

The first thing I learned about cultivating yams was it could not be done alone. I had done cassava planting myself, but that was considered easy, so easy it was considered locally to be a lazy man's crop. For cassava, all you needed to do was cut up the stems in short pieces and stick them into the ground. The main thing was to know which end of the cassava stem to stick into the ground. I made a lot of people laugh and started a new traditional story in the village, because in my first cassava patch, I stuck the wrong end of the stems into the ground. How dumb can the Whiteman be!

I really did not like to eat cassava because of its high acidity level and low nutritional content (except for the leaves), but it was very resistant to drought and grew well in poor soils. Cassava tubers were a good food reserve. They were always there in the ground to dig up when you needed them. I was told the ancestors never knew cassava, and thus, it was not used in any food offerings, as this frequently eaten food was a foreign import, originating in Latin America.

In contrast with cassava, cultivating yam tubers required a lot of work, and a high and steady level of rainfall on rich soils. It also required buying seed yams from those who specialized in their production. Once certain of obtaining seed yams, the earthen mounds in which they were to be planted could be made. The making of mounds was a specialty. It was best practiced by workers from another ethnic group who had the oversized hoes required to dig and pile up the earth in a conical form. Their large hoes were triple the size of the traditional African hoes used for all cultivation work. I doubted agriculture in Africa could advance as long as the main instrument of cultivation remained the short-handled, locally forged African hoe. Moreover, I could not see how yam cultivation could possibly be mechanized.

The making of yam mounds would begin after the first big rain of the season. Yams needed to take advantage of the full length of the rainy season to mature. Low rainfall meant no yams at all, or small yams. These earthen upside-down cones needed for yam planting were about three feet high, with a circumference of four to five feet. Several workers were engaged and paid a modest sum for each mound they built. They were also provided lunch and drinks. After a hard day of labor by three workers, I had about fifty mounds, one next to another, sprouting upward in my backyard like oversized anthills.

One of the costs of cultivating yams was the hiring of a fetish priest specialized in the blessing of yam mounds. Planting could only begin after this priest had completed his yam-blessing ceremonies, including the usual offerings to the ancestors and relevant gods, and the sprinkling of the blood of a freshly killed white rooster. With these obligatory ceremonies completed, a woman specialist hired to plant yams could begin her work. As fertile humans, only women were allowed to plant yams. The hope was their fertility would help result in a very good crop. Planting yams was a tedious, time-consuming task, and yams had to be carefully tended almost daily throughout the growing season.

The woman would slice off the top few inches of a mound, dig a shallow hole, and position the seed yam into the hole. The seed yam would then be covered with a light layer of straw, which in turn, would be covered with a thin layer of the earth. It was important that the seed yam have access to some air, but not too much. It could take over fifteen minutes to properly put in place a seed yam. Once the yams were in place, they would stay dormant until the next good rainfall. With moisture, vines would sprout from the seed yams. The growth of healthy and large yams required the vines to climb straight up and away from the mound.

The need for the vines to grow upward entailed yet another cost. Straight sticks over six feet long had to be purchased. These sticks were usually made from the cuttings of young saplings. There were men who specialized in the cutting and transport of these sticks from distant woods. These sticks had to be planted deeply into each mound so they could stand firm during the rainy season. The vines would wrap around the stick as they climbed upward. Each mound required daily tending to keep the mounds firm, weeds removed, and the vines required assistance to climb up the stick, sprouting a leaf with each turn as they grew around the stick and upward.

It would take six months or more for the yam within each mound to mature to the size needed to harvest it. But no yam could be harvested until the chief of the land and the head yam fetish priest had informed the village chief of the day harvesting could begin. Once this date was determined, the date of the annual yam festival at the end of the rainy season could be set. This festival had to take place before yams were sold or consumed. In the meantime, harvested yams were stored in a shaded, dry, and cool place, on top of a grass mat supported by lengths of tree branches so air could circulate around them. Some yam tubers were very large, weighing five pounds or more, and measuring more than a foot in length. In the right conditions, yams could be stored for months, just like potatoes in Kansas.

***

To announce the date of the annual yam festival, the town crier rose before dawn to begin making his rounds to every part of the village, stopping every twenty yards or so to tap briskly with a small iron bar on his metal, two-pronged iron gong-gong, which looked like a double-barreled bicycle horn. The loud, clanging sound alerted everyone that he was about to deliver an important message, so they should listen closely. After repeated clanging the crier blurted out: "The yam festival will be held five days from this day. Be there and ready to participate." In reply the people would yell out loudly they had heard and understood.

A huge open place in the center of the village was scraped clean of all vegetation, and thatched hangars were erected along three sides of the rectangular space. In the middle hangar, at the deep end of the open space, a special throne was built for the chief. Plastic chairs were placed around the throne for the seating of elders and special invitees. The arms and legs of the throne were wrapped in yam vines. Yam tubers were piled high around the throne. Additional male volunteer workers came to tamp down and flatten the earthen surface with heavy iron round plates attached to wooden handles. They pounded the earth hard, making it look as if it had been paved.

Very early in the morning of the festival day, all the women of the village brought yams for the blessing of the chief and the designated fetish priests. Among them were a few older women who barked out orders as to what needed to be done. The yams were piled in the center of the large opening like a stack of wood for a bonfire. It was important that each family contribute at least one large, recently-harvested yam to this pile. The women bringing the yams also came with their short bush brooms and swept the entire area clean, being careful to throw all debris and dirt collected to the east, behind where the chief would be seated.

When they completed their work, the women stepped into the adjoining bush to change into the new clothes they had brought with them. These were fancy clothes they would be wearing for the first time. They also put on all the jewelry they possessed, including old Venetian bead bracelets, which generations of grandmothers had handed down to them. They covered their faces with heavy makeup. The older women followed the old tradition of coating their faces with white kaolin clay or talcum powder. When they had finished dressing, they took their places along the perimeter of the open space to indicate where their families should join them. The placement of families was according to their rank within the different clans of the village. There were also some people from other villages and a few foreign tourists in attendance.

Once the women were in place, everyone in the village began to arrive, joining their respective family members. Before long, a crowd of several thousand had gathered. Everyone was singing and praising the gods. They all waited for the arrival of the chief and his entourage. Suddenly, a man dressed in old bark cloth appeared in the center near the stack of yams, blowing mightily on a noisemaker made from the horn of a cow. Upon hearing this bellowing sound, the crowd fell silent. They knew the chief was near. Next, a scantily dressed man ran through and around the open space, screaming the praises of the chief as loud as he could.

This man wore only a loin cloth; blood and white chicken feathers covered him. His body was streaked with white ashes. He wore an unsightly crown composed of a mixture of wild animal bones. His eyes were oversized, bloodshot, and protruded wildly from their sockets. He ranted and raved in a quite mad and bizarre fashion.

Just when the people were braced for the arrival of the chief, a group of traditional hunters emerged from their hiding places and fired their ancient muskets into the air. They caused quite a fright among the crowd. Some babies began to cry. Their muskets had been made by local blacksmiths who slowly drilled their barrels by hand through a solid iron bar. The muskets were probably more a menace to the hunters than the prey they hunted, as they often blew up and injured hunters. The hunters wore their traditional hunting vests, which their forefathers had passed down to them. All kinds of amulets to protect them from danger and make them invisible to wild animals covered these leather vests. The hunters formed a special secret society with customs only they knew.

As the hunters faded into the bush to protect the festival from ferocious animals which no longer existed, the sounds of a brass bugle were heard, announcing the imminent arrival of their chief. First, the most powerful fetish priests arrived, sweeping a path before the chief with special brooms made from yam vines. Behind them were young girls spreading yam vine leaves they carried in straw baskets on the path before the chief. The chief arrived about twenty yards behind these girls. He was held aloft by strong young men of the royal clan in what looked like a nicely decorated open casket. The chief sat in one end of the casket and a girl sat in the other end facing him. This young girl was slowly fanning the chief with a fan made from yam vines.

The casket was set gently on the ground in front of the chief's throne. When all the elders and members of the royal family were seated, the chief was helped to step out of the casket and onto his throne. All the time his aides worked to keep him covered by a large, multi-colored cloth parasol. I was honored by being assigned a seat at the end of the line of seats joining the front line where the chief sat.

After a few moments, the chief rose to his feet and the crowd grew silent. The chief's messenger instructed all to be quiet while the chief offered the annual yam harvest prayer. The chief begin speaking in a hushed toned and in a dialect nobody understood. People knew he was speaking in a tongue understood by the grandfathers and a select few, and that he was thanking the ancestors and spirits for the yam harvest in the same way all the chiefs before him had done. The chief prayed for about fifteen minutes. When he had completed saying his last word, large calabashes full of fresh palm wine were brought forth by ornately dressed young girls.

He poured some wine on the ground before him in thanks to the grandfathers. Then he and a few of his most senior elders walked up slowly to the pile of yams. Next to the chief were young girls holding the calabashes of palm wine. The chief dipped a miniature broom into the wine and raised the broom in the air, flipping wine drops onto the yams. Like a Catholic priest, he circled the yam pile five times, dousing the yams in drops of blessed palm wine. All the time, he repeated over and over the secret yam festival words he had been taught by his father, the previous chief, and his senior elders. There seemed to be something significant about the number five but its meaning, like so many other things, had been lost from memory over time.

As the crowd focused intensely on the chief, the day became increasingly hot and humid. The chief walked back to his throne in the most regal fashion in the company of the parasol holders, selected elders, and the calabash carriers. As soon as he was seated, he raised his right hand with his palm facing outward. This was how he communicated his best greeting to all participants. Upon seeing this hand sign from the chief, the crowd let out a loud shout of praise. This shout was immediately followed by singing and dancing in unison a special number used only to express thanks to the yam for all it had done for these people and their ancestors for generations. At the end of this musical interlude, each family proceeded in order of prominence to circle the yam pile five times while shouting out its thanks for the harvest.

It took some time for each family to proclaim its appreciation to the yams. When the last family returned to its place, all those sitting near the chief did the same as all the families had done. I was asked to join in this group and I gladly did so. At this juncture the chief's messenger asked each family to retrieve its yams. The women of each family passed by, one by one. It was amazing to me they could identify the yam they had placed in the pile. These blessed yams would not be eaten, but saved as sacred yams until the next yam harvest. One woman surprised me by asking the chief's permission to offer me one blessed yam. The chief said, "Bobovovi, you are now a yam farmer. You should keep one blessed yam in your compound." I was quite pleased and honored by this exceptional gesture.

The chief's crier was then instructed to pass in front of all the families and communicate to them the annual yam festival was over, and they should all return to their homes and enjoy a feast of fufu made from new yams. Upon hearing these words, the crowd again broke out in songs of praise and thankfulness. The chief was gently placed again in his royal casket with his young girl attendant, and five strong young men lifted them again above their heads. The chief's procession headed back to his compound for feasting and more celebrations.

People began to dance spontaneously in groups, maintaining perfect timing and unity of motion. With the chief's departure, the largest and most important annual event in the village was over. It was like starting a new year. I believed I had reached a milestone in my long stay in the village. Yet, at the same time, I saw this as a good time to plan my final exit from the village. This exit was long overdue. It was time for me to decide what I would do for the rest of my life. Sooner or later I had to get back to my life in Kansas.

CHAPTER TWENTY-EIGHT
TO STAY OR NOT TO STAY

F or many days after the yam festival, I was involved in an intense conversation with myself over how to extricate myself from the village and go home to Kansas. I had tried to leave several times in the past, but each time, events and the villagers conspired to keep their Bobovovi with them. I needed to go back to my own life and follow up with my plans to complete my university studies and settle down near where I was raised in Kansas.

It was as if I was no longer living in the real world. I wanted to get back to my own world where I belonged. I needed to live among my own kind and in an environment where I was not a stranger and understood all that was going on around me. I was determined to inform the chief I would be leaving the village soon to return to my American home. I was learning much, but almost all my new knowledge had little or no practical application to the life I planned to live in Kansas. I was happy with my life in the village, but I did not see any future for myself in this remote, impoverished corner of the world.

On the very day I planned to ask for an audience with the chief to tell him of my obligation to leave the village, I had early morning visitors. Shortly after dawn I could hear the murmuring of people in front of my house. I was still in my bed and not in the mood to deal with any favor seekers, but I knew they would not go away until I talked to them. I slowly got out of bed, washed my face with cold water from my shower bucket, and dressed in my old clothes. As I was in my own compound, I knew I could wear what I wanted as long as I was in long pants when receiving visitors. Even though I was living in a tropical climate, the wearing of shorts was frowned upon except for when doing manual labor or when in your own compound. I steeled myself for yet another early morning exchange with some people in need of help.

I was not prepared for what I saw when I opened my front door. There in my front yard was Chief Yofu and all the chiefs from the surrounding villages. I now wished I had dressed in my better clothes, but I tried to save the moment by welcoming them warmly, saying, "I am honored by your unexpected visit to my house."

A chair was brought for the chief and a stool for me. All the other chiefs sat around us on the ground. My chief spoke first, saying, "More than anything else we have come to thank you for staying in the village for so long and for all you have done to help us. It is very important to us that you stay among us. The grandfathers and many spirits are especially happy with your presence in our district."

After a long pause, the chief continued, "We have come to see you this morning to ask if there is anything more we can do to encourage you to stay among us."

I was indeed very surprised by all this. It was as if they had known in advance, in some occult manner, of my plans to leave.

After the chief finished speaking, his secretary rose to read an open letter all the chiefs, including the chief of Aniko, had agreed upon. The letter read roughly as follows:

To All Authorities Concerned,

We come before you very respectfully to ask you do all in your powers to maintain the presence among us of the one we know as Mr. Ataku Bobovovi Amerika. It is very important to all the chiefs and the some fifty thousand inhabitants of the twenty villages of this district that he stay with us.

Thanks to Bobo's laudable efforts a number of solutions have been found to our development problems. His departure would have catastrophic repercussions on us and our development hopes.

We, therefore, plead with you to help us maintain progress and harmony in our district by lending all your support to keeping Bobovovi among us.

We also fear the anger of our grandfathers and the spirits if he leaves, as they have shown us many signs since his arrival that they like him very much.

Thanking you in advance for all your help. We send to you our most respectful and friendly salutations.

Chiefs of the District of Ataku

The letter was then handed to me. I could see it had been signed and stamped with official seals of all the chiefs who had also added their inked thumbprints on a second page. I was overwhelmed and left speechless by this unprecedented action on the part of the chiefs. For sure, there was no way I could go ahead with any plans to announce my departure. I would have to delay my departure for some months and plan very carefully how I would extricate myself from the village. For now, all I could do was thank them heartily for this moving gesture, and say I had no plans to leave them and I was busy working on more ways to help them.

Every chief then stood, one after another, pleading with me to stay with them. Each plea was followed by each chief shaking my hand and telling me how thankful he was for me as a person and for all of my good works. I asked myself how all this could be. I had actually done very little to help anyone. After all the chiefs had departed, my village chief held my hand for a long time, looking deeply into my eyes, and stated emphatically, "I know you will be staying with us for a long time to come."

I replied, "This could very well be the case. I like living in the village. I feel at home here."

He said, "This is good. We like you. The grandfathers and spirits want you to stay. I think all of our country and Africa likes you. I believe there are many good things yet in store for you here."

His words gave me a sense of anticipation that both troubled and excited me. I waved good-bye to the chief and returned to my room to contemplate what possible fate was in store for me. I was afraid of what I knew but even more afraid of what I did not know.

CHAPTER TWENTY-NINE
CHRISTMAS SPIRITS

T ime passed quickly after the momentous visit of the chiefs. I wanted to plan more assistance projects, but I lacked donor funding and remained unsure of how long I would be in the village. I knew I needed to do some projects or the villagers would suspect I was preparing to leave. I came up with two project ideas I thought people would like, but before promising anything, I drafted some proposals and sent them off to potential donors. One project was setting up a corn-grinding mill in a village in need of one, and another project was for supplying more water, and perhaps electricity, to both Ataku and Aniko. Based on previous informal surveys and discussions with village leaders, I believed both of these projects would be easily accepted by the villages when funding was obtained.

I made sure all knew when I left for the post office to send an envelope to America with my two proposals. I let everybody know I was looking for funds to do more good work for them, but before saying anymore, I had to be sure to obtain funding. Everyone knew it would take time. It would take over a month for my letters to arrive in America and more time for me to receive any replies. There was nothing I could do now but wait for the mail.

The days slipped by quickly. The next thing I knew it was December and we were approaching Christmas time. A number of people were stopping by to tell me they wanted to organize a party to celebrate Christmas, but they did not have money to celebrate their own party. After hearing this many times, people started coming to tell me how nice it would be if I could hold a party at my house. This prompted me to analyze my meager resources to determine what kind of party I could pull off.

I sat down with some people who often came to sit in the shade in my compound to play, in a deadly serious manner, a simple board game called Ludo. They helped me put together a holiday event which would be modest by almost any standard but had the potential to be the best Christmas party ever known in the village. I scraped together some money to pay for a ten-gallon wicker-wrapped bottle of cheap Algerian wine at Chez André's, and some yams and chickens for the preparation of fufu. I saw right away the key thing was (as with any party in the world) to have ample food and drink for the thirty or more people who would be invited. Also essential would be playing some popular dance music.

I brushed off my old battery-powered Philips record player and purchased the eight size-D batteries required for its operation. As the sound it produced was not sufficiently loud, some people showed me how to amplify the sound by placing the two speakers on top of huge dried gourds, especially harvested from calabash trees and dried for such a purpose. As the party had to be at night, there was the problem of providing adequate lighting. I was encouraged to splurge and buy an Aladdin lamp from a little store in the village that could, if properly operated, make my living room as bright as day.

The big day finally arrived. A group of women came to prepare a feast. The pounding of fufu could be heard for hours, and when the music began, the pounding was in tune with the music. The village was scoured for popular "33" long-playing dance records. This included music by James Brown, Jimmy Cliff, and the colossus from the Congo, Franco, and his OK jazz band. At sunset people began to gather around my house.

Early in the evening, people began to eat and drink as much as they could hold. The twenty liters of red wine was quickly consumed and palm wine and its stronger relative, distilled palm wine, appeared out of nowhere. Like magic, the compound filled with an exuberant group of people, some known and some not, as people began to dance two steps to the right then two steps to the left, again and again. My small house was filled to overflowing and took on a very different appearance.

It was as if my entire house began to levitate, going up and down with the dancing steps of the crowd which moved in a mesmerizing unison of movement. For a few hours, I was convinced the entire world was swaying with the sounds emitted from the little Phillips record player, which sounded impossibly loud. I was carried away to some never-never land only to wake up the next morning wondering what had happened. I was not the only one to feel like this. The village was abuzz with rumors of how the spirits from the mountain had invaded our party and transported us to a state of ecstasy alcohol alone could never achieve.

My stature in the village was elevated to a higher level, as people were not only thankful I had organized such a wonderful party, but everyone was impressed by the way the spirits looked favorably upon me. Increasingly, the local fetish priests began to look at me differently. This event added to the talk in the village about how

I possessed occult powers that were acknowledged by the spirits they worshiped and respected.

Many began to say, "You are a very special white Tuesday's child."

My reply was, "My old Phillips record player must have been blessed by the gods."

When people heard me say this, they laughed, reminding me the party had occurred when there was a full moon hidden behind the clouds. Somehow this fact instantly explained many things which were beyond easy comprehension.

CHAPTER THIRTY
STOLEN FOOTPRINTS

We moved deeper into the dry season. The world turned a reddish brown. The shriveled leaves dropped from the trees, providing some of the organic matter needed to enrich the land. The savannah grass dried to a crisp, and farmers burnt the grass and their fields to diminish the snake and insect populations, as well as add potash to the soil. Yet, in reality, this annual traditional slash-and-burn approach to agricultural cultivation impoverished the soil. It was hard for me to see how a higher standard of living could be achieved in an agrarian society when the level of soil fertility was constantly falling.

The hunters also burnt the tall grass to force animals into the open so they could shoot or club them to death. The smoke of their fires mixed with the fine, white dust carried south by the desiccating northern Harmattan wind blowing off the Sahara Desert. This cool, dust-laden wind lowered visibility and increased respiratory ailments. The land cracked and groaned from a thirst that would not be satisfied for months to come. The air was so dry everyone's skin cracked. The cooler, dust-ridden 'Saharan' air also transported ailments like meningitis. This was considered an evil, merciless time of year. People were vigilant, ready to fend off the bad things which often happened during this harsh and unhealthy period.

Contrary to most people, I liked this cool part of the dry season. I did not perspire and I could sleep well under a blanket during the cool nights. It was too cold for most people. There was much competition in the used clothing market for the heavy winter clothes imported from North America. It was not unusual to see people bundled up in winter parkas and wearing woolen stocking caps. As it was never cooler than seventy degrees Fahrenheit, I was amazed people could bear wearing clothes made for an arctic freeze. On the other hand, people were very impressed by the way I could comfortably go about my business in my shirt sleeves in what they considered freezing weather.

Late one night I was snuggled comfortably under my green army blanket when a strange noise woke me from a deep sleep. I shined my flashlight on my tiny battery- operated clock and saw it was about 2:00 a.m. I did not like to see this time, as I had been told several times this was when evil spirits came out to torment the world. This thought increased my alertness and made me listen more carefully for any more noises. Then I heard a loud grunting noise. It sounded like a warthog rooting grub out of the earth. The noise seemed so close I sprang from bed and stepped toward my window to see what was making this startling sound.

It was a pitch black night. I could not see a thing from my window. I shined my flashlight in all directions but saw nothing. Just as I was about to go back to bed, I spied on top of my front wall a small, reddish light blinking like a car turn-signal. My wall was twenty yards away but the light was clearly visible. I stared intensely at this blinking light and was frightened to discern the ugly face of a disfigured creature, with huge bulging eyes, a large nose droop-ing over the wall, and oversized ears, which seemed to flap slowly. Hideous, red warts covered the entire face of the creature and a steady stream of foamy, white saliva dribbled from the swollen, protruding lips of the creature's hideous mouth. In a flash, the creature's eyes locked on mine, and before I could react, a spar-kling fireball the size of a grapefruit shot like a rocket from his right eye straight at me.

I quickly jumped to one side and dodged a fireball that buzzed by me to smack my bedroom wall with a crackling sound. I turned quickly around in time to see another fireball shooting from the creature's left eye. This burning ball of fire came again through my screen window. This time it stopped in front of me and began moving slowly toward my chest. I tried to move out of the way, but it followed me. I was so filled with fear I could barely move. The fireball hovered directly in front of my chest and edged slowly toward me, pressing me back onto my bed and down deeply into my mattress. For some unexplainable reason, I formed a cross with my arms and pushed back with all my might against the force emanating from the fireball. I pushed as hard as I could with my crossed arms and shouted for the fireball to leave me alone. I knew I had to be totally committed to preventing the fireball from enter-ing my body and possessing me.

I became angry. I was convinced that I was fighting for my life. I was ready to do battle and use all my strength to repulse the fire-ball. Suddenly, the fireball released its grip on me and flew back out the window. I saw it fly back across my front yard into the eye of the creature. I was shaken but very upset. I wanted to pursue the creature and beat it into a pulp. I grabbed my big walking stick and ran outside and through my front gate ready to smash into pieces this evil creature. I arrived at the spot where the creature had been, but there was only emptiness. It was so dark I could not see, and in my panic, I had neglected to bring my flashlight. The night was eerily dark and still. I stood quietly, not knowing what to do. I could hear in the distance a sound like a lame man dragging his leg behind him as he walked down the path leading to the cemetery. From this sound and the direction the creature was going, I surmised the creature was lame and dwelt near the cemetery.

I returned to my house, and despite the cool weather, I was sweating profusely. I found it odd that all the nocturnal commotion had not woken anyone in the compound. My dog was fast asleep on my front step. Had nobody heard what I had heard or seen what I saw? I sat on my one cushion chair the rest of the night waiting for Assi and Aba to wake up so I could tell them what had happened. Dawn finally broke, and I could hear the women stirring as they began to sweep our compound. I stepped outside to talk to them. They were very surprised to see me so early in the morning. I said, "Something strange happened in the night and I need to tell you about it."

My feeble mastery of the local language was not sufficiently adequate to describe what had happened. I used many gestures in my excited effort to communicate what I wanted to convey. They stood and looked at me with blank eyes and faces. Their uncomprehending stares made it clear to me that they did not understand what I was trying to say. I finally mimicked the part where the creature made a leg-dragging sound as it walked away. I dragged my leg along the ground like a lame man to demonstrate the noise I had heard. When I did this, the women became quite agitated and said excitingly to each other one word: "Ajaja." As soon as they said this word, the oldest one, Aba, ran off toward the village as fast as her bare feet could carry her.

The remaining woman, Assi, gently told me, "Go into your house to rest. I will bring your breakfast."

I still was trying to figure out in my own head what really had happened. It now seemed like a weird dream. How could such a thing happen and nobody else hear anything, not even my dog? It was all beyond my wildest imagination. I was so tired and weary. All I wanted to do was sleep and hide from the world. Just as I thought I might take a little nap, there was clapping at my front gate. I looked through the window and was surprised to see the chief, his key elders, and all the head fetish priests. I exited my house to greet them. We sat on some benches under the cool shade of a teak tree growing near my house.

The chief lost no time in telling me, "We came immediately upon hearing about your encounter with Ajaja. We need to hear every detail you can recall about this encounter. Ajaja is an ogre only known to us through our oral historians."

He pointed to one man among them and said, "He is our top historian and can recount village history from the time of the first grandfather. There is no living person who has ever seen the feared Ajaja. As I said, we only know about him from oral history. Your encounter with Ajaja is the first to occur in several generations. Therefore, it is of the utmost importance to obtain from you every detail of the extraordinary experience you had last night with Ajaja."

He sharply added, in a serious tone of voice, "You must be very strong in your soul to have withstood the powers of Ajaja. Oral history tells us that if the fireballs enter your body, your heart stops or you are totally paralyzed. We continue to be perplexed by why so much from the other world of the grandfathers and spirits is attracted to you. Many things have happened in the village since you arrived that have not happened before. Somehow, your presence has stirred up a lot of commotion in the other world. Obviously, the spirits want very much for you to stay here. We hope we will learn in time why the spirits are so agitated by your presence. My elders and I believe more strongly than ever that one day the village will benefit from a great revelation the spirits will send through you."

I conveyed carefully to them everything the best I could and with as much detail as I could muster. I was interrupted many times as they thoroughly discussed every point I made. I was making village history and they needed to get all the facts recorded accurately. When I had finished my recounting of last night's close encounter with the village ogre, they asked me to show them the place on my front wall where Ajaja had stood. They could see Ajaja had elevated himself by standing on an old termite hill. On top of this hill could still be seen part of a print from his odd-shaped foot. Just over the other side of the wall, there were scummy white tracks left by the saliva he drooled.

They asked, "Show us the direction in which you heard him walking?"

I led them along the wide dusty path passing in front of my house. This path headed straight to the cemetery. We walked along this path for about thirty yards until we came to a place where they could see marks on the ground of someone who had dragged his lame leg behind him. They analyzed and discussed these tracks for some time.

The chief confidently said, "We are not surprised he headed toward the cemetery. Our oral history has always been consistent in telling us this detested ogre lives among the remains of the dead."

We walked slowly back to my house. On the way I could see the chief was having a serious discussion with his entourage. When we arrived at my front gate, the chief stated, "The most preoccupying thing for us is why the mischievous Ajaja came after you. It is obvious to us somebody has gone to great lengths to manipulate the spirits which control Ajaja so he would do you harm. The evil nature of this despicable deed is very serious and it is urgent for us to find the person responsible. We must apprehend and judge this person as quickly as possible to prevent anything like this from happening again."

The chief firmly instructed me, "Stay in your house until we are able to get to the bottom of this very troubling case. I will send one of my guards to watch your place every night."

Before we parted ways, Kontor pointedly asked me, as he had done once before, "Have you been careful to dispose of your hair and fingernail cuttings?"

I replied, "I always flushed anything coming off my body down the toilet."

He then asked, "Have you gone walking anywhere recently in soft ground?"

I thought this over a moment and then softly responded, "I recently walked in my bare feet along the sandy banks of a small stream running through a nearby cocoa field. I visited this field to see a new variety of cocoa that is resistant to the swollen shoot disease, which is devastating most cocoa fields."

In a troubled voice, Kontor loudly commanded, "You must immediately show us where you walked."

Honoring this request, I led them through patches of banana and plantain trees growing near my compound to a nearby cocoa field I had visited a few days before. We entered the field, and I led them to the sandy place along the streambed where I had enjoyed walking barefoot. Many of my footprints were still clearly visible. Surprisingly, also visible were my missing footprints and the sandal prints left by someone else. Upon seeing some of my footprints were missing, it was obvious to the chief's delegation that someone had stolen my footprints and taken them to a distant, powerful sorcerer, paying money to awaken Ajaja and send this dreaded monster against me.

The chief ordered one of his men, "Stay behind and guard this sandy stretch with all the footprints. I will send someone soon to replace you. Nobody should disturb this place until we have completed our investigation of this extremely important case. It is our top priority to find and quickly punish the culprit. There is no time to lose!"

The chief sent me home. He and the rest of his men returned to his compound to determine how they would proceed in their investigation. The first thing for them to determine was if anyone held any kind of a grudge against me.

It was hard to keep any secrets in the village. Everyone knew everyone else's business. One could not make the slightest move without someone else knowing it. This was a communal society where introversion and shyness were discouraged, as anyone quiet and reserved would be suspect of doing something behind everyone else's backs. The chief's investigators trotted from household to household, demanding in the strongest terms any "truths" anyone knew about any negative comments said against me. Everyone was scared. They knew the harsh consequences for not telling the truth or withholding information. They also knew what they said was important because the entire village was very much aware of my confrontation with Ajaja.

After some days of this collective grilling, some evidence the chief could act on was discovered. It seemed one village man, known as Kpodo, with a history as something of a troublemaker, had been overheard saying I should leave the village as I was causing too much disruption. Kpodo was therefore not happy when the chiefs requested I remain in the village.

The chief's bodyguards captured Kpodo and paraded him like a dog through the streets with a rope tied tightly around his neck. He was taken to the chief's compound and soundly flogged and intensely interrogated. His treatment was brutal and without mercy.

Fearing even worse torture, Kpodo confessed, "I am the one who was behind the ogre trying to maim Bobovovi and scare him away. I wanted him to leave the village because I wanted to reclaim the land his house had been built on. My grandfather was the original cultivator of that land, and therefore, I have full rights to the land. I confess I stole his footprints and took them to a strong sorcerer in Kpolomo who did costly ceremonies to animate Ajaja to attack the one who left the footprints. I paid almost the equivalent of fifty dollars for the services of this strong fetish priest."

With this confession in hand, it was easy to pronounce Kpodo guilty. The chief ordered him stripped and flogged again with the rubber strap made from an engine fan belt. While Kpodo was screaming for mercy, the chief and his elders determined his ultimate punishment. They decided his case was so exceptionally wrong that they would apply the heaviest possible penalty.

This penalty involved banning Kpodo forever from the village. Indeed, to be ostracized from one's home village was the worst thing that could be done to anyone. To be forced to leave the village, and cut all contacts with it, was a fate worse than death. This unprecedented penalty also carried with it great shame for Kpodo and his family. Kpodo was released and told to go home, gather his things and leave the village by sundown. The chief angrily told Kpodo, "If you do any more evil against the village after your departure, we will beseech the grandfathers to condemn you in the next life." From this point on, Kpodo was *persona non grata* in the village. He had ceased to exist for all villagers. His name would never again be mentioned. His existence would be collectively deleted and erased from memory.

Kpodo stared at the ground as he plodded slowly to his compound. The people he passed along his way turned their backs to him or acted as if he was invisible. For all the villagers, he was like a dead man they no longer recognized or acknowledged. When I heard the news of this drastic punishment, I felt sorry for him, although I did not know him. I was also sorry for his family, as his relatives might also feel obliged to move away because of the great shame brought upon them.

Personally, I was disturbed. It was obvious my presence in the village was the source of much upheaval and too many unsettling events. I wished that for the rest of my time in the village things would be tranquil and routine, and all the grandfathers, gods, and spirits would get used to me and stop allowing my presence to agitate them. I was thinking I should consult with one of the village's fetish priests about what I could do to cease being such a nuisance, while promoting peace and stability in the village and the 'other' world.

CHAPTER THIRTY-ONE
PLANT MEDICINE

F or a few days, I took it easy, mostly staying at home to rest and think, trying to figure out my next move. Early one morning I awoke to find a small boy waiting for me just outside my front door. My women caretakers, Aba and Assi, told me the chief had sent him to accompany me to see the old woman who knew everything about the medicinal powers of plants. I quickly understood that this was related to my overdue course in learning about the medicinal values of plants.

Aba and Assi were like identical twins, except that Aba was much older and talkative. They were cousins who had been raised together by Aba's mother. They were wise beyond their years, but they never had benefited from any formal schooling. They were like so many of the very intelligent people in the village who had not had the opportunity to go to school. I have always believed many potential Einsteins existed in Africa, but the failure to go to school obscured their talents. Assi and Aba had children who lived elsewhere with extended family members and visited frequently. They were both short, middle-aged, and of dark complexion. Their clothes were composed of the mere basics, a threadbare cloth to wrap around their bodies like a long skirt and a matching blouse.

They were always barefoot except for special occasions when they would wear old rubber flip-flops that had been repaired many times. They lived very simply, struggling to obtain the essentials needed to survive. They had hearts of gold and took good care of me. I could not survive without their help. I also depended on their sage advice and counsel. In recognition of their indispensable services, I gave them as much as I could, and they were very thankful for all that I did for them. We were almost like a family.

I joined the boy who had come to fetch me. He led me silently along a path I did not know to a rundown compound some distance from the village at the edge of the forest where the slope of the mountain begins to climb steeply. I peered into this very odd compound. It was very unkempt, overgrown by weeds and covered with dangling vines draping down from ancient trees. The place was a mess and in total disrepair. Scattered everywhere were clay pots with a mosaic of plants of all kinds. There were birds perched and flying about everywhere, and strangely, many cats. I did not know so many cats and birds could live together peacefully. The smell of all the bird excrement, feline odors, and all the decomposing vegetative matter was overpowering. My mind was taxed to the limit to make any sense of the dirty and foul-smelling, confused jumble spread before me.

The boy left soon after we arrived at what I assumed was the entrance of the compound. I clapped my hands to announce my arrival by making the usual loud vocal inquiry, asking if anyone was home. I heard a feeble, squeaky voice come from somewhere within the weedy compound. I wound my way around a few bushes, dodging a few birds and cats, trying not to step on the bird droppings, to find an aged, lumpy pile of brownish human flesh seated in a rickety wooden chair shaped like a wheel barrel. As I drew closer, I could make out a pair of tiny eyes sunken deeply in their sockets and a broad, elongated nose that fell below her upper lip. The most arresting facial feature was a huge set of ears that seemed to cover the entire side of her head and flap involuntarily. A multi-colored cloth made from patches of discarded material covered her from chin to toe. I asked myself what kind of creature I was encountering and what I was really getting myself into.

From the head sitting atop the pile of flesh came a crackly voice welcoming me and informing me she was Mama Atiwono, the keeper of all plant secrets, just like her mother and grandmother before her. She was toothless and had trouble enunciating, so I could only understand a few words that bubbled out of her small, fish-like mouth, as drops of saliva rolled slowly down her almost invisible chin. Standing behind her was a strongly built young man who was her caretaker and interpreter. He picked up the arms of her wheel-barrel chair, pushing her closer to me so I could hear her better and she could see me more clearly. In a halting voice, she said, "I will start by describing the use of many of the plants in my compound."

She saw me eyeing one leafy plant growing in a patch of similar plants along one side of her exterior wall. She bubbled, "This plant I cultivate mainly to treat my sore gums and arthritis."

On closer inspection I could see the plant looked like marijuana. I asked her through the interpreter, "Can the leaves of this plant be dried and smoked like tobacco?"

"I mostly consume the leaves in my soup, but sometimes I dry and smoke them in my small wooden pipe. Would you like to try it?" she asked.

I politely declined, saying, "Not now, but perhaps some other time."

The front wooden wheel on her wheelbarrow made a screeching noise, and she asked the man pushing her to stop. She reached to her side to pick some weeds for him to rub between the wheel and the round wooden axle on which it turned. She gave me the name of this slippery weed, saying it contained a lot of oil that was good as a skin cream and for dermatological problems like psoriasis. I took out the small notebook and ballpoint pen I carried in my shirt pocket and noted in phonetic writing the name of the weed. I asked her caretaker for the French or English equivalent. He said he did not know; they only knew the local names of the plants. I realized then I would only learn the plant names in a language I barely understood; therefore, I would never be able to research the scientific name of any plant I was presented.

Mama Atiwono made some grunting noises and the young man reacted by pushing her rapidly around to various plants growing in her compound. She would quickly tell me the names of the plants, the properties they possessed and their use. I noted everything she said the best I could and tried to sketch the shape of the plant and anything else to help me identify it in the future. I was very much interested in traditional medicine and how the plants were used in its practice. I wanted to dwell longer at each plant, but Mama Atiwono seemed to be in a great hurry, acting as if she was wasting her time with me and only showing me around because of the chief's request. I certainly did not impress her as possessing any knowledge about plants.

She spoke a few slobbery sentences again. The young man interpreted, "She apologizes for her immobility. She has not been able to walk for over twenty years, and her health has been failing for many years. She is well over one hundred years old and thinks she is facing her final days before passing to the other world."

Upon hearing this I asked, "Who is she preparing as her replacement?" I was astounded to hear she was an only child and had been training the daughter of her aunt, but this young woman had run away to the city. I was troubled by this. It looked like all the in-depth knowledge Mama Atiwono possessed about plants, which had been passed down to her over generations, would be lost forever. I had often heard, "Every time an old person dies in Africa it is like a library burning down."

We completed our hurried tour of the plants in her compound and headed for the way out. I was told she would normally spend some hours with me outside her compound, showing me more plants and describing their uses, but her poor health and age did not permit her to do that today. We did visit a good number of plants just outside her compound exit, and as I ran out of paper to take notes, I thought it was just as well she could not give me the full tour. We passed some trees, mango, eucalyptus, and neem, but she did not stop to tell me about these trees, so I asked her why. She said, "These trees were brought by the Whiteman, and thus, they are not native to our land."

"But," I said, "They also have medicinal uses."

She crackled, "Those uses are common knowledge, and therefore, not needing my specialized knowledge of the secret properties of indigenous plants."

I sensed we were at the end of our tour. My eyes met an intense stare from Mama Atiwono that made me feel uneasy. Our eyes locked for a split second, and I felt some strange tingling within my chest. I thought maybe my heart had skipped a beat. She mumbled something and the young man robotically said, "She wants you to know she excuses your ignorance of plants because she can see her plants like you, and therefore, she recommends you spend more time with plants and learn about them. She invites you to come back anytime. She said there is something about you that has the trees talking to each other. She is astounded and confused over how your presence has raised so much excitement among all the plants."

I began to express my appreciation and wave good-bye when I saw a wide and constant stream of army ants blocking my path. She saw this as more evidence of the disturbing effect my presence was having on the natural surroundings. She warned me, "Do not try to divert the direction the ants are headed or try to step over them. Be patient and let them pass, then go on your way."

It took a long time for the ants to pass, as their advance entailed decimating all the vegetation standing in their way. Finally, the last tail-guard ant passed by and I bid farewell, saying thanks again. I began walking quickly back to the village so I could get home before dark. I could already see the big fruit bats flying off their roosts in some giant mango trees to begin a night of scavenging. These bats would migrate from one place to another, according to the season. They were targets for a specialized group of hunters who would kill them for sale in the local markets. Fresh bat meat was a highly regarded delicacy. There was a big demand by those addicted to eating the little flesh there was on a bat. I once tasted fried bat meat and that was enough for me.

The night falls quickly in the tropics and tonight was no different; the last rays of the sun were almost gone as I stepped inside my compound. I was immensely relieved to be back in my house. I thanked God for keeping me safe in Africa for another day. I found my dinner already on the table; I ate every bit of it quickly, took my bath, and retired to my small bedroom. Somehow, I felt very tired from all I had done today. I lit an extra candle so I could review the notes I had taken, reinforcing my memory of all I had observed.

At some point, I unknowingly fell into a deep sleep. I awoke abruptly upon hearing my dog yelping loudly. I was surprised I had fallen asleep without putting out the candle now burning its last flicker in a pool of hot wax. My dog yelped again a loud cry of pain. I hurried out of bed, throwing on my shorts so I could investigate what was wrong. I duly noted it was 2:00 a.m., the hour of the bad spirits. I gulped as I tried to swallow my fears. I grabbed my big wooden club and swung open my front door, prepared to do battle with all enemies, seen and unseen. I hesitated when I stepped out my front door as I could see it was a night brilliantly lit by one of the brightest full moons I had ever seen. I feared this could be a trap to expose me to the powers of the full moon, but I had to act. My dog was going crazy, whining in great agony.

I took my flashlight, pointed it at him, and saw he was covered by the same kind of army ants I had seen earlier in the forest. The ants had entered his ears, causing him excruciating pain. Ants were everywhere. It was as if they were angry because my house was in their path. I started stomping on them. Assi and Aba were up and defending themselves. They yelled at me not to further anger the ants by killing some of them. They were busy gathering debris and pieces of firewood to build small fires around my house saying, "The only thing that can make the ants deviate from their path is fire."

Once all the fires were lit, the ants moved to the side of my house and continued on their peculiar nocturnal journey. I asked the women, "Is it normal for ants to travel at night in this area like they are doing now?"

They said in unison in a most definite tone, "No, and we have never seen or heard of anything like this before."

It was obvious to them something had disturbed the ants, and they were either fleeing the source of their fears or pointing the way for those forces which had commanded them to march at night. Either way, their strange behavior was worrisome and had implications the chief, his elders and the high fetish priests must consider. There was no doubt in their minds this strange visit of ants had a meaning needing discovery.

Meanwhile, the only known treatment for my dog was the pouring of hot wax into his ears to kill the ants which had burrowed deeply into his middle ear. I held my dog down tightly as the women poured hot candle wax into his ears. At first he whelped and squirmed mightily, but as soon as the wax killed the ants and the pain inside his head stopped, he fell quietly to the ground. I am sure all was quiet around him, because this effective treatment would leave him permanently deaf. I was deeply saddened over my dog's painful ordeal. I knew I would have to get another dog to listen for him.

I wished I still had my cat as he had been my dog's best companion, but he had been eaten by my neighbors because of a failure in communication. I thought they had asked me if I had a cat, but they really asked if they could eat my cat. I said I had a cat and thought that was the end of the subject. But later in the day, I could not find my cat, named Yuki. When I asked where Yuki was, all that was conveyed to me were some creepy grins, giggles, and funny "meow" sounds. I would never forget again that cat meat was also a much-appreciated dish.

CHAPTER THIRTY-TWO
GOODWILL FOR ALL

The long awaited mail brought good news. Funding was available for my two project proposals. I was happy I would again have the opportunity to do good deeds and help improve the lives of many. I practically jogged to the chief's compound and asked for an audience to present some good news. I was lucky. He sent word he could meet with me shortly. I waited for about thirty minutes and was shown a stool in front of him and a few of his elders, who sat in a line next to him. I was welcomed with the usual courtesies, and then the chief asked, "So Bobovovi, what good news have you brought us?"

I gleefully announced, "I am very pleased to inform you I have received a letter from a potential donor who says he is prepared to fund my last two project proposals."

The chief happily agreed, "This is great news, but we need more information on these projects."

I easily and excitedly replied, "Both of these projects are winners. One is a relatively small project involving setting up a corn-grinding mill in Muvosho, the only village in the district without a grinding mill."

The announcement of this project was met with assenting grunts and repeated exclamations that sounded like "ah ha." These utterances communicated to me their firm agreement with this project.

I was also elated to inform them: "The other project is big and ambitious. It involves providing running water to both this village and the neighboring village of Aniko. This project will provide ample water to each village, and thereby avoid inciting any envy from either village. In addition, this project will also be able to generate some electricity to provide lighting in the two villages at night." The news about this project was met with serious looks, raised eyebrows and prolonged silence.

They discussed among themselves for a few minutes, and then, the chief turned to me and calmly said, "We are pleased with the Muvosho grinding-mill project. You should go ahead and work out the details with the chief of Muvosho. As for the water project, we need some time to consider it in more depth. We must meet with my cousin, the chief of Aniko, to discuss it. However, I cannot go to Aniko or send any of my messengers there. I want you to see the Aniko chief and arrange a meeting time under the big kapok tree located between the two villages."

I quickly agreed, "I will do as you ask as quickly as possible."

He smiled and said, "This is a time for some celebrating."

He, then, pulled from under his ample toga-like garment a small brown gourd. He jerked a small stopper from the top of the gourd and poured some fine, dark brown powder on top of the thumbnail of his right hand by gently tapping the bottom of the gourd with his finger. He brought this powder close to one of his nostrils and inhaled sharply while he held the other nostril closed with one of his fingers of his left hand. His eyes began to water immediately after partaking through his nose the contents of the gourd. I assumed it was some kind of local snuff. He passed the gourd to his elders, who also inhaled some of its contents. When they were done, I was passed the shiny brown gourd. I saw this as a great honor and I desired very much to accept this honor by showing them how able I was to inhale their snuff. I poured on the top of my thumbnail a tiny amount of the powdery brown substance, inhaling deeply as soon as it was near my nose.

Immediately, I felt like my head was going to explode. I fell off my stool. I was in total agony. I thought I had been poisoned. I wanted to keep my composure, but there was no way I could do this. I was gasping for air and believed I was in a fight for my life. I asked myself what kind of powerful drug I had been given. I thought maybe this was some sort of test or special punishment for something I had done wrong. It took me ten minutes to recover enough to re-gain my composure. My embarrassment was made greater because my agony caused them great laughter. Deep down I was hurt and upset by the fact they would do such a thing to me and laugh about it. As they could see I was not happy and almost in tears, the chief half-apologized, saying, "We did not think you would react so badly to a snuff we have been taking for years."

Fortunately, the effects of their wicked snuff wore off quickly without leaving any ill effects. It reminded me of a time when I was a child in Kansas and my grandfather gave me a piece of his chaw tobacco to chew on. I took a bite and swallowed hard. I was sick for days. This experience with snuff was more violent, but the effects did not last long. Certainly, this snuff experience reinforced my lifelong tendency to avoid drugs and all tobacco products.

I left the chief and elders feeling lightheaded, and oddly, my feet felt like they hardly touched the ground. I felt refreshed, invigorated and a little dizzy. It was as if I had had one beer too many. By the time I arrived at the foot of the mountain slope, I was feeling almost giddy and laughing for no reason at all. It felt as if I loved everybody and needed to hug all those I encountered. People laughed at my funny behavior. It seemed everyone knew (except me) that I had been drugged by the chief. I liked the "high" I was on high but not enough to partake of the chief's potent snuff again.

By the time I returned home, I was ready to crash, although the effects of the snuff had completely worn off. When the women in my compound saw me, they laughed. They knew the chief had shared with me his wonder drug made from a plant only he and Mama Atiwono knew. I did not take time to bathe or eat and dove into my bed clothes (old shorts and a worn T-shirt), and I was out like a light. I slept like a log all night and was stunned when I saw daylight creeping through my window and heard the sound of the women doing their morning sweeping. I asked myself how the night could have passed so fast. It quickly dawned on me I had a lot to do; this thought propelled me out of my bed.

First, I would go see the chief of nearby Aniko to ask for a time he could meet with the chief of my village. Then, I would go see the chief in Muvosho to discuss the details of installing a grinding mill in his village. I ate and bathed quickly and readied my moto for a good day's work. My spirits were riding high. I was pleased to be able to do some meaningful work that would result in benefiting people. My humanitarian heart was happy with doing such good works. I could not wait to get these projects completed so the quality of life for many villagers would improve. I knew Africa was a tough place for the application of goodwill, but this time, I thought I had true assistance winners.

I was able to gain quick access to the chief of Aniko. He readily understood my proposal for improved water, and possibly, electrical lighting. He was much younger than Chief Yofu and had a much higher formal education level. He took time to formally introduce himself, giving his Christian name, John, and explaining his chief name, Gyasi, which meant he had been a "delightful baby."

Chief Gyasi dressed in a spiffy, dark gray safari suit as if he were a civil servant. He wore nylon socks and his shiny black leather shoes were well polished. His face and head had been closely shaven. He was tall and an attractive man. He was all business and kept a regular office. His desk was very well organized with paper, pencils, and pens neatly arranged. He wore horn-rimmed glasses and kept an expensive fountain pen in his breast pocket. He exuded modern ways and habits. I could not have found a person more different than Chief Yofu. It was as if the two chiefs represented a striking clash of traditional and modern ways. After our brief conversation, he said, "I will send word to you when I can meet with my cousin."

In spite of the contrast between him and his very traditional cousin, I hoped this time they could work together and lead their sister villages to collaborate together to realize the water project. It was surely in their common interest to take advantage of this funding opportunity so they could enjoy some progress in their respective villages. Although it would have been out of place for me to say it, I wished they could bury the hatchet and put their ancient feud behind them for the good of their people.

It took me about an hour to cover the twenty miles around the base of the mountain to Muvosho on my moto. The road was very rough and parts of it were full of sand. At one point, I had to walk my moto through a shallow stream, and at another place, I slid into the sand, burning my leg on the exhaust pipe. It was difficult to drive straight and true with my twisted handlebars. All the time, I had to keep a lookout for any snakes or migrating crocodiles crossing the road, which was really nothing more than a wide dirt path. In this area, it was not uncommon for crocodiles to be on the move as they searched for ponds or rivers with plenty of fish.

I kept telling myself I needed to wear pants, high-top boots, and a helmet on these kinds of bush trips, but doing all this was hard to do. Finding such equipment was almost impossible and prohibitively expensive, and wearing such gear would be unbearably hot in this tropical climate. I knew I would continue to do like everyone else and wear my cheap, locally made sandals, knee-length khaki shorts, and a colorful open shirt made from cotton cloth by village tailors. (God forbid wearing any synthetic cloth in this climate!) This perfectly adapted, cool, and simple attire was "de rigueur," no matter what the risk.

CHAPTER THIRTY-THREE
MUVOSHO MILL I

I arrived at the small and very poor village of Muvosho late in the morning. Its extreme level of poverty was indicated by the absence of any house with a tin roof. Most houses were not built of mud bricks but were constructed of mud and wattle. The latter seemed to sprout like dusty mushrooms from the same color of reddish-brown earth. When people heard the sound of my moto, they all came out of their compounds to welcome me. I walked directly to the chief's compound and was quickly ushered into his audience chamber by his gatekeepers, who took my moto to a protected area.

The chief was a very young, educated man, who I had heard did not want to be chief since he wanted to continue his studies. I had been told that he had been taken from his classroom in the capital city by a determined group of village men and forcefully brought back to the village to undergo all the ceremonies and orientation required to be a chief. Once selected, he had no choice but to accept or flee his village forever.

The Muvosho chief, Osakwe, rose to meet me, asking me to sit on a very large stool obviously reserved for special guests. Of course, he had seated next to him his top group of elderly advisors. After welcoming me heartily and asking how everything was going with my family and village, he asked, "Why have you come to our remote village?"

I spoke in a loud voice, "I will skip the usual protocol and go right to the reason for my visit. Your village is the only one in the district without a grinding mill. I am prepared to resolve this problem and help you install a grinding mill in your village."

This news was received with great joy. This good news spread immediately from the chief's compound to all others in the village quicker than a flash of lightening. Upon hearing this exciting news, there was dancing and singing. The chief had a large clay pot of fresh palm wine provided to us so we could drink to this good news and thank all the gods, lesser sprits, and the ancestors with many libations poured on the ground.

After enjoying an hour or so of this very festive reaction to the news of the arrival of a grinding mill for the first time in their village, I told Chief Osakwe and his entourage, "I will start tomorrow procuring all the items needed to install a grinding mill and arrange for their transport to the village for safekeeping until the mill can be set up. I will solicit the technical help of the operator of the grinding mill in my village. I hope everything will be in place by the end of the month. In the meantime, you should find a good place in the village to install the mill and make some mud bricks for the construction of the walls of the small hut needed to house the mill."

He and his elders nodded and exclaimed their agreement to all I had said. Chief Osakwe ensured me by saying, "We are prepared to do all we can to facilitate the installation and operation of the mill."

I left the village feeling very good about how the mill would do much good for the village, particularly for women who spent long hours each day hand-grinding corn kernels into meal flour. The introduction of village grinding mills many years ago by the colonists was perhaps one of the most important improvements they offered. Upon returning to my village, I headed directly to the location of the village grinding mill and told the mill operator, Kokumo, "I need your help to know what to buy to set up a mill in Muvosho. Can you help me set up a mill and instruct someone in Muvosho on how to operate and maintain the mill?"

He said, "I cannot leave my mill, but I could loan you my very experienced apprentice boy, Ebo."

As it was late in the day, I told Kokumo, "I will be back first thing tomorrow morning to collect all the necessary details."

Early the next morning, I wolfed down my breakfast and returned with my notebook to the grinding mill to get all the information I needed to install a mill in Muvosho. In spite of the loud noise made by the mill, as it was always in constant operation, we discussed for almost two hours what I needed to make a mill work and keep it working. First, Kokumo, who was clad in only khaki shorts, took me inside the small hut where the mill was located and pointed to everything I would need to buy to install a mill.

In a clear and no-nonsense manner, he instructed, "The first thing needed is to pour a concrete slab to anchor the mill and the motor that powers it. This slab must be a foot thick, reinforced with steel rebar, and perfectly level and well cured; otherwise, the mill will not work properly. I cannot stress enough that the success of the mill depends on constructing the foundation exactly as I have explained."

He noted firmly, "You cannot pour the slab until you have the exact dimensions of the base of the mill and motor because bolts must be implanted in the wet concrete at the exact locations of where the bolt holes are located on the bottom of the mill and its motor. These bolts must match up perfectly with the holes in the base of the mill and motor, so they can be solidly fastened with sturdy steel nuts. You will need to engage the services of a local blacksmith to fabricate these special bolts. You must procure the mill and the motor that drives it according to the exact specifications I am telling you. I insist that you must accept nothing less than a British-made Lister motor, which is very strong and lasts for years. Be sure to buy an extra set of the circular grinding blades for the mill. These blades must be changed and filed often to stay sharp. You already know the Lebanese store in the regional capital, Kpolomo, where you can buy all these items."

He tapped lightly on the long rubber belt I would have to buy. He indicated how this belt would be wrapped tightly around the driver wheel on the motor and run to a similar wheel on the mill. This was how the motor turned the mill so it would grind corn and eject it out a large spout protruding from the opposite side. He stressed how important it is to maintain the right tension on the conveyor belt. More important than this was keeping the motor cool; this required setting up a large reservoir of water to circulate through rubber hoses to and from the motor.

He took me outside to show me two old metal oil barrels welded together, top to bottom, to create a tall sort of water-cooling silo hooked to the motor with tightly fitted rubber hoses. He said, "One important task of my apprentice is to make sure that the water reservoir is constantly full of water and always flowing in and out of the motor along the hard rubber pipes passing through the mud brick wall."

I was seeing there was much more than met the eye when it came to setting up a grinding mill, and at this point, I only knew about half of what I should know. For sure, I could see this would not be as easy as I thought, and maybe, if I had known beforehand all that was involved with setting up a grinding mill, I would have looked for a different project to do.

When I left the mill, I had several pages of notes and the start of a long shopping list. I lost sleep that night as I ran through all the details in my head and how I would go tomorrow to the regional capital, Kpolomo, to order all the things I would need trucked to Muvosho for the installation of the mill. I knew the Lebanese store owner, Aziz, from buying stuff at his store before. He impressed me as someone who could provide me with all I needed and deliver my order directly to Muvosho. I also thought I would not be required to pay him until my bank transfer arrived. I knew I could count on Aziz. He never failed to do as he said.

The next day I got up earlier than usual, skipping breakfast so I could get an early start on my trip to Kpolomo for the big mill-shopping day. I arrived in Kpolomo without mishap. I grabbed breakfast at one of the many roadside stands in this small town. When I arrived at Aziz's store, it was still closed, so I waited for Aziz on his front step. I did not have to wait long, as Aziz arrived shortly after I did, greeting me like a brother. This middle-aged, pudgy, bald-headed Lebanese man was of short stature. He had spent all his life in Africa and was a real entrepreneur. He was known to make money where others could not see any business opportunities. He owned several businesses and it was rumored he was also involved with the illicit diamond trade. He invited me to his back veranda and offered me coffee and crackers. As we began to sip our coffee, I explained to him the reason for my visit.

He lost no time in saying in his heavily accented voice, "You have done the right thing by coming to me. I have supplied many villages with all they need to set up a grinding mill."

I read to him my list while he made notes with a stubby pencil on a discolored sheet of paper. In his broken French, he quickly rattled off much advice, "You need five bags of cement to make the slab. I will buy you tar to paint your two barrels inside and out, making them rust-resistant. Barrels are hard to get, but I will find them and have them welded together, fitted with pipes and tarred. No problem. I will haul the barrels and everything else directly to Muvosho in my old, but strong five-ton truck. I know a blacksmith who can make bolts for anchoring your mill to the concrete slab."

I was pleased. It looked like he could provide and deliver everything I needed, and he would give me the bill later. He promised to deliver everything within a week, and when the truck came through my village, it would pick me up. Aziz had a way of making you feel good by reducing your worries.

When I left Aziz, I felt relieved of many burdens and was satisfied that I had achieved much. While in Kpolomo I passed by the bank where I was supposed to receive a fund transfer to pay for the grinding mill and the water supply project. I found the funds had not arrived yet and told the clerk I would be back in a week to check again.

I had reason to celebrate so I decided to go to the town's one semi-modern restaurant, Café Nasser, for a meal of chicken and rice. Afterward I walked across the street to Bar Truman for the coldest beer in town. This was something of an upscale bar, but the people in it were down to earth and the traditional kind who still opened beer bottles with their teeth. I enjoyed my bottle of beer very much. After some small talk with some of the other clients, I climbed on my moto, tilted my crooked handlebars to a thirty-degree angle to the left, and headed straight toward my village, feeling very good about myself.

Just after I entered the village, I stopped at the grinding mill to tell Kokumo about my dealings in Kpolomo and advise him the truck with everything needed to set up the mill in Muvosho should arrive next week. I asked him again to loan me Ebo, his apprentice boy, to help set up the mill in Muvosho and teach some people there how to operate and maintain it. I would need his apprentice for a week or two.

He confirmed, "I am okay with loaning Ebo, but the people of Muvosho will have to take care of his lodging and food, as well as pay him a small allowance for his services."

He also reminded me, "The people of Muvosho must provide sufficient sand and gravel to make the concrete slab for the placement of the mill."

As this was something I had overlooked, I asked him, "Is there any way we can find someone to take this message to the chief of Muvosho?"

"This will not be a problem. People from Muvosho come to my mill every day. I will send your message in this regard with my next Muvosho customer."

I thanked him again for all his help and continued on my way. Before I had gone too far, I encountered one of the chief's messengers who said, "I have been looking for you to let you know the meeting under the big kapok tree with the two chiefs to discuss your water project is to be held first thing tomorrow morning."

I welcomed this news and confirmed I would be there bright and early. I could not wait to get these two chiefs working together on this very promising project. I was thinking this would truly be a terrific breakthrough and make life so much better for these two villages. My hopes were running high, and for sure, I would stay here as long as it took to complete this important project.

CHAPTER THIRTY-FOUR
WATER FAILS

After a fitful sleep, I woke up feeling reinvigorated. My constant whistling of old songs from my youth in Kansas was a good indicator of my high level of contentment. Things were finally going my way, and today I would move to a whole new level of humanitarian assistance when the chiefs approved the much-needed water-project proposal. I was so eager for today's meeting and the subsequent approval of this wonderful project, I was the first one to arrive at the meeting place. I sat on the bamboo benches placed at the base of the kapok tree and waited for the chiefs and their entourages to arrive. There were some delays, as the handlers of the chiefs squabbled as to whom would sit where. It was agreed the chief of my village would arrive first and sit on the stool his elders had brought, and as soon as he was seated, Chief Gyasi would arrive. Everyone was looking to save face and maintain their pride.

Chief Yofu arrived dressed in all his regalia. Accompanied by well-dressed young girls who sang softly his praises, and who held high over his head a large multi-colored cloth parasol. His ostentatious arrival contrasted greatly with the simple, business-like arrival of his cousin, who dressed and acted like a senior government civil servant. It was as if Chief Gyasi viewed his traditional cousin as backward in his ways and wanted to remind everyone he was a modern, educated man. He sat straight in his modest chair, clutching his pen and notebook, while Chief Yofu slumped comfortably on his royal stool. Neither chief looked at each other or acknowledged the presence of the other.

After everyone was seated and a crowd had gathered around, Chief Yofu raised in the air his ornamental staff and all became silent. He greeted the group and spoke in a slow but melodic manner. "I want to express my happiness about meeting with my brothers to discuss the water project Bobovovi is prepared to help us realize. My counselors and I have discussed at some length this project and I am sure my brothers from Aniko have done the same. But before announcing the results of our deliberations, I would like Bobovovi to describe briefly the project and the benefits it will provide to both villages."

I started my sales pitch by speaking in my own simple, broken way, using all the words of the local language I could muster. "This project is a great opportunity for both villages to resolve their water shortage problems and make water collection easier by locating water taps within the villages. Women and children will no longer have to walk long distances to fetch pails of water, which would be much cleaner. As you know there are many natural springs dripping out of the sides of the mountaintop and much water is lost as it seeps into the ground. This water can be collected and stored for delivery by pipes to water-storage reservoirs in the villages. We could excavate a large hole under one of the bigger springs and construct a large concrete, catchment basin to store water. This water could then be piped from this basin the approximate two thousand five hundred feet to the villages."

When I finished Chief Yofu authoritatively inquired, "Does anyone in the crowd have any questions?"

A number of hands flew up. The chief called on a man who put his hand up first. This person asked, "Will the pipes be polyethylene or galvanized? It has to be the latter in order to resist bush fires in the dry season."

Another man asked, "How will the surrounding cocoa fields be affected, as they are dependent upon water dripping from the mountain springs? This water seeps into the soil and travels long distances down the slope of the mountain."

Out of turn, one unruly elder muttered, "Many costly ceremonies will have to be conducted to satisfy the spirits affected by this change in the natural flow of water."

I did my best to answer all the questions raised, and people seemed to be satisfied with my answers. The tough, unanswered question was over how villages would work together to control the distribution of water. I tried to answer this challenging question by explaining, "The basin will fill up with water and flow down two different pipes, one for each village, and each village would have its own water distribution system."

One old man rose and commented, "This is okay, but sometimes the water inside the mountain dwindles and hardly drips at all. Which village would get the water first in this case?"

I proposed, "Both villages should set up a joint water committee to govern the use of water and maintain the system."

This suggestion raised many eyebrows and people fidgeted nervously. The two villages had never been able to collaborate together. I was under the impression the entire project could be rejected because of water-control issues. I was learning that water control was a real development issue.

After some more back and forth, Chief Yofu raised his hand and all fell silent. He dryly provided a concluding statement, "Everyone appreciates Bobovovi's effort to provide water to the villages, but it will not work because our particular circumstances require each village to have its own separate water system to manage. Bobovovi needs to redesign the project so separate water systems are constructed for each village at the same time. Also, we like the idea of using falling water to generate electricity at night for the villages, but this is not necessary."

When I asked why they did not want electricity, the chief informed me, "There are enough hours of daylight. We do not need more light at night. The night is for other things and must stay night. Introducing light in the night would be too disturbing and create commotion among the spirits."

Chief Yofu added, "This old kapok tree was brought to Africa by the colonists. It symbolizes in many ways the challenges our two villages face in collaborating together. The tree marks the boundary of our two villages. For many years we quarreled over which village should benefit from the annual harvest of the cotton fiber pods it produces. We resolved this quarrel by alternating the years each village harvests the produce of this tree. In that way, we can take turns in benefitting from the income generated by the export of the Kapok cotton of this large and fruitful tree. We are happy that the demand for the silky cotton fiber contained in the kapok pods is still in high demand in Europe for stuffing pillows and mattresses. Bobovovi should keep this in mind as he redesigns the water project."

All these discouraging words left me speechless. I hung my head in defeat. My mood was dark. A wave of depression swept over me. I was devastated by seeing all my efforts to raise money for the good of these villages shattered because of some backward thinking and the stupid history that had separated these two villages for generations. I could hardly hear Chief Yofu and Chief Gyasi when they thanked me for all my efforts and wished me well in the design of new projects to help the people of Ataku and Aniko.

As I walked home, my thoughts were somber and I asked myself how I could like Africa so much if this is how it was. If people were not ready to make the changes needed to improve their lives, it was useless to try to help them. I was upset by a popular attitude that seemed to accept impoverishment and reject changes which could improve the quality of life. I was convinced that as long as they accepted their circumstances, a sustainable improvement in their living conditions was not possible. The case for development assistance seemed lost, even before it was given a fair chance.

By the time I reached my house, my mood was better, but I had firmly decided it was indeed time for me to leave the village and Africa forever. Enough was enough! I was fed up! I had given up on finding a way for the villagers to benefit from my goodwill and sincere desire to help them. It was wrong and very sad that I could not make a positive, lasting difference in the life of even one individual.

CHAPTER THIRTY-FIVE
MUVOSHO MILL II

I had only been home a short while when a boy came running from the center of the village to tell me a truck filled with all the grinding mill supplies had arrived. I quickly rushed off to find the truck and made sure it was carrying all the items needed to install the mill. I did a rapid inventory of everything on the truck. I noted Aziz had added a couple of jerry cans of diesel fuel, five cans of engine oil, and two cans of grease. All this would be needed for the initial operation of the mill.

As it was already late in the day, I asked the young truck driver, "Can you find a safe place to park and stay overnight so we can leave early in the morning for Muvosho?"

He agreed with my proposal and pledged, "I will sleep in the truck and protect it and all it carries from thieves."

I walked over to the grinding mill to advise Kokumo the truck was here, and therefore, I would need Ebo to come with us to Muvosho tomorrow. He said that this would not be a problem.

Positive forward movement on this project was putting me in a better mood. I was glad the people of Muvosho were so receptive to my helping them install a grinding mill in their village. I did my usual nighttime routine and prepared to rise extra early to join the truck for the trip to Muvosho. The night was peaceful and I slept soundly. I was feeling very good about myself when I arrived the next morning to see all was well with the truck. The driver, Anani, and Ebo were standing by the truck and ready to go. I made one quick check to see if all items were intact and in the same condition I had observed the day before. All was well. I climbed in beside the driver. Ebo rode in the back truck bed to make sure the bumpy road did not damage any of the goods.

The truck started with the first turn of the key and we were off. The truck was indeed old but sturdy. However, its tired motor only allowed moving at a slow speed. It took us two hours to reach Muvosho. Once in the village, we came to a sputtering halt next to the site where the grinding mill would be installed. The loud noise produced by the truck alerted the villagers to our presence and they rushed to gather around the truck to gaze in wonder at what it had brought to their village. Before doing anything we waited for Chief Osakwe, so he could accept responsibility for all the goods being delivered. The chief arrived and the people loudly sang his praises (and mine). This was certainly a joyous high point in the history of the village.

As soon as Chief Osakwe arrived and the customary greetings were exchanged, he asked for all the young men to come forward to help with unloading the truck. All the lighter items were unloaded first and placed on a spot that had been cleared for the mill. It took a half dozen strong young men to lower the heavy grinding mill to the ground, and an even greater number to coax down and carry the very heavy Lister engine. As each item was lowered to the ground, the chief yelled out what it was and all those assembled applauded and cheered. As each item was taken off the truck, I checked it off my inventory list.

I introduced the chief to the apprentice, Ebo, noting he was very experienced and would be staying in the village for a week or so to set up the mill and train someone to operate and maintain it.

The chief warmly welcomed him. "I promise to take very good care of him. I will also take good care of everything you have delivered. The cement and other items will be kept in my house while all else will be covered by a tarp and roped down. I will have someone standing guard night and day. Also, please see over there the gravel and sand we have collected for the concrete slab."

I was pleased. Everything looked in good order. I announced to all, "I will be going back with the truck and returning in a week to see what progress has been made." I bid farewell and climbed into the truck for the slow and bumpy return to my village. I was happy that all had gone so well. I was looking very much toward the day this mill ground its first bucket of corn.

A week zoomed by quickly, and almost before I knew it, I was heading out of the village on my moto in the direction of Muvosho. I could not wait to see how the work on setting up the mill had gone. I drove carefully this time, as I did not want to fall again. When I was about a mile from the village, the road was blocked by a huge tree that had fallen across the road. As I looked for a way in the bush around the fallen tree, I could clearly see the tree had not fallen on its own accord but had been chopped down intentionally. I could not understand why anyone would chop down a tree when they knew it would block the road. At first, I thought it might be charcoal makers. They often made charcoal in open pits they would dig in the middle of roads, but this was not the case this time. Charcoal makers used only small trees and branches they could easily cut into small pieces.

Try as I may, I could not find any way to get around the felled tree. It was with the greatest chagrin I found myself obliged to turn around and head back home. When I arrived in the village, I stomped straight toward the grinding mill and in exasperation asked Kokumo, "Have you heard anything from your apprentice in Muvosho?"

He said, "No, I haven't."

I explained to him about the tree blocking the road. He reassured me, "Just wait another week and I am sure the tree will be removed and the road will be passable."

I pleaded, "Please inform me if you meet anyone from Muvosho who knows anything about progress being achieved with setting up of the new mill."

Another week zipped by, and I set off for Muvosho again. I could not believe the tree was still blocking the road and no effort had been made to remove it. I parked my moto and tried to walk around the tree. I was bound and determined to get to Muvosho, even if I had to walk there. It was a difficult place to walk through the bush because as far as the eye could see the land was thickly covered with thorn bushes. I tried to wind my way carefully through the thorns, but it was hard to avoid being scratched. The scratches raised big red welts on my skin. The thorns contained some kind of toxic substance, quickly stinging and infecting my skin. After many scratches, I retreated backwards the same way I had come, getting scratched many more times. I knew I needed to get home soon to wash my wounds and cover them with mercurochrome to avoid serious infection.

When the women at home saw me, they ran excitedly to me and asked what had happened. I was scratched all over and my clothes were torn. I looked like I had been flogged. They escorted me to a place near a washbasin behind my house. They took off my shirt and washed my wounds with a strong local soap made with palm oil and the ashes of cocoa pods. Later, they applied a greenish cream made from a special plant they said Mama Atiwono grows.

They were adamant. "You should rest and avoid touching your scratches."

I was equally adamant. "I need to go to Muvosho!" But it was obvious I could not go until my scratches healed. Hurting and feeling miserable, I limped to my room to take a nap.

A few days later, I was feeling better and I walked to the village mill to relate my ordeal and ask Kokumo for his advice. I also wanted to know if he had seen anyone from Muvosho or heard from his apprentice. He did not know what to tell me. He had not seen anyone from Muvosho. I found it odd he had not seen anyone from Muvosho in two weeks.

He tried to comfort me by noting, "Muvosho is a remote village and it is not unusual for it to be cut off for weeks in the rainy season, as the road to it becomes impassable. I am sure the tree will be removed soon."

I suggested I would hire some guys to remove the tree. He thought this was a bad idea, as it was clearly the job of the people of Muvosho to remove the tree and it was in their direct interest to do so.

I was at a loss over what to do. I consulted with the chief and his elders, but they told me this was outside their jurisdiction. It was between me and Muvosho. Days sped by as I pondered my next move. I continued to drive to Muvosho, but each time I found the tree blocking the passage. Nobody in my village had seen anyone from Muvosho. It had been over a month since the mill materials had been delivered and I still could not get there.

I was beside myself with frustration and angst. I feared I was developing an ulcer. Every week or so, I continued my efforts to go to Muvosho, but the road remained blocked by the huge tree. The donor was asking for a report on my mill project, but there was nothing I could tell him. The road was becoming more difficult to use. The lack of traffic had allowed the bush to encroach onto it. I feared the onset of the rainy season would cut Muvosho off for months.

Deep down I also feared the entire village and others in my own village were pulling a well-orchestrated scam on me. I knew that in traditional culture it was acceptable to enact elaborate schemes to deceive someone, particularly outsiders, as long as you were not caught doing a "lie." Involving a cast of numerous people to act out a "lie" was often used in colonial times to fool the new white masters. Successfully executing a great lying scheme was a highly regarded achievement. I could not bring myself to believe that the people of Muvosho were subjecting me to such a scheme.

My main project had been rejected by two villages and the status of another project, upon which funds had been expended, was unknown. There was no doubt that my track record for helping the people of this district was dismal. Given these failures and my lack of any more project ideas, I was thinking it was indeed time for me to leave the village and move on. Enough was indeed enough! I had already stayed twice as long as I had planned. I had fully paid my dues to the humanitarian cause. I was under no further obligation. It was time I moved on with the rest of my life!

I had found that helping people was just too hard, especially if they were not ready to help themselves. It was not possible to change the nature of the people or re-engineer entire societies. It was useless to pursue more assistance projects until they requested assistance and were ready to devote themselves to improving themselves and their village. I was thinking the best way to get away was to pretend I was going on one of my usual jaunts but never return. Soon, I told myself, I would be gone, on my way back to Kansas and the life I left behind long ago.

CHAPTER THIRTY-SIX
BAOBAB FOREVER

The days passed as I carefully planned my escape from the embrace of the village and Africa. I had to be careful not to make any sign that would indicate I was preparing to depart. I had decided I would leave behind my few belongings and just ride off one day on my moto. I knew it was very bad manners not to say good-bye, but doing so would be too stressful, and moreover, I feared the villagers would again find a way to persuade me to stay. I especially feared doing anything to alert the spirits to my departure as I, too, was now convinced they did actually like me and would not want me to leave them. Keeping the spirits unaware of my escape plans was the most troubling challenge of all.

I tried hard to go about my business as usual. I kept trying to go to Muvosho. I even talked about trying to raise additional money so I could do two separate village water projects simultaneously. Soon I would say I was going to Kpolomo on business, but I would board the train there and go to Melomti to catch a flight out of Africa forever. I tried to keep my cool and wear a happy face. My escape would occur at the last minute and nobody would be the wiser. The day before I thought I might take off I made everyone know I needed to go to Kpolomo to settle my account with Aziz. That was true, but what they didn't know was after leaving the money for Aziz, I would start my final exit from Africa.

I found it difficult to sleep the night before my great escape. I was troubled, because I would be leaving without saying goodbye, and I worried about my dog. But there was no other way to consummate this divorce from the village and Africa. I had to be emotionless and coldly cut the cord of attachments and leave, or not leave at all. It was now or never. With this convincing rationale firmly set in my mind, I fell into a deep slumber for the remainder of the night. I slept so soundly for a few hours I did not hear the unusual rain that fell during the night.

I woke up feeling refreshed and committed to putting my escape plan into effect right after breakfast. I had not counted, however, on the strange sight I beheld when I peered through my bedroom window. Everywhere in my yard were plants sprouting up from the ground. Somehow, overnight, my house had been surrounded by a dense patch of plants of a variety I did not know.

I exited my front door to find these leafy plants poking up through the ground everywhere. There were hundreds of them. They were already six-to-twelve inches tall and standing very erect. I thought some birds must have flown over in recent days and their droppings contained the seeds that germinated with last night's exceptional dry season rain. It reminded me of the time I found hundreds of small fish in my yard after a huge cloudburst. Maybe a similar thing was possible under the right conditions for this kind of plant.

I sought Aba and Assi to chat about this amazing wonder, but they were cowering in their shack and did not want to talk. All they said was, "We cannot do anything until the chief and those he chooses arrive to see the plants."

Just at that moment I heard clapping at my front gate. I opened it to see the chief and the oldest of his elders and the most experienced fetish priests in the village. After quickly greeting me, they brushed by me, saying they had come to investigate the plant phenomena in my compound.

I asked, "Isn't the same phenomena happening all over the village?"

The chief replied, "There are only plants growing at your compound."

"I am sure the rains that made the plants grow in my yard also did the same in other places in the village," I replied.

They gave me a serious look, and Kontor said, "It only rained on your house and nowhere else."

I was stupefied when I heard this. I immediately knew this was serious business that would delay my escape plans. I began to feel sick in my stomach.

The chief and his group of wise men walked around my house and closely examined many of the plants as they meandered around my yard. They spoke among themselves, and then, approached me. The chief asked me, "Do you know what kind of plants these are?"

After my crash course with Mama Atiwono, I should have known the answer to this question, but I did not. They pointed to the five-leaf cluster of leaves growing out of the top of each plant and asked me again if I knew this plant. Again, I thought I should know the answer to their question, but I did not know what to say. They again gave me penetrating stares that seemed to possess both fear and respect, and said these plants were baobab tree seedlings. I found this absolutely amazing. I, too, began to be enveloped by a thick layer of fear and deep puzzlement.

In a trembling voice, the chief said, "We know from our oral history of such baobab miracles, but one has never been observed in living memory. The growing of these baobab seedlings in your yard is an important sign. We will form a special council of the wisest and most powerful fetish priests in the village to determine the meaning of this phenomena and what actions we need to take. In the meantime, I ask you to stay at home among the seedlings and not go anywhere."

I swallowed hard upon hearing the chief's words. For sure, these unusual events had indefinitely put on hold my escape plans. I kept asking myself how such a thing could happen just on the eve of my departure. I wished I had left some days earlier before any of these weird events had occurred.

I did like and admire the old baobab trees that stood tall and mighty here and there in the bush. These odd trees were considered sacred. People often said prayers in front of them, giving them offerings of food and drink. No one dared harm a baobab tree. Their fruits and leaves could be harvested only after special ceremonies had been performed to thank the tree for the bounty it was providing the people. The leaves were very nutritious and used in making special sauces. The fruits have high vitamin A content and are eaten raw or made into drinks and medicines. The fruits were called "monkey bread." This made me think they must have been a favorite food of monkeys when they still inhabited the area. The wood of the baobab tree was mushy and not useable. I had heard that when cloth was in short supply during the last world war, bark cloth was allowed to be made from the baobab as long as it did not harm the tree.

In truth, the baobab is the ugliest of trees. It looks like it has been turned upside down and its roots, instead of its branches, are pointed up into the air. Its trunk appears as if it has suffered from a severe disease; it is pockmarked and has many tumorous-like bumps protruding from its gnarled, grayish surface. I knew these trees were ancient and could live to be several thousand years old. They could grow to great height with their girth exceeding seventy feet. The older the tree the more it was considered a repository of wisdom. It was also believed the spirits of the ancestors dwelled within the old baobab trees. I had heard highly respected chiefs used to be buried inside baobab trees. The people believed the baobabs possessed many secrets once known by the people but were now forgotten after the passing of many generations.

It was easy for me to see why anything connected to the baobab was taken very seriously by the chief and his council. I waited at home as the chief requested, but I needed to eat so I called to the women in the compound to make me some food. I could hear them stirring in their outdoor kitchen, so I knew they were reacting to my call and soon would bring my food as usual and place it on the table. Later, I heard loud clapping at my back door, so I looked to see what this was all about. I opened the door to see my food sitting on the ground in front of it. For some reason, the women were too scared to face me and bring my food to me.

This unprecedented action on the part of Aba and Assi made me think again about why all these little baobabs were growing in my yard. I was increasingly convinced this was serious stuff and I had to be prepared for some heavy edicts coming from the chief. I tried to imagine what their conclusions about all this would be, but I could not come up with anything that satisfied me. So I sat down and read a book while I waited for some instruction from the chief. I was deeply concerned, but somehow I was uncannily comfortable with all the baobab seedlings around me. For no good reason at all, I moved my chair outside to sit among them. I wished I had a camera to take a photo of this special moment.

Several hours had gone by and I had dozed off in my chair when I was awakened by the chief and all the fetish priests, men, and women, who descended on my compound to witness the baobab miracle and inform me of what I must do in response to this powerful sign. I was told by the chief in no uncertain terms, "This is the way the ancient baobabs communicate. Apparently, they have chosen you to receive their secrets."

I was shocked by this unbelievable news. I rudely said in a loud voice, "Why have I been chosen, a Whiteman and a foreigner, who knows so little about local customs and beliefs?"

The chief ignored my remarks and ordered, "There is no time for discussion! We must act quickly so as not to anger the ancestors and spirits. Bobovovi, prepare to leave immediately!" He then pointed to a group of five fetish priests who would take me to see the oldest baobab tree in the district.

Like a sheep that had no other choice but to submit to its destiny, I said, "I have nothing to prepare. I can leave now."

The chief was pleased by my reply and said, "Excellent. Follow these five men."

I quickly fell in the middle of the five men who led me to a westward leading path. As I left my compound, it seemed people were hardly breathing and not a sound was uttered. As I moved out of my gate, I was stunned to see the baobab seedlings begin to wilt and fall to the ground. Upon seeing this inexplicable wilting, people rapidly fled from my house. I thought this was indeed strange, but I was too busy watching my step as we walked along a bush path I had never been on before.

It was not a short walk. I think we must have walked a couple of miles before I spied above the tall savannah grass the top branches of a majestic old baobab tree. I could also see clearly, just above the branches in the fading light of the late afternoon, the sketchy outline of a full moon. The fact of being out under the light of a full moon added immeasurably to my concerns over what lay ahead for me.

As soon as we arrived at the base of this huge baobab, two of my very solemn companions began providing offerings to the tree and chanting its praises. This baobab was the largest I had ever seen, but it looked dead, as it was barren of leaves and any fruit, and its bark had turned a dark gray. I was handed a small bottle of filtered water by one of the men who softly told me, "Drink and keep the remaining water with you."

They walked me around the tree five times as they poured drinks on the ground and offered thanks to the mighty baobab, saying they had brought the one it had selected. As we slowly stepped around the tree, I could see the trunk had a wide split in it, revealing a deep hollow space inside the base of the tree. After our fifth tour of the tree, we stopped in front of the opening in the trunk of this holy tree.

At this point, I was given some instructions and told in a sympathetic manner, "It is very important that you stay relaxed and prepared to fully submit yourself to this tree. You must go inside the tree and stay there until sunrise tomorrow morning."

I thought this was crazy. I fought the urge to run away. I was scared. Yet, at the same time, I was curious. Oddly, there was a strange attachment growing within me for this tree.

Kontor said, "We will stay here all night and wait for you to come out in the morning."

They hoped the tree and the ancestors dwelling within it would share with me some secrets the village could use. In particular, they were interested in re-gaining the knowledge of the five-leaf secret that had been lost generations ago. They noted the baobab produced leaves in a cluster of five and each leaf in the cluster represented an important secret. I reluctantly said, "Okay. I will do my best." I, then, slowly stepped through the wide opening in the tree to find a place to sit for the night.

Although this was a very creepy experience, I was surprised to find it was very roomy, cool, and clean inside. I searched for any signs of bats or other creatures, but there were none. It looked like I was the sole inhabitant of this tree. I found a place where I could sit and lean my back against the inside of the tree. I was scared and a little breathless, but I told myself I could do this. If nothing else, I wanted to do this as one last favor for the village. I tried to pass the time by meditating and going over all the days of my life, and what I would do after I left Africa.

As I sat there, it dawned on me I was really nuts for doing this and so many other things I had done in the village. I was really feeling stupid and regretting I had allowed Africa to throw me off my life's track. I should have been living a happy and successful life in Kansas, but here I sat in the hollow of a tree in the African bush in the middle of the night. So many thoughts crossed my mind. This was crazy! What am I doing here? I do not belong here! At that moment, I realized that my mind had been progressively perverted by a constant and prolonged immersion in Africa. I knew I was in desperate need of some kind of professional post-Africa trauma counseling.

The hours passed slowly. It was very dark inside the tree, except when the full moon arrived in a position that made the inside of the tree glow for a few minutes. I appreciated the light, but as usual, I was wary of the light of the full moon. This time the moonlight seemed to make my skin hot, and I broke out in a brief feverish sweat. I worried that I would never escape the unexplainable powers a full moon had on me. I needed counseling for this too, but who would believe me? I could see I had to keep quiet about many things or my sanity would be questioned by those ignorant of how Africa could remake your psyche and the way you looked at the world.

Soon the moon was gone, and it was again so dark I could not see my hand in front of my face. I could hear the men outside continuing their chants. Soon, I became so tired I fell asleep. Later, the sound of birds chirping outside woke me up. I was very groggy, and there were words sounding inside my head that had not been there before I slept. I could clearly hear in a soft whispering voice many secrets, including the five-leaf secret. I thought this was marvelous. I could not wait to go outside and tell the men who had accompanied me what I had learned. I stood up, but it took me a while to find my bearings, as I was dizzy and lightheaded.

I squinted as I stepped out into the broad daylight. Everything seemed to be covered with some sort of weird smoky, yellow-green mist. I walked around to the other side of the tree to find the five men transfixed, as they stared silently in the air at the giant baobab. I found it strange I could no longer see the opening in the tree. Even more mystifying was, somehow, during the night this magnificent tree had sprouted leaves and fully grown fruit hung from its rejuvenated branches. I could see this ancient tree had not been dead but had been lying dormant for many years.

I cleared my throat noisily so as to alert the men to my presence. They were dressed in different clothes, so I assumed they had brought a change of clothes with them. I made more noises so they would acknowledge my presence and I could tell them all the secrets I knew they wanted so very much to know. I was so pleased that I was in a position to share with the village these secrets and other pieces of lost wisdom magically communicated to me during the night.

They acted as if they did not hear me and continued to stare at the rich bounty offered by the father of all baobab trees. I lowered my gaze and saw something I had not seen before. At the base of the baobab tree, I could see that a small white marble stone had been erected. I moved closer to read the words that had been engraved on it. I was surprised to see many more bowls of offerings had been brought and placed around the tree and near the stone. I stepped near the stone and read words that meant something like the following:

"Here Dwells Forever the White Baobab

His Destiny Fulfilled

Born in Kansas for Africa"

I was stunned by what I read. I now knew why the men did not see me. I searched deeply for the answers to what had happened to me, but there were none to be had. I could only hear what the tree was saying and the soft song a little white bird was singing in the uppermost branches of the tree. Next to the bird was a rare chameleon with a red splotch on its head. As the bird sang, the chameleon swayed its head and rolled its eyes in time with the bird's melancholy tune. I was deeply moved and soothed by the lovely act of this odd, but striking pair. The bird's sweet song told me there was no escape. This was indeed Africa's final embrace.

***